Pepper Adams

Pepper Adams
Saxophone Trailblazer

GARY CARNER

Foreword by
CHICK COREA

**EXCELSIOR
EDITIONS**

Cover Credit: Photo by Erik Lindahl, Pepper Adams in Goteborg, 1978, copyright by Erik Lindahl.

Back cover photograph of Gary Carner with Barry Harris taken by Daniel Olson in 2010.

Published by State University of New York Press, Albany

© 2023 State University of New York

Excelsior Editions is an imprint of State University of New York Press

For information, contact State University of New York Press, Albany, NY
www.sunypress.edu

Library of Congress Cataloging-in-Publication Data

Name: Carner, Gary, author.
Title: Pepper Adams : saxophone trailblazer / Gary Carner.
Description: Albany : State University of New York Press, 2023. | Series:
    Excelsior editions | Includes bibliographical references and index.
Identifiers: LCCN 2023002655 | ISBN 9781438494357 (pbk. : alk. paper) | ISBN
    9781438494340 (ebook)
Subjects: LCSH: Adams, Pepper, 1930–1986. | Saxophonists—United States—
    Biography. | Jazz musicians—United States—Biography.
Classification: LCC ML419.A25 C37 2023 | DDC 788.7/165092
    [B]—dc23/eng/20230120
LC record available at https://lccn.loc.gov/2023002655

10 9 8 7 6 5 4 3 2 1

For Nancy

Ya gotta be original, man.

—Lester Young

How many musicians out there are *really* different?

—Ran Blake

Because jazz demands that musicians find their own sound and stamp their performances with a singular individuality, those who succeed in music tend to be distinctive, singular individuals.

—John Gennari

Contents

Illustrations

Foreword

Pepper Adams was my "elder" when I came to New York City in the 60s. I got close to him when I briefly held the piano chair in the Thad Jones/Mel Lewis band. What a thrill for me! I was too shy to get to know Pepper personally but my admiration for his playing was always out the top. His every note and every solo while I was with the band is part of my life in a beautiful way. Pepper's work on Monk's live at Town Hall recording is also memorable for me.

Thanks for taking care of Pepper's legacy,
Chick Corea
October 2019

Introduction

On September 28, 1986, our first wedding anniversary, my wife Nancy and I attended Pepper Adams's memorial service at St. Peter's Lutheran Church in New York City. Adams had waged a courageous battle against an aggressive form of lung cancer that was first diagnosed in March 1985 while he was on tour in Sweden. On that somber yet bright Sunday afternoon, St. Peter's ash-paneled, multi-tiered sanctuary, tucked under 915-foot-tall Citicorp Center, was packed with friends, musicians, and admirers. Reverend John Garcia Gensel presided over the service and many jazz greats performed and paid their final respects.

Adams was a friend of mine, but I knew him only during the last two years of his life. We first met in 1984, while he was recovering from an auto accident that had kept him immobilized for six months. Then afterwards, while separated from his wife, he was diagnosed with the illness that would take his life. Although a miserable time for him, it was an exciting ride for me. I was a twenty-eight-year-old grad student, a passionate jazz fan and record collector, who was trying to interest a jazz musician in working with me on an oral history to satisfy my thesis requirement at City College of New York. Adams, I soon learned, was an ideal subject: a major figure who, from the late 1940s onward had played with virtually everyone in jazz.

Because he was homebound that summer, we met several times in Brooklyn, discussing his career, listening to music, and once going out for lunch and running some errands. Our conversations yielded eighteen hours of documentation, captured by my trusty Sony microcassette recorder. The depth and historical sweep of his recollections were stunning. I knew right away that I had the makings of a valuable co-authored autobiography. But seven months later his cancer was diagnosed. Because cancer treatments and international travel made our autobiographical project an impossibility,

1

I decided that writing a full-length biography would be the more sensible approach. When Pepper was home between gigs, I watched football games with him while going through documents, eating pizza, and dubbing copies of his cassette tapes. Although I was trying to gather as much information as I could in the little time that remained, it was improper to pry about the minutiae of his life. Despite my curiosity, I had to respect the fact that he felt lousy, and his leisure time was sacrosanct.

The following summer I moved to Boston to further my studies and Adams research. No longer able to visit, we stayed in touch by telephone and postcards that he sent me from the road. Our final conversation took place eight months later, only a few weeks before his death. In August 1986, when Adams was bedridden and under the watchful eye of a home-health aide, I called to see if there was anything I could do for him. His caretaker answered and asked me to hold for a moment. While I paced anxiously for at least five minutes, Adams somehow dragged himself to the telephone. In a sentence or two he acknowledged that time was short, thanked me for calling, and hung up. That was right around the time that Dizzy Gillespie called him on Mel Lewis's behalf to say that Thad Jones, one of Pepper's dearest friends, had just died of cancer in Copenhagen.

A year later, once I began interviewing Adams's colleagues for this book, I spent a memorable afternoon with pianist Tommy Flanagan, Ella Fitzgerald's longtime music director. One of the last to see Pepper alive, he wanted me to know that transcripts of my Adams interviews were stacked on Pepper's nightstand days before he died. Flanagan told me that at one point, while he was perched on the edge of Adams's bed, Pepper awoke and tried to push those interview materials towards him. As if Flanagan was brushing crumbs off a tabletop with the backside of his fingertips, he accentuated his story by imitating Pepper's feeble attempt to move the heavy pile of papers in Tommy's direction.

As you can imagine, I was overcome by the implications of Adams's gesture. At first, I was astounded, something I must have communicated via my astonished gaze and stunned expression. Then my heart sagged, and eyes watered, as I realized that our months of work together had comforted Pepper at the end of his life.

Flanagan's interview was one of more than 250 I conducted. Repeatedly, interviewees affirmed Adams as a complex individual—a hero, a genius, a model of grace, an intellectual, a virtuoso stylist—yet someone also very hard to read. The contradictions they depicted intrigued me. Adams, they said, was an unworldly looking sophisticate, a white musician who sounded like a black one, and an exuberant saxophonist who was soft-spoken and mild-mannered off the bandstand. Many told me of his unprecedented agility on the baritone, that he played it like an alto. Before Adams, baritone sax was a cumbersome, fringe instrument. Today, because of his innovations, it is no longer viewed as a novelty.

Throughout his career, Adams told interviewers that the baritone's low pitch was like his speaking voice. He felt this, to some extent, explained his affinity for the horn. But more can be divined from his adoption of the instrument. For one thing, he greatly prized originality. Becoming a baritone saxophonist in the late 1940s gave him an opportunity to create a unique style on an infrequently heard instrument. Like Duke Ellington, whom he greatly admired, Adams believed he could similarly stand apart from everyone else.

Paradoxically, despite enhancing the idiom and securing his place in history, Adams's fealty to his instrument also hurt him. The public's disregard for low-pitched instruments and his resultant status as a sideman prevented him from both fronting his own band and recording far more albums as a leader, particularly any with widespread distribution. Moreover, refusing to double on bass clarinet disqualified him from studio work that could have helped financially when jazz gigs were sporadic.

When I began collaborating with Adams, I knew he was a superb instrumentalist but had no idea of the breadth of his contribution, how much his colleagues adored him, nor the degree to which his life intersected with some of the greatest poets, writers, painters, and musicians of his time. Thanks to our working relationship, the door to the international arts community burst open for me right after his death. As a result, I have had the remarkable privilege of speaking with so many of his esteemed colleagues, all of whom honored my interest in such a deserving artist.

Without a doubt, my interviewees are the heart and soul of this book. You will read some of them speaking, at times with surprising tenderness, of their fondness and admiration for Adams. His death was a significant loss, and their remembrances of his last few years are filled with sentimental accounts, sometimes with them breaking into tears. Besides helping me grasp the totality of Pepper's character and accomplishments, Adams's friends have given me a profound sense of interconnectedness with the jazz world. I'm grateful for their kindness and support, particularly when writing this book seemed insurmountable.

Despite Pepper's eagerness to share aspects of his career with me, he was reluctant to discuss his personal relationships or his time in the US Army.

Radio appearances and magazine articles, too, were of little use regarding his private life. So, I had to start from scratch.

Unraveling the complexities of such an enigmatic individual, plus digesting his thousands of hours of recordings, conceptualizing a narrative structure that suited his life, and transferring my personal observations and mountain of data into prose, took me thirty-seven years. Discounting some promising fits and starts, I waited until I felt ready to write the kind of book he deserved. That began in April 2017, after I gave a series of lectures about him, including a memorable residency at Utah State University.

Because chronological storytelling is hackneyed and outmoded, I always intended to write the book thematically. As Milton Lomask has argued, "The cradle-to-grave approach in biography is strictly a literary convention. Only in biographies and never in life do we get to know another human being in that consecutive fashion . . . No human life is so tidy, so uncomplicated, that you can construct it by simply reciting the events of it in sequence."

Biographer Leon Edel expressed the same point of view: "Biography need no longer be strictly chronological, like a calendar or datebook."

> Lives are rarely lived that way. An individual repeats patterns learned in childhood, and usually moves forward and backward through memory. . . . Chronological biography tends to fragment and flatten a life. A chronological recital of these facts reads like a newspaper; we jump from one item to another, and the items seem unrelated. . . . The task and duty of biographical narrative is to sort out themes and patterns, not dates and mundane calendar events which sort themselves.

After writing a few chapters with that in mind, it occurred to me that Adams's life would best be rendered in two parts. I decided to entitle the first half of the book "Ascent" to delineate his early years in Detroit and Rochester, New York, while becoming a virtuoso. "Dominion" could then cover the remainder of his life as a full-fledged musician based in New York City.

I further resolved that divulging Adams's death within this prologue freed me from ending the book with his demise, yet another banality. Insofar as "Ascent" could mostly proceed topically from Pepper's youth to his relocation in New York, I decided to defy common practice by beginning "Dominion" with a full account of Adams's terminal illness, then work my way back thirty years to his arrival in New York. Going backward, a device often found in cinema, not only struck me as a writing challenge, but seemed consistent with Adams's distaste for cliché. Emboldened by historian Doris Kearns Goodwin, who regretted not crafting her Lyndon Baines Johnson biography in reverse-chronological order, I liked how inverting "Dominion" circled me back to 1956, setting up my conclusion (chapter twelve).

Before I began writing, my years of research allowed me to comprehend Detroit's jazz culture and socioeconomic history. I was interested in understanding its automobile economy, profound racial problems, and illustrious jazz history. I was most curious about the extraordinary postwar "band of brothers," that clique of world-class jazz musicians who descended on New York City in the mid-1950s and reinvigorated the music.

Regarding Rochester, New York, where Adams attended public school, I wanted to know how that city came to be, why its economy was better off than the rest of the country during the Great Depression, and what took place there during World War II when Adams was a teenager. New York City's jazz scene in the 1950s and '60s, of course, intrigued me. I especially wanted to understand how jazz cross-pollinated with other arts and Adams's place within that world.

Inasmuch as biography is "a portrait in words of a man or woman in conflict with himself, or with the world around him, or with both," I sought to understand my subject's personality traits, strengths and weaknesses, how he behaved with others, and the inner myths he guarded and outer myths he promulgated. I wanted to explore his genealogy, learn about his childhood, get my arms around his relationship with women, and penetrate the veil of secrecy about his mother and tenure as a soldier. I strove to grasp why, despite his exceptional gifts and the universal respect he received from his colleagues, he wasn't financially successful. Was it because of his instrument, the way he conducted himself, or other factors?

Undoubtably, writing about Adams satisfied my wish to contribute something tangible to the music I love. But truth be told, my work over the years morphed from a passionate hobby to a raison d'être. After building pepperadams.com, in 2012 I produced a five-CD box set of Adams's entire oeuvre. The anthology was co-branded with *Pepper Adams' Joy Road: An Annotated Discography.* A sixth CD, produced separately, featured big-band arrangements of ten of his tunes. Now, with this companion study I, at long last, have fulfilled my original promise to him and myself.

Please visit the Instagram page (instagram.com/pepperadamsblog) that serves as the repository of Adams photographs and documents. More importantly, whether you are encountering him for the first time or are already hip to his career, be sure to listen to his glorious saxophone playing, some of which is posted at YouTube and pepperadams.com.

Part 1

Ascent (1930–1955)

Chapter One

In Love with Night

We had a beautiful scene in Detroit.

—Barry Harris

On a chilly Detroit evening in mid-April 1949, eighteen-year-old Pepper Adams and two Wayne University friends made their way to the Mirror Ballroom to hear alto saxophonist Charlie Parker. Eager to see jazz's new leader with his working group, all three met at the theater, only a mile from campus. They purchased their tickets, walked upstairs to the balcony, folded their coats, and waited patiently for the show to begin.

The Mirror, above Majestic School for Dance, was well known among Detroit's jazz community. "I knew of its significance even then," said drummer Rudy Tucich, who used to ride past it every day on his way to high school. "It was on the second floor. You went in—door on the right side of the building—and walked the stairway up. It was a place of wonderment to me." Along with the Grande, Beach, Graystone, Jefferson, Vanity, and Monticello, Mirror Ballroom was one of seven majestic dance palaces constructed during Detroit's early twentieth century Art Deco architectural boom. In 1941, it moved from its historic building on the Near West Side to 2940 Woodward Avenue, on midtown's central artery, two blocks from the palatial Masonic Temple.

For quite some time that memorable night there was considerable doubt whether Parker would show up. With their star attraction unaccounted for, management convinced trumpeter Dizzy Gillespie—scheduled to appear later that evening at the Paradise Theatre, only six blocks away—to front Parker's ensemble for the opening set. His surprise appearance, it was thought, would temporarily satisfy the audience while the Mirror's staff anxiously awaited their headliner.

Eventually, Parker arrived, albeit more than an hour late. After placating the theater's distressed crew, he exchanged words with his group, assembled his saxophone, and readied himself for the next set. The room was dark except for stage lights directed upon the bandstand. At long last it was finally time for him to count off his first number. "It was a night to remember," said Oliver Shearer, who, along with Pepper and Bob Cornfoot, watched the electrifying spectacle unfold. "Pepper was ignoring everybody in that whole room but 'Bird.' I've never seen anyone so excited in my life! He said, 'Can't you *hear* this, man?' He knew where he was going from that night on, I think."

Adams had been playing baritone sax for a little over a year. Paying his way through college by working local gigs, he was searching for his own sound and musical conception. But Parker's transcendent performance that evening gave Adams the paradigm he sought. He decided that his mission was to assimilate the many dazzling attributes of Parker's style and adapt them to the baritone. Not by copying Parker's licks and phrases, as so many others would do, but by refining a completely personal approach immersed in Parker's lexicon. As with Parker before him, his efforts would take a full decade to flower, necessitating thousands of hours of solitary practice and performing with others in a multiplicity of settings.

Adams held Charlie Parker in the highest esteem. "The greatest I ever heard" was how he would assess him in 1984, thirty-five years after seeing Parker at the Mirror. By 1949, Bird's revolutionary approach was a new way of playing jazz; highly virtuosic and intended for listeners as opposed to dancers. Sometime after his epiphany, Adams and Parker attended a Detroit jam session where each learned that both were classical music aficionados. "Somehow the name Arthur Honegger came up," remembered Adams about their very first conversation. "I said, 'Oh, I love Arthur Honegger,' and immediately I was Bird's friend because in Europe Bird had heard quite a bit of his music, but he'd never before met an American who'd ever heard of Honegger."

To attract Parker's attention as a teenager reveals Adams's emerging confidence and musicianship. For the next few years Parker would serve as a sage and confidant, in time becoming a trusted colleague. Even with his encouragement, it took a leap of faith for Adams to think that one day he could become a virtuoso jazz soloist on an instrument that, as Stanley Crouch wrote, had "the stand-off qualities and the resistant fury of a stallion that dares you to break him." In the late forties, most baritone saxophonists still had trouble playing in time with the rest of the band. To complicate matters, with the advent of Parker's audacious new music, far more harmonic sophistication and instrumental proficiency were expected from jazz soloists. Undaunted and resolute, however, Pepper was convinced that not only was the baritone an instrument he could master, but that no style would be too demanding. Moreover, he was certain that the horn was the ideal vehicle to forge a unique identity and make an enduring contribution to the art form. "I saw it as a wide-open field," said Adams many years later when recounting his early days as a musician and assessing the big horn's appeal. "No one was playing jazz in the way that I felt jazz could be played on the baritone. I thought I had a chance to do something entirely different."

⌐

In April 1947, two years before his watershed moment at the Mirror Ballroom, Adams had moved back to Detroit. When he and his parents left in the fall of 1931, America was coping with an unprecedented economic meltdown. Sixteen years later, though, the United States, with its allies, had won a world war. After two decades of deprivation and geopolitical instability, "she sits bestride the world like a Colossus," wrote historian Robert Payne about America's postwar dominance. "No other power at any time in the world's history has possessed so varied or so great an influence on other nations. . . . Half the wealth of the world, more than half of the productivity, nearly two-thirds of the world's machines are concentrated in American hands."

No US city was more emblematic of the country's mid-century financial and industrial might than Detroit. Its position as the country's economic powerhouse, begun forty years earlier with the inception of the auto industry, had remained intact after the war. Although Detroit's foundries had been converted into munitions plants during World War II, they had reverted to producing cars and trucks for American consumers soon after Japan's surrender, and jobs were being created in a wide range of allied industries. For that reason, Detroit attracted the attention of many throughout the country who were seeking employment.

Adams's mother was no exception. Her return to the city of her son's birth was primarily due to her new job in suburban Roseville's school system. Not only was the opportunity for a better life too enticing to pass up, but the move allowed her to reunite with old friends she had not seen since she left. Other circumstances, too, played a part in her decision. In 1943, three years after the death of her first husband, Park Adams, after a lengthy period of decline, she married Harold Hopkins, an employee of Langie Coal Company. They were married only two years before his death in 1945. Burying two spouses within five years, plus the strain of living during the Depression and war years, certainly made a complete change of scenery desirable.

One thing that she could not have anticipated was that Detroit's extraordinary music culture would in time embrace her only child as one of their own, functioning as a creative laboratory that would catapult him to greatness. Returning to Detroit was the best thing that could have happened to him, Adams recalled in 1984:

Going to Detroit at that time turned out to be a very positive thing as far as I was concerned, as far as developing as a player. I already had some background and could play pretty well. There was certainly a lot of room for improvement. And by moving to Detroit right at that time, I found myself almost immediately within a milieu of fine young players, people pretty much my own age, who were all very eager to play, and get together, and teach one another, and then just hang out together. It was a terrific atmosphere in which to learn music.

⌐

Before relocating to Detroit, Adams and his mother stayed all of March 1947 at Hotel Edison in New York City's theater district. The reason for visiting was to give her son a chance to study with tenor saxophonist Skippy Williams. Four years earlier, Williams took Ben Webster's place in Duke Ellington's orchestra, and Pepper first met Williams in Rochester the following year, after attending an Ellington performance.

During his four weeks in New York City, Adams learned about phrasing, how to listen to and blend with other musicians, and how to use dynamics to increase drama. He also learned how to build a set by playing some tunes softer or louder and how to vary tunes from night to night on a gig. Williams's basic formula was straightforward. First learn the melody and the chords, then analyze the chords and learn to play everything at the proper tempo.

Williams urged his young protégé to evoke different moods on the saxophone. He told Adams that some musicians play with different tone qualities in the upper and lower registers, and to aim instead for consistency: "Some guys take a solo and they play everything loud, and they don't know when to slow down or make it softer or louder. When you start a solo, you start it and get people's attention. Sometimes you have to play soft to get people to listen to you and then you bring it up."

Overall, Williams's approach to playing jazz encompassed both musicianship and self-awareness. "Those things make you a better musician and a better person," Williams said. "If you're a better person you're going to play better." With years of accumulated wisdom and indisputable credibility as a musician, Williams gave Adams a master class on the basics of playing jazz while also instilling in him a sense of proportion about other important things in life. Serving a pivotal role as a male mentor at a time when Adams was fatherless, Williams recognized that this special young man was a bit adrift and needed a helping hand. "Pepper was a lonesome person," said Williams. "There was something he wanted in life, and he lived for that horn."

Adams was forever grateful for Williams's mentorship. Although in interviews throughout his life Pepper fostered the conceit that he was a self-taught musician, he was fully aware that the adage is a myth, and in no way should his comments be misconstrued as impertinent. "I consider myself self-taught," he told his audience at Rochester's Eastman Theatre in 1978, "but anyone who is self-taught has had an awful lot of help from a bunch of people." What Adams was really saying about being self-taught is that, as a rugged survivor of the Depression, he was proud of what he was able to accomplish, considering his many constraints, and that he did so mostly on his own terms.

As for his mom, "She'd come by and watch me teach him, show him some little things. She would listen to what I said, and she'd go back to the Edison Hotel and she'd get on him," he chuckled. "His mom wanted him to be the greatest and he was. He was. He was great. But he wanted to be better, and he worked and worked. Then I didn't see him for a few years. Then I did start hearing him and I could tell that he accomplished it." A recent widow, Cleo Adams was a "lovely person," said Williams. "I never heard her curse. Once or twice, she would drink. I had some champagne at the house." If her time in New York City was marked by a fling with Williams, it was initiated years earlier in Rochester. "She told me personally that she really went with him for a while," said Oliver Shearer. A dalliance with Williams in New York City continued a pattern of maternal over-involvement that was just beginning to cast a shadow over Adams's life as he moved into manhood.

⌐⌐

During his first few weeks in Detroit Adams pursued employment and attended as many jam sessions as possible. The previous year he had quit high school halfway through eleventh grade so he could work full-time as a musician. Adams's first job was at a Dodge automobile plant, followed by a gig assembling auto bodies at Briggs Manufacturing. If Briggs was anything like what Walter Reuther experienced there twenty years earlier, it was back-breaking work with long shifts and a thirty-minute lunch break.

Adams had been very much aware of the Reuther brothers and the social unionist struggle for worker's rights since childhood. As a socialist and egalitarian who believed that America was intrinsically unjust, Pepper revered the Reuthers's work to bring about economic justice. Adams "didn't like the system in this country," said saxophonist Ron Kolber.

> He thought it was unfair. I used to call him "the great socialist." He said, "There's too many people that don't have things that they should have in this country, and they can't get them because of what they are." He was very adamant about that. . . . I think that deep down in his heart he was a rabid socialist. With those kind of wry witticisms that he had, he always sort of made fun of the system here. He'd always make some kind of remark like, "Oh, yeah, it's 'the land of the free and the home of the brave' if you happen to be free and brave."

In mid-November 1947 Adams left Briggs for a six-week stint at Grinnell's, Detroit's largest music store. After years of listening to classical music recordings and concert broadcasts on the radio, by age seventeen he was so knowledgeable about the repertoire that he was able to function in their record store department as its "classical guy." While employed throughout the holiday season, Adams worked next to the instrumental repair department. As a saxophonist keenly interested in what was going on there, he became friendly with one of its repairmen. Over lunch one day, Pepper's coworker told him about a Bundy baritone saxophone, essentially a student-model American-made Selmer, that had come in on trade. "It really plays well," he told Adams. "You should take it home and try it." Curious about the instrument, and eager to find a way to become more employable as an underaged musician in a city with competition aplenty, Adams loved the horn. By December he accumulated $125, enough money to buy it, thanks to his employee discount. Just as he hoped, he started getting hired right away.

Adams counterbalanced baritone gigs with a day job on the assembly line at Plymouth's body plant. It may have been here that Adams participated in a labor strike. Ron Kolber said that Pepper showed him a big scar on the palm of one of his hands, the result of a wound he incurred when he was on a picket line, participating in a strike at one of Detroit's factories, where he was assaulted by a chain-wielding counterdemonstrator.

That summer Adams first met tenor saxophonist Wardell Gray, initiating an important mentorship that lasted until Gray's death in 1955. By 1948, Gray had already recorded with Charlie Parker and possessed an international reputation as a jazz player of the first rank. His lyrical melodic lines, magnificent tone, sophisticated use of time, and strong sense of swing had a profound effect on Adams's emerging style. He and Pepper enjoyed trading horns when they gigged together in Detroit, and other than Sonny Stitt, Adams credited Gray as the finest baritone saxophone soloist he ever heard.

⌒

Dissatisfied with his menial factory jobs, Adams felt it was time to pursue a college degree to train himself for a career outside of music. By passing Wayne (later Wayne State) University's entrance exam, he was admitted as an English literature major that September. Adams was part of a group of about ten Wayne students who lived at Webster Hall, the school's only dormitory, got together for meals, went out to hear jazz, and fraternized well after the clubs closed. The gang often met in the student lounge to listen to records. "We practically lived in there listening to music," said Bess Bonnier. To the "long, gracious room with big, tall windows," each day Bob Cornfoot lugged his variable speed Bogen turntable and a fistful of 78s.

During the week Adams and Cornfoot watched movies that were playing at the Center or Forest theaters, about six blocks from campus. If Laurel and Hardy with Charlie Chase, or comedy shorts with Bobby Clark,

Charlie Chaplin, Buster Keaton, or the Marx Brothers, were playing at the Mayfair or elsewhere, they would grab a few laughs before going to bed.

"I always thought of him as kind of unhealthy," said Jack Duquette about Adams. "He was always a little bit pale," agreed Mike Nader. "It's as though he never saw the light of day." Duquette could never understand how Adams was able to play baritone and smoke as much as he did. A chain smoker throughout his life who smoked as much as four packs a day, Pepper began smoking cigarettes in Rochester when he was ten or eleven years old. His mother, too, was a habitual smoker. Camel was his preferred brand, and throughout his life he smoked those without a filter. "When he'd buy a pack of cigarettes, he would turn it upside down instead of just opening up a little flap, open up the whole thing, and then just dump them all in his shirt pocket," said Tom Fewless. "He'd put a Camel in his mouth, he'd smoke it, but he would never flick the ashes off," said Hugh Lawson. "When he'd light it and put it in his mouth, he would not put it out until it was *all* over." By 1984, after forty years of smoking, he had yellow nicotine stains on his right-hand index and middle fingers, between his fingernails and middle knuckles.

Most of Adams's university classes took place in Quonset huts that had been erected during World War II to accommodate its expanding student body. His favorite was Fran Striker's history of film course. Covering motion pictures from its infancy, it gave Adams a chance to see silent films such as F. W. Murnau's *Nosferatu* (1922) and early talkies made in the US and abroad. For other classes, Adams borrowed Bob Cornfoot's notebooks. "I was on the GI Bill, so they paid for my paper and my notebooks and that," said Cornfoot. "I'd come back from a class, [then] Pepper would take the notebook and go to his class and make his notes." At one point, when Adams was taking a musical appreciation class, they were covering Haydn. "No wonder the guy wrote 104 symphonies," Pepper wrote in Cornfoot's notebook. "The son-of-a-bitch only scored in octaves!" Adams did his term paper on Stravinsky.

〜

In 1947 and '48, before Adams drove a car, his mother would drive him to his gigs and stay to hear the music. "She kind of hung out," said Jack Duquette. "She wanted to be where Pepper was. She was alone. She tried to be not his mother when she was in that context." Instead, Cleo asked her son's friends to introduce her as Pepper's sister "Pat," another shortened form of her first name. A sure sign of his distance from her, Adams already addressed his mother that way. "It was a little different for me because I never knew anybody who called their mother on a first-name basis. I always felt a little funny about that," said Hugh Lawson.

Cleopatra Adams was a petite woman, about five-foot-four, with red hair and a broad, round face. Her eyebrows were arched above penetrating eyes, perched atop firm, wide cheekbones. "She looked pretty English or Irish," said Shearer. "She had a nice figure. She *really* liked the music. . . . There weren't too many parents letting [their kids] get to the real source." Bassist Charles Burrell also acknowledged Cleo's good looks. Ten years older than Pepper and twenty years younger than Cleo, Burrell, an African American, dated her in 1947. He admired her courage to do so, feeling that she was forty years ahead of her time.

An unfortunate carryover from Rochester, Cleo's over-involvement was a source of irritation for her son. Now, however, he was a college student and his nearly fifty-year-old mother, trying her best to look thirty years younger, was ingratiating herself with his university-age friends or seducing older musicians that he worked with in Detroit. Finally, his mother's flings became too exasperating. "She started going with a friend of his and that fucked him up," said Curtis Fuller. "I knew personally that it bothered Pepper. Pepper moved out because of it—her irrationality—and moved in with Elvin somewhere in Black Bottom when Elvin was [engaged] to [Pat Mead,] a skinny white girl." This experience made Adams more introverted than he was beforehand.

⮌

Throughout 1949, Pepper maintained his intense schedule, practicing his instrument, sitting in with various groups, and regularly jamming at Barry Harris's house at 4721 Russell Street. Apart from his studies and a part-time job at Music Box, a record store, during the first half of the year he had a steady gig with Willie Wells and drummer Charles Johnson. By fall there were Monday night jam sessions in the front room of Elvin Jones's house at 129 Bagley Street in Pontiac, as well as guitarist Kenny Burrell's Wednesday night sessions at Webster Hall.

In 1949 and early 1950 Adams often worked at Club Valley. "That was the best gig in town if you weren't old enough to work in a bar," said Pepper. "In Detroit in those days, you had to be twenty-one years old to work in a bar—not just the musicians, but the dishwashers, the night porter—and a lot of us were ready to work well before we were twenty-one," said Adams. "There was a lot of playing in people's houses, but there were places to play as well. Because of the fact that people under twenty-one could not get into bars, there were special places for them that didn't sell whiskey. Actually enough, there was a big audience for this sort of thing."

In virtually all the ensembles he played with in Detroit, Adams was the only white musician in the band. He was scorned by Detroit's white players for several reasons. First, they chided his full, commanding sound on an instrument that was more commonly played in a restrained manner and with far less wind. Second, "They objected to my harmonic things," recalled Adams about his early experimentation with chord substitutions that were unusually dissonant for its time. Third, they criticized his choice of material. "Absolutely no respect for Duke Ellington," Adams said. "Ask them to play an Ellington tune and they would say, 'That corny shit?'" Fourth, "was drugs, which was part of their social milieu. I was excluded from that automatically." Consequently, acquiring better-paying gigs was doubly out of reach. Besides ostracization by Detroit's white musicians, who generally received higher wages from club owners, Pepper was still underage in a town where most of the best-paying gigs took place at clubs where alcohol was served.

Figure 1.1. Duke Ellington. Recorded for Bethlehem in the mid-1950s. Public domain.

For some time, car production accelerated after the war. By 1950, the US auto industry alone accounted for one-sixth of the nation's employment. With the best paid blue-collar workers in America, Detroit was at its economic zenith, and its success provided discretionary income that benefited Adams. But major changes would soon occur that would degrade the city's fabric of life. First, coinciding with the last wave of millions of blacks moving north to escape racism and mechanization of the southern agrarian economy was the start of the gradual decline in the number of factory jobs. Additionally, restrictive housing covenants forced them to live primarily in Black Bottom and Paradise Valley.

Originally named for its rich black soil, by 1949, Black Bottom, a sixty-block area near downtown Detroit, was still the oldest and poorest section of the city. Half of it had substandard housing, and due to the recent influx was more overcrowded than ever. In Paradise Valley, the nearby entertainment area wedged between Gratiot Avenue and Grand Boulevard where almost a third of black Detroiters lived, housing was just as dilapidated.

Compounding their problems, racist lending regulations maintained by the city's banks continued to deny African-American homeowners the loans they needed to refurbish their homes. Because of that, housing deteriorated further, and it was difficult, if not impossible, to acquire any wealth. Exacerbating the situation was construction of the federal interstate highway system. Promulgated as an urban renewal project that would resuscitate downtrodden areas of the city, the massive highway project instead obliterated black neighborhoods and drove residents away.

While Detroit's freeway construction eviscerated inner-city black neighborhoods, the suburbs to the north and west became for white residents an increasingly attractive alternative to city living. The new expressways, spreading out from Detroit like an outreached, welcoming hand, granted relocated suburbanites' easy access to their city jobs from pristine communities built on newly developed farmland that they could access quickly in new-model cars assembled, they thought, in their hometown. But "white flight wasn't the only force emptying Detroit," wrote Scott Martelle. "During the 1950s, the Big Three automakers and other leading industrial concerns embarked on massive decentralization plans to build factories closer to regional customer bases around the country, but also to try to reduce one of the main pressures on profit margins: the cost of labor." As a result, Detroit's blue-collar factory jobs began to wane in the 1950s, adversely affecting neighborhoods that had been built around the plants to support such work. While half of all autoworkers remained in Detroit, decentralization led to the exportation of many allied industries that had once been central to Detroit's economic stability. By 1960, the transformation of America's auto industry was well underway. Only one-third of all cars were built in Michigan, much of Detroit's factory work had moved to other states, and most white-collar auto jobs had moved to Detroit's suburbs.

⌇

Since he purchased his Bundy at Grinnell's, Adams had been experimenting with mouthpieces to develop a sound on his instrument from which he could be heard without the aid of a microphone or amplification. In autumn, 1949, Wardell Gray returned to Detroit with a Berg Larsen mouthpiece that he was using on his tenor. Adams decided that Wardell's setup was the perfect solution for getting the kind of "firm and penetrating sound" he sought. He promptly mail-ordered one that would fit his saxophone, eventually having to drive across the border to Windsor, Ontario, to pick it up, because Berg Larsen at that time wasn't distributed in the United States.

Soon thereafter Adams decided to trade in his Bundy for a new, top-of-the-line Selmer "Super Action" B-flat baritone sax. B-flat horns were considerably lighter in weight than Low-A models and possessed improved intonation across its entire range. Adams bought his new instrument in January 1950 at Ivan C. Kay, Detroit's Selmer distributor. Because it would oblige him to spend several years paying for it, he brought an expert to the store with him to vet the instrument: Duke Ellington's baritone saxophon-ist Harry Carney. Adams had maintained his friendship with Carney and other members of Ellington's band since he first met them in Rochester in 1944.

By the time he was fully grown in 1950 or so, Adams hardly looked like the prototypical musician who grappled with the big horn. At five feet, ten inches and 155 pounds, with a wiry frame and a narrow chest, he more resembled a bookworm than a jazz musician. His complexion was sallow, his eyes blue, his lips thin. Brown hair closely cropped on each side of his head abutted a thick tuft on top. He wore horn-rimmed glasses beneath his high forehead. Big ears hugged his head, and his front teeth were crooked from insults received while playing ice hockey. Adams projected an owlish mien, with arched eyebrows and a pointed, slightly curved nose that aimed downward above nostrils that flared out in a triangle above a firm, rounded jaw. His face, with its peregrine intensity, belied a very gentle soul. "He was interesting," said saxophonist Beans Bowles.

Adams was soft-spoken and polite without any hint of aggression. His folksy, northern US accent was an amalgamation of upstate New York and central Indiana dialects that he acquired from his parents, with added flourishes obtained from transplanted southern factory workers and musicians who lived in Detroit. "He reminded me of Coltrane, in a way," said drummer Arthur Taylor. "He spoke really nice English: '*Hello, Arthur, how are you?*' Very proper. This guy was great. Coltrane was like that too . . . It has a sweetness about it."

According to Bowles, Adams "was kind of sheltered. A very studious guy. Very Caucasian." Nonetheless, his mild-mannered affect and understated appearance wasn't the look of someone timid or naïve. He was keenly aware of the intricacies of the world, firmly grounded as an individual, and intensely loyal to the music. A resilient child of the Great Depression with a laser-focused mind, Adams had the capacity to envision his future as an artist, the exuberance to design his life ahead of him, and the tenacity to make it happen.

Sometime before the spring 1951 semester, Adams withdrew from Wayne University. He had gotten busier as a musician and was promoted to manager at the Music Box, taking Bob Cornfoot's place. It's possible that he felt he was being pulled in too many directions at once, with little time left over for his studies. As part of his decision, it's likely he considered reapplying to Wayne as a full-time matriculating student to avoid the draft and the possibility of getting ensnared in the Korean War that had begun the previous June.

On July 12, Adams reported to Detroit's Army Draft Board. "I had a chance for a gig in Sweden and I wanted to take it, but I couldn't leave the country while my draft status was what it was," he said. After seeing his name on a list of forthcoming inductees, and aware that volunteering entitled him to request a specific post, "I just went on and volunteered, hoping I'd be turned down on the physical," said Adams. "Unfortunately, I passed the physical."

Once officially a new enlistee, Adams applied for an assignment with the military band so he could continue to practice his instrument and perform in live shows. With six years of professional experience as a musician, dating back to early 1946 while still in tenth grade, Adams's request was approved after he passed his audition. A few days later, as a new member of the Sixth Armored Division's Special Service Section, Adams was ordered to report for six weeks of basic training at Fort Leonard Wood in Waynesville, Missouri, two hours south of St. Louis and Kansas City, in the blazing hot and humid Ozarks.

Chapter Two

Now in Our Lives

I always felt that he was a little bit of a disembodied spirit.

—John Huggler

Pepper Adams's paternal lineage in the United States stretches back eight generations to James Adams, his sixth great-grandfather. Of Scottish origin, he arrived in the Massachusetts Bay Colony as an indentured servant in 1650. Only fifteen years old and fighting on behalf of Scotland during the final years of the English Civil War, he was captured on September 3, 1650, by Oliver Cromwell's forces at the Battle of Dunbar.

James Adams's voyage aboard the *Unity* began on November 11 and took six weeks. Many arrived in Charlestown in poor health. Adams and sixty-one others were bought by Saugus Ironworks in Lynn, Massachusetts. Their term of servitude was seven years. Adams worked the land four days a week and toiled in Saugus's foundry the other three. Ironworkers endured twelve-hour shifts. "The work was hard, dirty, hot, and dangerous," according to Geni.com. "More than likely, many ended up deaf or at least hard of hearing because of the constant hammering."

After obtaining his release in 1657, Adams and a few business partners founded the Scots' Charitable Society, the Western Hemisphere's oldest philanthropic organization. Five years later, he married Priscilla Ramsdell, a Puritan settler, in Concord, Massachusetts, who bore him seven children. One of his sons, James Jr., moved his family to Rhode Island where Nathaniel, Pepper's fourth great-grandfather, was born in 1708. Nathaniel likely died in Groton, Connecticut, where at least one of his ten children, James III, was born in 1732. James III would move his family inland to central New York, where the Adams clan would be based for the next four generations.

By the mid-nineteenth century, Pepper's ancestors had settled near Rome, New York. In 1879, his grandfather, Nathaniel Quincy Adams, married Alice Frances Cleveland in nearby Verona Mills. She gave birth to five children: Mina, Harry, Rita, Marguerite, and Park, Pepper's father. The youngest of five, Park was born in Rome on January 19, 1896. Listed as a boat builder in the 1880 census, Nathaniel Adams's trade was no doubt influenced by his proximity to Oneida Lake and the Erie Canal that passed directly through Rome. Mercifully, Pepper's grandfather died a few months before the Stock Market Crash of 1929. He would be spared the misery that his wife and children would endure during the 1930s.

~

After graduating high school, Park Adams's first job was at a Victor Talking Machine store in Chicago. Promoted to management, he was transferred to Detroit and tasked with opening a new outlet. In 1917 he married Lillian Miller, and a year later their daughter Mina was born. The marriage didn't last long. Lillian's accusation that her husband was "playing around" precipitated their divorce. Her granddaughter, Joie Gifford, said that Lillian later regretted her decision, feeling that her jealousy was unfounded.

By the late 1920s, five foot seven, slightly pudgy Adams lived with his second wife in Detroit's affluent suburb of Grosse Pointe Village. Adams was employed as general manager of Pringle Furniture Company. At 431 Gratiot Avenue in downtown Detroit, the massive store boasted that their sixty-five showrooms featured painstakingly chosen pieces by America's most renowned artisans.

It's not known whom he was trying to impress, but one of the only stories that Pepper heard about his father was the time his dad rode a horse up the marble grand staircase of Detroit's opulent Book Cadillac Hotel. "That's a hell of a feat of horsemanship to convince a horse to walk up a marble staircase," said his son. His father's colorful description of a hangover—"The inside of my mouth feels like the inside of a motorman's glove"—is the only expression that Pepper would remember him saying. But life changed radically when the giddy optimism of the 1920s ceased in those traumatic last days of 1929. By the time of Pepper's birth on October 8, 1930, eight months of back salary remained unpaid because those who bought furniture on credit were unable to make their monthly payments. Soon thereafter, Pringle's declared bankruptcy and all of Adams's expected salary vanished. With no work available and Detroit in a freefall, Adams exhausted his life savings and could no longer afford to pay child support to his first wife. Soon thereafter, he defaulted on his mortgage and his house was forfeited to the bank. Park and Cleo had no recourse but to pack their belongings and relocate to their respective family's homes in upstate New York and Indiana, since neither household could accommodate all three of them.

◡

Adams's mother, Cleopatra Marie Coyle, returned to the agricultural community where she was raised. Born on March 25, 1899, in Columbia City, Indiana (now Etna-Troy Township), she lived there throughout her teenage years with her older brother, James Rollie Coyle, and then again with her son for nearly three years. During the dark of the Depression, while the nation dealt with catastrophic starvation and unemployment, the Coyle homestead provided food and shelter for the two Michigan transplants.

At the farmhouse owned by Pepper's grandfather, there was a piano that young Adams began playing when he was three years old. He remembered one of his cousins, who played trombone, as "kind of crazy, a terrible lush." In 1934, during his last year in Indiana, his mother worked at a pharmacy owned by her cousin while Pepper attended nursery school at a one-room schoolhouse with about fifteen kids, some twelve years old.

The Coyles hailed from Connemara, Ireland's most Celtic area. Abutting the windswept Atlantic coast, Connemara is "a vast, archaic, hectic kingdom of stones and boulders and pond-studded bogs, of endless reaches of undulating hills and soaring mountains; of plunging waterfalls and wide, charging rivers," wrote Jeannette Haien. To this day most of its residents still speak Gaelic as their primary language. Their intense animosity for Britain dates to at least 1652, when Cromwell, under the threat of death, forced Catholic landowners to relocate from England to this remote, barely arable region.

Adams's maternal forebears left Connemara for America sometime before the Great Famine of 1645–1652, when one quarter of Ireland's population fled the country or died from disease and starvation. Those who stayed were victims of England's malevolent scheme, begun in 1647 and enforced by 100,000 British troops, to export nearly all Irish grain, meat, fruit, dairy, and vegetables to both protect its own proletariat workforce from hunger and sustain its overarching colonial aspirations. More than three hundred years later, resentment about Britain's genocide and shameless "Potato Famine" misinformation campaign is still felt intensely by the Irish. About this, Pepper's family was no exception. As a boy, Adams was told how a blight on Ireland's potato crop was used as a smokescreen for England's larger machinations. He was instructed that it was his responsibility as an Irish American to set the record straight with anyone he met who remained misled about Britain's evildoing.

One set of Pepper's maternal great-grandparents, James and Joanna Coyle, were born in Ohio and Indiana in ca. 1843 and ca. 1851 respectively. Adams's maternal grandfather, Charles, born in 1869, passed away in 1916. His wife Minnie Belle Burnworth, born in Indiana in 1872 and died in 1941, is buried next to Pepper's mother at South Park Cemetery in Columbia City. The Burnworth set of great grandparents—George W. and Martha J. Coggshell—were born in 1843 and 1837 and perished in 1916 and 1923.

Two of Pepper's maternal relatives were famous Americans. His cousin, Henry F. Schricker, was twice elected governor of Indiana, delivered Adlai Stevenson's nominating speech at the 1952 Democratic National Convention, and ten years earlier had declined Franklin Roosevelt's offer to serve as his running mate. Cleo and Rollie's great uncle, James Whitcomb Riley, from the mid-1880s until his death in 1916 was America's most widely read poet. Known for his children's verses, John Singer Sargent painted his portrait, and a large bronze sculpture of him still sits on Greenfield, Indiana's courthouse lawn.

Apart from Indiana politics, a love of reading is a trait deeply embedded among the Coyles. "Our whole family was kind of Irish intellectual types," said Pepper. "This goes back to the tradition of the family being quite literate." Cleo, who taught third grade, was well regarded as a reading teacher. "Everybody used to send problem readers to her," said Adams. "She really had a gift for that." Even adults benefited from her expertise. If they spent an hour with her, he said, "they were able to get a whole lot more out of their reading."

⌐⌐

During the summer of 1934, Adams and his mother were preparing to move to Rome, New York, six hundred miles away, to finally be reunited with Pepper's father and half sister. In anticipation of the family's reunion, Pepper's father suffered a heart attack, and, as a result, was out of work for the rest of the year. Before his illness, he was employed by McCurdy's, one of two major department stores on East Main Street in downtown Rochester. He had been recruited by the store's owner, Gilbert McCurdy, to re-establish the furniture department that closed at the Depression's onset. That Rochester had department stores that sold furniture in 1934 is one indication of the city's economic solvency as compared with the rest of the nation. According to David Cay Johnston, this was almost always the case. "For more than a century," he wrote, "Rochester was to industrial America what Silicon Valley is to the digital age."

In January 1935, with his father back on his feet, the family moved to an apartment at 627 Park Avenue in Rochester, and, by September, Pepper began kindergarten. Each day after school he enjoyed listening to Fats Waller's fifteen-minute radio show. "The earliest influence?" Adams was asked. "Fats Waller is the earliest one I can remember. . . . He played some harmonically very interesting things, and from him I got interested in [Art] Tatum."

By the summer of 1937, after years of renting, Adams's parents bought a two-story, five-bedroom house at 128 Belcoda Drive in Irondequoit, a pretty Rochester suburb wedged between the northern city limits and Lake Ontario. That September, Adams began second grade. "I was taught sight-singing," said Adams.

It was a great help. I'm all in favor of that. They should do a lot more. I was fortunate when I was in grade school. I was in a pretty affluent town in Rochester, New York, where even in the real hard times they did have music and art teachers for the very young children, which got me interested in both at an early age. They could afford these frills, like having a music teacher in grade school, for example, and had they not, my life would have probably been entirely different.

In 1938, before entering third grade, Adams started listening to Sunday radio broadcasts featuring John Kirby's Sextet. He also enjoyed listening to Fletcher Henderson's band on the radio. "There was a period there, I'd catch them five nights a week. I'd get an hour of Fletcher Henderson every night from a hotel in Louisville."

In February 1940, Pepper's paternal grandmother died in Los Angeles. Her body was transported back to Rochester for burial alongside her husband. Pepper's grief-stricken father died three months later. On May 21, nine-year-old Pepper Adams attended his father's funeral, his second one that year.

At that time, Pepper was in fourth grade. "I was doing everything I could to make money and put food on the table from the time I was nine, like selling candy and cigarettes door-to-door in a cardboard box. I'd make a few extra bucks in the course of a week. It was pretty regular after school."

In the fall of 1941, more than a year after his father's death, Adams began sixth grade at Hoover Drive Middle School. Rochester's schools loaned musical instruments to any student who was interested. Although instruction wasn't provided, one could gain entrance into the school's band, taught by Prescott Whitney, if you learned how to play an instrument on your own. With that as an incentive, Adams first borrowed a trumpet, then a trombone, before settling on clarinet, and he joined the school band by the winter of 1942.

By midyear, Adams began taking saxophone lessons with John Wade at Columbia Music Store on South Clinton Avenue in downtown Rochester. Adams may have started on C melody saxophone, said his friend Chris Melito, and probably took lessons there for six months or a year at most. After his lesson, Adams often bided his time by listening to jazz records at McCurdy's, where his father and half sister had worked several years before. Eventually, he sampled their entire jazz collection. Mrs. Gates, who managed the record department, took notice of this special boy who was so interested in jazz. In learning more about him, she discovered that he was fatherless. She told him that her husband Everett had an extensive jazz library and invited Pepper to their home for dinner. He accepted her invitation, and after dinner both her husband and Adams retired to his study where they listened to records and discussed music theory. These informal get-togethers continued seasonally until Adams moved to Detroit, and throughout his life, whenever Adams returned to Rochester, they either got together or spoke at length on the telephone.

At their first meeting Adams asked Gates, a saxophonist, Eastman graduate, and violist with the Rochester Philharmonic who would later join Eastman's faculty, if he knew the tune "Baby, Won't You Please Come Home." He wanted to know if it was a blues. Gates, familiar with the tune, thereupon taught Pepper the basic 12-bar blues structure. "He had a real keen intelligence," said Gates. "He had a way with words. He had kind of an instinctive feel for putting words together. He had a sly smile that was marvelous. He captivated both my wife and myself."

> He did not have much formal study. . . . Among all the things
> that he had as a talent was the ability for critical listening. He
> could listen, and he would be able, for instance, to be critical of

intonation. Listening to Pee Wee Russell on clarinet, he said, "He doesn't really play too well in tune, does he?" I said, "Well, he does sometimes, when he's sober. . . ." His ability to concentrate on what he was listening to—for a ten-year-old, eleven-year-old kid to be able to do this—this is quite remarkable!

On January 8, 1943, a half a year after Adams began studying with John Wade, the Rochester Red Wings announced that they had signed Pepper Martin, a star member of the World Series champion St. Louis Cardinals, to play with and manage its squad. Adams acquired his lifelong nickname soon after his schoolmates saw Martin's picture on the front page of Rochester's newspapers and claimed that there was a facial similarity.

꙰

March 3, 1944, was another school day in Rochester's very long winter, but this would hardly be an ordinary day for thirteen-year-old Pepper Adams. Duke Ellington's orchestra was playing the first of three nights at Rochester's Temple Theatre that evening and Pepper had tickets for the show. Because of his interest in contemporary classical music, Adams at a young age developed an affinity for music with dissonant textures and audacious percussive elements. With his musical preferences very much in place, he was excited to hear Ellington's orchestra for the first time in a concert setting. It embodied many of the musical attributes that Adams prized: rhythmic drive, virtuosity, astringent harmonies, complex orchestral writing, and nuanced instrumental color. Plus, it showcased an exciting array of soloists conversant in New Orleans jazz right through the Swing Era and beyond.

Ellington opened the show that evening with his customary four-bar piano introduction to Billy Strayhorn's "Take the 'A' Train." Had Rex Stewart, the band's cornetist, scanned concertgoers before playing the tune's opening strains, he would have noticed Adams's enthusiastically applauding, broad-smiling, young white face in the theater's balcony. The two first met on Saturday afternoon, March 4, when they were introduced by Skippy Williams, whom Adams had first met at a nearby luncheonette. Adams told Stewart that he was his favorite soloist in Ellington's band. Touched and flattered by this exceptional young man, Stewart invited the no doubt astonished teenager backstage so he could meet Harry Carney, Johnny Hodges, and other bandmembers.

As Adams explained thirty years later, "Rex was my favorite soloist in the band because he was the most inventive harmonically."

He was playing the things I was searching for. Of course, there are some marvelous soloists in that band. I don't want to denigrate anybody, but Rex's harmonic approach in those days was what set him apart. . . . Stewart had this kind of a bleak harmonic and rhythmic approach that no baritone player had, but, hell, that's what I liked, so I adopted some things from Rex. Rex Stewart could play some very off-the-wall notes and make them fit very well because of the context in which he put them. I found that really exciting, listening to the way that things that are not part of the harmonic structure could be made a part of it, and then figure out why it worked.

Adams had been playing the piano since he was three and studying clarinet and soprano saxophone since 1941. Because he had saved enough money to purchase a tenor saxophone six months before Ellington's performance, however, Adams's new preoccupation was trying to make sense

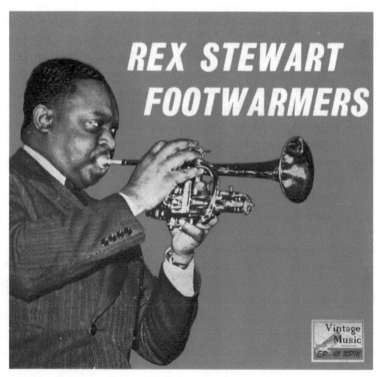

Figure 2.1. Rex Stewart. Recorded in Paris ca. 1939. Public domain.

of the technical and harmonic achievements of Don Byas and Coleman Hawkins, two of the period's illustrious tenor sax practitioners. Hawkins's "approach to chord changes was fascinating, and particularly during that time, well, the beginning of the forties on through the forties," Adams told Marc Vasey. "He was at the peak of his game, zipping in and out of chord changes, and doing it in such a musical way. It was like a magician, with a trompe l'oeil kind of thing, where something happened and you say, 'What was that?' But it went by so smoothly, you didn't realize that something very unusual had just happened there until you started to try to analyze it."

As Pepper told Peter Danson, "I was studying more classical music at the time. Although I enjoyed jazz, which I listened to on the radio—which is what you did in those days—it was really classical music which interested me first. Then, when I started to hear Ellington and all those chords and voicings, I knew immediately: . . . Debussy, Ravel, Elgar, Delius, the tonal palettes of twentieth-century music were all there. You know, the rough kind of excitement of the Basie band could be a lot of fun and I certainly liked them as soloists, but Duke's band was an entirely different ballgame."

It's hard to overstate how valuable meeting Rex Stewart was for Adams, especially considering the role he assumed as a lifelong father figure. By taking Adams backstage, Stewart was perpetuating the tradition of established musicians supporting young, aspiring ones. Coleman Hawkins was another musician who encouraged Adams. "When I was a kid, Coleman Hawkins exhibited a great deal of fondness for my playing on tenor, and I played a completely different way than Coleman played," said Adams. "But he apparently saw validity there and he was an early advocate of my playing." Hawkins, Stewart, and bassist Oscar Pettiford each heard Adams play at Rochester jam sessions and praised his musicianship. Much later, in January 1956 when Pepper first moved to New York and was still unknown, drummer Kenny Clarke invited Adams to sit in at his Café Bohemia gigs. Then, by virtue of his influence as house drummer at Savoy Records, Clarke produced *Jazzmen: Detroit*, Adams's first great recording. A few weeks later Pettiford, one of Jimmy Blanton's successors in Ellington's orchestra, recommended Adams for the baritone saxophone vacancy in Stan Kenton's band. As a result, Adams stayed with Kenton—his first tour with a nationally known group—for six months until he, trumpeter Lee Katzman, and drummer Mel Lewis quit Kenton in San Francisco to form their own quintet. Adams's stay on the West Coast led to his first substantive write-up in the jazz press, three months of recording in Los Angeles's studios, and two albums as a leader for West Coast labels.

While a youngster, other benevolent elders stepped in to help. Most notable, of course, was Everett Gates, Rochester's respected pedagogue. But Stewart's profound act of kindness was the most transcendent event of Adams's boyhood. Ellington's Temple concerts also catalyzed Adams's enduring love affair with Duke's music. In 1977, thirty-three years later, when Adams's friend Gunnar Windahl stayed for six weeks at Pepper's home, "Every day I think he listened to Duke Ellington," said Windahl. "Duke Ellington meant a lot to Pepper." As a professional musician Adams often performed selections from the Ellington/Strayhorn songbook, his ballad writing incorporated characteristics of Strayhorn's compositional style, and Strayhorn classics such as "Day Dream," "Chelsea Bridge," and "Star-Crossed Lovers" are lovingly treated on some of Adams's most exquisite commercial recordings. Adams also maintained another connection with Ellington's band. Many years earlier, in admiration of his extraordinary improvisational ability, Harry Carney deputized Pepper as his understudy. Carney, however, only missed one two-week gig in forty-five years. Because it wasn't practical for Ellington to use Adams for that brief stretch of time, Pepper was never able to relish playing with Duke's band.

In many ways Adams's life mirrored Stewart's, who had early success as one of jazz's premier trumpet soloists before his career stalled. Similarly, Adams was a sensation in New York upon his arrival in 1956, created a stir in Los Angeles while based there for a few months in early 1957, but, eventually, his career, too, also languished. That's not in any way to diminish their considerable achievements, nor imply that their musical growth stagnated. It is simply a measure of how much both struggled financially and how little attention they received from record companies and the international press. "Pepper was a very talented cat," said saxophonist Doc Holladay. "I always had the feeling that Pepper really knew how talented he was, and it was always a frustration for him to realize that people didn't appreciate him." Because of this, Adams identified with and had fondness for struggling artists and unsung heroes, such as Stewart, Strayhorn, painter Lyonel Feininger, or composer Arthur Honegger. They were special because, like Adams, they were unique, accomplished, and neglected.

⌣

During the summer of 1944, Adams stopped by Columbia Music Store, where he had worked the previous year. He told Joe Weinstein, the store's assistant manager, of his interest in jazz. Weinstein suggested that he speak with Raymond Murphy, who was managing Columbia's mail-order jazz record business. Murphy was eighteen years old, between high school and his freshman year at the University of Rochester. Adams was thirteen, between junior high and high school. "I collect jazz records and I'm very much interested in jazz," Murphy told Adams. "So, I invited him to come over, and that began a friendship that lasted until he went to Detroit."

Just arising in the 1930s and '40s was "the emergence of a collector's culture, in which young, mostly white men . . . engaged in fraternal associations around and through rituals of intense listening and verbal expression," wrote John Gennari. "We talked about jazz, we listened to jazz, we read books about jazz," said Murphy. He remembered Adams as one of the few he met at that time who completely immersed himself in jazz. "My biggest impression was the intense devotion he had to it; I mean right from the beginning."

Besides developing a small group of friends who were equally devoted jazz fans, Adams at the time also met accomplished musicians in addition to those in Ellington's band. In 1944, for example, Adams sat in at Golden Rooster with pianist Meade Lux Lewis. In mid-1945 he met Oscar Pettiford, who was touring with Coleman Hawkins, and later met drummer Denzil Best and pianist Thelonious Monk, Hawkins's other sidemen. Equally significant was Pepper's friendship with saxophonist Bob Wilber.

Adams first met Wilber in 1944 at a Max Kaminsky gig at New York City's Pied Piper (later renamed Café Bohemia). For only four months in late 1945, two years before Adams left for Detroit, Wilber was enrolled at Eastman School of Music. Pepper and Bob, sometimes with John Huggler, spent Saturday afternoons listening to and playing along with jazz records at Wilber's apartment. Although "he didn't have much facility, he really had a feel for it," said Wilber about Adams, "You could really tell that this guy was not just fooling around. He was serious about it. You can tell when a guy listens to a record, he's digging the right things, he's hearing the good things. You could tell that he had that sensitivity to music." Adams had never practiced with a player of Wilber's ability. At age eighteen, just a year after he quit Eastman, Wilber was recording with Sidney Bechet in New York. Wilber's example of how to play jazz spurred Adams's development and laid the foundation for his steady gig in 1946 and '47 at the Elite.

↬

It's the prevailing view of psychologists that the early loss of a parent is often a harbinger of cancer, depression, substance abuse, isolation, or intimacy issues. Ultimately, Adams manifested each of these conditions, with isolation remaining a constant throughout his life. An only child raised by a single parent, he spent a lot of time on his own, listening to records and the radio at the expense of playing outside with kids in the neighborhood. As an adult, he didn't teach saxophone as so many of his peers did, thereby developing a coterie of admiring students. Rather, he preferred to spend idle time in solitary pursuits such as reading fiction, doing crossword puzzles, or going to art museums by himself. By 1971, he moved from Manhattan's vibrant West Village, where he had friends and fans, to a brick row house in Canarsie, an area of Brooklyn cut off from New York City's subway system, its major highways, and its jazz scene. He didn't marry until he was forty-five, and by the time of his death ten years later—at home alone, only in the presence of a hospice aide—he had separated from his wife, with whom he had no children. By then it had been many years since he'd contacted relatives from either side of his family, primarily due to his deep-seated resentment that they didn't help in any tangible way after his father's death. Instead, in a very real sense, his family consisted of fellow musicians and jazz fans scattered around the world.

Self-reliant Adams went at it alone. He didn't marry into wealth, never had a benefactor, wasn't part of jazz impresario Norman Granz's stable of well-paid musicians, and rarely had the support of a record label or management to promote him and book his gigs. Off by himself, perusing art books and listening to classical music while chain-smoking Camel "straights" and drinking whiskey, he empathized with overlooked artists like himself who were deserving of widespread acclaim. Perhaps later in life, had he adopted a child, dedicated himself to a cause, or made himself available to teach up-and-coming baritone saxophonists who would have given just about anything to study with "The Master," he may have freed himself from his self-inflicted imprisonment of isolation.

By the time he left Rochester for Detroit, sixteen-year-old Adams had already experienced several traumas. Within five years, his father, step-father, and two of his grandmothers died. The general atmosphere of the country during the Depression and war years, too, had a sobering effect on his outlook. People throughout the country were suffering, citizens were fraught with anxiety, and it was hard for his family to plan when work was so hard to acquire.

Moving from city to city, sometimes every year, was a constant throughout his early years and served as a dress rehearsal for his adult life as a musician. Much like brief jazz gigs, not staying in one place for any length of time made it difficult for him to make intimate friendships. As a result of moving so often, Adams acknowledged that he had some gaps in his education. Mathematics, however, was an exception. "Math I never had any trouble with," said Adams. "I had a natural aptitude there so that was no problem." The more profound holes for him were structural: a childhood taken from him by constant relocation and the need to work long hours after school.

"You know where you have some precocious kids, and some mothers don't know how to deal with it?" asked John Huggler.

> She sort of pedestalized him. He kind of took it but I could tell that there was a kind of reticence about it. I think that jazz was giving him a way out rather than a way into something. . . . He was terribly close to his mother, meaning that I thought there was something unwholesome in it. I think there was a lot of pain there, and I think he may have been trying to find an out; that the closeness was of a suffocating nature for him. . . . I gather that she was a doting mother, too. She was just inordinately proud. She treated him a little bit as if he was already a man doing great things.

Despite being such a kind, sensitive person, Pepper never knew true, unfettered intimacy. "My, he was a little lost soul!" recalled Mrs. Everett Gates. "I'm glad we befriended him." Her heartfelt act of love at McCurdy's was precisely what Adams needed throughout his life but didn't receive. "I think Pepper was always a loner, and I think that he would have carried the seeds of that loneliness even in the middle of Detroit and a totally [liberating] black experience," said Huggler. "I think it was fundamentally in Pepper: Sad and alone. I don't feel his playing particularly projected that."

For Huggler, a conversation with Adams could be difficult:

> He didn't have very much of a sense of spontaneity about him. When he thought, and when he spoke, it was very deliberate, as though he were really paying attention to his inner mind as to how he should phrase things. He was very much a stickler for not being misunderstood. I would get tired of that. You had the feeling that he spoke when spoken to, and when asked for an opinion he was very careful and deliberate, and even plodding and slow, about getting it out. Not from any sense that I got of dull-wittedness or anything like that. It might have been

a holdover from the attention he'd gotten early on. If he was going to speak when he felt unprepared, he would want you to understand that he was saying exactly what he thought, and he had thought that out. It was a little difficult. It didn't trip along the way people do when they feel lighthearted. I certainly got the feeling that Pepper was at that time a rather sad person.

In addition to his emotional baggage Adams chose an especially challenging occupation. According to psychologist Frank Patalano, high psychosocial stress may be one of the chief reasons why jazz musicians of Adams's generation (or earlier) died prematurely. "The main stressors were severe substance abuse, haphazard working conditions, lack of acceptance of jazz as an art form in the United States, marital and family discord, and the vagabond lifestyle that most jazz musicians lived," wrote Patalano. In his informal survey of the life expectancy of jazz artists, he deduced their average lifespan was fifty-seven years. Adams almost made it to fifty-six.

⌐

The dearth of local jazz musicians created an opportunity for Adams to perform at a young age with seasoned musicians who were either too old to be drafted or had been discharged from the Armed Forces. In January 1946, only a few months after the war in the Pacific ended, Adams began a steady six-nights-a-week job at Elite (pronounced EEE-light), on West Main and Ford, near West Broad Street. The working sextet was "a hip jump band," said Adams. "We had a terrific drummer, Teddy Lancaster. He was killed in Korea." Pianist Jimmy Stewart was the leader. Saxophonist Ralph Dickinson, who had just returned from the Army, joined the group in October 1946. (Huggler replaced him in 1947.) Walter Washington, the bassist, had worked previously with Lucky Millinder. At one point, Frank Brown played drums. A guitarist nicknamed "Spoons" would sit in from time to time. He used a dime for a pick and a long cigar would hang from his mouth when he played. Adams played soprano sax, still in a Dixieland style, and the band gave him a chance to solo, though he was struggling to articulate his ideas.

In the spring of 1947, Elite went out of business, ending an extremely rich year-and-a-half musical experience. It was Adams's only steady gig in Rochester and, as a budding sixteen-year-old soloist, one of his last chances to play in front of an audience before he left for Detroit. Because he was gigging six nights a week, it was difficult to wake up in time for school or be attentive in class. In December 1946 he dropped out of high school. Adams wrote about that period of his life in 1953, while on a troopship returning from Korea:

> One of the major reasons that I only completed two years of high school was my independent attitude. I held my own opinions and did not necessarily change them merely because a teacher told me they were incorrect. Several teachers appreciated my viewpoint and were very kind and helpful, but others deplored my attitude and predicted that I would come to a bad end. If a teacher would say, "We must respect our God and our country above all else," I would say, "Why?" This is not only inconvenient; it is embarrassing since it is a difficult position to support, especially when I added, "The philosopher Rousseau says that one must respect one's personal integrity above all else and I am inclined to agree with him." On the occasion when this happened, as on many other occasions, I was sent to the office of the Boy's Councilor, Dr. Wishart, for "punishment."
>
> Wishart was a kind and honest man. If he believed I was wrong, he would argue with me, clearly and logically, not forcing me to accept any conclusions; if he believed I was right he would say so. On this occasion he agreed with me that the "God and country" bit was a meaningless cliché and an emotional trap for fools. He showed me other references to support my belief. I particularly remember his showing me an E. M. Forster article.

Although there was less demand for entertainment directly after the war, Rochester's nightclubs continued to present talent. Starting in 1945, pianist Joe Strazzeri ran Squeezer's at 420 State Street, across the street from Kodak's world headquarters. Typically, gigs were followed by open jam sessions. "Pepper used to stop in there and just get on the stand," said trumpeter Leo Petix. "He was looking to get with a group and get on the road." Even though he was hardly an accomplished player, pianist John Albert felt that he already had a conception of what he was doing as a soloist. "He played quite well, and for a person his age (middle-teens), he had already developed a style, certainly different than anyone there that day," wrote Albert.

He was playing a soprano sax. The rhythm section, I don't recall who they were, responded to his playing. He was a good "time player," and left holes they could fill in. That's what I remember most about his style. He would blow a single note or a phrase and then wait for the rhythm to come to the next change or even go by it, and then he would dig in and catch up with great time and ideas. This to me was different than the other horn men. They seemed to stay on top of the beat and didn't seem to use the rhythm [section] to their best advantage or let them have some fun, too, on the chorus. So, I guess what I heard that made him different and new was a thinner, biting sound. [He] played more notes and more interesting melodic flights, and used the rhythm section like Miles Davis. . . . The musicians were half and half in their comments. The horn men weren't that "gassed," but the rhythm section was impressed. I know that later, when other horn men were changing their ideas and sound, I thought back to that day and I wondered if any of them remembered where they heard it first.

Chapter Three

Inanout

His practice regimen was from the time he got up until the time he
went to sleep. He'd rather do that than anything else because he didn't
see anything else in the army that was worthwhile.

—Ron Kolber

Throughout his first eighteen months as a soldier, Pepper Adams was
stationed at Fort Leonard Wood in Central Missouri. A bustling place,
swelling with 100,000 people at any one time, this sprawling 61,000-acre
military installation in the Ozark Mountains had once served as both a
training facility for American soldiers and a work camp for German and
Italian POWs during World War II. A year or so prior to Adams's arrival,
it was chosen as an ideal site to prepare American troops for the Korean
War because its scalding, humid summers, subzero winters, and rocky terrain were much like the harsh weather and rugged landscape of East Asia.

From mid-July through the end of October 1951, his initial fourteen
weeks in the army, Adams experienced activities at the camp that were
completely alien to him, such as firing bazookas, running through obstacle
courses, learning how to build airstrips, and being taught how to repair
bombed-out pontoon and trestle bridges while under fire. "We all had to
go through the same training," said saxophonist Norb Grey: "Six weeks of
infantry training and then eight of combat engineer."

In mid-August while still in basic training, Adams unexpectedly received
an emergency furlough concocted by Charlie Parker. Bird had called the
base, posing as the physician of Adams's mother, so that Pepper could play

a gig with him on August 24. Before that time, Pepper had only played with Parker at a few Detroit jam sessions.

"He managed to get me called to a field telephone during Bivouac Week to say he was playing in Kansas City the following weekend," said Adams. (Bivouac Week is off-base encampment training, during which soldiers learn to improvise temporary shelter.)

> It's near the end of the month and I don't have any money left. So, he says, "If you can get there, stay with me and I'll give you the bus fare back to Leonard Wood." It's about 180 miles or something. Come the weekend, I hitchhike to Kansas City, arrive around seven on a Friday evening, call up the club, and say, "Is Charlie Parker there?" "No, and the son-of-a-bitch will never work here again!" *Clang!* [The irate club owner slammed his telephone handset onto its base.] Here I am in Kansas City. $3!

As a backup plan, Adams brought with him the telephone number of a mother of one of his army buddies. With the money he borrowed from her, Pepper got enough to eat, saw the film *Roman Holiday*, spent two nights at the YMCA, then returned to the base on Sunday. Despite his disappointment about not gigging with Parker nor spending a few days with him, Adams forever remained proud of Bird's invitation.

Two months later, once he finished combat engineer training, Adams joined the Sixth Armored Division's Special Service Section, the largest of Leonard Wood's three bands. Typically, Adams's company played while the American flag was raised in front of headquarters. On Monday morning at six o'clock, they would play the "Star Spangled Banner" and a few marches for a new group of soldiers who had just gotten their uniforms. A 4:30 p.m. band rehearsal was occasionally called to play a tune or two for a few battalions. And on Saturday mornings, Pepper's troop was required to play for the graduation ceremony of those bivouac groups who were off base for seven days. Usually, soldiers were finished with their duties by mid-morning on Saturday. If nothing was planned that afternoon, they were free until 7:00 a.m. on Monday morning.

According to Doc Holladay, the common tasks that soldiers were expected to accomplish each day, such as neatly making their bed or perfectly marching in formation, Adams did with little care. "A shirt has to be hung up in line, right after a certain coat and trousers, and when you open up your footlocker at the end of the bunk bed there's compartments on the top and there's stuff on the bottom," said Grey. "Everything is supposed to be put in a certain order, rolled up a certain way. It's kind of a regimentation that some guys just won't put up with."

Adams ignored such standardization. "He never went out of his way intentionally to do it," said Kolber. "He just didn't give a shit." He would grouse, "No one's sleeping in my bed but me so why do I have to make it? I can't understand why you have to make your bed so tight that you can bounce a quarter off of it, and then you jump in and go to sleep." When marching in formation, he was lackadaisical. Pepper wasn't breaking rules per se, nor in any way retaliating in a passive-aggressive manner. "I think his whole point was just to keep his mind free," said Holladay. "The tendency there is to program *your* brain to be responsive as they want you to be responsive. I think he stepped back from that." Consequently, some soldiers would avoid being seen with him, afraid that by associating with Pepper they'd somehow risk being shipped to Korea, something every musician was doing their best to avoid.

Although being a band member gave them more latitude than other soldiers, Pepper pushed the envelope further. In his own way he was standing his ground, much as he did in high school. Similarly, he would be admonished for his infractions, "but the only people that were reprimanding him were Army people, which he didn't pay any attention to," laughed Kolber:

> It had absolutely no importance to him whatsoever! In his rationale, if it didn't seem to be good sense, he just didn't do it. He never antagonized even the officers or the sergeants or the people in power there, because he was such a likable guy and he always came up with really common-sense reasons for not doing what he was supposed to do. It was amazing how he [would] get out of these things. When he used to get dressed for bed, he used to drop his pants and step out of them, and the pants used to sit there on the floor, and then he would get into it the next morning. He said, "Listen, you don't give me enough time to get dressed. It's hard for me to get up in the morning. We get up and everything is always rushed. This way I just step in, pull them up, and [Adams snapped his fingers for emphasis] it's *there*, man! I'm on time and you're happy. What difference does it make where I keep my pants?"

"But you can't leave your clothes on a dirty floor," was one officer's response. "How can it be dirty when you're making us scrub it every day?" Pepper replied. "He never got into direct confrontation with them," chuckled Kolber. "He was always too nice of a guy, and if something that they said made sense, then he would accept it. He sort of went along with most things. But when it started infringing on his personal habits, *then*—"

> Whenever we took physical training, he was beautiful! When we had to jump and meet our hands above our head, he would never jump. He said, "Listen, I can play. That's what I'm here in this band for, to play, and I can't do all these other things." He says, "It doesn't take that much physical energy to strap a baritone sax around your neck." He told the sergeant that. The officers always used to call him into the office, so I never heard too much about what they did. But he always came out smiling, smoking a cigarette, saying, "It's *all* straight." And they never bothered him, but they did shake him out. He was too well liked. No one could really dislike him because he was an intelligent man, knew what he was talking about, so people didn't monkey around with him too much. They knew that, whatever he did, there was a good reason for doing it.

↬

Throughout the first half of 1952 Adams stayed on base, practiced relentlessly, and performed with Special Services only when required. Although at heart he was an introvert, who practiced alone in his bunk with a near monomaniacal fervor, when called upon to do so he was also an enthusiastic team player. It's possible that his practice routine was based on what he learned from Charlie Parker. In his teens, Bird practiced fifteen to sixteen hours a day for three to four years, learning the blues and "I Got Rhythm" in all twelve keys, playing scales in each direction, and mastering "Cherokee" at a super-fast clip. Adams "had all these tunes, just the chord changes," said Kolber. "They were all in 'concert.' He got them from Barry Harris." As Doc Holladay remembered, "Pepper used the service as a school, in a sense":

> He'd pick a tune and he would learn that tune to where he really had it by memory. . . . He'd start playing it in all different keys, so he had that [melody line] in all kinds of keys and be comfortable with it. Then he'd start playing off the changes of the tune, and he'd . . . [do] that until he'd get the changes down to where he could run the changes on the tune. Then he'd start

to run that in all the keys. He would digest a tune, just take it apart, make it his own, and then he would go on to the next tune. All the time he was in the service, in the band where I observed him, he was constantly doing that. A new tune every day or two. He could play for hours. The rest of the guys would go out to hang out and party, and Pepper would be in there taking a tune apart.

When Adams practiced chord changes, "He attacked them [with] what scales he could use against the changes, what arpeggios he could use, and then he would try to attack every note in that change from every angle," said Kolber. After some time doing this, Adams told Kolber, "I don't even think of changes anymore. When a piano player plays a chord, I know what it is. I can hear all phases of it and I can fit it into what I want to do. I don't let technique hang me up because I practice all the scales going in all different kinds of directions, going up one scale, coming down another scale, and then doing them in fourths." He said, "I've done this to such an extent that I can attack any change from any direction and go to any direction I want to go." He was just progressing until it got to a point where he would have so much under his fingers, he could do anything he wanted with it.

On July 11, after completing his first year in the army, Adams received a two-week furlough and went home to Detroit. Sometime between July 13 and 26 he recorded eight tracks for Vitaphone in Ann Arbor, Michigan, led by drummer Hugh Jackson. This was Adams's first commercial recording in which he could be heard soloing on baritone saxophone. At age twenty-one, Adams was beginning to display some of the hallmarks of his mature style: a unique sound; a consistent swing feel; precise articulation; melodic paraphrasing; tasty, harmonized counter melodies; freedom in articulating the theme; long, flowing lines and beautiful pacing; tremendous drive on up-tempo tunes; and an amazing wealth of ideas. If the session were released in 1953, it would have signaled that a new voice on baritone saxophone had arrived. Unfortunately, the world would have to wait another three years.

Before returning to Missouri, Adams attended a jam session at Elvin Jones's house, where he first met Elvin's brother Thad. Initiating one of the most important relationships of his life, one that would in years to come be central to jazz, Pepper realized that his and Thad's musical approaches were very much alike. "Here's a cat proceeding on many of the same aesthetic lines that I've been doing for a number of years, but in the same way of combining beauty and humor," Adams told Albert Goldman. "He, too, was playing harmonies that were certainly not common among jazz players." At the time, said Adams, Charlie Parker "played some very interesting and very complex harmonic substitutions but the Bird-influenced players mostly did not."

Back at Fort Leonard Wood in August and September 1952, Adams practiced his saxophone, drilled with his outfit, and bided his time. Adams's rank was PFC (Private First Class), said Kolber, "one of the newer people in the band, so, therefore, that meant that he had a lot of time left in the army. The army couldn't ship you any place unless you had at least six months to go. That's the main reason he got sent out because they needed people fast in Korea."

Before traveling to San Francisco and awaiting orders, Adams was granted his one-week "terminal leave." He returned to Detroit, did some playing, and visited with Thad Jones, one indication of their deepening friendship. Jones, in fact, was one of only two people to write to him while he was stationed briefly in Japan.

In early October, after his transfer to San Francisco, Adams traveled to Asia, disembarking first at Seattle's Fort Lawton. There were 2,900 soldiers aboard the ship out of California. The deck was so crowded at times, they couldn't move in any direction. "About the second day out, the motion of the vessel makes many of the men ill, and the sight of these men heaving their guts is enough to sicken most of the rest of the men," wrote Adams. "Before long, everywhere you go you are met by the sight of men being violently ill, and pools of puke drying on the decks, in the stairways, the latrines, and the compartments. The smell alone is enough to make you sick."

Aboard the troopship that departed from Seattle, Adams was part of a small combo who entertained soldiers twice a day. The band was granted better sleeping quarters and a small practice space. "The first day out of Seattle was very calm and there were only a few scattered cases of seasickness," wrote Pepper.

The second day, however, we hit the ground swell, and the monotonous rolling of the vessel sickened many of the men. As I came out on deck after breakfast, the rail was lined with men desperately ill. The sight was more than I could take; I joined them and felt miserable all morning. . . . After noon chow I began to feel better, and gradually the majority of the troops recovered. There were a certain number of men, however, who were sick the whole seventeen days of the crossing.

In Japan, Adams was stationed for almost three weeks at Camp Drake in Saitama while awaiting reassignment. Finally, in mid-November, he boarded the Sgt. Joseph E. Muller troopship for Incheon, Korea, then was ordered to report to Tenth Special Services headquarters in Seoul. After one rehearsal he was taken by jeep to his first performance with its Second Platoon.

Traveling nearly every day for the next six months, Adams performed in about 250 shows for US troops and their allies. "We'd pitch in an open area someplace, or anywhere near where these different groups were," said platoon member Al Gould. Where there were fifty men or more, we'd put on a show." Adams's Second Platoon consisted of twenty-eight to thirty-three men depending on the rotation. About two-thirds were entertainers. Others maintained the trucks, put up tents, and set up the stage and generators. "The one vehicle that was the main one, that we carried a lot of our uniforms and that kind of stuff in, looked like a metal-covered, two-and-a-half-ton army truck," said Gould. "We would always throw a tarp over it which said 'R&R.' R&R stood for the name of the show: 'Road to Ruin.'"

The roads that the convoy navigated were unpaved and rocky, producing clouds of dust and only allowing them to plod along at a top speed of fifteen miles an hour. Sometimes they had to travel at night, making their journey even more treacherous. The slow pace during the day would enable soldiers to observe the rugged terrain, including marijuana that was growing near the road. Someone would yell, "Pot!" the convoy would screech to a halt, and the excited soldiers would jump out. "Marijuana was growing all over the place," said Gould. "They'd run out and get whatever they wanted."

Living conditions were substandard, and cigarette rations were one of their few luxuries. Sometimes there'd be latrines available, but for the most part soldiers would relieve themselves alongside the road, using toilet paper that was provided. They rarely had a chance to bathe, only occasionally having access to cold showers when asked to do impromptu performances for officers at the front line.

Every so often Pepper was able to break away from his squadron. "A couple of times I hitched along the front line, carrying a carbine in one hand and my alto in the other, to visit Frank Foster," said Adams. "Frank was in the Seventh Infantry Division band. We sure had some good sessions."

Despite the joy that soldiers derived from smoking pot and playing music, danger lurked everywhere. Three members of the Second Platoon were killed prior to Adams joining: one by a sniper and two by land mines. "When the enemy broke through at times at night, we were there but I don't think you could say we did any actual fighting," said Gould. "We were riding with the infantry guys at the time. We were prepared. We carried M-1s or M-2s." At one point, Pepper's horn got battered when his truck rolled over due to airplane fire. The full extent of his injuries isn't known, though one of his legs was hurt. Years later he told saxophonist Mark Gridley that sometimes before an attack the enemy would play trumpets to create a sense of dread. "Can you imagine how haunting an experience that would be?" asked Gridley. As novelist Philip Roth explained, "Chinese Communist soldiers, attacking sometimes by the thousands, communicated not by radio and walkie-talkie—in many ways theirs was still a premechanized army—but by bugle call, and it was said that nothing was more terrifying than those bugles sounding in the pitch dark."

Apart from being on edge, Adams witnessed plenty of suffering. One of his duties was to function as a backup stretcher bearer. If the infantry was shorthanded, he was responsible for carrying wounded soldiers on stretchers to where they could be taken for medical care. At MASH units he saw soldiers with missing limbs. On one occasion he had the horrifying experience of witnessing a gunner, carrying a box of ammunition and wearing a bandolier around his torso, suffer a direct hit and explode. Periodically, Adams also functioned as an ammunition bearer and risked the same fate.

Korea was such a ghastly experience that Pepper chose not to discuss it, though he did acknowledge how fortunate he was to survive. "Going over on a troopship and having it jammed to the gills, and then coming back on a troopship and having it half full, made me realize something about casualty rates," he said. For other reasons, too, Adams's military experience was vexing. In his journal, addressed to Kim Byong Joo, the houseboy who served his platoon while based in Seoul, he vented his exasperation: "You might not realize (as I didn't before I came into the army) the vast, sheeplike stupidity that so many people are capable of. My time in the army has certainly lowered my estimation of humanity; I never realized there were so many idiots in the world." Nevertheless, his army stint "gave him a lot of time to work on what he wanted to do with his horn," said Jack Duquette. Furthermore, Adams gained a perspective that he didn't have before he enlisted. At the outset, it was his goal, should he survive, to return to college, finish his degree, and become a journalist. Once he realized that four years of musical training in Detroit made him far more advanced than all the professional musicians in his platoon or those in other units who were considerably older and had toured with name bands, he concluded he should instead become a professional musician. Adams explained his decision in his journal:

Three or four years ago I frequently went for several days at a time without practicing, but it is no longer possible for me to do this. Formerly, while I enjoyed playing greatly, there were other things that I enjoyed equally. Now, however, if I go for any length of time without playing my horn, I grow restless and anxious to blow again. It is this fact more than anything else that has convinced me that I must try to make it musically when I get home. Logically, I should do otherwise; music is an extremely overcrowded and insecure field. I have enough schooling available under the GI Bill to enable me to finish college. I believe that I could be quite happy in life as a college instructor, and I am sure that I would be a very good one. I am equally sure that I could be successful at several other occupations, too, but I realize that I could never be at peace with myself unless I first make every effort to satisfy my musical ambitions. There is no shame in defeat; the only shame would be in premature capitulation.

At long last, in late May 1953 Adams stepped aboard the Marine Phoenix troopship in Busan for his return home. In early June he disembarked in Seattle, then arrived in Detroit a few days later. On June 5 at Fort Custer, Michigan, Adams, with the rank of Corporal, submitted his paperwork, was transferred to the US Army Reserve, and was relieved from active duty. Meanwhile, "A brief recession at the end of the Korean War gave automakers the opportunity to merge, close, or relocate scores of Detroit-area factories," wrote Nelson Lichtenstein. "Hudson, Motor Products, Packard, and Murray Body closed their doors, Chrysler took over Briggs, and Ford slashed the Rouge payroll by twenty thousand. Ford won worldwide attention when it moved engine-block production to an 'automated' factory in Brook Park, Ohio." It was in this climate, when the automobile business started moving out of town, that Adams returned to Detroit.

Chapter Four

Twelfth and Pingree

In Detroit, every instrument that you could imagine playing, they had
someone that was really special on their instrument. On the baritone
saxophone, Pepper was that person.

—Louis Hayes

When Pepper Adams returned to Detroit in mid-1953, it was America's
richest city. Its median family income was higher than New York,
Chicago, or San Francisco. Because of concessions that the United Auto
Workers secured from the automobile industry, Detroit's factory workers had
the best-paying manufacturing jobs in the nation, and its black population
was wealthier than anywhere else in the country.

The US was still primarily a manufacturing economy, and that jug-
gernaut was led by Detroit. "If the auto industry had a good year, that
meant a good year for the steel industry, for the plate glass industry, for the
chemical industry that supplied the paints," said author Roger Lowenstein.
Due to pent-up consumer demand for automobiles after the Second World
War, Ford, Chrysler, and General Motors were awash in money, even though
labor agreements had compromised some of their profit. GM had record
earnings for ten years in a row, thanks to its wildly successful Chevy Bel Air.

Back in his civilian clothes, Adams spent his first few weeks in Detroit
getting reacquainted with musicians he hadn't seen since he enlisted. Most
were impressed with how much Adams had improved as a soloist. In recognition of Adams's newfound prowess, Billy Mitchell deputized him as his
full-time sub at Blue Bird Inn.

On January 1, 1954, Mitchell went on the road for an extended period, ceding the leadership of Blue Bird's house band to Beans Richardson, the group's bassist. Adams replaced Mitchell, joining Richardson, Thad Jones, Tommy Flanagan, and Elvin Jones. The quintet would work together six nights a week until mid-May, when Thad joined Count Basie's band.

Those 135 magical nights were a peak experience for Adams, a once-in-a-lifetime opportunity to play Thad Jones's new small-group music every night with him and two-thirds of his all-time favorite rhythm section. In the previous year Thad had written a provocative book of originals, including "Zec," "Scratch," "Let's," "Elusive," "Compulsory," and "Bitty Ditty," compositions that Adams considered masterpieces and continued to play and record throughout his career. Thad had originally joined the Blue Bird band in late 1952. At that time, Roland Hanna asserted, only Dizzy Gillespie was Thad's equal. "Miles would stand under the air conditioner with tears running out of his eyes when he heard Thad play," said Hanna.

At 5021 Tireman Avenue on Detroit's Near West Side, the Blue Bird "lasted quite a few years in a black, working-class neighborhood," said Adams:

> It was a working man's bar with great jazz. It was very common to have the band in there swingin' like a son-of-a-gun, and half the people at the bar were sitting there in overalls with their lunch pails on the bar behind them, either on their way to the late shift at the factory or on their way home and stopping by the bar for a taste. . . . Great place, great atmosphere. Nothing phony about it in any way. No pretensions, and great, swinging music. Certainly not the same thing as paying a $12 cover and sitting down at an aluminum table for a blenderized drink. The clientele at the Blue Bird was 99½ percent black. It was strictly a black scene in which I felt no uneasiness at all.

As an aspiring fifteen-year-old saxophonist, Charles McPherson spent a lot of time outside the Blue Bird listening intently to Adams. "I learned a lot," said McPherson in 2018:

> First of all, some articulation things that I could hear slightly Bird doing on records. But records can't really show you everything. The technology back then isn't what it is now, and records can show only so much anyway. But I could notice certain things that Bird was doing with his tongue in terms of articulation

on the horn. When I heard Pepper in person, right in front of me, I could hear that same approach to articulation that he was doing on the baritone. And, in fact, it seemed like all guys that were playing this kind of so-called "modern music" were using this tonguing and slurring kind of thing on their horns when they played long lines. . . . This impressed me because this takes some virtuosity to bring this off.

⤷

As ethnomusicologist Mark Slobin wrote about his hometown of Detroit, "In the first half of the twentieth century, the auto industry produced cars and culture, but in the second half the city manufactured musicians." Whereas Detroit has good reason to boast about its long history of important musicians of all types, extending well past the Motown hit factory of the 1960s and early '70s, never before the postwar era or since has this city produced such a concentrated group of world-class musicians, all approximately the same age, who would burst onto the jazz scene at the same time and profoundly influence the music's history. This tightly knit, unofficial collective of like-minded musicians born around 1930, refined their skills in Detroit's vibrant 1950's nightclub and after-hours scene. For almost ten years, from 1947 through 1955, this extraordinary generation consisted of a dizzying roster of now legendary musicians.

One way to gauge the degree to which these Detroiters influenced jazz is to acknowledge the well-known bands that some of them joined once they first left Detroit. Frank Foster joined Count Basie. Paul Chambers was hired by Miles Davis. Curtis Fuller recorded with John Coltrane. Barry Harris played in Max Roach's quintet. Donald Byrd joined Art Blakey's Jazz Messengers. Kenny Burrell joined Oscar Peterson's group and toured with Jazz at the Philharmonic. Tommy Flanagan worked with J. J. Johnson, Miles Davis, and Sonny Rollins. Elvin Jones toured with Charles Mingus and Bud Powell. Pepper Adams recorded with John Coltrane, then toured with Stan Kenton and Chet Baker. Doug Watkins worked with Blakey and Rollins. Louis Hayes joined Horace Silver's group.

Philip Levine, who served from 2011–2012 as poet laureate of the United States, was deeply impressed by the Detroit jazz musicians he knew in the late forties and early fifties. "I had no idea that somebody not born with millions could make a life out of art, but I saw these people doing it in the face of all kinds of discouragement," said Levine.

It gave me a model. You do the work and you don't whine. You do it for the sake of the work. They played because that was what they were meant to do. All of these guys to me were real eye-openers. I was starting to write poetry, and here are these guys who were about my age . . . and they all knew what they wanted to do already. Not only did they all know what they wanted to do but they were very serious about it. There wasn't any [romanticized] get up in the middle of the night and write poems shit. It was, "You got to master an instrument, you've got to master the classical aspects of the instrument." I remember Tommy, and Bess, and Barry. You'd sit down and hear them play Chopin. They loved this stuff! Kenny Burrell would play classical guitar. The literature for the instrument they were out to master. All of them. Pepper too. And they were into it with such seriousness. I thought, "Jesus!" They were the greatest thing in the world for me. When I looked at these guys, and women, I saw what real dedication was all about. I would say, at that time Pepper (and Tommy) were just *totally* into what they were doing. It was, "Out of my way. Nothing is going to derail me. I know what I want to do. I'm gonna be the best goddamn baritone saxophonist in the world."

Interlude

DETROIT'S JAZZ EDUCATIONAL ECOSYSTEM

How did Adams's remarkable generation of Detroit jazz musicians come to be? First was the influence of Grinnell's, a special retailer and piano manufacturer. Second, a great industrial city's affluence was leveraged to create a first-rate public-school music program. Third, the longstanding custom of informal jazz education was a well-established means of passing the tradition's vocabulary from Detroit's professional musicians to those on their way up.

The Grinnell brothers always had big ambitions. At the turn of the century, when they first opened their factory in Holly, Michigan, an hour's drive northwest of Detroit, they proclaimed it the world's largest piano facility. Eventually, with more than forty stores in Michigan, Ohio, and Ontario, Grinnell's became the nation's largest music supplier and piano distributor. "Grinnell's had this thing where you could take lessons down at the store on

Woodward, but the other thing you could do is buy a piano 'on time,' on layaway," said historian Dan Aldridge. "So, you have all these working-class families in Detroit who had their own piano. It was because of Grinnell's." Their business model of supplying pianos to so many Detroit families is one of the main reasons for the city's dazzling success in producing such an abundance of influential musicians. "The family piano's role in the music that flowed out of the residential streets of Detroit cannot be overstated," wrote David Maraniss:

The piano, and its availability to children of the black working class and middle class, is essential to understanding what happened in that time and place, and why it happened. . . . What was special then about pianos and Detroit? First, because of the auto plants and related industries, most Detroiters had steady salaries, and families enjoyed a measure of disposable income they could use to listen to music in clubs and at home. Second, the economic geography of the city meant that the vast majority of residents lived in single-family houses, not high-rise apartments, making it easier to deliver pianos and find room for them. And third, Detroit had the egalitarian advantage of a remarkable piano enterprise, the Grinnell Brothers Music House.

Coinciding with Grinnell's start-up, Emma A. Thomas, Detroit's first supervisor of music, established a visionary elementary-school program that emphasized singing. Due to her influence, "public school music programs in Detroit had been recognized among the country's best by the mid-1920s," wrote Mark Stryker. "Elementary students had specialist-taught music classes three or four times a week, and it was common in the 1930s and '40s for students to start playing an instrument in the third grade."

Ultimately, four high schools—Cass, Miller, Northern, and Northeastern—produced the bulk of Detroit's greatest jazz musicians. Lucky Thompson, Yusef Lateef, Art Mardigan, Kenny Burrell, Willie Anderson, Lorenzo Lawson, Frank Rosolino, and Milt and Alvin Jackson attended Miller. Situated in Black Bottom on Detroit's Lower East Side, Louis Cabrera was their band director and the main reason for so much of its success.

Sam Sanders, Barry Harris, Alice Coltrane, Ernie Farrow, and Bennie Maupin attended Northeastern. The school had a glee club, marching band, and instrumental music instruction. "There was a strong emphasis on learning the basics of the language of music," said Maupin. "I had been in the glee club. Everybody sang. There was no way you could ever go to that school and not sing on some level."

Charles Boles, Claude Black, Sonny Red, Donald Byrd, Paul Chambers, Doug Watkins, Roland Hanna, Teddy Harris, and Tommy Flanagan attended Northern High. Northern's jazz program started in ninth grade and was run by Orvis Lawrence, who had played with Glenn Miller and the Dorsey Brothers. "Lawrence [was] a very good Teddy Wilson-type piano player, a very good musician," said Boles.

Pepper Adams didn't attend public school in Detroit, but many of his colleagues attended Cass Tech, and the school exerted a strong influence upon Detroit's musical culture that invariably shaped Adams. Cass functioned as a magnet school for the city's most gifted young musicians, including Doug Watkins, Paul Chambers, Wardell Gray, Donald Byrd, Bobby Byrne, Hugh Lawson, Ron Carter, J. C. Heard, Bob Pierson, Major Holley, Roland Hanna, Gerald Wilson, Al McKibbon, Howard McGhee, Lucky Thompson, Billy Mitchell, Sam Donahue, Julius Watkins, Dorothy Ashby, and Alice McLeod Coltrane. (Byrd, Watkins, Chambers, Hanna, Thompson, and Coltrane transferred to Cass.) Its music program was as rigorous as graduate-school programs are today. "You got there at something like seven in the morning and you were never through before 9:30 or 10:00 p.m.," said Charles Burrell. According to Burrell, "You started taking piano, harmony, theory":

On your respective instrument, all the principals of the Detroit Symphony taught there. You did all your academics on top of that. You started with those, and then you had Orchestra three nights a week and you had Jazz Band two nights a week. . . . In the meantime, you'd listen to the big guys who were playing in joints and things. You'd go out to these joints. A part of your experience was getting to hear them play. You had your mother's consent.

Cass was a total immersion. "When you finished Cass Tech, you could go out and audition for any symphony in the world," said Burrell. "You were a finished musician."

⏚

Detroit's jazz players were extremely charitable when it came to passing the tradition onto younger aspirants. "There were a lot of private lessons going on, and all kinds of opportunities to hear some of these guys and be exposed to their playing," said saxophonist Bennie Maupin. In 1944, for example, when Ted Buckner returned to Detroit from Lunceford's band to lead a small group at Three Sixes, he tutored Yusef Lateef. There were the Jones and McKinney families passing down their musical traditions. "I had good teachers," asserted Curtis Fuller. "I didn't have trombone teachers necessarily. I had people like Pepper, and Miles, and Coltrane." Joe Henderson, Maupin's tutor, invited his acolyte to work alongside him on local gigs. "Detroit was like that," said saxophonist Mike Coumoujian. "Even when you are learning, you can get a chance to play with Barry or somebody like that. They would always let you come up and play."

In 1949, when Frank Foster moved to Detroit from Cincinnati, he taught many young musicians, including Barry Harris, how to work with tritone substitutions. "I think Frank Foster was probably one the best things to happen to Detroit when he came," said Barry Harris. Before joining the army in 1950, Foster mentored some of Northern High's budding musicians. "He was becoming a pretty astute arranger," said pianist Teddy Harris. "He would get Donald Byrd, Sonny Red, and myself and Claude Black, and take us to his house where he would teach us how to read his arrangements."

Although Foster during that period influenced Detroit's jazz players, and other musicians, such as Sam Sanders, Teddy Harris, Harold McKinney, and Marcus Belgrave, would later serve as important local mentors, no Detroit jazz musician has had a greater intellectual reach than Barry Harris. As a theorist and sage, Harris influenced his entire generation of musicians, both in and outside of Detroit, as well as many younger and older musicians. "I learned more about improvisation from him than any one person I studied with," said Yusef Lateef. "We called him the 'High Priest.' He's a brilliant man."

Beginning in the late 1940s, the workshops that Harris led at his home every week became so widely respected in the jazz world that they drew established touring musicians from around the US, including John Coltrane and Sonny Rollins, who would stop by when they were working in Detroit. Harris's salon was a place for the exploration of all sorts of ideas. "They discussed literature, politics, philosophy," Charles McPherson told Richard Sheinen. "I would hear these names batted around: Spinoza, Schopenhauer. I thought, 'Man, these people are really different.'" Harris, a taskmaster who took education seriously, at one point asked McPherson to show him his high school report card. He had a C average and Harris was unimpressed: "Oh, you're an average kind of guy," the pianist told

McPherson. "It won't work because this music is complicated and you're not going to be able to play it if you're a C kind of guy." The admonition continued: "You have to read more. You have to broaden everything about your mental capacity. You can't be in this narrow, skinny bubble here. You have to expand, because when you play this kind of music, the bigger your view is, the better you play. It's not just notes and chords."

Detroit's workshop environment was extremely supportive despite its earnestness. "We would exchange music, we would transcribe music and share it, we would rehearse a lot," said Kenny Burrell. Adams remembered that time as such a great environment in which to thrive, "because the contemporary kids—I was growing up and playing in kid bands when we were in our teens—were such great musicians. And having so many good musicians in a city like that provides an incentive too. There's so many highly efficient players that one has to get pretty good on one's instrument or you have no chance of ever getting a gig. You really got to work at it."

There was a genuine brotherhood; a sense of being a part of something together that was culturally significant and much larger than themselves. "Every musician I know from Detroit has said this," remembered Eddie Locke in 1988: "I saw Donald Byrd not too long ago. He said, 'I never got the same feeling that I got in Detroit.' There was something else going on there."

What Byrd and Locke were referring to was Detroit's non-judgmental approach to teaching the art form, and the profound connection that bound all of them together because of it. "The friendship [shared by Detroit's jazz musicians gave you] the feeling that you could go ahead and *play*," said Locke. "There were so many little, funky joints that had music in it. . . . When you're in [those] joints you could go ahead and do your thing!" Although young musicians knew better than getting on the bandstand until they had acquired a certain level of technical mastery, playing alongside Detroit's older musicians was a liberating experience. Coupled with the down-home informality that was found in the city's many cozy neighborhood venues, it allowed aspiring jazz musicians to take risks in front of an audience. It gave them a chance to develop their identity as soloists without the fear of both embarrassing themselves and of dealing with the suffocating machismo that was customarily meted out by aggressive musicians in other cities. Thus, the hallmark of Detroit's jazz apprenticeship model was its nurturing way of passing down the tradition. Its jazz musicians became so accomplished in part due to the city's remarkable, truly anomalous, female-centered educational culture that contrasted so dramatically with the prevailing male-dominated, cut-throat ethos, historically a part of America's jazz culture since its infancy.

That's not to say that playing jazz in Detroit was a lighthearted walk in the park. Quite the contrary. "Pepper was a *player!*" inveighed Locke.

He was *serious!* There was no bullshit up on that bandstand! That was another thing about Detroit. When you got on that bandstand there was no fucking around! *Play!* When the cats would play, [they] would tell you [if] you weren't playing. They would try to show you when you weren't doing it, not just say it. They'd say, "Come over to my house." They cared enough about the music to do that. That's what Pepper was involved with and that's what made him such a beautiful, beautiful cat.

The immutable bond that connected Detroit's jazz family lasted well past the time they left town. "A large number of musicians, and people who are friends from Detroit, have continued to be good friends here for thirty years or so," Adams told Ben Sidran. "I can sit and name forty or fifty people that I've maintained friendships with consistently over at least a thirty-year span. I doubt if there are many people in other walks of life that could do that."

If a Detroit musician needed money, another Detroiter provided it. "I can remember many times when we've helped each other out," said Billy Mitchell. "One just gets the money and walks up to the other and says, 'Hey, I had a couple of record dates today. Here, you take this.'" If someone needed a homie for a gig or recording date, they willingly showed up. When Tommy Flanagan was busy touring the world with Ella Fitzgerald, he was happy to fit into his dense schedule an Eddie Locke recording date in New York. "He didn't say, 'How much money you got?'" said Locke. "He said, 'Where? What's it gonna be, man?'" The love and loyalty that Detroiters felt for each other, based upon so many hours of working, eating, and laughing together in Detroit, was in their bones, something they carried with them forever.

Twelfth and Pingree

PART II

On March 6, 1954, a few weeks after Adams began his steady Blue Bird gig, Kenny Burrell formally established the New Music Society. Its dual mission was to produce ongoing Monday-night jam sessions, held at World

Stage Theater, and to organize occasional Tuesday-night concerts elsewhere in town. Adams played there every Monday. Because it wasn't far from Wayne's campus, many college students would attend, and before long it was packed with excited jazz fans, many of whom were underage and couldn't get into other clubs. Much like the Blue Bird, the crowd was enthusiastic and respectful. "One hundred fifty people would have been a really large crowd because the place wasn't big," recalled Elvin Jones. "It was just as if you were in Carnegie Hall. It was the same kind of reverence, the same sort of atmosphere."

That July, Wardell Gray returned to play the Blue Bird. Nine years older than Adams, Gray served as one of Pepper's most important mentors. When they exchanged horns on the bandstand for their own amusement, it gave Adams a chance to hear Gray on baritone, an instrument he rarely played. Other than Sonny Stitt, Gray was the only improviser at that time who played baritone saxophone with precise articulation and a confident time-feel.

On either horn Gray was a magnificent soloist whom Adams greatly admired. "There existed a certain kind of elegance in those long, smooth, swinging phrases," wrote Mike Baillie. From Gray, Pepper learned "playing in various ways to break up the feelings, having different approaches, different sounds on the instrument, like playing a lyrical phrase with a lyrical sound and then being able to alter your sound to play something else." Besides emulating Gray's long lines, gorgeous tone, timbral variations, use of quotations, adroitness with the time, and his unparalleled melodic gift, Adams similarly adopted his use of a Berg Larsen mouthpiece.

Gray's shocking death on May 26, 1955, when he was found dead by the side of the road outside of Las Vegas after playing Benny Carter's first set on opening night at brand-new Moulin Rouge hotel, was a personal tragedy for Adams. "The night when he heard about Wardell Gray, if Pepper had known who it was that took Wardell out, Pepper would have [taken] a gun and killed him," said Doc Holladay. "He was pained, he was angry, and by his own admission, he was violent." According to Buddy DeFranco, Gray "OD'd and the guys around him panicked, threw him out in the desert." Bassist Red Callendar, in agreement with DeFranco's account, blamed dancer Teddy Hale for not acting responsibly: "If the guys he was with had any brains, they would have taken him to a hospital. They could have saved him. Instead, he died and they dumped him in the desert. . . . Had he lived, he would have been one of the truly amazing players of our time. He was anyhow."

Figure 4.1. Wardell Gray. Recorded at the Hula Hut Club, Los Angeles, August 27, 1950. Public domain.

Other than Gray, the only other baritone soloist that Adams admired was Sonny Stitt. Widely respected for his alto and tenor saxophone playing, Stitt also played baritone from 1949–1952 when he co-led a group with tenor saxophonist Gene Ammons. "I heard them several times in person," said Adams. "Only three years later, Sonny and I worked together, and I tried to get him interested in playing my horn, but he said he didn't play baritone anymore. He just wouldn't touch it, wouldn't even consider it." Besides his swinging, fluid lines, Stitt's articulation made a deep impression on Adams and many other players. "Stitt set the pace for articulation on the saxophone," asserted saxophonist Gerry Niewood. "The clarity of his ideas and his technique [were] just at the highest level."

Harry Carney, Duke Ellington's baritone saxophonist for nearly fifty years, of course, served as a model of how the baritone could be played. "He was the baritone player that made me think of filling up the instrument with air, keeping the instrument full at all times," said Adams. Nonetheless, Carney wasn't the kind of soloist that Pepper aspired to become. "Carney I always admired, still admire greatly," Adams explained to Lucinda Chodan in 1986, just weeks before his death.

> He was a master of the instrument: The way he could express himself on the instrument, and the range that he was capable of. . . . He had technical facility, everything. He was phenomenal but he was not your jam-session-type player who would go and play "Perdido" for twenty choruses in a club. His solos with Duke: He would compose a solo that would fit where it fell in the arrangement, and to enhance the arrangement around it. He was marvelous at that. He played marvelous solos but he did repeat himself. Every solo on the tune would be pretty much the same because it was geared to fit in the specific spot. So, he was not your basic improviser.

Two other bari players that Adams heard in Detroit though never cited as overt influences were Leo Parker and Tate Houston. Parker played at El Sino and other local clubs in 1947–1948, when Pepper was new to the instrument. "I think he played better than the records tend to indicate," said Adams. As for Houston, he "was a fine baritone player, a fine soloist," said Adams. "Tate was not very much into harmonic exploration, but just playing the simple changes and playing with good time, which, in itself, was extraordinary on the baritone."

Gerry Mulligan and Serge Chaloff, two prominent white baritone saxophonists at the time, held no appeal for Adams. Mulligan played in a Lester Young-influenced, Swing Era-type style, not the intricate Charlie Parker approach that Pepper was busy mastering. As Adams told Bill Rhoden, Mulligan's "light, airy tone, which was supposed to be hip at the time, I never liked." Regarding Chaloff, Pepper heard him play in the summer of 1955. "I found [him] extremely disappointing," Adams told Brian Case. "His lack of swinging, for one thing, and I think that's largely because he didn't play the instrument very well, so that he was always technically behind, had to struggle to catch up, and that made his time uneven." As Pepper told Peter Danson, "I think it's a common tendency for uninformed people to think of me as a bebop baritone player influenced by Serge Chaloff. But I don't care for Serge Chaloff at all. That nanny-goat vibrato, the flabby rhythmic approach to playing, turned me off something terrible, particularly contrasted with the way I heard Wardell playing."

～

In the summer of 1954, Adams felt it was time to test whether he could land his first record date. Elvin Jones had recorded three quartet tracks for bari and rhythm section, and by September, Pepper had an acetate pressing that he could bring with him to New York. Taking a few days off, he headed east to play the recording for Bob Weinstock, owner of Prestige Records, and Alfred Lion, who ran Blue Note. It's likely that Adams secured the meetings thanks to Miles Davis's recommendation. Davis had recorded for both labels, and only a few weeks before, during his six-week run as guest soloist, had worked with Pepper at the Blue Bird.

Nothing in the short run arose from Pepper's meeting with Weinstock, though it initiated a relationship that led to various dates he would do for Prestige beginning in 1957. Similarly, beginning in 1957, Adams would participate in his first of many dates for Blue Note. Interestingly, although Pepper was always treated by Blue Note as a sideman, from 1957 until the company was sold in the early seventies, he would become the only white musician who would consistently record for the label during its golden era.

While in New York City, Adams sat in at Birdland with Miles Davis, playing Sonny Rollins's tenor saxophone. Pepper's appearance, dress, and affect once again fooled someone into thinking that he was not what he at first glance appeared to be. "When I was working with Miles Davis at the Birdland nightclub in New York, Pepper came by," said Rollins.

> He was going to sit in with the band. I thought, "Oh, gee, this guy is probably some guy that can't play." Miles knew him, I didn't. Miles likes to be the instigator of a lot of things, so he said, "Oh, let him play." Miles knew that Pepper would sound good and would surprise me, and, so, he did. I mean when he played it was really great! It completely flabbergasted me! He played with all the requisites of that time: energy, ideas, drive, and swing; everything! And Miles was looking over there like he told a joke on somebody.

Alto saxophonist Phil Woods recounted a similar incident that took place at a Paris restaurant about fifteen years later when he, Adams, and Swiss drummer Daniel Humair had dinner. This was one of Pepper's earliest visits to Europe, so very few musicians there knew him. "Humair is quite conversant in the arts, and on wines, and on food," said Woods.

> Pepper was over there on tour, just happened to be passing through. . . . Daniel was kind of making fun of Pepper, figuring this cat was a rube, and didn't know anything about French culture and all that. Pepper kind of took it and then proceeded to do a diatribe on Daniel. He discussed art to its fullest, proceeded to order an eight-course meal in . . . French, checked the wine list, knew exactly what the good wine was. Daniel felt like disappearing. He had no idea that Pepper was so hip.

According to Ron Ley, "Pepper may well have encouraged Humair's misimpression so as to set him up for the take-out humiliation that Humair finally suffered." Although Adams's soft-spoken politeness and unassuming looks fooled some into thinking that he was an unsophisticated bank clerk or the like—certainly not a hip jazz musician—"meek is not a word that applies to Pepper," said Ley. "The ferocity of his playing gets closer to the strength and emotion that underlay his personality."

᠆

From mid-1953 when he returned from Korea until late 1955, Adams lived with his mother because he was saving money so he could relocate to New York City. Despite the convenience, he was aware that staying with her increased her codependency. Sure enough, when he told his mother in December 1955 that he was moving out, it caused a row that was brewing for some time. On December 12, a few days after he moved to a Detroit boarding house at 640 West Hancock Street, and weeks before his permanent move east, his mother wrote him:

Dearest Pepper:

Please don't destroy this without completely reading it!
    In the first place, I can't understand any of this; you know and knew at the time (Thursday evening) that I didn't mean what

I said, and I was rushing home Friday to tell you so and beg forgiveness. So, if you didn't do this to assuage your temper, or to hurt me, then why? I need you if I'm going to have a home. (I bought this because of you, remember?) And you need me (or a home), the car, piano, home cooking, et al.

Secondly, won't you try to understand that you have removed from me the reason for working and living? I would not deter you if you wanted to leave the city, but, please, as long as you are here, don't live in a hole. (Think of the money you can save!) And, you do know that "to err is human, to forgive divine!" (We were both too tired to argue—you certainly said things you didn't mean, too!)

No doubt your friends will encourage you in this course of action, but did it ever occur to you that they possibly don't want you to have a nicer home than they? They want to put you in their category! But you are fully aware that they won't pay your bills!

Let me pay for your day lost last Friday, and help you move back. I must reiterate, I can't go on living this way. Try and think back, and you'll remember the times I seemed to be projecting my motherly interest (perhaps too forcibly), when I was concerned regarding your health—staying out all night—not getting enough rest, etc; that interest seems quite natural to me; but it won't happen again! I realize and am so sad that I've been so wrong, but *please* let me make amends, and try again!

I'll always love you,

Pat

P.S.: Please call and tell me when you will come out to dinner (I have so much food); I'll come and pick you up at work, or that address!

P.P.S.: Do you want me to give the purse to G. for her birthday, or for Christmas?

Love,

P.

P.P.P.S: Please come (move) home for Christmas! I can't do anything at all regarding it in this state of mind; I can't go to school; what happens if I lose my job?; you know, there's no charity granted if there's a living child, do you not? Believe me, I'm not threatening, just stating facts. I might be able to teach another ten years and get good retirement, if I could regain my mental equilibrium. But this way, I'll be both physically and mentally ill, then what? (I'm *afraid* to take my own life!)

Honey, you can come back on your own terms; I'll only speak when spoken to, or however you want it; now I know where I was wrong in many instances and I'm so sorry!

Please be magnanimous and save my health—you won't be sorry! You'd help an old dog as bad off as I.

I have food you can take in chili, curry, juice, etc.—please call.

I still love you, will never stop,

P.

Pat's letter reveals personality traits that her son grew to resent over the years and from which he desperately needed to flee. Her need to meddle in his affairs, for one thing, especially after he came back from the war and was well into his adult years, was more and more difficult to withstand. "She never could quite get that idea that he was a grown man, able to manage his own affairs and do things on his own," said Bob Cornfoot.

Surely, her suicide threat and manipulative approach were equally troubling; a behavioral repertoire reminiscent of the lead character in Billy Wilder's legendary 1950 film *Sunset Boulevard*. Released a few years before Pat's letter, Gloria Swanson portrayed Norma Desmond, a delusional former star of the silent-film era who ensnares a struggling screenwriter and kills him in a jealous rage. Throughout the movie she is pushy, fragile, clinging, jealous, anxious, possessive, demonic, controlling, devious, flirtatious, conniving, agitated, domineering, and histrionic. So, too, over the years, was Pepper's mother, who bandied guilt, offered money, and begged for kindness when it suited her needs.

Her parental style and emotional volatility are the likely reason why her son never felt safe nor unconditionally loved. Why else would he tell his wife many years later that his mother "detested me since the day I was born," possibly the most damning thing any child could say about its parent. If anything might explain the derivation of Adams's remoteness, intimacy issues with women, and the need to conceal his deepest feelings, it was the absence of unconditional maternal love. That Pepper became one of America's most original musicians while shouldering such a burden is a testimony to his extraordinary intelligence, musical aptitude, and his intense desire to be an innovator.

Adams withstood his imperious mother for nearly half his life. He was aggrieved by her urging him, against his wishes, to become a symphonic clarinetist. And his anger was compounded by the fact that he blamed and never forgave his mother for his father's death. He believed that she, a practicing Christian Scientist, willfully denied his father the medical care he needed because of her staunch religious beliefs.

A final confirmation of their strained relationship took place in the mid-1960s, about ten years after Adams left Detroit. While Pat was visiting her son in New York City for the last time, they accepted a dinner invitation at Ron and Cindy Ley's apartment on Horatio Street in Greenwich Village. "Their relationship was unlike other mother-son relationships I had known," wrote Ley. "They didn't show any signs of affection. I was left with the impression that they were not close." Gunnar Windahl agreed: "He did not like his mother at all." Several years later, though, out of a sense of duty, Pepper stayed with his mother at 16850 Martin Road in Roseville, Michigan, during her final illness. She died of cancer in 1971.

↩

From at least the beginning of 1955 until early January 1956, Adams was a weekend fixture at West End Hotel's early morning jam sessions. What I loved most about Pepper "was his sound," said Bennie Maupin. "He had this beautiful sound and he had already some great ideas. There was continuity to his playing. There was something about it. Every time I heard him I really liked it. . . . He inspired me, just listening to his ideas and his command of the instrument. It was just great to hear what he could do! It gave me perspective. He had an influence on me and I certainly loved what he did." Gerry Niewood felt similarly about Adams's playing. "Something that really turned me on was the continuity, from the time he started to play 'til the end of the solo":

> There was a real continuity, one continuous invention, that was
> tied together. It wasn't little, short phrases, or little ideas that

were not connected or kind of peppered the landscape. I think of him more as a person who would tell a story. Maybe start with an idea, and then explore that idea in many different ways over the time and through the harmony. He would let his mind explore that idea and let it unfold through the solo. The state of his craftsmanship got higher and higher and higher as it went. It's difficult to do. What separates the best players from the not-so-great players is their ability to connect it all and have that logic. That gets back to his intellect. His intellect was at such a high level that he could really be so inventive with his thought.

At 515 South West End Avenue in Delray, a Hungarian industrial neighborhood downriver from Detroit, the Friday and Saturday late-night get-togethers gave Detroiters an opportunity to work with each other and play opposite visiting out-of-towners. No matter how illustrious a jazz musician might be, he had better be at the top of his game when he came through Detroit, warned Major Holley. "They were in for a rough time. Detroit musicians were like hyenas, vultures, buzzards, sitting around, waiting for these guys to come in and devour them!"

Gerry Mulligan was one of many touring musicians who got manhandled at West End. "Pepper really cut him!" said Mike Nader.

There was a lot of excitement in the air. Gerry Mulligan's there. Pepper is playing his horn. Pepper's going to cut him. Everybody was rooting for Pepper. It was almost as good as an athletic event. It was a contest. Two titans on that huge instrument. . . . Pepper outshone him. It was nothing overtly hostile. Pep outplayed him. Pep was really, really on! He was in top form. [Mulligan] was, I think, at times bemused because of the stridently partisan attitude we were displaying towards Pepper. It was very exciting for those of us that were there, and we were all rooting for the hometown guy.

This event may have occurred on the same night that Mulligan and trumpeter Chet Baker descended on Klein's Show Bar. "Him and Chet Baker came in on us one night and he demolished the guy!" said Curtis Fuller about Adams versus Mulligan. "We went from Klein's to the West End. He totally embarrassed him and made him look like a kid with that saxophone."

Just after Christmas, about seven months earlier, Pepper had left his yearlong Blue Bird gig to work with Kenny Burrell, Tommy Flanagan, and Elvin Jones at Klein's Show Bar. "That was a wailin' little band," said Adams. At 8540 Twelfth Street (now Rosa Parks Boulevard) at the corner of Pingree, it was "a very unique place," said Curtis Fuller. "If you bought a mug of beer, you got free corned beef sandwiches. The kids loved it. They could play chess." Like the Blue Bird and World Stage, the audience mostly consisted of respectful jazz listeners who came to hear the music and quickly silenced those in the audience who transgressed.

Around May 1955, drummer Hindal Butts assumed leadership of the band, Adams became music director, and Pepper brought in Curtis Fuller, forming the group they called "Bone and Bari." During the day, Adams and Fuller would often practice together at Pepper's house. "He heard a little something in my playing that he wanted to cultivate," said Fuller. "Race relations being what they were then, he had to pick the times that I could come out to his house because the neighborhood he lived in was all white." To drive Fuller from his place to Adams's house at 19637 Ryan Road, close to Eight Mile and less than a mile away, he'd put Fuller in the trunk of his car, drive to the back of Pepper's house, then the two would slink in so that Fuller wasn't seen by his neighbors. "He liked to run over a lot of Thad Jones, teach me a lot of things," said Fuller. "Anything that Thad wrote. He just loved Thad!"

One of Adams's littlest known influences is his mentorship of Fuller, and how, by doing so, he influenced the lineage of jazz trombone playing. "Coming up with Pepper on the Detroit scene, he inspired me, taught me to reach, [to] try to get more out of the trombone without the slide," said Fuller.

Pepper inspired me with his selection of material to play on trombone, and he wouldn't release me. He was *determined* to make me play it by playing it over and over again. Of course, that took me in another direction. I sort of released the path of J. J. Johnson, who was a master, and found a direction where I started listening to saxophonists. That's due to Pepper Adams. I used that to take me down a path that would lead me to a better place on that instrument. . . . At that time, it wasn't being done on trombone. He kept telling me the advantage, that no one else is playing like this: "You have the ability. . . ." I can actually say that [Pepper is] responsible for a lot of things I'm playing.

As he reiterated with Mark Stryker, "Playing with Pepper was pivotal. I can't impress upon you how much I respected and admired him. If I hadn't met Pepper, it never would have happened for me." Thanks to his tutelage, Fuller would refuse to accept the limitations of his instrument, just as Adams had done with the baritone. In the next decade, Fuller would record with many of the major musicians of the period and become one of jazz history's greatest trombonists.

As impressive as the 1950s Detroit jazz scene seemed to Bill Crow, he was left with the impression that Detroit's musicians weren't making any money. That might very well be true, particularly for Adams. In 1955 he still lived at home and worked a day job at Al's Record Mart. Moreover, Detroit had no recording industry of its own and its illustrious radio orchestras were long gone.

The allure of joining a major group based in New York, or, better still, being in such a band and freelancing in New York City—with its exciting recording and studio scene, and the opportunity to earn a living and play on any given day with countless extraordinary musicians—was too enticing to keep these great Detroit musicians in town much longer. New York's magnetic draw, of course, wasn't a new phenomenon. The Big Apple had served as America's musical hub since the 1920s, when "centralization of recording and radio studios, booking agencies, and publishing companies had," in the words of journalist Otis Ferguson, "turned New York into a 'microphone to the nation,' making it necessary for promising musicians around the country to migrate there if they were to parlay their talents into lasting professional success."

Many of Adams's colleagues left Detroit within just a few months of each other. "It was looking for broader horizons," Pepper told Ted O'Reilly. "Some, like Elvin, got a gig on the road and then just decided to stay in New York. Some others of us, like Tommy Flanagan, and Kenny Burrell, and I, all moved to New York at the same time. That was really in search of professional advancement, which I think in the long run has been good." And so, just after New Year's Day, 1956, with his life so full of promise, twenty-five-year-old Pepper Adams packed his belongings and moved to New York.

Dominion (1956–1986)

Chapter Five

I Carry Your Heart

He had no concept at all that he was right near the end.

—Bob Sunenblick

Pepper Adams died on Wednesday morning, September 10, 1986. As per his wishes, his body was cremated, and his ashes were scattered in New York Harbor. Since early July when he returned from his triumphant Montreal Jazz Festival performance, Adams spent his last ten weeks at home in bed, either sleeping, doing crossword puzzles, listening to his Arthur Honegger cassettes, or reading George MacDonald Fraser's *The Flashman Papers*.

His final concert on July 2 at Montreal's Spectrum was a fitting tribute to an extraordinary career. Before a demonstrative audience of seven hundred people, Adams performed four originals ("Dobbin,'" "Ephemera," "Conjuration," and "Bossallegro"), Thad Jones's lullaby "Quiet Lady," Harry Carney's "Chalumeau," and Jones's out-theme "'Tis." Adams had played "Chalumeau" at New York's Town Hall a week earlier. *Down Beat* reported that it "was perhaps the evening's most poignant moment." It was particularly emotional for Mel Lewis, who sat in the balcony and heard Adams's Carney dedication. "It was so beautiful," said Lewis. "The place was so quiet, and I started crying because I knew then that was the last time I was going to hear him." Pianist Dick Katz, also there that night, "couldn't believe that a man that sick could play that well."

Before Adams's Spectrum concert, trumpeter Denny Christianson came by the backstage trailer to wish Pepper well. "I walked in, and he looked at me, and his eyes lit up with a warm smile, like he was really happy, almost a relief, that I made it before he went on," said Christianson.

> It was just a wonderful feeling to know that he felt as warm about me as I did about him. We didn't want to break the moment. We hung together for about twenty minutes just to be with each other. People around him were saying, "Oh, he looks great!" But, my God, he couldn't even get up and down the steps without somebody holding each arm, and his eyes were real red all around his eyes, and they were bloodshot and sunken in his head. As soon as I looked at him, I knew he was in bad shape. I knew from February how much a toll it had taken. By the time I had seen him in July—and people had said, "Oh, he looks better"—and I looked at him, I said, "Bullshit! He looks much worse." When I saw him in July, when I said goodbye, I knew that was the last time I was going to see him.

Adams, too, acknowledged his precarious health. "It's getting so bad, the horn weighs more than I do," he joked. When drummer Cisco Normand assisted Pepper up the short flight of steps from the trailer onto the bandstand, Adams received a boisterous standing ovation, the first time he had ever received such a response. Pepper's "sound in the hall was really big," said saxophonist Charles Papasoff, and the incongruity of his robust playing with the gaunt way he appeared on stage intensified its dramatic effect. The enthusiastic crowd remained effusive the entire night, finally ceasing when he stopped them to say a few concluding remarks and reintroduce the band. Too exhausted to perform an encore, he said, "Thanks, folks, you've been really beautiful. Let's do this again soon."

Sixteen months earlier, on March 21, 1985, Adams had returned home from a two-month European tour with chest x-rays and test results. Before he was able to discuss his condition with his oncologist, he traveled to Newport, Rhode Island, to play two nights at Treadway Hotel. "It was a very emotional time," said his friend, Mike Jordan.

> I think he really wanted to just talk to somebody. Other than the fact that he wanted to play, he was glad to be back in this country. He did a very long European tour. Being sick it really kicked the shit out of him. I know he was glad to see me, and it was a great time. But [by] the same token, he was upset with

the situation with his wife and, of course, how could you not be worried about your physical status when you would've been told you have spots on your lungs? . . . He had a few drinks with me. He said, "What do you want to hear?" I said, "Play a ballad for me, will you?" He said, "All right." He got up there and played "A Child Is Born." It was the most beautiful ballad I may have heard anybody play. The drummer was in tears.

As Ray Mosca pointed out, "Pepper'll make you cry with a ballad. There are very few cats that can do that." When Adams and Jordan embraced and said their goodbyes, Adams had tears in *his* eyes. He was very anxious about what he was about to face in New York and knew his future was uncertain.

On March 26, the day before he was admitted to New York's St. Luke's Roosevelt Hospital, Pepper met with Dr. Edward Gelmann at his office on Fifth Avenue. According to singer Lodi Carr, who met Adams at Gelmann's office, Pepper was still in the dark about his cancer's severity. When he left the consultation, however, he was a changed man. Understandably, Adams was overwhelmed when his physician explained the dire nature of his illness, that he would need to begin chemotherapy immediately if he hoped to extend his life. As planned, after his appointment Adams and Carr went to lunch at a nearby Chinese restaurant. In shock about his diagnosis, Pepper was barely hungry and noticeably trembling.

Weeks later, when Dr. Hugo Haugstad in Sweden received confirmation of his original diagnosis and Gelmann's recommended protocol, he shook his head. Haugstad doubted that chemotherapy and radiation upon small-cell carcinoma, the most pernicious type of lung cancer, was worth the misery that Adams would endure. "They shouldn't treat that," he told Gunnar Windahl. Pepper would be far better off, Haugstad said, trying to enjoy his last few months of life. "Put him on a steamer to the South Seas, where he can play and enjoy some women or something. You can never cure that."

A month earlier, after Haugstad's examination at the Hospital of Boden, Windahl suggested that Pepper consider getting medical treatment in Sweden since it would be far less expensive than in America. Adams decided against it, both wanting to satisfy his commitment to play his forthcoming gig in France and get a second opinion in the US. That turned out to be a wise decision. As Bob Sunenblick, a practicing oncologist and his record producer affirmed, once disrupted by surgery, small-cell carcinoma can spread rapidly throughout the body. If Adams had undergone surgery in Sweden or refused cancer treatments in the United States, he would have died in a matter of months. Three important recordings that he made in 1985 and 1986 and his thought-provoking NPR radio show with Ben Sidran would not have taken place.

One of the three projects was Denny Christianson's big-band date, recorded on February 24–25, 1986. Christianson had been looking for a guest soloist, first for a nightclub engagement and radio broadcast, then a follow-up recording. When Denny researched Pepper's discography, he was surprised to realize that, despite Adams's many years of performing with so many great jazz orchestras, he had never been the featured soloist on any big-band recording. Nearly a year after his cancer was diagnosed, Adams trudged up to wintry Montreal for a rehearsal with Christianson's band, then the two-day recording session at Studio Victor. Battling a partially collapsed lung and cancer that had metastasized to his brain, Adams, in a great deal of pain, sometimes with a pounding headache, performed multiple takes of eight tunes plus a fifteen-minute suite. "I chose stuff that was compatible for him," said Christianson in 1987. "If it hadn't been for Pepper, I wouldn't have put this on record. . . . I [didn't] want to sound like what Thad was doing fifteen years ago but I had these charts. I love the charts, but as far as making a musical statement, I said, 'All right, that's something Pepper would like,' and he did."

The second important recording session done during Adams's illness was Joshua Breakstone's *Echoes*. Recorded in New York on February 19, 1986, less than a week before Christianson's session, it had been delayed for nearly a month because of Pepper's medical treatments. At the rehearsal and elsewhere, Adams continued to smoke cigarettes despite his insecure health. "He didn't just smoke a little," observed Don Friedman. "He was the world's biggest chain smoker." When musicians tried to talk him out of it or at least attempt to understand his point of view, Pepper typically replied, "My doctor said it was OK."

The Adams Effect, his final date as a leader, was the third significant recording that he completed while terminally ill. Produced by Uptown Records on June 25–26, 1985, it featured an all-Detroit band except for Billy Hart. "I scheduled the recording for eight, nine, ten days after he received his cycle of chemotherapy and he was in good shape when he came in there," said Bob Sunenblick. "He didn't look very well but he was in very, very good shape. If you shut your eyes, it was the old Pepper. He was very strong." With Frank Foster, Tommy Flanagan, and Ron Carter, the session featured five Adams originals ("Binary," Valse Celtique," "Claudette's Way," "Dylan's

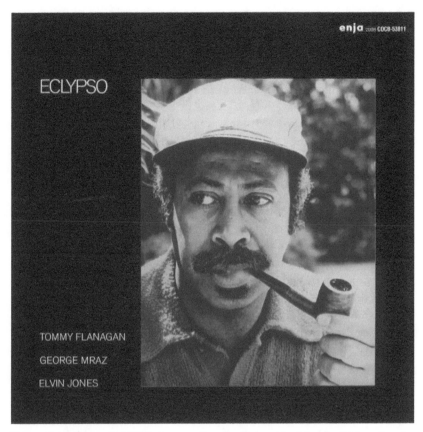

enja 2006 COCB-53811

ECLYPSO

TOMMY FLANAGAN

GEORGE MRAZ

ELVIN JONES

Figure 5.1. Flanagan's 1977 trio recording for Enja with Adams's all-time favorite rhythm section. Public domain.

Delight," and "Now in Our Lives") plus Foster's ballad "How I Spent the Night." Customarily, Adams never re-recorded his compositions on studio dates, even if they were recorded by other artists without him present. For his last recording as a leader, however, he decided to redo "Claudette's Way," "Valse Celtique," and "Dylan's Delight," the last two with faster tempos.

⌐⌐

On July 30, 1985, Adams wrote pianist Per Husby, updating him on what had transpired since his last gigs with him five months earlier:

Dear Per:

Sorry it's taken so long to get this back to you but there are plenty of extenuating circumstances. My life the last few months has contained all the elements of a soap opera save amnesia, and amnesia would have been welcome.

My next stop after Oslo was Stockholm, and my buddy Dr. Gunnar Windahl ("Doctor Deep") had worked out his schedule so he'd be there at the same time. He ghosted in my room at the Castle Hotel a couple of nights, and he was alarmed by how tired I was, as well as by a lingering cough that I had. The tiredness I could easily explain; my work schedule in England would have been considered inhumane by the courts of the Spanish Inquisition.

About a week later, I did a one-nighter (AWFUL rhythm section!) up in Boden, where Gunnar lives, and he had arranged at the hospital where he works to have me given a quick examination and a chest x-ray by Dr. Haugstad, the head of the chest department. (Nothing but the best for "Doctor Deep.") What they expected was to find lungs clogged by years of smoking, make me stop, give me some medication, and clear up the problem in two weeks. What they found was two amazing, healthy lungs, but with a mysterious black spot in the middle of the left one that was cutting off half its function.

Dr. Haugstad warned me that the spot could be a malignancy, gave me the x-ray and test results, and told me to take them to my doctor as soon as I got back to New York, less than two weeks later. . . . But Dr. Haugstad hadn't been very frank with me. What he'd told Gunnar was that the spot was almost certainly lung cancer, which has a very low rate of recovery; so that's what Gunnar told Claudette, who promptly packed all the valuables, took all the money from the joint accounts, and split.

Fortunately, I had about $5,000 cash when I got home. Unpaid bills took a lot of it, but I had enough left to get me into the hospital. Diagnosis: Oat Cell Carcinoma, inoperable but beatable by a combination of chemo and radiation therapy. After eleven days in hospital, I started the chemo part, getting infused every three weeks. It didn't affect me too badly: some nausea, some tiredness, but nothing like some of the awful stories I've heard. Which is a good thing because I was working most of the time . . . and, most importantly, making a decent income. The US is not where you want to be if you're sick and broke at the same time. . . . My doctor told me to not even think about working from the start of the radiation cycle until two weeks after it ends. So, my next challenge is surviving the next eight weeks. I'm trying to sell my backup instrument and car; if I manage to do that, I'll probably make it.

Gigs start again in October, and I'll be back on chemotherapy, so I'll be able to travel up to three weeks at a time. Eventual cure, if it occurs, will be next March or April . . . Still can't walk too good, but somehow it doesn't seem to matter too much right now. If you're having severe pain, it proves that you're still alive, right?

When you have time, wish me some luck.

Skal!

Pepper

After Adams's lung cancer was discovered, stories began circulating about his wife leaving him once she found out the news, that she cleaned out their bank account before his return home from Europe, and that Adams, stripped of his savings, was being left alone to die. An outraged jazz fraternity, inflamed by Claudette's selfish and callous behavior, stood unified behind Pepper and made him the talk of the town during his final illness. Yet Adams's account of his wife's behavior, as expressed in his letter to Husby and repeated by Lodi Carr and others, was only partially true. "I am sure the sequence of things doesn't work right, that Claudette abandoned him as soon as she knew he had cancer," asserted Diana Flanagan. "Before he had cancer they had separated. People were led to believe that Claudette cleaned out the house and bank account because Gunnar called her and told her about the cancer. But that's simply not the case. . . . I had dinner with her one time, and it was long before he had cancer. It was after he broke his leg." That meeting took place in early 1984, more than a year before Adams's cancer was diagnosed, at which time Claudette explained their intentions to separate.

Claudette found out about Pepper's illness after the Flanagans learned about it. "Gunnar called us in the middle of the night crying," said Diana Flanagan.

> He was heartbroken and really could not control himself. He called, sobbing, and said, "Pepper's gone, he's gone." I said, "What do you mean?" He said, "Well, he has cancer. It's incurable. He has a big tumor and it's inoperable." Then, it must have been the next day, he did call [Pepper's] house. The moving people had just left. The arrangement was that she was to move the stuff out when Pepper was away. That was a prior arrangement. They had just moved her stuff out. They were gone about five minutes and the phone rang. It was Gunnar and he told her all this. She said to me, "What could I do? Call them back and tell them to put all the furniture back in the house?"

Rightfully, Claudette was resentful of the rumors that circulated about her. As an admissions counselor at Brooklyn Friends School, she had served as breadwinner throughout their marriage, with robust health benefits plus alimony and child support for the benefit of her son. Despite her financial support, she was being accused of disowning Adams at his time of need. Whatever happened to funds in their joint checking account has never been clarified. Though Keith White was under the impression that Adams had saved about fifty-thousand dollars, there's no indication that Pepper initiated legal action nor in any way was aggrieved about its loss.

⌐⌐

In July 1985, four months after his cancer diagnosis, Adams was instructed to neither work nor travel while enduring six weeks of radiation treatment. The following month he attended a free outdoor concert, only two miles from home, featuring the Count Basie Orchestra with vocalist Sarah Vaughan. Thad Jones had returned to the US from Denmark earlier that year to direct the Basie band, and Adams and Jones hadn't seen each other in quite some time.

A few days before the performance, Jones met with Gary Giddins, who was in the process of forming the American Jazz Orchestra and needed his advice. At the meeting, Jones was worried about Adams. He had just learned about Pepper's illness and was, according to his son, Bruce, "really,

Figure 5.2. Thad Jones and Pepper Adams, August 12, 1985, Old Boys High Field, Brooklyn, New York. Photo by Mark Vinci.

really deeply disturbed." He asked Giddins, "Have you seen Pepper? How's Pepper doing? Is he OK? God, I really want to see Pepper."

The day of the concert, "the band is up there and I'm standing in the field, and who comes hobbling over but Pepper," said Giddins.

> He looked pretty bad, but he was in such great spirits! He was talking about the band and how great it was to see Thad up there. He hadn't seen Thad yet. We walked in back of the stage and Thad came over. Oh, it was beautiful! They just hugged and kissed. Thad was *so* concerned about him. Nobody knew it then, but Thad was dying. He got sick shortly after that. . . . I was getting goosebumps just watching the two of them.

By September 1985, Adams was cleared to work a gig in Memphis. While there, on September 29, New York's Universal Jazz Coalition hosted a "Tribute to Pepper Adams," emceed by Ira Gitler. An A-list of jazz musicians included Milt Jackson, Frank Foster, Kenny Burrell, Tommy Flanagan,

Dizzy Gillespie, and the entire Mel Lewis Orchestra. Adams personalized the audience's experience by writing the following letter, read to them by Lodi Carr:

Good evening and welcome:

I don't wish to intrude upon your time, which would certainly be better spent in enjoying the marvelous artists assembled here, but I feel that I should, in the interest of clarity, explain the nature of the event and why you are faced with the anomaly of a tribute without a reasonably fresh corpse. At the beginning of April, I was diagnosed as having a small-cell carcinoma of the left lung. This form of cancer grows and spreads rapidly and is therefore immune to surgery. The very speed of its growth, however, lends it an air of instability, and because of this factor it is susceptible to the ministrations of a combination of chemo and radiation therapy. The odds of recovery at the time were quoted as being 65%, which, with the Big "C," ain't too shabby. One major flaw in this beautiful theory is that the costs of chemical and radiation therapy are enormous. My hospitalization policy paid the major portion of it. But the remainder is by no means minor, and need I remind you we happen to live in one of the few remaining major nations that regularly allows its citizens to die because they can't afford adequate health care.

For the first three months of treatment, things went well. I was in chemotherapy, and, aside from an occasional visit to the doctor's office for an injection of the chemicals, I was able to travel and work normally. I may have even set some sort of record by playing consecutive gigs in Nouro, Sardinia, and Edmonton, Alberta three days apart! I was extremely fortunate in not having many of the debilitating side effects that affect many patients. Then I entered the radiation phase of the therapy, during which I could not work. Five days a week for six weeks I drove to Methodist Hospital in Brooklyn, registered as an indigent patient (since the treatment cost $97 a day and is not covered by hospitalization), and I received treatment. A rather lengthy process and a full day's work. Then, that series ended, and I was given two weeks to recover my strength before resuming the chemicals.

For a few days things seemed all right, but then I started becoming weaker and most alarmingly losing my motor skills. I called my doctor and he set up a brain scan. Now, whatever happened to the power of old jokes? I fully expected the people to say, "Mr. Adams, we've done a complete scan of your brain and we couldn't find a thing!" Instead, they found that cancer had spread to there, so now I'm going back to the hospital every day and receiving radiation of the head. The odds, of course, have changed, but no one is quoting them now.

From the very beginning of this, a number of people have always presented the idea of doing a benefit. But I've always opposed it on the strictly pragmatic grounds that this treatment is so expensive that no benefit will come close to covering the cost, and that in the long run I'd be much better off trying to earn the money myself without the onus of a publicly admitted illness. This resolve lasted at least until Barry Harris called and said, "We're doing one for you, whether you want it or not." Now, 35 years of arguing with Barry have taught me the futility of this exercise, so I merely asked that he not call it a "benefit." He settled on the word "tribute," so that's where we are today.

Barry's absence in Europe necessitated calling upon the services of Jimmy Owens as coordinator of the project, and Cobi Narita has very kindly donated her premises. To each of these people I am highly indebted, as I certainly am to the marvelous musicians who have volunteered their "services"—a wholly inadequate term for this evening. I'm truly sorry I can't be with you this evening, but I'm playing a concert in Memphis, motor skills or not. My deepest gratitude is reserved for you, the members of the audience, and I'd like to thank you for being here and being a part of this occasion. I very much hope to see you all soon, and you needn't worry about me. Long ago I adopted the ancient Roman motto "Illegitimi non carborundum": Don't let the bastards grind you down.

Apart from diminished motor skills, "as he was getting more involved in his chemotherapy and the illness was taking its toll, he had a number of problems which he was telling me about," said gastroenterologist and record producer Mark Feldman:

He never complained about a lack of breath, even though he was being treated for a huge accumulation of fluid around the lungs and being treated for pneumonia along with his chemotherapy and his radiation therapy. One thing he complained: He felt he lacked coordination at times . . . actual articulation. He felt that something was being lost there. . . . You're on some pretty heavyweight stuff, between the radiation therapy . . . plus, you get radiation therapy to the head. It's prophylactic, because very frequently small-cell carcinoma will metastasize to the brain. So, whether it was actual metastasis or whether it was the effect of the radiation, he was having his problems. But he was such a defiant guy to begin with that he just had to get out there. He just could not let this illness get in his way.

By early 1986, Adams's many rounds of cancer treatments had depleted his health benefits. To continue qualifying for hospitalization and the medical treatments administered there that he needed to stay alive, his only recourse was to declare himself a ward of the state. "We live in a catch-22," said Jack Kleinsinger, jazz promoter and former assistant attorney general of the State of New York. "If you have a little bit of money, you can't get medical attention the way you can if you're dead broke. I wore my lawyer hat. [Pepper] wanted to know what he could do legally. Put money in his wife's name; that's basically what he had to do." Accordingly, Adams spent down his assets, declared himself indigent, and qualified for Medicaid.

Half a year after the New York City benefit, a second fundraiser for Adams, organized by saxophonist Jackie McLean, took place on March 6, 1986, at Hartford, Connecticut's 880 Club. This time Adams was able to attend. Adams received an award from Artists Collective, the Hartford-based organization spearheaded by McLean's wife. Adams was still "playing as forcefully as ever," said Bill Barron. "I guess when he picked up the horn his strength came back, but you could tell that he needed to rest."

Nine days later, Pepper flew to Phoenix to attend Don and Sue Miller's annual Paradise Valley Jazz Party in nearby Scottsdale. Lew Tabackin assisted Adams whenever possible:

I tried to spend as much time with him as I could because he was really in bad shape. . . . I tried to get him to eat but he was having difficulty eating because he couldn't taste anything.

The scary thing was, man, when he got on the bandstand, I couldn't believe it! He could play with so much intensity, and then he'd finish playing and he'd be just wasted, just the way he was before. It was just amazing the way he could summon up so much energy. It was a spiritual thing; it transcended the physical. It was very inspirational. . . . Pepper wasn't even sitting on a chair. He was standing up and [a baritone] is a heavy thing.

From Arizona Adams flew to southern California for Costa Mesa's Orange Coast County Jazz Festival. The festival was overseen by Fred Norsworthy, who in late 1968 produced *Encounter*, one of Pepper's greatest studio recordings. Then, in early April, Adams flew across the North American continent and another six hours further to Dublin for a series of concerts. Regarding his workload in Ireland, Pepper wrote a letter to Ira Sabin, editor of *JazzTimes*, which was published in its July 1986 issue. The letter was unusual for Adams, who for so much of his life safeguarded his feelings:

I'd like to thank you for the kind words in the current *JazzTimes* and thank you particularly for stressing the fact that I'm continuing to work. People have been exceedingly kind, and their contributions have been quite helpful. But opposed to the cost of the treatments that are, to put it bluntly, keeping me alive, private charity can only go so far. The bulk of the costs have been offset by my own efforts in being able to work and work effectively. And, if I may say so myself, I've done remarkably well for fourteen months, and the next three months appear quite secure.

And this despite the efforts of a few unscrupulous agents who have used my name to secure work and then, when the job was secure, informed the purchaser that I was too ill to perform and substituted someone else. I've learned about these incidents when the purchaser (club owner, festival executive, etc.) would call to commiserate about my health when I was sitting home, feeling fine but out of work. I wonder if these agents considered that by eroding my reputation for reliability, they were diminishing my chances for survival; if they *did* think about it, they were obviously not deterred. Which is why I consider it important that people be reminded occasionally that I'm still a credible working musician.

I must report, though, that my string of playing every job I had contracted for has finally come to an end. It happened on my last trip to Europe, in April, which ended in near disaster. It started at the Dublin Festival, where they drove me into the ground like a tent peg. I had five concerts with five different bands (four of them requiring lengthy rehearsals), a 2½ hour master class, and a live television show, all within three days. I was already in a lot of pain when I arrived in Paris to work seven straight nights at Le Petit Opportun; after five nights the pain became so overwhelming that I had to sit out the last two nights.

When I got home it was discovered that I had a severe case of pleurisy, which was raging out of control since it had been there, untreated, for ten days or so. My oncologist held off the chemotherapy while I was in such rotten shape, but finally the point was reached when it had to be administered, ready or not. I could tell that the doctor was worried and, frankly, so was I, but it's worked out well. I'm recovering nicely. I've felt nearly myself for several days, and still have a couple of weeks to recoup my strength before I resume work. My itinerary through the middle of September is sprinkled with nice paydays, and at no point so burdensome as to tempt a return bout of the pleurisy, nor of the pneumonia I went through twice last winter. Things are definitely looking up.

Despite his optimism, Adams's health continued to decline, and by the time of the letter's publication he would never work again. In July 1986, Sunenblick called Adams's oncologist for an update:

Gelmann told me that the usual way with treating cancer patients is that they get the first round of chemotherapy. Now, in this disease, almost 95 percent of people will get a complete response for the first round of chemotherapy. When this cancer recurs [from] the second line of chemotherapy, very few get a response. About 40 percent. Pepper wasn't one of them. He had two cycles of chemotherapy the second time around and he didn't respond. I called his physician shortly after this because Peter Leitch or

Sylvia Levine asked me to call and find out how he was doing. So, I called, and he said that Pepper wasn't responding and that he wasn't going to treat him anymore. That was the end. He was going to die soon afterwards.

Adams was living alone. When Sunenblick called him, the phone rang twenty-five times before he could answer. He was very weak, could barely talk, and wasn't eating. "He would have died all by himself," said Sunenblick. Alarmed by Pepper's isolation and tenuous health, Sunenblick called Gelmann's office. After consulting with its nursing staff, Gelmann's office scheduled a hospice to provide Pepper with a home health aide.

As much as his closest friends sensed that the end was near, it became too difficult for some to visit and comfort him. "The last two times I went to his house, he had this cancer and it was eating him up," said Roland Hanna. "I couldn't go to see him anymore after that. I didn't want to remember him like that. I wanted to remember him the way I knew him. The last time I saw him he looked so much like a ghost. I just couldn't go out there anymore. I talked to him on the phone, but I couldn't go to see him anymore." To ease his pain, Adams was taking dilaudid, a powerful narcotic that caused him to become constipated. Mark Feldman, who called Pepper each week, advised him to eat certain foods to improve his diet and ameliorate the condition. "Whenever you talked to him, he was always 'hanging in there,'" said Feldman. "The very last time I talked with him," however, "he just came out and said, 'Why is this happening?'"

> For a guy who was very realistic and so perceptive, with a question that came out of the blue, he really wanted an answer. I took a couple of deep swallows and said, "Look, Pepper, you have to hang in there. . . ." I think that last phone conversation where he said, "Why is this happening? Why am I not getting any better?" I think it was sort of like, "I've done my part and I've done what I could." I took a couple of very long swallows. It's something I deal with every day but talking to someone like him was very painful.

When the Flanagans visited Adams in late August 1986, Diana Flanagan tried to connect intimately with him about his impending death. "I thought maybe I should try to give him a chance to say something realistic about it, not to just avoid it," she said.

I asked him, "How are you feeling about it? It must be a very strange feeling." He said that he was scared, it was very weird, and he was anxious. I said, "You don't have any peace about it at all?" He said, "No . . ." I think there was kind of a resolution with Claudette, but about dying he felt very uncomfortable and strange. . . . You would think that an artist at some point *could* reconcile a lot of disparate feelings and come to something, you know? It's *so* sad that he never did that. It's a very painful way to die. He was very bitter. . . . He'd say little things that had that sound of resentment.

Chapter Six

Claudette's Way

We two were dressed for a day so bright; we two were dressed for the night but gave way to thorns of fright, the little, subtle thorns of fright.

—Barry Wallenstein

Pepper Adams first met Claudette Nadra in Detroit sometime between the twentieth and the twenty-fifth of September 1960. A few weeks shy of his thirtieth birthday, he was working a week at Minor Key with Donald Byrd. Adams was introduced to Nadra, of French-Canadian descent and around twenty-one years old, by Hugh Jackson. Pepper was obviously taken with her. Because of her attire, he dedicated "Alice Blue Gown" to her, and before the night ended, he "was lining her up," chuckled Jackson.

Claudette was equally interested in Adams. She wrote him on January 6, 1961, four months after they met, asking that he forward his phone number. Five months later she wrote again, saying how pleased she was to hear from him. A letter to Adams a month after that expressed how surprised she was that they didn't have a chance to meet again, followed by two more letters, reiterating how eager she was to hear back from him.

About a year after they were introduced, Nadra sent Adams a Valentine's Day card after visiting him in New York. Three months later, on May 21, 1962, she wrote again, thanking him for the copy of *At the Half Note Café* that he mailed her as a gift. In August, she said she'd be visiting New York the following month. Obligated to spend her time with a suitor, she would try to visit Pepper. Should Adams's prior invitation still exist, however, she would instead "bunk" with him when she returned during the Christmas holidays.

THE COMPLETE BLUE NOTE
DONALD BYRD/PEPPER ADAMS
STUDIO SESSIONS

Figure 6.1. Donald Byrd. Public domain.

Nonetheless, by March 1963 Claudette had married Harvey Bresler. Eight months later she wrote Pepper, wondering if they could stay in touch despite her marriage. After a gap of two years, during which time her marriage collapsed, Claudette wrote Adams on July 1, 1965, thanking him for helping her move to New York City. But a year and a half later, whatever they may have shared as a couple had ceased. Claudette moved back to Detroit and in 1967 married George Hill.

On December 17, 1971, as the mother of a twenty-two-month-old son, she wrote Adams a Christmas card, revealing that she often thought about him and hoped to see him soon in Detroit. From New Year's Day 1973 through mid-1974 she wrote several postcards, apprising him of her and her son's whereabouts. Then, on July 18, 1973, she visited Pepper in New York. Two years later, they got engaged and she and her five-year-old son moved in with him.

One of Pepper's friends felt that Claudette's choices for a husband, with a black child from her second marriage, were somewhat limited. In his view, Adams became a logical choice for two reasons. First, he was completely accepting of her son. Second, he was ready to live with someone who could "keep house" with him. More than anything, he said, this was a marriage of convenience. She would enjoy being associated with an esteemed musician, by association tasting fame for herself, would be grateful he was such a good father, and would somehow find a way to overlook his awkwardness as a lover. And so, after so many twists and turns since they first met, Adams acceded to marrying Claudette. At age forty-five it was his first marriage. For Claudette, age thirty-six, her third.

Pepper and Claudette were married on Valentine's Day, 1976, by Reverend Harold Moody, who for many years served as pastor of Judson Church, the landmark building opposite Washington Square Park. The Saturday afternoon wedding and reception were hosted by Roz and Marshall Allen. Attended by Thad Jones, Mel Lewis, Ron Carter, Jerry Dodgion, Roland Hanna, Al Porcino, and others, e. e. cummings's poem "I Carry Your Heart" was read as part of their vows, food was served, champagne was poured, and the house piano may have been played by some of the guests. Patsy Ryan, Pepper's former neighbor, was also in attendance. According to Ron Ley, Adams's best man, Ryan "had very strong maternal feelings for Pepper," and was troubled by his decision to marry Claudette, feeling that her self-centeredness would eventually spell disaster. A most unpleasant scene took place before the guests departed, when Ryan expressed her opinion about the marriage to the newlyweds, which brought Claudette to tears.

⤺

In the summer of 1977, after eighteen months of marriage, Adams found himself at a crossroads. For twelve years he had languished in Thad Jones/ Mel Lewis Orchestra's reed section, one of jazz's greatest big bands, but desperately needed to reinvent himself. Adams never wanted to be in the group in the first place. After accepting section work for too many years, he was eager in the mid-1960s to break free and perform exclusively with small ensembles so he could flourish as a soloist. But Thad Jones, one of his dearest friends, whom he admired more than anyone, needed him in his newly formed orchestra, reminded him of all the things his mother had done for him in Pontiac, Michigan, in the early 1950s, and eventually convinced him to stay. That happened in the summer of 1966. Now, after hundreds of Monday nights at the Village Vanguard and countless tours of the US, Europe, and Japan, Adams was more restive than ever.

Pepper had voiced his frustration a year prior to the band's 1977 summer tour, telling Thad that he was unhappy with his lack of solos. Citing the baseball adage, "Coach, play me or trade me!" as some indication of his discontentment, his use of the phrase, so characteristic of his understated sense of humor, has since become part of the band's lore. When it was uttered, Jones laughed and ignored it. This time around, Adams wasn't joking.

His conflict came to a head in Stockholm at the midpoint of the band's two-month European tour. Before their evening performance at Tivoli Gardens on August 3, Adams met privately with Jones and Lewis. He told them that he wanted a pay raise and top billing as a featured soloist. Claudette especially wanted greater fame for her husband, which she felt was long overdue and richly deserved. Both, however, were unaware that it was predetermined never to give inordinate solo space nor pay any musician in the band more than anyone else. Steadfastly adhering to protocol, Thad and Mel declined his request. "This was a very sad moment for Pepper," said Ron Ley. "He loved Thad and held him in high esteem." Left with no alternative, an aggrieved Adams said that he'd be leaving the band at the end of the month when the tour concluded.

Adams returned to New York and began forging his identity as an itinerant soloist. In no time he found himself in demand throughout Europe and North America. Then, in 1978 and 1980 he recorded *Reflectory* and *The Master*, featuring Adams's newly written compositions. Both were nominated for a Grammy Award for Best Instrumental Album of the Year by a Jazz Soloist.

At last, the American recording industry was acknowledging Pepper's brilliance as a performer. His 1979 project with singer Helen Merrill, *Chasin' the Bird/Gershwin*, was also nominated for a Grammy, his third such nomination in three years. And four years later his 1983 album *Live at Fat Tuesday's* was nominated, his fourth in six years. In honor of his impressive run, Pepper appeared on the prestigious, nationally broadcast 1982 Grammy Awards telecast. Clad in a tuxedo, he performed (appropriately enough) the jazz standard "My Shining Hour."

In addition to being a personal triumph, his high-profile television appearance was an epiphenomenon of cultural and political forces sweeping the globe. Just a few years earlier, radical Islam had toppled the Shah of Iran, and both Margaret Thatcher and Ronald Reagan had begun dismantling "progressive" social programs. In the jazz world, as in politics, a return to conservative values was becoming a fact of life. The altered landscape that suddenly favored hard-swinging acoustic jazz more than at any time since the early sixties helped Adams. He was working steadily, winning polls as the world's premier baritone saxophonist, and had the ongoing support of a record company. A younger generation of musicians, too, was choosing him for their gigs. And due to numerous radio and television appearances, the public was starting to become familiar with this gentle, soft-spoken, erudite man who let his big horn and bigger sound speak for him.

Moreover, beginning in 1976 until he became disabled in mid-December 1983, Adams wrote nearly half his oeuvre of forty-two compositions. Although fifty percent of them were written scattershot from 1956–1975, Pepper's robust book of original tunes included seven magnificent ballads, some of his greatest compositional achievements, five of which he composed since his wedding. In 1982, when assessing the trajectory of his career, Adams acknowledged how dramatically his life had changed for the better since leaving Thad Jones/Mel Lewis:

What has been happening to me in the last three or four years is like starting a new career in a sense, because there were so many years there, a long period of time, where I never recorded. Eight or ten years, and being pretty much overlooked in general, and hardly ever working as a soloist. It was my ability to read that kept me alive. Doing hack work. Really, European contacts are what got me back into playing as a soloist again, which is what I've always wanted to do but was always denied the opportunities. And hardly ever getting written about or talked about in the press. Just a couple of years ago I picked up a book, *The Biographies of 3500 Great Jazz Musicians,* in which my name was not mentioned. And receiving a circular letter from George Wein's office about a jazz repertory company with all the great jazz musicians in New York, which listed five baritone players and not me. Things of that nature, you know. Feeling as if I was completely out of it and being totally disregarded. It's starting to swing around again. It's a good feeling.

What led to his marriage's dissolution? Foremost was Claudette's frustration with Pepper's drinking. Adams didn't start boozing until after January 1956, when he moved to New York. "I remember running into him at Jim & Andy's," said Hugh Lawson. "I went in there one afternoon, man, and Pepper was in there drunk. It was unbelievable! It bothered me because I had never seen it before." In 1960, on their weekend gig in Montreal, "I went around with him during a couple of breaks and, Christ, he could really pack it away!" said Keith White. "I could drink a little bit in those days, too, but I couldn't keep up with him. He'd have two glasses to my one, or three glasses to my one, and he'd be ready for three more."

When Adams was living in Greenwich Village, he spent time with Thad Jones, trombonist Bob Brookmeyer, and trumpeters Richard Williams and Jimmy Nottingham, who were heavy drinkers. According to Mel Lewis, the only time he and Pepper got into an argument was when Adams was drunk. Otherwise, whatever was irking him he kept to himself, sometimes for years.

"Pepper spoke more freely after a few glasses of liquor," said Gunnar Windahl. "He was no easy-speaking man when he was sober. It was not that easy to get in touch with him. A few sentences, then he picked up a cigarette and lit it. But after a few glasses, he thawed and was very easy to speak with. He very generously presented good stories from his fantastic life. . . . He was so controlled, otherwise, when he was sober. An introvert." By the mid-seventies, Adams drank every day at home. He and Claudette would have a drink together before dinner, then Pepper would have another. "When he used to drink a lot, he used to get very moody," said Dylan, Adams's stepson.

> If he was happy that day and he drank, he'd just be more happy. He'd tell jokes. He had a very unique sense of humor. Sometimes he was very, very funny with the humor he had, and other times he was just utterly [gross]. I used to feel uncomfortable because, if he was not in a good mood and he drank, he'd just kind of be off the wall. If there was something on television that he didn't like, and my mother and I were watching, he'd sit there and talk pretty loud about, "Oh, this is bullshit! You don't know what you're watching. This is trash." Just make us feel pretty uncomfortable. . . . Usually when he drank, he'd get in a bad mood. I always felt that he was depressed.

In April 1979 when Gunnar Windahl stayed with Pepper and Claudette for several weeks in Brooklyn, Adams was drinking just as heavily.

> It was not always joyous. You could see that he had no jobs for long periods of time. He went smoking around, reading and so on. When we were approaching the cocktail hour, he shone. His frowning forehead cleared up, and he went deep into the Kentucky bourbon bottle and we had a few drinks. Just two drinks before dinner. That was a very rigid rule in that house. Really, it was like two bottles of hard liquor. He could really *pour* a drink, I assure you! So, I was deadly drunk when I came to the table. I was not accustomed to a very fast drink before. . . . It was, of course, a problem that Claudette had to behave like a policeman sometimes, so he didn't drink too much.

Occasionally, alcohol got Adams in trouble. In late July 1980, after a gig in Paris with Elvin Jones, Adams and bassist Andy McCloud went out drinking. Pepper was carrying $2,000 worth of cash that he had amassed from various European gigs since his arrival on June 21. After carousing into the wee hours of the morning, "finally, we parted company," said McCloud. "Somebody mugged him, and they took all his bread. He came to my room. He said, 'Look, man, I got mugged.' He had a lump over his eye. I gave him $100." Three years earlier, just prior to sitting in with Jones's group in Aix-en-Provence, France, he was carrying all his earnings from three weeks of gigs and was punched in the face during the day. Again, he lost all his money, plus the camera he was carrying around his neck.

Pepper, when asked, perpetuated the myth that he had his drinking under control, though he admitted, "Occasionally I get *out there*." The truth, however, is that, by the 1970s, alcohol had a firm grip on him. Prior to a Jones/Lewis performance in Rochester, Chris Melito noticed him trembling from the effects of alcoholism. In the early 1980s, "I got a letter from Claudette that upset me a lot," said Windahl. "[Pepper's] blood counts were not very good, and he had to stop drinking. But I couldn't see any of *that* when I met him. That was the first signal of their relationship getting worse."

Aside from heavy drinking, three other factors that precipitated their separation were Adams's lack of emotional intimacy, Claudette's misperception of her husband as a philanderer, and Adams's dejection about the state of his career. Pepper was an "enigma, closed emotionally," Claudette complained.

"He wouldn't let me in. He didn't let anyone get close to him." Although extremely voluble when recounting an incident from his life, he wouldn't use words to "tell what was happening inside of himself," said trumpeter Jon Faddis. "He'd tell you what was happening inside of himself with his horn, with his music." That said, human relationships are a two-way street. Mel Lewis felt that Claudette was a "hard lady." Both Ron Ley and Rose Cornfoot agreed. Ley described her as "straitlaced," and Cornfoot said, "It just seemed that there was no warmth."

Perhaps due to his inherent aloofness, Claudette felt her husband was fooling around with other women. "Claudette seems to think that I have a mistress in every town," Adams grumbled in 1985. In March 1986, he told vocalist Ruth Price that Claudette felt "he was a womanizer, which he thought was preposterous," said Price. "He was adamant about the fact that it was her imagination, but she was, apparently, very jealous." Based on her own experience, Claudette should have known better. Adams as a skirt chaser runs contrary to his long history as one who didn't pursue women. Instead, Claudette was probably wary of his lighthearted, platonic friendships with many women; some who, like her, were fans that admired him for his intelligence and extraordinary artistry. Ironically, she seemed to have forgotten that she and Pepper began their relationship in 1960, that it took sixteen years of pursuit before they were married, and that she too had had (in part) a platonic relationship with him for many years.

Unquestionably, Adams's long-simmering frustration about his finances soured his mood and adversely affected the marriage. Nevertheless, according to a friend, Pepper's dejection about his career was situational; a normal response by someone "frustrated in their efforts to achieve something they deserve to have. Pepper's depression was a consequence of societal conditions and his naïve sense of fairness and modesty. He felt that truth would out, and that extraordinary ability would be recognized by sheer pluck." As his friend further observed,

> I suspect a lot of his frustration was exacerbated by Claudette. I suspect she felt greater disappointment than Pepper in terms of lack of recognition. She had more personal ambition than Pepper. I suspect that she tried to motivate him by constantly reminding him of his failure to attain the status she wished for him and herself. This led Pepper to become angry with her, angry with others, and angry with himself. Pepper's celebrity was, no doubt, a part of her motivation for marrying him. I

suspect that she was more than a bit disappointed with what she discovered after they lived together for a while, and then set about trying to shape him by pointing out directly, or indirectly, the shortcomings in his career. I doubt that she ever gave him the sense of a warm, understanding, and supportive person. Pepper could have benefited from a woman in his life, but Claudette wasn't that person. I had never known him to be so angry with anyone as he was with her. It was, perhaps, the one aspect of his life in which he lost his cool.

⟿

A combination of fatigue from his late-night Hartford gig, his stressful drive home afterwards through a formidable winter storm, and the disillusionment about his marriage may have contributed to his car accident in mid-December 1983. Sometime around the fifteenth, Adams was leaving his house in the morning to run errands for most of the day. As he always did, he backed his car up his driveway from his below-grade garage to the sidewalk where it was level, then walked back to shut the garage door. This fateful day, however, his old Volvo didn't wait for him to return. Instead, it rolled down the driveway towards him and he didn't react quickly enough to get completely out of its way. Pinned between its front bumper and the garage door, Adams's car crushed one of his legs.

Whether a result of negligence or an automotive malfunction, Adams was unbelievably lucky that morning. First, his stepson was home playing hooky from school. He had just lit a joint at their dining room table moments after Pepper left the house, thinking that he had the place to himself. A few minutes later he noticed a faint sound coming from outside that seemed vaguely familiar. Realizing that the muted cries for help were uttered by his stepfather, Dylan ran outside. "He seemed to be in excruciating pain and was about to pass out," Dylan said. Dylan immediately alerted their next-door neighbor, who was not only home on a December morning but also able to rescue Pepper by reversing the stick-shift vehicle back up the driveway. Once their neighbor got involved, Dylan sprinted back inside to call for an ambulance. Within fifteen minutes, Adams was whisked away to nearby Brookdale Hospital.

Due to the accident's severity, Pepper's leg was wrapped in a long, heavy plaster cast that had to be elevated around the clock. All winter and spring, 1984, Adams convalesced in his dreary basement, chain-smoking cigarettes and self-medicating with booze when he could get it from Dylan. Since his family was away most of the day, Adams, with a bedpan by his side, was confined to a wheelchair, nibbled on breakfast and lunch that was left for him, and awaited his stepson's return from school for assistance and his evening meal.

Because he couldn't speak on the telephone or listen to his vast record collection, both upstairs and impossible to reach, his connection with the outside world was limited to an occasional visitor. Lee Katzman was probably Adams's first friend to come by, get him out of the house, and cheer him up. According to Katzman, Pepper regarded his auto accident as somewhat of an embarrassment.

Adams was upset that his marriage had collapsed, thinking he squandered his one opportunity to sustain a family of his own. Although his leg pain was intense at times, worse than anything was the fact that he couldn't work. His accident had forced him to cancel seven months of employment in 1984, including a week at Lush Life, his first prominent New York City club date in years. Like a sandcastle at high tide, the forward momentum that was propelling his solo career to that point, built up since he left Thad Jones/Mel Lewis's orchestra, was slowly ebbing away.

By the time of his calamity, Pepper and Claudette hadn't been sleeping together for several months, and their crumbling marriage had a corrosive effect on her son. Sometime after Adams's misadventure, Dylan set their bathroom curtain on fire. Pepper considered it a childhood prank but Claudette, over his objection, regarded it as a cry for help. By fall, Dylan was sent away to a Massachusetts boarding school, paid for by his father.

The cumulative effect of Adams's setback, the unhappy family environment, and her son's behavior had pushed Claudette to the edge. With her son out of town, she found her own apartment on Berkeley Place in the Park Slope section of Brooklyn, a quick subway ride from work. She was undergoing psychotherapy to cope with her troubles, and, according to her husband, was also exploring witchcraft and the occult. As a condition for any reconciliation, she told Adams that he too must seek therapy and stop drinking. Neither took place, though earlier that year she could have weaned him off alcohol by discarding all the liquor in the house. In time, Dylan would attend Morehouse College and start building a life of his own. Conversely, Adams's bizarre car accident was the beginning of the end for him. His disability and its aftermath, lasting more than a year, dovetailed into his cancer diagnosis, making his last three years utterly miserable.

Chapter Seven

Joy Road

He should have been playing in the greatest concert halls in the world.

—Don Friedman

In September 1977, with word out that he was available on a full-time basis to tour the world, Pepper Adams began the most productive six-year period of his career. Somewhat uneasy about being on his own, his wife's stable financial situation gave him the sense that he could at least in the short run begin developing a career as a touring soloist without too much risk.

In March 1978, Adams once again worked at Gulliver's, Amos Kaune's intimate West Paterson, New Jersey club facing the Passaic River. On the gig was Ron Marabuto, who had come east from California in 1977. Pepper "pretty much took me in," said Marabuto. "He was family." Adams "was putting a book together," said Marabuto. "He was always writing tunes. He was getting better at pacing sets. He was getting so he could pace a whole night." Adams often called dance tempos that Ellington played in the thirties and forties. "They were the same tempos as some of these old foxtrots, the way a real square band will play dance ballads," said Marabuto. "They weren't played very often; real in-between tempos."

Three months later, Adams recorded *Reflectory*, the session he regarded the best of his career. This would be the first of several Adams dates in which he would use drummer Billy Hart since Elvin Jones by then lived in Japan much of the year. *Reflectory* included four original compositions, "Claudette's Way," "Reflectory," "I Carry Your Heart," and "Etude Diabolique," which he wrote for the session.

"Etude Diabolique" is an exploration of the diminished scale, by the late 1970s a characteristic of Adams's style. A few years earlier, his diminished approach inspired Cecil Bridgewater to adopt some of that vocabulary in his own playing. "He opened up my head to that way of playing," Bridgewater said. As Pepper grew as a soloist, "he got trickier with it and more playful with it," said pianist Harold Danko. "He could take what a lot of us would use, that would sound like a cliché, and just turn it into a wonderful thing of beauty," said Phil Woods. "That's a rare gift to take common material like that, just common clay, and mold it into pure platinum."

Adams headed back to California in mid-November 1978, his third West Coast trip in a little over a year, for a series of gigs and recordings. On November 20, in Hollywood, he recorded *Confluence* with Bill Perkins. To make a small-group recording with Adams "was one of the great ambitions

Figure 7.1. Pepper Adams, November 5, 1978, Museum of Fine Arts, Montreal. Courtesy of André White.

of my life," said Perkins. One indication that fellow musicians were taking note of his recent work as a composer, *Confluence* is the only date during Adams's lifetime not led by him in which at least half a recording is made up of his compositions.

Nineteen seventy-eight turned out to be a great year, capped by his Grammy Award nomination for *Reflectory* as Best Instrumental Album of the Year by a Jazz Soloist. The first quarter of 1979 would be just as eventful, capped by Helen Merrill's *Chasin' the Bird/Gershwin* project. In April, however, his schedule thinned out. At that time, Gunnar Windahl visited for the entire month. "Sometimes I was very sad because he had no job and you saw that he longed for a call," said Windahl. "Now and then he had a gig and I went with him: to Washington, up in Connecticut, and, of course, in New York City, but not the main places. I think Pepper was very disappointed that he wasn't invited to play at Fat Tuesday's more often, at the Village Vanguard, Seventh Avenue South. We talked about that when we were a bit drunk. Otherwise, I didn't dare take up the topic."

⤳

His career in full bloom, 1980 would be Adams's busiest since he left Thad Jones/Mel Lewis. With two Grammy nominations in each of the previous two years, Pepper was increasingly seen as an attractive draw for club owners. Adams returned to the studio on March 11 to record *The Master*, his second date as a leader for Muse. For his follow-up to *Reflectory*, he wrote four new compositions, "Rue Serpente," "Bossallegro," "Lovers of Their Time," and "Enchilada Baby." *The Master* derived its title from bassist Milt Hinton and others from his era who referred to Adams by that nickname, a demonstration of the esteem they had for his intellect and vast knowledge of the jazz literature. It's quite rare in jazz, a music that at least prior to 1990 seemed to go through major stylistic transformations every decade or so, for colleagues twenty years older to revere someone two decades their junior. Adams came of age in the mid-1950s. Milt Hinton, born in 1910, toured with Cab Calloway beginning in the late 1930s.

A half a year after recording *The Master*, in 1980, Adams worked the Halloween weekend at Far and Away in Cliffside Park, New Jersey with the piano and bass tandem of Earl Sauls and Noreen Grey. This would be the first of twelve gigs with them, stretching all the way to 1986, that Sauls would record on his portable machine. In time, Adams would affectionately refer to Grey/Sauls, always with an added drummer, as "my Jersey band."

Figure 7.2. The Master. Public domain.

Adams regarded Noreen Grey, the daughter of Norb Grey, as a gifted all-around musician. He enjoyed her harmonically complex tunes, knotty textures she contributed to the ensemble, her swinging solos, and the irrepressible joy she exuded on and off the bandstand. Her husband at the time, Earl Sauls, an equally talented ensemble player and soloist, played with great time and undergirded the ensemble with a steady, hard swinging, foundational groove, sometimes at the very bottom of his instrument.

Urban Dreams (1981) was Adams's third date as a leader in four years, quite a departure from 1968–1977 when he had led just three records under his own name. Although he had received industry-wide acclaim for writing and performing his own music, Palo Alto Records "did not like original material, so I had to talk my ass off to get them to do two of my tunes," said Adams. "They were dictating really clichéd, hackneyed tunes and I had to talk them out of that." One tune they could agree on was "Time on My Hands" (1930). Adams loved old tunes, said Ron Kolber:

> He would send me a tune, an old tune. Every time we'd see each other he'd say, "You know this one?" We used to try to stump each other with old tunes. One of his favorite tunes was a tune by the name of "Says My Heart." It's an old tune. Always digging for old tunes; that was a little hobby with him. He said that some of the early tunes were really great. . . . He had great interest in the old-timers, any of the old-timers. He would listen to all of the old records. He said, "That's where we're from." He said, "If we listen to that, we're gonna get to where we are and maybe beyond, but you can't start in the middle and go. You gotta go all the way back."

In 1982, while working in England, Adams visited mouthpiece fabricator Geoff Lawton, where he chose a new metal mouthpiece that he would play for the rest of his life. Adams would experiment with softer and softer reeds to try to recreate the growl that he got with his Berg Larsen, but with a clear plastic reed, his sound, according to saxophonist Scott Robinson, was still quite "edgy and bright and buzzy." Adams's new sound was distorted even further by the advent of CD recording technology, still in its infancy in the 1980s.

Adams returned to Europe in December for a Metropole Orchestra radio broadcast. For Adams to have an opportunity to perform as the primary soloist with a forty-four-piece band was long overdue, and another indication of his increasing stature as a major jazz figure. A weeklong booking at New York's Fat Tuesday's in August 1983, culminating with a live recording at the club, was yet another. On that date, Kenny Wheeler's lonesome sound made for a very interesting contrast with Adams. "Wheeler was a real individual," said saxophonist Kirk MacDonald. "Not a bebop player, but a very creative player . . . I think that was the attraction for Pepper." Wheeler's playing was most effective on ballads; on waltzes such as "Doctor Deep" in which his slurs, swoops, large intervallic leaps, and wounded sound enhanced the mood; or when his staccato playing didn't interfere with the groove.

Conversely, Adams's playing was steeped in Charlie Parker's approach. But unlike others, Pepper had a unique way of creating tension with the beat. "He never struck me as being a guy in the pocket, like Bird was, or Coltrane, right dead center in the pocket," said bassist Gene Perla:

> He had a certain way of placing the rhythmical notes that were at one point tugging at the time and at the same time propelling it. He would play lines that would sort of start at one relationship to the beat and wind up on the other side of it. Sometimes he'd start late and wind up in front of it. Other times he'd start in front of it and wind up behind it. Other times he'd play lines and phrases that would sort of swim, an elastic approach across the rhythm. He had his own time that would float on top of the time.

Keith White agreed with Perla. Adams's "sense of time was uncanny, like Bill Evans. They seemed to have a built-in metronome. Actually, that's what the expression 'big time' means: the guy's a 'big time-guy.' That's what separates the men from the boys, their sense of time. There's lots of good players, but unless they have big time, forget it. But he had that. Often, Adams pulled back the time when stating the theme or playing a ballad. "Back-phrasing," as Denny Christianson defined it, is an older aesthetic, far more common among singers, or musicians who came up in the 1930s and 1940s.

Regarding Adams's pliant time-feel, in 1986, a few older musicians, who were active in the forties and fifties, advised drummer Phil Hey on how to best accompany Adams at his forthcoming gig in Minneapolis. "His time is very snaky," they told him. "He doesn't land on the beat a lot, and they said he plays real long, cool phrases. They said you just have to hear the phrase and learn how to play a little more legato on the drums, which," said Hey, "is evidently why he loved Elvin Jones so much. That elastic feel and that real legato sound. That gave me a good clue about how to play with him. Not quite so quarter-note oriented, but phrase oriented."

Chapter Eight

Conjuration

I love playing with Thad.

—Pepper Adams

Ever since 1954 when they worked together for nearly four months at the Blue Bird, Pepper Adams longed to front a quintet again with Thad Jones. As Adams told Ben Sidran in 1986, he enjoyed working with Jones in a small-group setting "because sometimes the slapstick kind of humor starts flowing. Musical, of course, but so broad as to approach farce: Making fun of a style that we don't care for by exaggerated vibrato, taking a well-known phrase from something and distorting it, or, particularly, playing it in another key and creating the tensions that occur when you play something that is totally recognizable as a melody except that the whole rest of the band is in an entirely different key." Pepper admired far more than Thad's sense of humor. When asked by an interviewer in 1980 if Thad was a genius, Adams replied, "I think that is underrating him."

Jones was both a paternal figure and a force of nature. Pepper once remarked that next to Thad—seven years his elder—he felt like a "small little boy." Conversely, Thad admired Adams's erudition and was flattered by his unstinting loyalty and reverence. Regarding their very close bond, saxophonist Seldon Powell told Bob Rusch,

> I heard Pepper say a couple of things that made me know that he and Thad had been very close in their lives. There maybe was a rub or two here and there: . . . when he figured that he

wasn't getting his share of solos. . . . Somebody said something about that to Pepper and he turned and said to him, "When I was in the army and they sent me to Japan during the Korean War, I received two letters the entire time I was over there. One of them was from Thad Jones." The inflection that was in his voice told me something about how he felt about him. They might have had a conflict here or there, but I'm sure they felt very close to each other as human beings and as musicians, and they were the giants of their time.

Marvin Stamm saw Thad and Pepper in a comparable light. "There was a tremendous rapport between these two guys," he said.

They were musically and personally a great match. There was the bear and there was Pepper; thin, skinny Pepper. There was the composer and there was the interpreter. When they played together—and they did do small-group things together—I just thought they were a great complement of one another. I thought their relationship personally, as far as I know, was quite warm. I think there was a *tremendous* love that existed between these two men, both musically and personally, and I think it served them both well. I think they created a tremendous amount of music. I think they laughed a million laughs.

By the summer of 1977, the quintet that Thad and Pepper did finally establish in 1964 had long since dissolved. Although they played an occasional quintet gig during that time, their group had many years earlier been eclipsed by the formation of Thad's extraordinary orchestra. For Adams, it was a hard pill to swallow. And it was a big loss for jazz that Jones couldn't sustain both aggregations during the twelve years that Adams anchored the reed section in his big band.

Pepper and Thad's first collaboration in the 1960s, during Jones's final year with Count Basie, was their work on Adams's Motown recording *Plays the Compositions of Charlie Mingus*. One of Pepper's finest recordings as a leader, the September 1963 date is matched in quality by a second recording, made three months later to satisfy the remainder of his contract. For that unreleased session, Adams chose Jones to write four septet charts for him as 45 rpm jukebox showpieces. The masters to them were likely destroyed in Universal Music Group's calamitous warehouse fire of June 1, 2008.

The twin Motown projects, done for its Jazz Workshop subsidiary, were the beginning of Adams and Jones coalescing as a unit. Within a year they would form the Thad Jones–Pepper Adams Quintet. But not before Thad (and Mel Lewis) accepted a job with Gerry Mulligan's reconstituted Concert Jazz Band. Mulligan's orchestra disbanded in mid-1964, after a run of less than a year. Soon thereafter, Thad and Pepper reconstituted their quintet. Its debut performance took place on September 20, 1964, at the Scene in New York City. Six weeks later, on November 2 at New York's Palm Gardens, the quintet, with the formidable rhythm section of Hank Jones, George Duvivier, and Elvin Jones, played their second gig. Then, a week later Thad and Pepper appeared on Oliver Nelson's influential recording *More Blues and the Abstract Truth*. Around that time, Thad Jones led an octet at the Scene including Adams, Mel Lewis, Jerry Dodgion, and trombonists Quentin Jackson and Benny Powell. The first four would, a year later, form the nucleus of the Thad Jones/Mel Lewis Orchestra.

By 1965, the Jones–Adams quintet was working throughout New York City. In March they played Amos Kaune's Clifton Tap Room, with Ron Carter and drummer John Dentz in the group. In April, they possibly worked the Five Spot, then returned to Clifton Tap Room for two consecutive weekends in early May. Gaining traction as a working unit, from mid-May to mid-June, the band, with pianist Duke Pearson added, worked a month at the Five Spot, then a week at Slugs'. The ensemble was also featured at two outdoor concerts in New York City that summer, sponsored by Jazzmobile, before returning to Slugs' for another week in October.

These were the quintet's glory days, for Adams a dream come true, when Thad was focused on the band and its future. Much to Pepper's dismay, though, things were about to change. During the 1965 Thanksgiving weekend, Thad Jones and Mel Lewis held their first midnight big-band rehearsal at Phil Ramone's A&R Studio on Seventh Avenue at Forty-Eighth Street. The session was organized to run through several orphaned Jones arrangements that Count Basie had commissioned but rejected. After the first rehearsal, word got out that Thad's extraordinary charts—swinging, majestic, sanctified, at times featuring just the rhythm section, with amazing saxophone-section solis and magnificent shout choruses—were something entirely new. "Harmonically, it was more modern, but it always swung," said Jon Faddis. For those reasons, there was considerable excitement about Jones reinvigorating the big-band idiom, at that time in decline.

Adams attended some of the rehearsals but missed the band's premiere engagement at the Village Vanguard on February 7, 1966, and was crestfallen about the band's sudden, cataclysmic fame and the way it usurped their quintet. In the short run Pepper assigned Marv Holladay as his sub while he took small-group gigs and pondered his future. Until that summer, when Thad persuaded him to permanently join the orchestra, a disappointed Adams resisted playing with the band, not wanting to be involved in yet another large group in which he'd be lucky to play one solo a night. "You couldn't hire Pepper to come in and just play baritone saxophone in a band," said Mel Lewis.

> You'd hire him as a jazz soloist, which limited him because a baritone chair in most bands was just a chair that a body just filled, just a part. How many bands wanted a jazz baritone player? They didn't want that. They wanted a jazz tenor player. Sometimes the alto player didn't matter either. They wanted a lead alto player, a jazz tenor player, and the rest were bodies. So now you're stuck with a baritone player that plays jazz . . . I think that made it very difficult for Pepper to go on the road with bands . . . Playing with these bands was boring for him.

In April and May 1966, several months after the big band's Vanguard premiere, the Jones–Adams Quintet taped their only recording, the brilliant *Mean What You Say.* They also managed to fit in a gig in Hackensack, New Jersey, with the big band's rhythm section of Hank Jones, Richard Davis, and Mel Lewis, another week at Slugs', and a live Friday night broadcast for WABC radio, hosted by Alan Grant. By then, Lewis had taken over for Dentz, who had moved to California. But the die was cast. Thad's creative juices would soon be diverted to his big band. Whereas the orchestra would obtain a ten-record deal from Solid State, record two of them during their first year, and perform at the Newport Jazz Festival that summer, the only quintet activity in 1966 would be a week at the Vanguard, beginning in late November, opposite John Coltrane's septet.

By 1967, the orchestra was ensconced at the Vanguard and starting to tour regionally while the quintet was an afterthought. Going forward, an average of one or two gigs a year would become the norm. One factor that limited the quintet's ability to tour was the recording and studio commitments that Thad Jones, Duke Pearson, Ron Carter, and Mel Lewis had in New York. Ultimately, a work-around was to use Thad and Mel's current rhythm section as subs. Thus, most small-group jobs outside of

New York included either Roland Hanna with Richard Davis, Gene Perla, or George Mraz; Walter Norris with George Mraz; or Harold Danko with Bob Bowman or Rufus Reid.

Playing Gulliver's in 1972 with Thad and Pepper's quintet was "one of the greatest experiences musically that I had," said bassist Gene Perla. "Every day we'd play a certain number of these same tunes, except that every night they were in a different key. You'd just start playing and you'd have to get it together. It was a marvelous experience for ear-training and forgetting about memorizing changes because you just had to really go with your ear and remember the feel of the tune."

Because the Jones–Adams Quintet did not fulfill its destiny as one of jazz's greatest ensembles, Adams's career didn't take off in the mid-1960s as he expected. Instead, each week for the next twelve years he would sit in Thad's orchestra and pine for his own gigs. Even worse, because promoters continued to define him as a big-band musician not on the traveling circuit, he was offered very few opportunities to record as a leader, greatly compounding his disgruntlement.

⤺

The Thad Jones/Mel Lewis Orchestra gigged every Monday night at the Village Vanguard, previously an evening when the city's jazz clubs were closed for business. Initially, trumpeter Nick Travis and trombonist Willie Dennis were on board, but they died before the band's first rehearsal. After a few run-throughs, trumpeter Jimmy Maxwell got ill and backed out, but lead-trumpet concertmaster Snooky Young stayed until 1970. Phil Woods was slated to be the orchestra's lead alto player, but Jerome Richardson convinced Jones to accept him instead. Because of Woods's superiority as a player, "You couldn't very well ask Phil Woods to play second alto to Jerome Richardson," said Mel Lewis. "Forget it, you can't do that."

With Richardson chosen, Thad and Mel hired Jerry Dodgion for second alto. Thad and Mel hoped to hire saxophonist Wayne Shorter, but he wasn't available due to his commitment to Miles Davis. Shorter recommended Joe Farrell, who was hired. Both Thad and Mel agreed on saxophonist Eddie Daniels, and the baritone chair was always Pepper's. Mel chose bassist Richard Davis, and after a few months Roland Hanna permanently replaced Thad's brother, Hank. Roland and Thad "complemented each other and inspired each other," said Lewis.

Apart from Dodgion, Farrell, Daniels, Adams, Davis, Hanna, and Richardson, "There was a preponderance of CBS members because those were Thad's drinking buddies," said Lewis:

> I didn't know Cliff Heather, I barely knew Jack Rains, you know? I came up with [Garnett] Brown and Brookmeyer. Thad came up with [Jimmy] Nottingham. We chose Jimmy Owens, but Jimmy burned us. He did something to us that we didn't like. Right when we needed our band, he went and hired everybody for Gerald Wilson to go and work at Basin Street. So, we got angry at him for it. . . . We got rid of Jimmy and hired Richard

Figure 8.1. Solid State Thad Jones. A pre-1969 photograph of the orchestra. Public domain.

Williams. And Richard's problem was drinking, so he got fired for drinking, and so did Nottingham.

❧

It didn't take much for jazz deejay Alan Grant to convince Max Gordon, Village Vanguard's owner, to take a chance on Thad's new band, especially on a night that his club was dark. In early 1966, Gordon was struggling to keep his club open. "Max's club was in pretty dire straits," said Grant. Gordon knew that he had to take a risk if he was going to resuscitate his business. He also knew that Grant offered to promote the band's upcoming Vanguard premiere for several consecutive weeks on his live radio show from the Half Note. What Gordon didn't anticipate was that, because of the orchestra's instant success, his fortunes were soon about to change, precipitating a successful run of more than twenty years.

At the band's first public performance, Max Gordon "was going to charge $2.50 per head at the door for us and he was going to get the bar action," wrote Doc Holladay. "By 10:30, the place was pretty well filled up and stayed that way the rest of the night. Now, Max didn't get rich by being a philanthropist for down-and-out musicians. He saw a good thing brewing the very first night, and during the first break we took he made a deal with Thad and Mel to pay everybody in the band [$17] every Monday night, whether the people came or not, and they went for it." After more than fifty years, listeners are still filling up the Vanguard on Monday nights to hear the band.

When Thad's band opened in February 1966, they only had nine arrangements. "We played those nine charts and stretched them out," said Mel Lewis. Thad elongated the tunes by improvising riffs and asking his soloists, much to their delight, to play lengthy solos. "Even when the chart was the same, he'd change it when someone was playing a solo," said trombonist Steve Turre, who served as a sub in 1973. "He'd have us go to a different place. He'd call audibles like a quarterback and things would happen. You never knew what to expect."

Jones "used hand signals to select soloists, signal members of the rhythm section to drop out, control dynamics, change tempos, repeat sections, cue a written insert, or select an individual to improvise a background," wrote Chris Smith. "He used to do things like he'd be suppressing the trombones, bringing them down, and bringing us up, with two different hands, one hand pressing downward, the other one kind of lifting upward," said alto saxophonist Don Palmer, who was a frequent sub for Ed Xiques or Jerry Dodgion in the early 1970s. "He used to do things on held chords, chords held at the end of a piece, where he'd bring different sections up and others down, and then up and down again, so you'd hear the different colors of the chord coming out, being accentuated at different times," said Palmer. Indeed, "There was something magical when he was leading the band," said Dick Oatts. "When he would count off the band, he was as much an improviser as when he was playing. . . . What he had on the page was just an example. He would take it each night and make it something different."

At six feet tall, with skinny legs yet massive as a redwood tree from the waist up, Jones conducted his band with boundless energy. "No one ruled a band with such love as Thad Jones," said trombonist Bill Watrous. "He loved us all like his sons, like his own children, like people that he wanted to have around him at all times. We got a feeling from Thad that we were all special." Bassist Steve Gilmore said that Thad "had an aura about him, and everyone had tremendous respect for him."

Figure 8.2. Thad Jones conducting, August 18, 1975, at Atlantic, Stockholm. Photo by Christer Landergren.

Due in large part to his unparalleled creativity with his big band, Jones to this day is still undervalued as an instrumentalist. That was never the case with musicians. Adams said that Thad was his favorite trumpet player because he surprised him the most, and Miles Davis once said, "I'd rather hear Thad miss a note than hear Freddie Hubbard hit twelve." Thad's band always had the most respect for both Thad and Pepper as soloists, said Dick Oatts. Mel Lewis concurred: "The two best soloists in the band were Thad and Pepper."

Trombonist John Mosca agreed that Jones is among the greatest of all jazz trumpeters. "In terms of taking the revolution that Dizzy did to the music and taking it somewhere else, another step, it would be Thad," he said. "His harmonic concept and his rhythmic conception are totally original. There's nobody else that thinks like he does." Mosca noted that Jones "would take incredible chances. He would get out on the thinnest limb you can imagine as an improviser. He would start a phrase that would lead someplace but you can't imagine how he's going to get back. And he would! Even the audience knew it. The audience would be on the edge of their seats, really. It was almost like they could not breathe."

Just as Adams oscillated between Art Tatum's flamboyance and Wardell Grey's brand of lyricism, so too did Jones seesaw between Dizzy Gillespie's pyrotechnics and Rex Stewart's melodicism. But that grossly oversimplifies these two unique, multifaceted stylists. To ascend to their exalted plateau, one that so few jazz musicians reach in their lifetime, you must spend many years working at it. "Anybody who really loved this art has to have known the history of the art," said drummer Tony Inzalaco.

And so, you study everyone that preceded your arrival. If you want to become something, you have to understand the styles: the sound that they got, how they did what they did. And, of course, whatever in their playing is attractive to you, you assimilate that and use it with your own viewpoint. That's the only way that people can be part of the history. Nobody comes along and plays anything that's really new. It's a synthesis of all the [players] before . . . and what [you've] come to because of that. So, I think that's part of the challenge of this art; to come up with what history has provided for you and come out of that with your own voice. It takes time, and it takes a lot of love, and it takes a lot of courage, and it takes a lot of hard work.

Throughout 1967 and early 1968, Jones's band continued to receive favorable press and perform before enthusiastic audiences. Despite so much forward momentum, a crisis during the summer of 1968 nearly put an end to the orchestra. Thad's brother, Elvin Jones, was living with a Japanese woman, Keiko Okuya, who came from a wealthy Nagasaki family. With no professional experience as a concert promoter, but with access to successful Japanese businessmen due to her pedigree, Thad and Mel entrusted her with organizing their first tour of Japan.

With so much money at stake, it's a pity that Thad and Mel didn't do their due diligence. Had they paid closer attention, they would have uncovered Okuya's earlier failure in bringing Pepper Adams to Japan for a month of concerts with her boyfriend. Thad and Mel, though, had no experience with the mechanics of international travel. Consequently, on July 9, 1968, accompanied by a great deal of fanfare, the band and many family members convened at JFK Airport for a triumphant send-off. Much to their shock, at Northwest Orient's ticket counter Thad and Mel were informed that the airplane tickets promised to be waiting for them were not there. When their lawyer tracked down Okuya in Japan, she assured him that tickets would be delivered to the airline the following day. A much smaller group reconvened at JFK on the tenth, but, once again, no tickets were supplied. With their entire band promised two weeks of work, and with some of the musician's spouses anticipating an exciting trip with their husbands, Thad and Mel had no recourse but to charge the airplane tickets on their American Express cards.

Because most of their promised gigs throughout Japan were illusory, Thad and Mel scrambled for work once they arrived in Tokyo. During the first three days, they worked two nights at tiny, cramped Pit Inn and once at the two-thousand-seat Kunikiniya Hall. That bought them some time to fill out the rest of the tour. With the assistance of photographer K. Abé, they booked a television show, a performance at a US military base, a follow-up concert at Kunikiniya, three nights at Golden Getsusekai, one more night at Pit Inn, and a third concert at Kunikiniya where 1,500 patrons were turned away. Because the band was stranded in Tokyo, Abé, in an extraordinary act of generosity, loaned Thad and Mel $15,000 ($64,000 in today's dollars) so they could return to New York. Jones and Lewis paid him back once their secondary mortgages were approved.

What happened to the original tour? According to Jerry Dodgion, Japanese businessmen who were financing it took exception to Okuya, by then an independent-minded, Americanized woman who was attempting to function as an entrepreneur in a fiercely patriarchal society. When she told one of her investors to "fuck off" when he demanded a kickback, he advised his cronies that they couldn't expect payoffs, and all withdrew from the enterprise. Band members, of course, were sympathetic to Thad and Mel's plight but were understandably upset that they weren't touring the country, weren't getting paid $100 per day, nor fitted for a new pair of shoes, allegedly part of the package. Okuya's father, whose factory would have provided the footwear, disowned her when he learned she was dating an African-American musician.

The band returned to New York on July 22, 1968, were back at the Vanguard on the twenty-ninth, and Thad and Mel's lawyer filed suit for breach of contract. Mel Lewis said that it took him a long time to pay off the debt, implying that nothing of substance ever resulted from their case against Okuya's Elvin Promotion Company.

The Japanese tour was the first of a long line of lost opportunities that led Adams to conclude that the band was never well managed, neither by Mel Lewis nor others. "Unfortunately, that band never had the proper management, in my mind, that could have made the band excel," agreed Rufus Reid:

> Thad and Mel wanted someone to do it, but they really didn't want anybody to do it at the same time. By and large, the band could have, and should have been able to do more, but somehow it just never did. Sometimes things would happen in Europe. Some of the business things, that shouldn't have been allowed to happen, happened. Some of the people that would book the band wouldn't pay on time, and, therefore, paychecks were late, etc. Things of that nature. You got too big of an organization. When something like that happens it's pretty devastating.

Saxophonist Ed Xiques felt that "the problem was both of them." Mel never wanted to be a leader. "He just wanted to be a sideman," said Xiques. "The drummer is the leader of the band musically, but he was not a leader in that sense of the word at all," said John Mosca. "He was one of the guys. . . . Mel had found what he wanted to do with his life. This was it for him. He couldn't think of anything he'd rather be doing than being out on the road with the guys playing. He was in heaven." Jones, for his part, would have nothing to do with business. "You couldn't talk to Thad about money," said Harold Danko. "You wouldn't talk to Thad about even bad conditions." But, as Jon Faddis pointed out, "with success comes a lot of responsibility," and to the orchestra's detriment, though Thad was the public face of the band, he remained solely on the artistic side.

Compounding Mel's lack of business acumen was Jones's penchant for getting in the way of the band's success. Thad "was always upset that he wasn't more acknowledged for his talent, but he would do things to sabotage that stuff," said Faddis. As Xiques saw it, "Thad may have had a classic case of fear of success." One example was his souring relationship with Philadelphia International Records, a black-owned, well-capitalized firm that Thad, with his terrific people skills, could have fertilized into a long-term deal. Instead, he let it be known at the outset that it wasn't his preference to arrange the label's pop tunes on his albums, thus alienating himself from the label's management.

Another example of Jones impeding his own success was when the orchestra had gigs in Florida. "Every time we went to Florida, for some reason or other, he'd make it up in his mind that there was going to be racial prejudice when we got down there and then he would create it," said Lewis. In February 1975, on one Florida trip with the band, Thad "had a preconceived idea before we went in," agreed Faddis. "Something happened in the restaurant and, the next thing I knew, Thad was gone." Such behavior must have bewildered promoters and club owners, just as it did those in the orchestra, damaging the band's reputation for dependability. "The guys in the band wouldn't even know what the hell—especially the black guys," said Lewis. "They'd say, 'What the hell is wrong with him? Nobody's bothering us.'" As it turned out, Jones's many frightening experiences touring the segregated Deep South as a young musician in the late 1940s caused lifelong trauma that he was never able to resolve.

⌒

By 1970, with the exodus of many television jazz orchestras to sunny California, Jones/Lewis's personnel were in transition. Joe Farrell had left the year before, Bob Brookmeyer the year before that, and Snooky Young, Bill Berry, and Jerome Richardson were moving west. Others would soon leave, or hire subs in their place, due to a change in the band's orientation. "We had a meeting one night in that kitchen of the Vanguard," said trombonist Eddie Bert. Thad and Mel announced that to continue the band, they would have to spend more time on the road. "We were all involved in New York scenes," said Bert. "I couldn't leave town." According to Bill Watrous "little by little, the band became a lesser band for it."

By early 1972, however, the trumpet, trombone, and reed sections were completely reformulated to accommodate international travel. With eighteen-year-old Jon Faddis as its new concertmaster, and sixty-three-year-old plunger master Quentin Jackson in the trombone section, the Thad Jones/ Mel Lewis Orchestra in a very real sense began its rebirth. Soon thereafter, the band's US State Department tour of the Soviet Union helped steady its personnel for another three years. Designed as a public relations strategy to pave the way for Richard Nixon's visit three weeks later, his visit led to two treaties that initiated the thawing of the Cold War.

Unlike the ill-fated Japan trip, the Russian tour was an "altogether very, very happy experience," said Thad Jones, and his musicians were elated by the outpouring of emotion that they experienced. Previously, jazz had struggled to be heard under the Soviet regime. After more than ten years, though, an American jazz orchestra had returned, and it created a response "as if we were a rock group here in America," said Billy Harper. "There were that many people."

While in St. Petersburg, the Soviet government opened the Hermitage Museum's private Impressionist Collection solely for Adams. As extraordinary as that experience was for him, his time in town was hardly idyllic. An afternoon jam session with members of the band and local musicians was violently squashed by the KGB and local militia. Another time, Adams's luggage was surreptitiously inspected. "They got into my room," he told Ron Kolber. "They took my horn out and put it backwards in the case." Hoping to see the results of a more equitable society, and the apotheosis of the socialist ideal first advanced by the French Revolution, Pepper was disillusioned by Russia's oppressive regime.

Although a subsequent Moscow jam session was tolerated, a jam session in Tbilisi, Georgia, also met with brutality. Americans were welcome to observe, but no one informed Thad and Mel's musicians that they were forbidden from joining Georgian ensembles. Once the musicians took a break, police ordered them not to reconvene because they had invited American musicians to jam with them. When local musicians tried to restart the session, officials in black leather coats intervened, assaulting them with leather truncheons.

Not all the band's dealings with the state-police apparatus were problematic. "There was a lady that Mel was with who I think probably was assigned to really watch and keep up with the band," said Harper. Although others in the orchestra had flings with women who weren't planted by the government as undercover spies, "with Mel I think they might have had a method," said Harper. Though the entire band was invited, a very special moment for Jones, Xiques, Adams, and Hanna took place in Kyiv, when all four attended a concert featuring violinist David Oistrakh. A place of honor was made for them on the stage, and they were introduced to the audience as special guests of the country.

⇨

Adams's solos always lifted Thad's band. "In that sax section there was a reverence for Pepper," said Don Palmer. "The only word you can use probably was he was loved, because he was such a sweet man and he played so fucking good! Rhythmically, he was a powerful player! It was as strong as anything I've ever heard." According to Earl Sauls, when you played with Adams, "you were just caught up in it . . . A lot of times he played pretty far behind the beat . . . [yet] he still had that momentum."

In his last two years with Thad and Mel, Adams only received an average of one or two solos per night, especially when they were on tour. "I felt kind of bad," said Harold Danko, who joined in 1976. "There's Pepper Adams only taking one solo and I'd have six." That sentiment was felt by everyone in the band: "[It] made no sense to me, and made no sense to anybody, yet this is the way that Thad did it," said Mel Lewis. "Sometimes [Adams] would go nights and nights without him ever playing":

> Now, all right, if it happens on a Monday night at the Vanguard, a couple of Mondays in a row, it's only one night. Then, when you go on the road, and you're going two and three nights and he ain't getting nothing to blow, they start thinking. After two or three days, Pepper figured, "Well, I'm not going to get anything to play anyway, so the hell with it. This is the greatest beer over here. Good beer, and I'll bring some whiskey and I'll really get bombed. Who's going to know?" So, when he'd get to a point where he could barely stand, then Thad would start featuring him. To me, that makes no sense. . . . Thad never

gave Pepper enough to play in our band. Pepper had more to play in Kenton's band than he had in our band.

Discounting his tours with Stan Kenton and Lionel Hampton, Adams's only long-term big-band gig was with Thad Jones/Mel Lewis. Although he got bored playing in most big bands, Jones/Lewis was different. New music would be brought in, and because Thad's writing for saxophone was so demanding, it was for Adams, at least at first, a welcome challenge. Also, in its early days, the band only performed on average six nights a month, Adams said, so "it's not running the book into the ground."

All in all, big-band work was "strictly for survival," said Adams:

> Certainly, there was very little pleasure involved except for rehearsals. I always like rehearsals with a big band 'cause you got something to react to: When you're seeing the music for the first time and learning to play it, and getting the blend within the section and with the other sections. All the stuff you can do at rehearsals, that's fine. . . . If I stay in a big band too long, once I have all that covered, then it becomes hack work and is no longer interesting. The next thing is to memorize all the parts and see if you can play all night with your book closed—and get dirty looks from the bandleader. After you have that covered, the only remaining challenge is to see how drunk you can get and still play the book accurately. That can be bad for you after a period of time.

During Adams's Jones/Lewis tenure, the band went through four phases. The first one existed from its establishment in late 1965 until several members left for California. From 1970–1972, with Marvin Stamm as lead trumpeter, there was a transitional second phase when the composition of the trumpet, trombone, and reed sections, plus bass chair, evolved and eventually settled down. Then, from 1972–1975, much like its first phase, a third one, with Jon Faddis as concertmaster and George Mraz on bass, featured a consistent roster, albeit with Roland Hanna's mid-1974 exodus. A fourth incarnation, begun in mid-1975 and lasting until Adams's exit, was akin to its second phase, but with even more disruption. Starting with Frank Foster and Gregory Herbert replacing Billy Harper and Ron Bridgewater, within a few months Al Porcino replaced Faddis, later replaced by Earl Gardner.

Steve Gilmore replaced Mraz, and a year later was replaced by Rufus Reid. Trombonist Janice Robinson replaced Quentin "Butter" Jackson, and still other personnel changes continued to be made each year, often in advance of lengthy European tours.

In its initial phase, Detroiter Snooky Young functioned as the band's lead trumpeter. Even with a handful of appointed subs rotating in and out, Young's presence unified the band's sound. After Young moved west with the *Tonight Show,* Stamm took over the lead trumpet role in his image. Stamm had started in late 1966 as a sub for Nottingham, but also served as first-call sub for any of the four trumpet chairs (Young, Bill Berry, Nottingham, or Richard Williams). When Berry left for California with the *Merv Griffin Show,* Stamm took his place, eventually taking Young's spot. Stamm stayed until 1972, when he chose not to travel with the band, and after it was decided that Jon Faddis should assume Stamm's lead chair so he could maintain his high-note chops.

In mid-1970, around the time that Young left, Jerry Dodgion assumed Jerome Richardson's lead alto chair after he moved to California. Adams considered Dodgion one of jazz's greatest sight-reading saxophonists, and much preferred Dodgion's phrasing since it was closer to his own. By 1971, Billy Harper was in the band in place of Joe Farrell, Eddie Daniels was transitioning out, and Ed Xiques took Dodgion's place as second alto after first subbing on baritone for Pepper. The saxophone section finally coalesced in 1972 with Dodgion, Xiques, Harper, Ron Bridgewater, and Adams, and it remained constant until mid-1975.

While the character of the reed and trumpet sections were shifting, so too was the bass chair. Richard Davis, Mel's original choice, was planning to leave in 1972. Davis's replacement, George Mraz, joined in early 1972 and stayed until 1975. About Mraz, Mel Lewis said that he had the best time of all the bassists who played in Jones/Lewis or any of its subsequent formulations.

Mel Lewis was present for almost every Jones/Lewis gig. He was the perfect choice for the orchestra in the way that he supported all the parts, playing "underneath" them as drummer Tony Faulkner once explained. "Mel never forced the band to play, like a lot of drummers feel that they have to force the band," agreed Dodgion. "He always allowed the band to play, and this went together so great with Thad's writing, which was somewhat unique. For it to not be played in a forceful way is to let the music be itself."

Although Lewis could play with a full kit sound and great energy or complexity if called for, he is known as one of jazz history's greatest big-band

Figure 8.3. Pepper Adams, probably August 13 or 14, 1973, at Grona Lund, Stockholm. Photo by Christer Landergren.

drummers partly because of his extraordinary ability to play "the perfect fill or setup," said pianist Jim McNeely. "It was really kind of like riding on a magic carpet," said trombonist Ed Neumeister. "You could say he was handing the figures to us on a silver platter. Never overplaying, and just laying down the foundation of a groove, and setting up what the big band needs without any flash whatsoever. It was really an amazing experience. I didn't truly realize how great he was until he was gone and there was that vacuum there."

As John Mosca said about Mel Lewis, "That space that he would leave made him different from everybody else. I never heard anybody else who got through arrangements that complex and still have that great feel. . . . A big-band drummer has to set up figures, and many drummers play the figure with the band":

But Mel would very rarely do that. In fact, you had to actually ask him to do it if you wanted him to play a figure, or [Thad] would write it in. The way he would set up the figure, he would imply everything, and then the horns would play it. So, Thad: You notice his writing for the horns is very rhythmical. It's almost like it's a drum part for the horns—all the horns, saxophones too. And a lot of it is very complex rhythmically. He could do that because Mel would be out. Mel would set us up. In other words, he would make it easy for us to play the complex things.

～

Beyond his profound influence on Adams, Thad Jones's impact upon jazz is substantial. His work an arranger and composer is still widely studied and performed at high schools, universities, and conservatories around the world. Mondays around the globe are often regarded as big-band nights because of Thad's long-time residency at the Village Vanguard. Jones enlarged the vocabulary of big-band writing to include sax- and trombone-section solis; shout choruses (those triumphant, climactic moments for full orchestra that conclude his works); a focus on the rhythm section as a unit, with an emphasis on bass and piano solos; use of soprano sax as a lead voice; bass lines paired with the melody; a far greater use of harmonic dissonance; internal voices that have their own distinct melodies rather than filling out an orchestration by doubling other voices; an emphasis on baritone sax as a solo vehicle; and hip, swinging, sanctified tunes with a heavy groove. When Jones "played" his band, he arguably improvised alterations to the band's arrangements more than anyone had done so before or since his reign. His legacy remains to this day the high-water mark that jazz orchestras, big-band composers, and arrangers aspire to more than fifty years after Jones/Lewis's first gig at the Vanguard.

Chapter Nine

Civilization and Its Discontents

There's about fifteen years of my life there I wish someone would give
me back.

—Pepper Adams

During part of the time that Pepper Adams was a member of the Thad
Jones/Mel Lewis Orchestra, he was also affiliated with Duke Pearson's
big band. Co-led by Donald Byrd until he left New York in 1968 to work
in academia, Pearson's orchestra convened every Saturday afternoon at Lynn
Oliver's Studio in Manhattan, where Blue Note held its band rehearsals a
week before recording them at Van Gelder's. "That band could have been
as good as ours, but Duke's personality wasn't as strong as Thad's," said
Mel Lewis. "He didn't push himself hard enough for that. He was too
busy with chicks."

Pearson was on Blue Note's payroll as their A&R man beginning in
January 1963. Through the mid-1970s, he was responsible for overseeing
the label's recordings and entrusted with writing arrangements for many of
them. Pearson "was different from other producers," said Joe Chambers. "He
was 'invisible,' never in the way nor obtrusive, attending all the rehearsals
and quietly ensuring that the recordings went smoothly." As Pearson told
Ted O'Reilly in 1973, "I'm only responsible for putting the product on
record and trying to see that comes out well."

Pearson's big band didn't work much. Occasionally, they gigged at
Club Ruby in Queens, or Dom in Manhattan, sometimes with Alan Grant
as emcee. They played a week at the Apollo Theater, a few Sunday nights

at the Village Vanguard, or on Mondays there, too, substituting for Jones/ Lewis when the band with Adams traveled out of town. Jazzmobile invited Pearson's group back from time to time, and there were a few out-of-town engagements, some that included singer Nancy Wilson.

Its lengthiest gig was Sunday nights at the Half Note. The band worked there from February through September 1967, and again from November 1972 until June 1973 at the club's midtown location, when Pearson reconvened the band to add some luster to the club's reopening. The idea of showcasing a big band at the Half Note may have been conceived by its owners, the Cantarino brothers, to capitalize on Thad Jones's success.

Pearson "was a romantic composer," said Tony Inzalaco. "He was like Puccini to me, the jazz Puccini." Pearson's Half Note gigs barely paid at all. "Maybe we made $3 apiece but nobody really cared," said Bob Cranshaw. "We just enjoyed playing the music."

Pearson hardly gets credit for overseeing so many Blue Note releases, nor for the label's acquisition of prominent new artists. Much like Thad Jones, Pearson is also overlooked as a composer and instrumentalist. Just as "A Child Is Born" is the only one of Thad Jones's many tunes now considered part of the standard jazz repertoire, Pearson's "Jeannine" is his only composition regularly performed by jazz musicians. And as an instrumentalist, Pearson is similarly ignored. Some of his finest piano work is on Donald Byrd's recordings with Adams, and on the Thad Jones–Pepper Adams Quintet's *Mean What You Say* (1966).

Interlude

New York's Turbulent Late '60s Jazz Scene

Because of New York's magnetic pull as jazz's finishing school, performers since at least the 1940s have routinely moved there to develop their craft and get better known. "I think New York is great because you develop very fast," said Lew Tabackin:

> You feel that you have to play good because you don't know who's going to be listening. You're not worried about your audience so much as the people you're with that you really respect. You never know who's gonna walk in. Coleman Hawkins could walk in, which he has done. Sonny Rollins, anybody, could walk in.

So, you have to be playing at your best all the time and try to be original because the person you're copying could come in. So, development is intense in New York, and that's why I think it's important for musicians to at least spend some time in New York. It adds another dimension to people's playing.

In 1964, New York's jazz scene was still bustling, the culture of musicians hanging out was still firmly in place, and American society was at least a year or two away from the social unrest that ultimately drove some jazz players to relocate in Europe. After work, jazz musicians converged at Birdland, and not just for its Monday night jam sessions. "Birdland was a big meeting place," said Nabi Totah. "It was like a social hall. Later on, at night, everybody would come down."

If you were a jazz fan, you could stay for the 4:00 a.m. set at any New York City club, drink to your heart's content, and socialize with those on the bandstand or with musicians who came by to hear the group. "Those who played the clubs had free access to those playing the other club," remembered Tony Inzalaco. Musicians, in turn, recognized the same loyal patrons who attended night after night and interacted with them. There was a camaraderie among jazz musicians, and with musicians and their audience, something that slowly leached out of the music business starting in the 1990s when draconian liquor laws opened new opportunities for attorneys to file negligence lawsuits against tavern owners and their staff.

But when Birdland closed in 1965 after filing for bankruptcy the year before, it had a seismic effect on New York City's jazz scene. "The music stopped almost," said Ray Mosca. "There were only a couple of places: the Vanguard, and the Village Gate, and a couple of joints in the Village. It got weird. There were not that many gigs." Increasingly, jazz musicians found themselves working out of town, if they worked at all, sometimes driving long distances. "You used to go out and play three nights in Philadelphia, two nights in Detroit, or two nights in Montreal," said Mosca.

Besides dwindling jazz venues, inner-city crime, black nationalism, and the Vietnam War made life increasingly difficult. "There were assassinations, social unrest, people afraid to go out at night," said trumpeter Art Farmer. "People felt that they were taking their lives in their hands if they went out to hear jazz. That had a bad effect on a person who tried to play for a live public."

Lew Tabackin also felt the pressure. "The late sixties and early seventies were a tough time, especially for white musicians," he said. "It was kind of like a revolution in America, and I had a lot of respect for the revolution; a black revolution, but it didn't do me any good. There wasn't much chance for a white jazz musician." Tabackin at one point was hired for a Broadway show, then let go the same day because its executive producer was instructed to only hire black musicians. "It got to be purely racial," said Tabackin. "Less and less opportunities were opening up. . . . That's one of the reasons I moved to Los Angeles. I had a job offer from the *Tonight Show.* I took it because I wasn't playing as much as I wanted."

It was equally hard for Tony Inzalaco, precipitating his move to Europe:

> Sometime in '67 there was some kind of a revolution in terms of black people, black musicians. I was one of the people that worked with Billy Taylor. I guess every drummer in New York worked with Billy Taylor at a certain point in time . . . One day, Billy called me and said, "Tony, don't be offended, but I was instructed that I can't hire any white people any longer. And so, I just want you to know that this is not my thing, but it's a movement."

Besides the racial politics and closure of so many jazz clubs, the youngest segment of jazz's audience, who had become infatuated with rock music, had been waning for some time. "The sixties saw the perfection of stereo LPs, the emergence of ever-more powerful FM radio stations, and the worldwide distribution of inexpensive 45 rpm records," wrote Lewis Porter and Michael Ullman. Whereas "in the late fifties the jazz club was a main pillar of New York City's cultural economy, by the late 1960s it's a niche site struggling to hold on to its relevance, but with an air of much-faded glory, as the city (and the nation) has moved on to go-go bars, prominent rock clubs, or concert venues with psychedelic light shows," said John Gennari. "Youth culture came to dominate urban public space, and 30–60-year-olds, who a decade earlier might have been going to the Vanguard or even the Five Spot, now largely have ceded the hip culture spaces of the city to 15–30-year-olds."

With radio and recording industries shifting to accommodate the demand, "jazz music went all to hell almost everywhere in the United States," said saxophonist Bud Shank. "I think musicians found themselves with maybe four alternatives: 1) become a junkie and hide away from other people; 2) go to Europe; 3) give up the music business; 4) go into some other form of music." To make matters worse, soon after some musicians chose Europe, the most secure New York City music jobs that jazz players maintained for years began ebbing away. First, prominent television shows with jazz big bands moved their operations to California. Then, with the advent of the synthesizer in the 1970s, studio work started to be outsourced to individuals who could do orchestrations on their own.

Civilization and Its Discontents

Part II

Beginning in 1969, Adams traveled to Europe on a yearly basis. He regarded Europe as only a day away from New York and was eager to obtain work overseas because small-group jazz in the US had largely dried up. "I had always gotten good press in Europe, which is very different from the United States," said Adams. "So, I didn't have to overcome these barriers of people coming to see me, having been told in advance that it wasn't worthwhile doing by people like Whitney Balliett, or Martin Williams, or Leonard Feather, or John S. Wilson who got on my case immediately and told the American public that they shouldn't bother."

Adams's first European gig as an itinerant soloist took place in mid-December 1969. After working with Thad's band in London, Adams worked for two weeks at Montmartre in Copenhagen. After a subsequent gig in Aarhus, he flew to Faro, Portugal, to visit David X. Sharpe, his friend from New York. Sharpe had relocated to this coastal city to open Godot's. Adams played a week there, then worked another week in Sweden before returning to New York in early February.

It's not known with whom Adams played during that week in southern Portugal, but "a real jazz man will play his instrument no matter what," said Eddie Locke:

> He's gonna play. He's not gonna make an excuse for not playing by saying, "Something is going wrong, I can't play." If you love it so much, it doesn't make any difference. No dollars, bad musicians, good musicians, mediocre musicians: You're gonna blow! Pepper just happened to also be a great *player*. But he was a real jazz man. . . . A real jazz man is rare. That's a lifestyle. That's not just going to school. And that's what Pepper was about. In Detroit, you played in the joints. Slop jobs in those old, funky

Figure 9.1. Pepper Adams, February 1, 1970, at Artdur, Goteborg, Sweden. Photo by Christer Landergren.

places. That's a jazz man. He wasn't trying to play in Carnegie Hall every night. He was just going to play some music because he loved to play. . . . People wanted to play with him because he was a jazz man. . . . I don't care who he was playing with; he's gonna sound good because he's gonna blow! He doesn't give a shit about the other cats. If they play the wrong change, he'll play the wrong one. That's a true jazz musician. Bird was like that. Coleman Hawkins was like that. I put him in some heavy company there but that's what I'm talking about.

In September 1973, while Thad and Mel's band were based in London for a week at Ronnie Scott's, Adams recorded *Ephemera*. "The opportunity to record was only in England and very much on the cheap," said Adams. *Ephemera*, recorded for Spotlite with Thad and Mel's rhythm section of Roland Hanna, George Mraz, and Mel Lewis, opened with its title track, the tune Adams considered his finest composition. "He thought it was underrated, that people didn't see that the structure was something like Coltrane's 'Giant Steps,'" said Gunnar Windahl. "He was very proud of that composition."

Also included on the recording was "Civilization and Its Discontents," Adams's first original ballad. As Pepper told Peter Danson, "I like to use a strong melody which does not quite relate to the chords but gives that feeling of tension across the chord, which in the end gives it a very bitter-sweet kind of quality." Though Adams, in Albert Goldman's view, "was a very brilliant up-tempo player [who] could run changes endlessly with far more invention than a vast number of well-known soloists, the beauty of Pepper wasn't in that stuff at all":

> That was more like "The Amazing Pepper Adams." The beauty of Pepper, the whole glamor of his style, lay in very slow, sub-tle, moody, and reverie-like stuff like "Chelsea Bridge," things like that, that were very subtle, very sensitive, very sort of close to an impressionist tonal palette. And it suggested a kind of a very introverted, shy, tender—never sentimental, or weak, or anything like that; far from it—but a guy in the shadows. Now, of course, that's not so far from a description of Miles Davis either, you know? [Adams's] classic works are soliloquies delivered in the shadows, off to the side of the stage. He's the Hamlet of the horn.

Despite his ballads' melancholic atmosphere, Adams's penchant was to depart from that ambience once he began soloing, as if to sidestep any vulnerability. Instead, he preferred to explore ornate embellishments and highly technical double-time runs. "I think that his tendency to double up is inspired by his mind being so fertile," explained Gerry Niewood:

> He's thinking of what's going on deeply inside the changes, his tendency to express all of that. Pepper was a florid player who could play a ton of notes as could a piano player, but he was a very vertical player, too, which you associate with the piano. A lot of his playing was from the bottom up, from top down, through the harmony, spelling it out, really letting his mind unravel it all for you. Rather than confining his thinking just to the melodic line on top, he would just run through the whole harmony, from the bottom up, and express all of what he was thinking—in terms of the flow of the changes, the inner

stuff—through his improvisation. . . . He would hear all the stuff between the changes, and in his solos you could hear how the inner harmony was moving. He had that all at his command. He would fill in the spaces. He would show you the direction of the flow of his ideas through the harmony very masterfully. He'd be playing with the clay. You could see every stage of the way he was hearing the harmony flow. He really was a master of that.

Undoubtedly, Adams, in Art Tatum's image, was a virtuoso instrumentalist who enjoyed expressing his abundant musical ideas. Major Holley once asked Pepper why he played so many notes. Miles Davis once asked Coltrane the same thing, and many years later criticized his guitarist for overplaying. "Like a lot of guys do, they play too many fucking notes," Davis complained. "Like Mike Stern. I tell him all the time. I say, 'Mike, you need to go to Notes Anonymous.'"

Although Don Friedman acknowledged this point of view among his colleagues, he never felt it was an appropriate criticism per se. "Some people say, 'Oh, this guy's good but he plays too many notes.'":

> I don't agree with that. I personally don't feel that should be a criteria. I don't think it matters if somebody plays a few notes or a lot of notes. It depends *how* they play the notes. If they play them great, and if the guy has a lot of chops, why not play a lot of notes if he's got the ideas and it all works out right? . . . Besides all the notes [Pepper] played, he got into the time-feeling and he helped the swing. Some players can play a lot of notes but they can't quite get into the groove. He could do both.

Looking at it another way, those who have criticized Adams's effusiveness "are of the same party as those who found van Gogh's canvas 'too full of paint,' a criticism Henry Miller once compared to the dismissal of a mystic as 'too full of God.'"

In 1975, the following year, just prior to Thad and Mel's European summer tour, Adams worked the Domicile in Munich for three weeks. After his quartet had nearly finished its engagement, Enja decided to record the group. For *Julian* and *Twelfth and Pingree*, Adams began a new phase of his compositional work: the use of bass and baritone as two horns. With George Mraz, one of his era's great virtuosos, Adams had the freedom to craft as tricky a strain as he wished. Adams and Mraz's intertwined, harmonized melody line on "Jirge," comprising the tune's entire theme, was, in a sense, Pepper's attempt at channeling "Jack the Bear" (1940), Duke Ellington's feature for bassist Jimmie Blanton. Not that "the pieces sound alike, just that the idea of using the bass in the theme goes back to Duke with Blanton," explained Lewis Porter. Pairing bass lines with the melody was a compositional technique that Thad Jones employed in tunes such as "Three and One." A few years later, "Reflectory" would become Pepper's second composition written in this manner, and five years afterwards he would write for Mraz a soli section for bass and baritone in "Rue Serpente."

⤹

Rather than stay with Thad Jones's orchestra, why didn't Adams take a leave of absence and move to Europe after the New York jazz scene deteriorated? Based on the success of other American jazz musicians, he might have carved out a new identity for himself as a soloist, worked consistently as a bandleader, gotten on the roster of a state radio orchestra, recorded for any number of European labels, and advanced much further as a player. One explanation might be that he didn't have any savings to afford him the peace of mind to give it a try. Still another reason may be that he regarded his commitment to Thad as sacrosanct. He once explained to a friend that he felt his role in Jones's band was to anchor it as Harry Carney had done with Ellington. Alternatively, perhaps he believed that penetrating the New York studio scene would finally allow him the opportunity to make a comfortable living. Unfortunately, that didn't turn out to be the case, though he did experience some degree of stability in the mid-to-late 1960s. In a 1969 interview for *Jazz Magazine,* Adams confessed about 1966–1968, "In the three years preceding this one I probably made more money than I ever had at any period in my life." What a welcome change, considering that his net annual income from 1956 through 1965, while living in one of the world's most expensive cities, averaged around $19,000 a year, adjusted for 2021 dollars. Between the years 1966–1968, and again from 1972–1974, however, it more than doubled to $48,000, though he still couldn't save any money. It was hardly the comfortable lifestyle he envisioned for himself that Thad Jones and Mel Lewis enjoyed.

Had Adams decided to double on bass clarinet, as he did on a 1957 Bud Shank date and again in 1958 with Benny Goodman, he could have improved his financial situation. Pepper's stubbornness to stay devoted

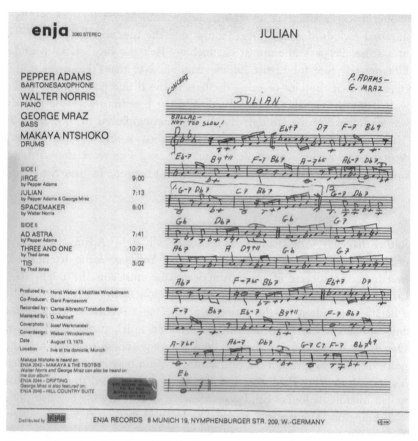

Figures 9.2 and 9.3. Julian, 12th & Pingree. Live recordings done at Domicile, Munich, both from August 13, 1975. Public domain.

throughout his career to the baritone sax revealed both a single-mindedness, reminiscent of his sixth great-grandfather James Adams's commitment to endure against insurmountable odds, and a stubborn streak that prevented him from pragmatically adjusting to circumstances beyond his control. "If Pepper would have bought a bass clarinet, at least he would have worked," said Mel Lewis.

> I think he was foolish, in a way, because there was no reason why a great jazz musician like him, who was an excellent reader, who was an excellent soloist—I mean, he was a giant baritone player—should be sitting around while guys that were inferior

enja₂₀₇₄

PEPPER ADAMS   TWELFTH & PINGREE

to him were doing the dates and getting to play baritone solos.
Guys would have written for him, but they needed that double.
The whole thing is, studio work required doubling. . . . There
was certainly room for Pepper. He probably could have averaged
three, four, to five dates a week, and you add that to his jazz
club work and all, you're talking two or three hundred dollars
a week, four hundred dollars a week, plus jingles and residuals.

Instead, he chose to accept whatever studio work remained available to
him. Considering his struggle to survive as a musician, moving to Europe
may have been too big of a risk, even for a few months. Nothing in his

experience would have given him the confidence to believe that he might succeed as a baritone soloist on his own.

While a member of Jones/Lewis, Adams averaged only three weeks of work per year as a bandleader. Added to his two weeks of European gigs, that left nearly eleven months each year in which he either played in Thad's big band, did unsatisfying "hack work" (his snide term for mundane gigs), worked as a sideman, or was intermittently unemployed. Is it any wonder that the sixties and much of the seventies were such an empty experience for him?

Although Adams was a private individual, his friends knew him as a funny guy with an extremely wry sense of humor. "That cat had one of the keenest and quickest wits," said bassist Ray Drummond. "He always had me in stitches," said Frank Foster. He felt that Adams, much like Danish pianist/comedian Victor Borge, could have very successfully combined music and humor if he had chosen that route. "I saw him as a great American humorist."

According to Bob Wilber, Adams "could see the funny things, the ironic things." One such example took place at a saxophone clinic, when a student asked members of Thad Jones/Mel Lewis's reed section whom they suggested aspiring players should copy. When it was Pepper's turn to respond, he broke up everyone in attendance by responding, "If you copy from one person, it's plagiarism. If you copy from everybody, it's research."

In the right setting, Adams enjoyed doing physical comedy. In 1960 at Montreal's Little Vienna, guitarist and harmonica player Toots Thielemans sat in at Pepper's gig. "Toots was playing harmonica and Pepper was doing some bits with his cigarette," wrote Keith White. "He would put it in his mouth by manipulating his lips, as if to swallow it, and then he would pop it out again. During one of these episodes, he inhaled deeply, the cigarette was flipped back into his mouth by his lips maneuvering it, and then he just looked at the audience for a moment, who didn't know what exactly to expect, when, suddenly, smoke seemed to shoot out of both of his ears! Everybody started to break up. Toots even had to stop playing for a moment."

Musicians were often amused when Adams infused his solos with clever quotations. One time, the Thad Jones/Mel Lewis Orchestra was playing for a large group of jazz fans in Belgium who rented space for their get-togethers above a police station. "Pepper's right in the middle of 'Once Around,' which is a fast, minor solo for him," said John Mosca. "He's burning away, really tearing it up, and a police car comes with a siren on and he goes right into 'I Don't Want to Set the World on Fire.' I swear, right in the middle of this solo, and it broke everybody up. It was very funny!" Another time, when Jones/Lewis was performing a concert at an amphitheater in Italy, the venue had been presenting Verdi's *Aida*. "Most of the stage had been cleared, but the props for the opera—Egyptian-style artifacts—cluttered one side, in full view of the audience," wrote Lucinda Chodan. "When it came to Adams's first solo, his big baritone blasted out a couple of bars of *Celeste Aida*, one of the opera's arias. The crowd was impassive. Thad Jones was laughing so hard he had to stop playing."

Adams enjoyed a hearty laugh, whether it was the result of an anecdote he told or a practical joke he engineered. At one of his early Detroit gigs with Tate Houston and Bill Hannah, Pepper pulled aside an obese, unsightly woman in the audience and told her that Hannah thought she was good looking. When the band took their break after the first set, she aggressively pursued Hannah, much to Adams's delight. To keep his distance, Hannah hid from her in the men's room. At another Detroit gig, Bess Bonnier, who was mostly blind, asked Pepper to escort her to the ladies' room. As a practical joke, Adams took her instead to the bar's phone booth. Bonnier got a big kick out of it. "He was lots of fun," she said. "He would "happily get into any kind of mischief."

For the most part, Adams was a tolerant, easy-going, self-effacing soul. "He could get a little short with things if he thought something was too mundane or blah," warned Pierson. "He would scoff at it; make comments he didn't care for it." Every so often, too, Adams exhibited a stubborn, dogmatic streak. "One musical discussion I had with him was whether melody or rhythm was the basic part of jazz," said Per Husby:

I said, "Melody," and Pepper just gave up on me. He said, "You can play a bad melody with great rhythm and it sounds great, but a good melody with bad rhythm is always horrible." I think he sung Ellington's "Johnny Come Lately" to me, snapping his fingers, demonstrating how the tune itself was ridiculous without the rhythm. I still don't know if I agree with him, but, again, he was just cutting me off. Rhythm was the most important part, then melody. There was no question about it.

Throughout his life Adams read widely and enjoyed all sorts of literature. "He was always buried in a book of some kind," said Frank Foster.

He liked Irish writers, such as James Joyce, Sean O'Casey, Frank O'Connor, and William Trevor. He read American satirists—Mark Twain, Terry Southern, Nathanael West—and Russian novelists Nikolai Gogol and Vladimir Nabokov. He enjoyed Evelyn Waugh's *Vile Bodies* and *A Handful of Dust,* relished Kenneth Patchen's poetry, read *Harper's,* the *New Yorker,* and other literary magazines, and in the 1950s was searching for novels written by American detective author Dashiell Hammett.

When he discovered a new author he admired, such as Nabokov or Anthony Burgess, he read their entire body of work. "I hope you're a reader of Nabokov, if only for his dissection of the American academic scene," Adams wrote in a 1963 letter to Ron Ley, a professor of psychology. "Touched upon rather lightly in *Lolita,* but amplified in *Pnin,* and particularly in *Pale Fire,* which is written in the form of a poem and pseudo-scholarly annotation thereof. 'Iffen' you ain't, they're all highly recommended, fascinating on many levels, and mighty funny besides."

When he traveled out of town, Adams stayed in touch by sending hand-written postcards. Moreover, he possessed an uncanny ability to remember the names of people that he met in faraway cities, often many years later, to which he tagged a remembrance of some kind. "No matter where he went, somebody would come up and talk to him and he'd remember their name and he'd remember where they were from," said John Marabuto.

One striking character trait was how Adams would drop away from conversation. Much like Gustav Mahler, "he would talk to you for a while and then fall silent," said Per Husby. "He would look straight-ahead, and you wouldn't quite know what to say to him." Such protracted silences were long and heavy, for some quite unnerving. His pregnant pauses, the antithesis of his voluble saxophone playing, were never unnerving for the Leys. "We could have periods of silence, and nobody felt the need to fill the gaps if somebody wasn't speaking," said Cindy Ley. After more than twenty years of friendship, each was comfortable with the conversational rhythms of the other, whether it involved quiescence or loquaciousness. "We were from the radio generation, and when you listen to the radio you don't talk," explained Ron Ley. "You listen."

༒

In December 1968, Adams recorded *Encounter,* his first date as a leader since 1963. Excited at the prospect of recording again under his own name, Pepper hired Zoot Sims and the all-Detroit rhythm section of Tommy Flanagan, Ron Carter, and Elvin Jones. Adams and Sims were good friends. They used to meet at Sims's Greenwich Village apartment, push back the furniture, and play ping-pong. They worked together on local gigs, too, particularly at the Half Note. Their first recording together was in 1959, on Chet Baker's *Plays the Best of Lerner and Loewe*. Sims also appeared on Pepper's 1963 Mingus tribute album. Adams chose Sims for *Encounter* because his style was so radically different from his own. The Adams–Sims pairing was a throwback to Count Basie's penchant in the late 1930s of contrasting a muscular Coleman Hawkins type "vertical" saxophonist with a lighter and lyrical "horizontal" approach of Lester Young. Hugh Jackson took the same approach in his 1952 Vitaphone session with Adams and tenor saxophonist Larry McCrorey.

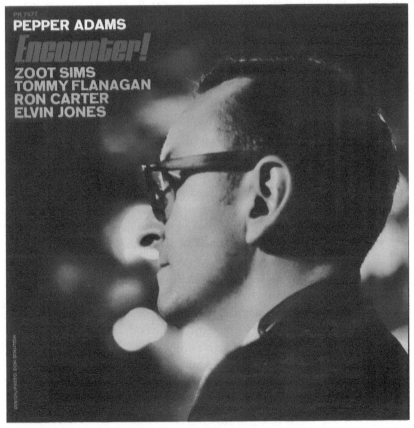

Figure 9.4. Encounter. Public domain.

Two years before, Adams and Thad Jones recorded *Mean What You Say.* Including Duke Pearson, Ron Carter, and Mel Lewis, it featured Jones's brilliant quintet arrangements. Although producer Orrin Keepnews was "horrified" by the band's attempt at musical satire on "Yes, Sir, That's My Baby," he still "thought that that was going to be the record that was going to put everybody over," said Gary Giddins. That never happened, in part due to the hoopla surrounding Thad's big band and the fact that the quintet could not follow up with either a promotional tour or a second recording.

More than a year earlier, Adams recorded *Pepper Adams Plays the Compositions of Charlie Mingus,* the only time in his career that he made a tribute album. "Mingus came to the date and just watched in open-mouth astonishment at the fact that a date could be done smoothly, without rancor, no screaming, no throwing things," said Adams. "Just professional musicians who have the music ready, and go in and play it, and get a good performance. He just couldn't believe that record dates were like that."

In 1964, the following year, Adams had moved into his studio apartment at 84 Jane Street. It was the first place of his own since 1961, when he lived across town on Jefferson Street. Pepper lived in #8, on the top floor of the four-story walk-up. "I remember walking up those steps thinking to myself, 'How does he carry that bari up these steps all the time?'" said saxophonist David Schiff. The air in his flat was stale and heavy from cigarette smoke. It had a "bachelor, alcoholic vibe," said Ron Marabuto.

During the eight years that he lived in the West Village, Adams maintained a curious balance as a public and private individual. Neighborhood merchants and residents knew him, and he was gracious to everyone who said hello. "He loved talking to writers," said Mike Jordan. "That's one reason why he liked the Village. He used to like to go to bars where writers hung out, like the White Horse Tavern, the Corner Bistro." But despite his time in pubs or strolling throughout the community, Adams was off by himself so much of the time reading fiction. Even during intermission at a New York City gig, he would often find a cheaper neighborhood bar where he could grab a beer and smoke a cigarette, thereby finding sanctuary from fans, hangers-on, or women. "I don't think anybody appreciates loneliness more than Pepper," Tommy Flanagan told Mark Feldman.

Despite his self-absorption, "he was a very caring person," said Per Husby. Just before Adams played with Husby for the first time, Pepper worked in Oslo with bassist Sture Nordin. On a subsequent trip to Scandinavia, Nordin "had a crisis in his marriage," said Husby. "Sture told Pepper about the difficulties, that they planned to split up. Soon after Pepper went back to the States, Sture's wife got a long letter from Pepper in which Pepper wrote about the way he felt by meeting the two of them; that he thought it was a shame that they should split because he certainly felt that there was something there to cherish, which actually resulted in Sture and his wife not splitting up. He just couldn't let go of that. He wrote this letter and cared about these people."

Adams also functioned as a confidant to younger musicians in Thad and Mel's band. One time he showed concern for a colleague was when he counseled Jon Faddis in Munich during the orchestra's 1975 summer tour. "I just remember Pepper coming up to me and asking how I was doing. I said, 'I'm OK.' He said, 'You really got to be careful with this stuff, with this depression.' I said, 'OK . . .' I think it was the caring that he had in him." Growing weary of life on the road, Faddis quit the orchestra a few months later.

Pepper served as a patient, encouraging mentor to aspiring musicians, either as a clinician or on the bandstand. His egoless, non-judgmental style, consistent with Detroit's way of teaching the jazz tradition, allowed musicians to relax, make mistakes, and learn from his example. Adams was "the first American soloist that I ever played with," said Husby; "a good man to start with because Pepper had an extremely friendly way of handling people." As Earl Sauls remembered, "It didn't feel like you were being pressured. It just felt like he respected you."

One developing musician that Adams took under his wing was David Schiff, a seventeen-year-old student at Wilmington Music School. During one of their saxophone lessons, he told Schiff, "You can mimic anyone you want but you've got to get your own sound and your own style." Near the end of the weeklong June 1970 workshop, Adams said to Schiff, "Can you come to New York? Why don't you come to my apartment? If you could stay a day or two, I really enjoyed working with you. Fish, come on. I really think you have a lot to learn, and you could be a great player."

Two days later, on Monday, June 29, Hal Schiff drove his son to New York City for the two-day apprenticeship. "I went up to his place and for hours and hours we'd play," said Schiff. Adams asked him if he wrote music. Schiff said, "No, not really. I just want to play." Pepper replied, "You can't play unless you learn to write." "He taught me basic theory stuff, how to voice for different instruments. As the day progressed, he said, 'You got to learn your pentatonic scales, learn all your harmonic minors, and all your majors.'" He advised Schiff to get *Patterns for Jazz* by Jerry Coker and master everything in it. "The patterns in here are great," Pepper told him. "Then form your own patterns."

> I said, "Like what?" So, he opened a page and he'd just blow through it like he wrote it. He said, "OK, so let's work on this." So, we worked on it, and he said, "OK, here's this pattern. Now take this line and make something of your own. Use it but create something of your own." So, I fiddled around with it but he said, "No, no, it sounds too much like what's written." He said, "Think of it like a book report. The notes on the pages are like the words in a book. You learn the words and the story, and then you have to do a book report. So, you can't read word for word. You have to tell the audience about what you're trying to say." You play the tune, and then when it's your turn to blow some, you're not going to play the tune again. You've got to do a book report. You've got to tell them what the song is in your own words. The light went on like a spotlight! I said, "Oh, my God, *that's* what this is all about?" I thought improvisation was play scales, play some patterns, and just move your fingers, or try to play the solo exactly like Sonny Stitt or Sonny Rollins. Pepper opened up my eyes and ears. . . . We spoke about how to improvise, and the importance of techniques of breathing and articulation, and phrasing of certain patterns and notes. He was very emphatic about playing, and being yourself, and not copying other people.

Schiff's father was concerned about his son being drafted, serving in the infantry, and dying in a Vietnam jungle or rice paddy. For that reason, he was trying to persuade his son to join an armed services band, as Pepper had done in 1951. Adams "agreed with my father that it would be a good idea to go into the military for both the experience and how hard it was to be a working musician and make a living. I thought that was unusual because of all the great things he had done and was doing," but Schiff nevertheless joined the US Navy Band in 1972.

Schiff's lesson and the pointers he learned from Adams at Wilmington's workshops in 1968–1970 had a lifelong reach. "I practice telling a story," Schiff said in 2015, twenty-nine years after Pepper's death.

I think that's the biggest thing that he taught me. You have to tell a story. You have to make your solos interesting. He said, "When you're playing, make sure you swing, make sure that you play a little on the outside to add color to your solo, and don't play linear all the time. Break it up with patterns. Break it up with large intervals: with fourths and sixths. Really make it interesting." He said, "Anybody can play the blues, but there are very few people who can play it and make it sound that it's the blues but it's not. It's something new. Always make your solos sound like something new." I said, "Pepper, how can I do that? There's so many monster, great players who have played every lick in the world." He said, "But that's where your individuality comes from. You have to find a way that you can do the same thing but sound a little different that people will notice." Every time I pick up my horn, I can hear his voice telling me that.

With such a nuanced, personalized approach to jazz instruction, it is hard to fathom why Adams felt insecure about teaching his craft. Unquestionably, as an autodidact, he never learned a proven method to best convey his ideas to a saxophone pupil. But what difference did that make? As jazz history's greatest baritone saxophone soloist, all he had to do was to show others how that came to be. Certainly, based on his experience with Schiff alone, beginning in 1970 he could have begun supplementing his income by teaching gifted, intermediate-level students. He needed the income, and by doing so, Adams would have closed the gulf between himself and the world.

Since he never taught students other than Schiff and Curtis Fuller with this kind of specificity, nor formally presented his methodology in a treatise or interview, Pepper's technical innovations and philosophical approach to playing jazz have never been explained. That made it harder for the next three generations of baritone saxophonists to learn from his recordings what it was that he did on the instrument. Fortunately, thanks to David Schiff, the key elements of an Adams method, and the wisdom he never shared with the world, have finally been brought to light.

Chapter Ten

Lovers of Their Time

He was guarded in his relationships.

—Keith White

In January 1964, while on tour with Lionel Hampton's band in snowy Lake Tahoe, California, Pepper Adams fell in love with singer Ruth Price. Although they only knew each other for a few weeks and were never physically intimate, Pepper nonetheless asked her to marry him by expressing his intentions in a letter. "I was very surprised to get that," said Price. "We didn't have that kind of a relationship where you would expect a proposal."

A former ballerina, with bright eyes, jet-black hair, and a warm, engaging smile, Price had worked with Stan Getz, Shelly Manne, and Charles Mingus, and at the time was gigging in town with Harry James's Orchestra. Although Price initially perceived Adams's overture as a practical joke, she soon deduced his earnestness. "He certainly was clear about what he wanted," said Price. "He said that he loved me and that he wanted me to consider being his wife. It was the sweetest and most formal letter." Pepper even itemized his assets as a way of reassuring her that by marrying him there would be at least a modicum of financial security.

Adams's written marriage proposal gets to the heart of his emotional distance from others. "He had a definite note of affection about him," said Albert Goldman. "He was very grateful that you came, and you dug him, and you could feel real vibes and warmth. But it was always coming to you over a gulf, over a gap. He was sending a message, like in a bottle. You can't imagine any physical warmth or hugging."

Although touched by his affection for her, Price could not accept Adams's proposal because she was engaged to pianist Dave Grusin. Nevertheless, from that point on, Adams and Price remained good friends. He often sent her postcards from his travels abroad and they frequently exchanged book recommendations. "We both read all the German modernists," she said, and it was likely her suggestion to explore William Trevor's novels and short stories.

Eighteen years later, Price was Adams's guest at the 1982 Grammy Awards dinner in Los Angeles. Then, at their final meeting in March 1986 when he was dying and planning his legacy, he asked her to consider writing lyrics to his compositions. He was always taken with her intelligence, shared her passion for literature, and was impressed with lyrics she had written to Chick Corea's "Tones for Joan's Bones." When he returned home, Adams mailed her lead sheets to all seven of his ballads, plus "Dobbin," "Trentino," "Rue Serpente," "Claudette's Way," "Doctor Deep," "Reflectory," and "Bossallegro." Included in his letter explaining the derivation of each title was a request that she rename "Claudette's Way." Unfortunately, Price never tackled Adams's project. By 1992, six years after his death, her attention had been diverted to Jazz Bakery, a performance space she established in Culver City, California, that over the years has showcased numerous jazz musicians and as of 2022 is still in business.

⌐

Still single after Price's rejection, Adams continued his long-distance relationship with Fran Kleinberg. "She was a very unusual, unusual girl, she really was, that at a very young age became involved with drugs," said vocalist Arlene Smith. As a teenager, Kleinberg drank, took narcotics, and slept with older musicians. "As far as sex was concerned, I think she was jaded early," said pianist Stan Patrick. "She had been through a lot too early in her life . . . It didn't have too much meaning; like playing scales." Additionally, she had a tortured relationship with her adoptive parents, who were old enough to be her grandparents. "These people did everything for her," yet she was "mean, nasty, and ugly" to them, said Bobbie Curtis Cranshaw.

Kleinberg was one of the few middle-class, Jewish, French-Canadian women of her generation who was passionate about jazz and involved in the culture. Of medium height and slightly cross-eyed, she had dark black hair and conveyed an Asian look. Like Adams, she played a little piano, wore eyeglasses, had no siblings, and was a chain smoker. "She just loved the music, and I think she loved the life," said Smith. As a groupie she ingratiated herself with Jackie McLean and other jazz musicians. "She knew everybody," said Patrick. Although she dressed stylishly prior to 1959, she wore baggy clothes once heroin became a preoccupation.

Adams and Kleinberg first met in New York City when Adams was new in town. She visited him in late 1957, when she drove from Canada with Stan Patrick, her lover at the time, and audaciously smuggled drugs over the border. Adams's sexual relationship with her began in the summer of 1958, when she returned to see him in New York. Soon afterwards she wrote, asking that he mail back her sandals and pajama bottoms.

In April 1959, seven months later, Adams and Kleinberg got together in Montreal while he was on tour with Benny Goodman. But by late November 1959, Kleinberg's addiction had overwhelmed her. She explained her situation in a letter that she wrote from Verdun Protestant Hospital (now Douglas Mental Health University Institute), Montreal's principal psychiatric institution:

> It was the only place in the city, Verdun being a district of Montreal, that would admit me to kick my habit. I've been here five days now and it seems like a long, dreadful nightmare. I had to give myself up. I was a dead human being, going through the motions of living but deriving not one small bit of pleasure from life . . . This place is similar to jail. The wards are locked at all times . . . The first three days were pretty bad. They kept me in a semi-conscious and/or unconscious state, however it was torturous kicking, even in oblivion . . . I'll never know how I got myself into such a mess. They want to keep me here for two or three months to be sure I won't leave and get high again.

In recognition of her plight, on November 29 Adams shipped her a box of Barricini chocolates to help deal with her craving for sweets. On December 1 she wrote him again:

> If I ever needed anyone in my life, I need someone (I'm afraid to say you) now. Would it upset you to think or to know that my thoughts are constantly of you and that I'm managing to maintain myself by leaning on you? If you want to not have anything more to do with me, Pepper, please don't spare me or be kind to me . . . This Thursday'll make it two weeks that I've been here. I count the days, the hours, and the minutes. It feels like I've been here such a long, long time . . . P.S: I sure would dig to dip right now! I dream of it, imagine it all the time. That's not too good, is it?

A week later she thanked him for his thoughtful gift and provided an update on her incarceration, foreshadowing future problems: "One very big advantage in being here is, if ever in the future I should get busted, rather than sending me to the joint, I'd be returned here." Kleinberg was finally released from Verdun in early May 1960 after a six-month internment, just prior to Adams's gig at Montreal's Little Vienna on May 13–15.

A year later, Kleinberg replied to a letter from Adams, acknowledging that she had been drug-free since at least September 1960. But despite her intention to abstain from heroin, she soon resumed her brazen, self-destructive ways. By July 1962 she was back at Verdun, this time for thirteen and a half months. "I don't feel that anyone in this world is really able to understand me," she confessed in a letter to Adams. Seven months later, after Kleinberg received both Valentine's Day and birthday cards from him, she sent Pepper a letter, dated March 18, 1963, addressed in care of La Tête de L'art, the Montreal club where he was working. She was eager to see Adams while he was in town, though their visit would be restricted to hospital visiting hours.

In early 1964, sometime after her release, Adams sent her three satirical books, Jules Feiffer's *The Explainers* and Terry Southern's *Candy* and *The Magic Christian*. By then she was embroiled in more legal problems, as explained in her letter of May 17. Written from Kingston Penitentiary, she had begun serving a two-year sentence for her third drug offense:

> This time, Pepper, I really hit *the* jackpot. At the end of January 1964, I got busted for scripts, out on bail, and busted again with six joints and two gimmicks [drug injection paraphernalia], plus I was charged with resisting arrest the second time . . . I was sentenced February 11, 1964, so my time's just begun . . . Pepper, I need you like never before. I need your moral support. Please write to me. Your letters always cheered me up in the past . . . I don't think you'll let me down at a time like this, Pepper. I sure hope not. Be living for word from you. Love, Fran.

Adams promptly wrote her back, which she acknowledged in her letter of June 2, sent to his Nevada hotel while on tour with Lionel Hampton:

> Thanks so much for your letter, which I received yesterday. It sure was a much-needed lift. And I'm glad I was right to assume that you wouldn't desert a sinking ship, no matter how slim chances may seem for an SOS! . . . Our last meeting remains

vividly in my mind. It was a bitter experience for me and, I imagine, you too. Never have I seen you so furious as that night (Monday at Birdland) . . . Do you still dig Rose? Was it a mutual misunderstanding? . . . Go easy with Old Grand-Dad! Be cool and I'm glad you're going to Europe at last! Love, Fran.

Six weeks later, on July 13, 1964, she wrote him at Jane Street: "Now that I have a record, do you still dig me even a little?"

Adams was loyal to Kleinberg over the years, in part due to his "very keen protective sense toward the underdog." Despite his anger with Kleinberg's recidivistic behavior, he visited her at Kingston Penitentiary in January 1965 and again in Montreal in September 1968, sometime after her release. Finally, her pursuit of the ideal heroin fix, and the bliss she hoped she might yet again derive from it, was her undoing. In 1969 she died of an overdose in New York City.

↩

Adams and Rose Cobb were a couple beginning in 1959, yet by Thanksgiving 1960 she had left him for another man. To what degree they stayed in touch since then is unknown, though in 1986 she attended Adams's memorial service, where she introduced herself to both Claudette and Dylan. That must have been a rare moment of tension for Claudette on a solemn day on which she seemed oddly ebullient. She had been aware of Cobb since at least 1983. "I found letters about a year before Pepper and I separated, and she is one of the many reasons for the separation," wrote Claudette. "No, the letters no longer exist. I was happy to destroy them."

According to Dylan, Adams's stepson, as early as July 1983, when he first moved from Brooklyn to attend boarding school in New England, Adams visited with Cobb in Virginia, where she had been living for years. One visit is hardly proof of Adams's philandering. Nonetheless, because they were lovers, Dylan was certain that Cobb would reveal much about his stepfather that no one else would know. Unfortunately, that was not to be. Since Adams's memorial service, she has never resurfaced.

"She was my ex-girlfriend," said Curtis Fuller. "I met her first. She met me. She was working at the Woolworth School for Boys in Harlem. I used to rehearse up there with the French horn player Julius Watkins. She worked . . . as a social worker, but she lived downtown, and Pepper was her neighbor. Very pretty girl. They became great lovers. I was just fooling around but Pepper was very serious with her. They were in love." Adams likely met Cobb in mid-1959 when she sublet Jon Hendricks's apartment on the top floor of 316 East Sixth Street. Adams was rooming with Elvin Jones at 314, apartment #10, also on the top floor. When Pepper and Rose visited each other, it was easier for them to step from their roof to the other and walk down a flight of stairs rather than trot down four floors and trudge back up in the other building.

At the time, the East Village neighborhood was alive with musicians, and people came in and out of both buildings all the time. Saxophonist Jay Cameron lived next door to Hendricks, and at one point Booker Ervin and bassist Eddie DeHaas lived in the building. Across the street was the Philadelphia contingent of Lee Morgan, Tootie Heath, Bobby Timmons, and Jimmy Garrison. Oliver Shearer lived at 312. "I had a small little place, but they would drop in on me because there was always somebody there: Sonny Rollins, or it might be Shafi Hadi or Wild Bill Moore," said Shearer. "There was always interesting conversation. . . . Elvin was always over there."

Adams rarely had a girlfriend during the time he roomed with Jones. "Guys who knew him well from Detroit told me that they thought it was partially due to the influence of his mother, who apparently had been a kind of a swinger on the scene back in Detroit; that Pepper had suffered something that gave him an attitude towards the whole sex scene quite different from the rest of the guys, where everybody was trying to get a piece of ass wherever they could," said Cameron. "It was just aloof . . . The fact that he was so above all that stuff and just didn't devote the same amount of attention to it that the rest of us did kind of seemed outstanding."

Lois Shearer felt that Adams had difficulty with female relationships. "Elvin was a little worried about him," she said. "Elvin felt that, even when Pepper had a relationship . . . they weren't sexual or sufficiently sexual." There was never any belief among his friends that Adams was a homosexual, fighting against his true nature. They simply wanted to help him get over his hesitancy with women. So, it must have been both surprising and a relief for the Sixth Street clique to see Adams and Cobb dating.

In mid-1959 Cobb left New York to attend Howard University. In early August she wrote to Adams, who by June had moved to his own place at 76 Jefferson Street on the Lower East Side: "You are rather nice, really. That laugh, the crazy way you smoke. How quiet you are. Perhaps I too shall learn to listen and not speak so much."

On September 11, most likely after a visit with him in New York, she wrote again, professing her love, saying how lonely she felt without him: "Tonight, there is no hand that will hold mine, no unshaven cheek to kiss . . . I only wish that at all cost I could remain with you . . . I love you so very, very much, Pepper. Perhaps someday you will ask me to share all of your happier and unhappier moments. I shall only wait and hope with all my heart that you do."

A few days later, in anticipation of his upcoming visit to Washington, she wrote, "Did I disturb you the other night by calling? I want so much to hear from you, to be close to you."

That November, when Adams worked a quartet gig at Washington's Statler Hotel opposite John Coltrane, Philly Joe Jones, and Shirley Horn, he visited again with Cobb. Two weeks later, they spent her Thanksgiving break together.

After her fall semester, Cobb dropped out of school, and by August 1960 had moved to 76 Jefferson, taking Studio #2 on the second floor. Pepper lived in Studio #4, a cold-water flat with a sink and communal toilet but no tub or shower. Their rent was around $25 a month.

"It was an old, dilapidated warehouse," recounted painter Emilio Cruz, who lived upstairs from Adams. Industrial lofts like these gave musicians a place to rehearse, and painters the space to create large canvases. Because occupying factories was illegal, it often took an annual bribe to have the city inspector look the other way.

"The front door was like the old refrigerator doors, the big ones," said Fred Norsworthy: "You go in. As you look on the left-hand side, there was the toilet system, but with the door cut out halfway over and the toilet was in back. You'd walk the whole length of the top of the warehouse floor, which was quite long, and Pepper had his bed on the end, on a bunch of bricks. There was no electricity, so his friend hooked up wires to bring in light from the streetlight outside." On August 11, 1960, Cobb wrote about a robbery at the building: "We all lost clothes, all my jewelry, Pepper's TV set, my radio, watch." On September third she wrote to Adams in Denver with good news. Their landlord was finally cleaning up the building and its pervasive stench was beginning to dissipate. Also, he was considering installing heat before winter. In her letter, she added,

> God, I sure am lonely. Pepper, when you go away, I have no one to talk to at all, no one to cook dinner for, even if I am a bad cook . . . Darling, I want very much to just kiss you . . . I love you, and after writing five pages of jibble, it's unnecessary, I know, to say that I miss you over and over again, but I do.

Nothing is fun without you. I am happy that you are working, and that you are playing with people you want to play with, etc. . . . I shall never fully adjust to your long periods of being out of town. I shall always miss you and shall always be completely happy to have you come home.

Two months later, on October fourth, she wrote to Adams, reaffirming her affection for him: "I love you very, very much, my darling, darling Pepper." But seven weeks later everything had changed. First, on November twenty-seventh she wrote him a perfunctory note, addressed to his Chicago hotel:

Pepper,

I can't come, I'm sorry. Enclosed please find money. Let's don't talk for a long, long time.

By December sixth she had moved from Jefferson Street and had a chance to explain what had transpired since late November:

Dear Pepper,

What can I say now . . . that I haven't already a million times tried to say . . . ? Last summer, when I was home for those couple of weeks from school, I wanted so much for us to really have something strong in a relationship. Perhaps as I begin to look closely at this thing and really analyze it, the relationship began to die then . . . In Smalls, before you left to go on the road, I even asked you, "What about us?" No response. As you have repeatedly put it, you couldn't afford it.

I met Ralph and suddenly I felt needed. There was no question of affording . . . We're going to have a baby. We don't always understand everything about each other but at least we work at it. I want to be happy. I desperately want to feel at peace with myself and everyone. It has never been my intention to hurt anyone, especially you.

Love,

Rose

Like Claudette, Rose required far more intimacy than Pepper was able to supply. When Adams told Cobb that he couldn't "afford" to commit to her, he was not merely expressing his autonomy. He was also revealing the inadequacy he felt in not measuring up to the prevailing norms of his era. Before the Women's Rights Movement of the late 1960s and its gradual effect on the US workplace, there was a great deal of pressure for men to serve as sole breadwinners. In the end, if Pepper was groping for attachment while adjusting to life in New York, Cobb longed for steady companionship with a mate, something Adams's profession and temperament at the time didn't permit.

⌐⌐

In early 1956, Adams moved to New York City with a woman who worked at Detroit's World Stage. After living for a few days in a New York City hotel, they rented a room at 410 West End Avenue on Manhattan's Upper West Side. The place had a sink, small stove, and refrigerator. Their bathroom was down the hall, and a rehearsal area with a piano and practice rooms was available in the basement.

While getting settled, Adams spent four days experimenting with heroin. He was most likely with Elvin Jones, whom he trusted, and some of his buddies. "I think he tried it," said Mel Lewis. "I don't think he ever got into it like his friends did." Around this time, Adams ran into Cathy Cooper, a friend from Detroit. She had become a heroin addict and Pepper was concerned about her well-being. After discussing with his girlfriend whether he should leave for another few days to assist her, he changed his mind. What's notable is the extent to which heroin was consuming the lives of their friends and how ready he was to assist them.

In May, just prior to his six-month tour with Stan Kenton, Pepper and his girlfriend met Oliver Shearer at a party. "The young lady followed me into the bathroom, pulled up her dress, and said, 'Aren't I a woman? I want to be fucked *tonight!*' I was floored," said Shearer.

> This is Pepper's woman. She came out of the bathroom and she was all upset. She was talking at the party that her man wouldn't fuck her. She was kind of out of her head. So, I said, "Pepper, what are we going to do, man?" He says, "I'm gonna go home. Come and go home with me." I went home with him. We were thinking, at that time, if she was going to do something stupid, let's smoke up the evidence. So, we smoked up the grass that

was there. What she did: she went down to Central Park and jumped over the wall and broke her leg.

Why she leapt over Central Park's perimeter wall that night must have been at least in part due to her drunkenness and agitated state. Certainly, if she gave it any thought whatsoever, she miscalculated the drop over the wall. On the west side of town, the park's surrounding walls are more than twice the height inside the park than they are from the top of the wall to the sidewalk. If fallen upon, trees and other objects inside the park can cause physical harm. True enough, her fall not only caused a fracture but necessitated surgery. A week or so later, after she received her diagnosis, she asked Adams if he would consider delaying his road trip for a few days to assist her after her operation. "You're asking me to choose between you and my music?" he replied.

Adams's response was reminiscent of the parting words from Duke Ellington's autobiography. "Music is my mistress, and she plays second fiddle to no one," he wrote. After months of waiting, Pepper had finally gotten his opportunity to tour with a name band, and he wasn't going to let a friend's ailment deter him, especially one that occurred the way it had. And why should he? Judging from his girlfriend's complaints, both were already disenchanted with each other. Sex, she grumbled, had always been "mechanical."

From the time he moved to New York until he got engaged to Claudette in 1975, Adams's female relationships were unfulfilling, and his girlfriends were equally dissatisfied with him. Due to his upbringing and experiences to that point, he didn't know how to honor their need for intimacy because he didn't innately trust them. As a kind of a rescuer, Adams sought and was particularly sensitive to the needs of people in trouble. In Kleinberg's case they were women in the shadow of his mother: pushy, needy, promiscuous, manipulative. Kleinberg "got what she wanted," said Stan Patrick. "When her mind was set on something, she could be very convincing when she wanted to be." So, too, was Claudette. Adams, aloof and blasé, responded to strong women determined to spur him to action, an attribute that both Cobb and his Detroit girlfriend lacked.

Part of his problem with women stemmed from his insecurity about being physically unattractive. "I think that was really a big issue with him," said Ron Marabuto. "I think Lodi [Carr] mentioned that to me a few times, that he was really uptight about his appearance, that he wasn't an attractive guy." Pepper's stigma took root in seventh grade, when he was nicknamed after Pepper Martin, the unsightly baseball player. Also, like Coltrane, Adams was self-conscious about the poor condition of his front teeth. "You think they grow this way?" he once joked. Sadly, he could never afford to get them repaired.

By his late thirties, the weight of a heavy saxophone around his neck was taking a toll on his physique. Adams's slouched posture made him appear two inches shorter, and he accentuated his seemingly poor looks, almost in defiance of it, by dressing with little care. His overalls and flannel shirt, for example, were more indicative of a laborer than a stage performer.

Figure 10.1. Pepper Adams and Raul Gutierrez, La Grande Parade du Jazz, Nice, France, July 13, 14, or 15, 1977. Photo by Barbara Conradi.

"He wasn't a guy who was striking, looking handsome like a Stan Getz," said Albert Goldman:

> He wasn't sexy like Elvin Jones. You have to understand that there's a kind of cultural history here. There had been, when he came on the scene, which was the end of the bop era, you might say, when the great idea among serious jazz musicians was to be a "wig;" was to be brainy and wear a goatee like a French artiste, and a little bop beret, and to profess way-out Eastern religions and weird philosophical beliefs like existentialism. Intellect was hip, just like in the sixties, intellect was shit . . . In the bop era there was blatant intellectualism, and with blatant intellectualism went wearing horned-rimmed glasses, and stooped shoulders and pale skin. But that too can have a certain glamour and cachet, and it didn't with Pepper. Pepper was homely, not necessarily to the bone, but it came off that way. So, that's a little self-defeating, because I don't give a goddamn how pure an artist you are. Jazz has a facet that can never be removed from it: that is, the entertainment business. Standing up in front of people in a club or wherever and making yourself the center of attention and interest, it doesn't hurt to have something that they can rest their eye on as well as their ear.

But "if people are coming to listen to you, are they coming to listen to you play or are they coming to see how you look?" asked Don Friedman. "That is, actually, one of the criteria. I see it all the time. People who make a big show about their playing are the ones who get a lot of attention." The Art Ensemble of Chicago, outfitted with colorful face paint and African tribal garb, Joshua Redman's histrionic knee lifts while squeezing out a phrase, or Keith Jarrett's sexual gyrations above his piano stool are three examples of extravagant behavior that Friedman might have cited.

Antithetically, "The external Pepper, the Pepper that Pepper presented to the world, was 'cool,'" asserted Ron Ley. In other words, his exterior mask was comparable to postwar American male performers from varied disciplines. "To be cool" was "synonymous with authenticity, independence, integrity, and nonconformity," wrote Joel Dinerstein. . . . [It] "meant negotiating a resistant mode of being in the world." According to Dinerstein, "cool" has four basic elements: "1) Control your emotions and wear a mask of cool in the face of hostile, provocative outside forces; 2) Maintain a relaxed attitude in performance of any kind; 3) Develop a unique, individual style (and sound) that communicates your personality or inner spirit; and 4) Be emotionally expressive within an artistic frame of restraint." Adams, the embodiment of unperturbed detachment, exhibited each of these traits.

In some respects, Pepper's cool onstage persona—his "version of self," to use Philip Auslander's turn of phrase—is more akin to classical music performers. With few exceptions, these soloists, without any accompanying stagecraft, focus on letting virtuosity convey their broad range of emotions. In much the same way, Adams let his music speak for itself. Never outwardly demonstrative on the bandstand, he preferred his playing to be judged on its own merits.

Although he was restrained and unglamorous, women over the years were nonetheless captivated by him. "He never was a ladies' man, but he always attracted ladies," said Hugh Lawson. "He had that nonchalant, indifferent attitude . . . A chick had to really be infatuated with him because he wasn't attentive." Throughout Adams's life, women admired and pursued him, some imploring him to be more forthcoming with his feelings. Others, he confided, had completely overburdened him.

Apart from Pepper's cool remoteness, there was a curious triangulation afoot that further enhanced his allure. Although his onstage disposition in the 1950s and '60s wasn't consciously sexualized, he was often the only white musician in all-black bands. As one of the few white members of jazz's black inner circle, his masculine, self-assured stature conveyed a privileged exclusivity and exoticism that women found intriguing. For them, the way he so unassumingly transcended the racial norms of the day elicited gratitude, admiration, and even desire. Off the bandstand, equally appealing was Adams's gentle, humble, soft-spoken manner. Women were drawn to the entire package, but especially his feminine attributes of politeness, compassion, and an eagerness to dive into a conversation. "I could see any woman that he was trying to talk to really being interested," said Rose Christianson, who first met him in 1984 when he was already looking like a septuagenarian. Whether his appeal to the opposite sex offset any self-doubt about his appearance remains a mystery.

Chapter Eleven

Urban Dreams

Pepper just loved to play.

—David Amram

Two months before Pepper Adams and Thad Jones formed their quintet, Adams worked in Europe for the first time. As the only white musician in Lionel Hampton's tentet, he toured France and Belgium for ten days, first playing the Antibes Jazz Festival on July 23, 1964. "Prior to the appearance of his first photographs in the jazz magazines, almost the entire European critical fraternity thought him to be black," wrote Joachim-Ernst Berendt. The French critics at the time "still followed the [Hugues] Panassié idea that only blacks could play jazz," said Bob Cornfoot. "When [Pepper] got there and turned out to be white, they felt they had been betrayed and they took it out on him . . . [He] said that they went out of their way to be particularly nasty and vicious to him because he was white." French jazz fans, more polite than journalists, were equally surprised when they saw him. "*You're* Pepper Adams?" was the first question often asked.

Nine years earlier, "when Pepper first came to New York, those were the days when there weren't too many young white players being influenced by black players," said Horace Silver. "He came in sounding black. I heard him first playing tenor saxophone at Birdland. He was sounding like Sonny Stitt . . . I was impressed with him because he wasn't playing that kind of cool, laid-back kind of style. He was playing that hard-driving kind of style." Adams confirmed his apprenticeship in an interview soon after he moved to New York. "I learned how to play jazz from the black musicians in Detroit," he said. "If you want to know how to play jazz, that's how to learn it." Concerned that Adams may have invited a racist backlash, Eddie Locke reprimanded him, saying that he should have never uttered such a naïve statement for publication. Adams replied, "I don't care, Locke. That's the truth."

Did Adams alienate himself from the white-controlled network of agents, editors, broadcasters, and promoters by stating his allegiance to black musicians? Perhaps so. "Maybe if he had gone on out and gotten in a nice white group, he might have made it," said Barry Harris. But joining a polite dance band or anything remotely similar wasn't of interest to him.

"The only thing that stopped him from being what you would call a star is that he hung out with black guys," said Arthur Taylor in 1987. "I know what was happening, and I saw [it] because I was there . . . He liked to be with guys who could play, and in this music the guys who can play are black. He was accepted by these guys, and they respected him. Any time I speak about him I speak about him with reverence, but that hurt his career. . . . He chopped his own head off." As Curtis Fuller acknowledged, "Pepper only associated with black musicians. *Only!*"

> That was his whole life. Only! It cost him. . . . I'm sure he was shut out by a lot of people. Hey, look: We *know* what a thing is, you understand? . . . He couldn't just come uptown and get high with the guys like Mulligan did. He *lived* it. He lived with us. We became one, like blood brothers . . . He realized he had to live it. He didn't just want to take something off a tape and get a guy's phrase or his lines. He became a part of it.

Adams, Locke insisted, was a "jazz man. You could never play like Pepper unless you *lived* it," he said. "He lived that life. He lived in those joints with us."

Besides any marginalization that Adams experienced due to his association with black musicians, he was also "a victim of reverse racial discrimination," said George Coleman, because some blacks were jealous of his excellence as a soloist. "Pepper's white and he's playing so black though, and he's playing so *good*," said Coleman. "When a cat plays so good, whether he's white or black, if he's playing too much like Charlie Parker, getting into the real guts of the music and standing out there alone being the only one who can do it, the envies and the jealousies entered into the picture."

Further compounding his situation during his early days in New York, Adams also suffered ostracization from black musicians due to peer pressure, said Lois Shearer. "Sometimes the wrong person becomes a victim," she said:

There was a real, almost unified talking, and resentment, and boycotting of white musicians by blacks. . . . If you can't get at Brubeck, and you can't hurt him, and you're not especially well developed as a human being, you might take it out on Pepper, you see. So, a young musician, just coming up and getting a gig, might not call Pepper because he was white; might call someone else. I think in that way it affected him. I know it to be a fact. I'm just explaining it in philosophical terms.

Despite the impediments, Adams forged ahead. He "rose above all the muck and mire of what cats have to go through with color and all the barriers," said Andy McCloud. "He busted them all because he could *play* and didn't give a fuck about who you were or your attitudes. All the negative stuff he seemed to just push aside, and that's why I think everybody liked him."

↩

Beginning in 1959, Adams, Elvin Jones, Wilber Ware, Bobby Timmons, Richard Davis, Randy Weston, and Clifford Jarvis often got together at Oliver and Lois Shearer's East Village loft. Not far from their former apartment on East Sixth Street, the new place had a piano, sometimes a drum set, but always a hot pot of coffee available for visitors. "They could rehearse, but mostly they wanted a refuge to talk, whether Oliver was there or not," remembered Lois Shearer. By the late 1950s, a great deal of bitterness was felt by jazz musicians, especially those who had recently arrived in New York and were trying to get established. They were exasperated by how the jazz press had anointed Dave Brubeck as jazz's star pianist while Earl Hines, Bud Powell, Erroll Garner, Duke Ellington, Thelonious Monk, and other black jazz pianists were still performing and, at the very least, deserving of equal attention.

"I made friends with Bobby Timmons at this time," said Lois Shearer.

Bobby was pretty militant on the subject of black music and the heritage of the music being black . . . Bobby was the first one who articulated that as part of a conscious elevation of black roots into jazz. It was a reaction to what had been going on, deliberate on Bobby's part. Oh, absolutely, we talked about it many times. This didn't last that long because the black power movement in the sixties came in later and, by that time, jazz was fairly through with it.

At the Shearer loft, musicians would gather around the coffee table, made of a jagged-edged, orphaned slab of marble perched atop a wooden base. The anger was freely voiced: "Whitey's taking the music away from us. They're taking gigs, they're making all the money, they're getting all the press, and they can't swing and they can't play." Although Shearer was white, she suffered no awkwardness about such talk. "Once you were OK, when they were talking about whites, it had nothing to do with you," said Shearer. "Pepper wasn't really perceived as white by the musicians, nor was I in that sense. That's why, in a way, my house was a meeting place for discussing these ideas, and it never occurred to them to feel uncomfortable around me, nor did it occur to me to be uncomfortable."

When they lived on East Sixth Street, Adams, Jones, Timmons, and the Shearers were all very close. "Bobby was very, very close to Pepper," said Oliver Shearer. "Among all of us at that time, there was a general sense of excitement about being in New York and a forthcoming life," said Lois Shearer. "A lot of our conversations among ourselves were happy." More than anything, Oliver said, they discussed music, "especially when Bobby was around. Bobby had all the records."

↩

From at least June until October 1963, about a year before Adams moved to Jane Street, he and Timmons shared an apartment at 339 East Sixth Street, #10, near First Avenue, only a block from where Adams had lived with Elvin. By then, Timmons had been a hardcore addict for some time, though most junkies for their own self-preservation go through spells when they quit. Adams "was trying to help Bobby out, keep straight," said Joe Baptista, former Village Gate maître d'. After Timmons's gigs "he used to go by, pick Bobby up, and get coffee. The whole impression I got was if he hung out with Bobby, Bobby wouldn't hang out somewhere else and get in trouble."

If Timmons was using heroin when Pepper was back in town, Adams would have noticed drug paraphernalia or seen evidence of Timmons taking his morning dose. As saxophonist Gary Bartz pointed out, "If you are a drug addict, every morning, if you don't have anything—what we call your 'wake-up'—you gotta have your wake-up just to get started. If you don't have that, you got to go out on the street and find it."

Heroin use among jazz musicians was a scourge in the era that preceded America's gradual academic acceptance of jazz. Beginning with Charlie Parker's usage in the 1940s, its adoption among jazz musicians was increasingly widespread over time, though no greater than what was found among healthcare workers who had ready access to it. "The Charlie Parker thing was hooked up with the idolization of Charlie Parker," said pianist Ronnie Mathews. "But Dizzy Gillespie never did drugs. So, again, it's an individual choice. But that certainly did not stop Dizzy Gillespie and Charlie Parker from working together. The doctor and the nurse are going to get impaired too. It's not just musicians . . . We'd have to get into the dynamics of what addiction is and what an addict is. That has to do more with personalities than professions."

Jimmy Heath witnessed heroin's widespread use among his colleagues in the forties and fifties but felt it had more to do with societal norms. "It had to be the pressures that caused us to turn to drugs," he said.

It was a social acceptance in our group because of being under so much pressure in the United States as a black person. This is my personal opinion. I think if Charlie Parker had been accepted for the genius he was, I don't think he would have turned to any drugs like that. Even his coming from the environment that he did at such an early age, he wouldn't have been exposed to that. It wasn't in all the neighborhoods. It was . . . in the black neighborhoods. Now it is in all neighborhoods! But at that time . . . it was almost like it was genocidal that it was placed in the neighborhoods, and that made it available to people who were oppressed. There was some degree of alleviating the pain by getting high. To space out on everything, you get away from things momentarily or however long you were high. You're oblivious to some of the things . . . Maybe the concentration level was enhanced as long as you wouldn't be sick. But there's always that Dr. Jekyll/Mr. Hyde thing, that you become sick, and that was terrible. It was the most horrible thing.

Unquestionably, heroin use is debilitating. "I think the wear and tear on one's kidneys and liver has caused the death of a lot of people that I was hanging out with," said Heath. He cited John Coltrane, Philly Joe Jones, and drummer Specs Wright as three casualties. Bobby Timmons, who died of cirrhosis in 1974 at the age of thirty-eight, was another.

Whereas Heath and Timmons grew up in Philadelphia, Ronnie Mathews was reared in New York City. "I never felt that you had to do drugs to be 'in,' " he said.

> I always thought that was a media thing. I've heard people say that "I did it because Charlie Parker did it," so I'm sure that there were people who felt that way and thought that way. I guess that if you're hanging out with the guys and you want to be "in" because you see them doing it, then, yeah, the influence is there and the availability's there *because* you're in that clique. So, maybe you're going to try it. But for the people who didn't get into that, I never saw anyone turn their back on them because they *didn't* do it. The first and most important thing was your ability to play. If you could play, you got the call. If you couldn't play, you didn't get the call.

Part of heroin's appeal was its ability to enhance a musician's concentration. In a conversation between Dexter Gordon and Michael Ullman, Gordon articulated the difficulties of performing in boisterous, distracting settings, the very antithesis of classical musicians' pristine recital-type environment. "What does it do for you anyway, for a musician?" asked Ullman.

> He asked me to imagine what a jazz musician does. Here he is, standing in a noisy, smoky club, facing people who are talking, drinking, walking about. Telephone ringing, doors opening and shutting. He has to listen to what is going on behind him . . . the other players . . . while doing this highly complex, intellectually challenging, creative activity. He told me that heroin allowed him to block out everything but the music. Of course, he knew that this sounded like an endorsement of heroin, which it wasn't.

Gary Bartz agreed that heroin can lead to insight. "It slows everything down," he said. "You see everything, you hear everything. You have enough time to make decisions while you're playing. If you're fortunate enough to stop, you still retain that level of *you see everything, you hear everything.* Now you can do it without the drugs. That's about the only thing I can ever say positive about it, and I would never encourage anybody ever to do it because you can meditate, you can get to that point without that."

Interlude

When Adams moved to New York City in January 1956 he was one of the thousands of transplants from all over the country who moved there to experience the dynamism of the big city and escape boredom, racism, and poverty. As historian Jon Panish has written, the move to Greenwich Village was an important reverse migration; a demonstration of the disdain felt by many during the 1950s regarding white America's conformist, middle-class, consumer-driven ethos. "Jazz was the music of New York in the fifties," wrote Panish, "at least of literary and artistic New York," yet experimentation in jazz, dance, film, theater, fiction, painting, sculpture, poetry, television, and photography seemed to be happening all at once.

"The capital of Western culture moved from Paris to New York, from an exhausted and depleted Europe to a nation mostly untouched by the ravages of World War II," wrote Joel Dinerstein. "The old American colonial complex—a sense of being on the periphery of things, still strong among the modernists of the 1920s—had been swept away by the triumph of abstract expressionism, by William Carlos Williams's appropriation of American speech as a basis for new poetry, and, of course, by jazz, the American art form *par excellence.*"

New York's cross-pollination of jazz musicians with painters was mutually beneficial. The painters David X. Young, Larry Rivers, and Howard Kanovitz, for example, hosted all-night jam sessions that Adams and many of his peers frequented. Painters regrouped daily at the Five Spot, near where most of them resided, because "they felt that what we were doing was serious music," wrote David Amram. As a result, the Five Spot became the center of bohemian life in New York, where writers, painters, and jazz musicians converged. "When you opened the door, the music rushed out, like a flood of color onto the street," said Hettie Jones.

In the literary world of the late fifties, the Beats made the most noise. Allen Ginsberg sought a new form of action poetry leaning heavily on improvisation. Jack Kerouac and John Clellon Holmes both referenced bebop figures in their fiction. "The Beats, as they came to be known, revered those who were different, those who lived outside the system, and particularly those who lived outside the law," wrote David Halberstam. "They were fascinated also by urban black culture, and they appropriated phrases from it: *dig* and *cool* and *man* and *split*. They saw themselves as white bopsters. They believed that blacks were somehow freer, less burdened by the restraints of straight America, and they sought to emulate this aspect of the black condition. An interest in African-American music of the time—the new sounds of Charlie Parker, Miles Davis, and others now seen as legends among jazz musicians—was almost a passport into Beat society."

Nevertheless, many despised how the Beats had co-opted jazz. "Most of the poets are slumming," complained Ralph J. Gleason. "They're cashing in on the jazz audience, but they won't learn anything about jazz." Kenneth Rexroth, a passionate jazz fan who for a few weeks recited his poetry at the Five Spot with Adams's quintet, disassociated himself entirely from the Beat movement and the East Coast literary establishment when he moved to California in the late 1950s. "How dare they use jazz as a background for their poetry and not even know what the music was about," Rexroth told Lois Shearer at a Santa Barbara literary party. "They used jazz as a background to make themselves look hip." Consequently, "most jazz musicians never got close to these people nor felt any kinship with them."

Urban Dreams

PART II

Bobby Timmons was still new in New York when he joined Adams's otherwise all-Detroit group at the Five Spot in late February 1958. The two first met in Chicago during the summer of 1956, when Adams and Mel Lewis were playing the Blue Note with Stan Kenton's Orchestra while Chet Baker, with Timmons as his pianist, was playing elsewhere in town. A wealthy friend of Baker's was hosting a barbecue and jam session at his home on Chicago's North Side, and the quintet that was hired included Baker and Timmons, Adams and Lewis, with bassist Jimmy Bond. While tuning up, Adams discovered that the piano was a half-tone flat. "I told him, 'Listen. On my solo, you just play in your key and I'll get it,'" said Adams. Timmons was amazed. He had never seen that kind of flexibility before with any horn player. Musically, said Mel Lewis about the predicament, "Pepper could do anything."

This was the first of many experiences in which Timmons was elated with Adams's musicianship. "At gigs, Pepper would play something, man. Bobby would laugh and be so thrilled he'd almost fall off the piano [stool]," said Oliver Shearer. "He'd play something hip for Bobby and it went all through his body. Anybody who'd play something really good, it would just thrill him like a shot of insulin. Pepper used to always do that to him."

Adams and Timmons made for an interesting pair. Although temperamentally similar, Adams wore flannel shirts whereas Timmons, a snappy dresser, loved stylish shoes. Pepper "used to wear off-the-wall shit, old clothes," said Mike Jordan. "He dressed like a farmer." One time, Timmons suggested that Pepper consider trading in his only suit for something more fashionable. With a sincere and surprised look on his face, Adams replied, "But I already have a suit." Timmons, laughing hysterically, felt that Pepper's response was delightfully innocent. Timmons "never maligned anybody unless it was in a humorous way," said Benny Golson. He "was just a real sweetheart, a sweetheart of a man," concurred Ron Carter.

"If you want to say that anybody represented that hard bop thing, his music did," said Ronnie Mathews about Timmons.

He used those minor thirds and flat fives and that kind of thing. It also was a sound that was commercially successful. That was what the record companies were pushing for . . . It's like sitcoms or talk shows on television. You get one that goes, and then you can't turn to any channel on television that doesn't have a talk show. The same thing was happening in the music industry. So, if you're looking for a name that represents that so-called Hard Bop Era, I would say it was Bobby Timmons. His writing during that period was pretty outstanding. But it's also hooked up in economics.

Due to his heroin addiction, Timmons's health declined from late 1963, when he and Adams found their own apartments, until 1974 when Pepper was one of the last to see him at St. Vincent's Hospital. "I arrived in Japan and there's an English language Japanese newspaper called, I think, the *Miyanishi Times*," said Adams. "There was this obituary on the front page. I was really shocked because, based on the three times I had seen him over the period of about ten days, I'd seen great improvement."

Only six months before, while still on his feet, Timmons and Lois Shearer took a long walk together in Greenwich Village until dawn, catching up on all the years that they hadn't seen each other since he first became

Figure 11.1. Bobby Timmons's first date as a leader, recorded in 1960. Public domain.

an addict. Although he had told her in the late 1950s that he could never get close to any white person due to his upbringing in Philadelphia and the status of blacks in a white-dominated society, there was one notable exception. "I love Pepper," he told Shearer that evening. "He's the only white man I ever loved, and I loved him."

〜

Adams and Donald Byrd's first New York City gig together likely took place on February 4–9, 1958, at Cafe Bohemia, with the all-star rhythm section of Hank Jones, Oscar Pettiford, and Kenny Clarke. Soon afterwards,

Thelonious Monk chose Adams and Byrd for a studio recording, just days before the tandem began their Five Spot residency. Their eleven-week run launched the Byrd–Adams Quintet, and by the end of the year the band had recorded the prophetically titled *Off to the Races*, the first of a series of recordings for Blue Note Records that cemented their place in history. Byrd's exclusive recording contract with Blue Note catalyzed the ensemble, and their status as a working group led them to be later signed by Shaw, who booked jazz ensembles throughout North America.

Because steady quintet work wasn't available from mid-1958 well into 1960, Adams and Byrd maintained careers as solo artists besides taking gigs as sidemen. In mid-1959, after Adams completed tours with Goodman and Chet Baker, Byrd and Adams recorded *Byrd in Hand*, their second date for Blue Note. As with the addition of Jackie McLean on their first release, "Blue Note seemed to want to add another horn, so of course it's not the band that's working all the time," said Adams. "We had to write new arrangements and change everything." Eventually, this approach would be mostly phased out in favor of showcasing the working group. Still, the label would continue to urge them to include at least one shuffle on each album. "They were very interested in trying to get something that was saleable," added Adams.

By July 1960, the ensemble's rhythm section of Duke Pearson, Laymon Jackson, and Lex Humphries had coalesced, and a three-month tour took the band to Cleveland, Chicago, Minneapolis, Salt Lake City, Denver, Detroit, Kansas City, and Pittsburgh, then back to Chicago and Detroit, before returning to New York in late October. Shaw's predilection for booking long road trips spelled disaster. Exhausting car rides, such as 1960's 2,900-mile stretch in less than five weeks, from Minneapolis to Salt Lake City to Denver, became the norm. "Several times there were road trips so long that the money from the gig didn't cover the travel expenses." Adams cited transportation costs as the main reason why the band ended its four-year run.

What made Byrd–Adams unique? First, it featured two great soloists backed by terrific, hard-swinging rhythm sections. Their repertoire was fresh and compelling; a blend of unusual standards, interesting originals, and cleverly adapted tunes, such as Henry Mancini's "Theme from Mr. Lucky" or its up-tempo version of "I'm an Old Cowhand." Additionally, trumpet with baritone saxophone was an exquisite pairing, more aurally spread than the customary trumpet/tenor sax combination of its time, and unusual in 1958, especially one playing their brand of small-group jazz.

Figure 11.2. *Minneapolis Star* ad. August 15, 1960. Public domain.

Still another characteristic was how well Byrd and Adams's phrasing meshed. When they stated each tune's theme, often using impressive dynamics and provocative counterpoint lines, it was beautifully rendered. "Phew! Boy! The way they orchestrated for just those two horns, and the solos!" raved Gerry Niewood. "It was just intense!"

Finally, their styles perfectly complemented each other. Byrd, at root, was a melodic, soulful, lyrical player who used space, nuance, and blues inflections in his solos. Adams, more rhapsodic, delighted in double-time playing and exhibiting other technical flourishes. All told, the Donald Byrd–Pepper Adams Quintet recorded ten dates—six studio albums, three tracks for a stereophonic showpiece, and three live LPs—assuring their place as one of the great jazz groups of its time. It launched the career of Herbie Hancock, and it gave Byrd, Pearson, and, to a lesser extent, Adams, Hancock, and Walter Davis a forum to write original compositions. Three of Byrd's tunes, "Curro's," "Bird House," and "Jorgie's," immortalized jazz clubs, Adams was heard widely throughout North America, and the quintet's Blue Note dates were reissued in the US and abroad during his lifetime. "When Pepper made those records, he really pushed the baritone into the middle of the hard-bop thing," said Gary Giddins.

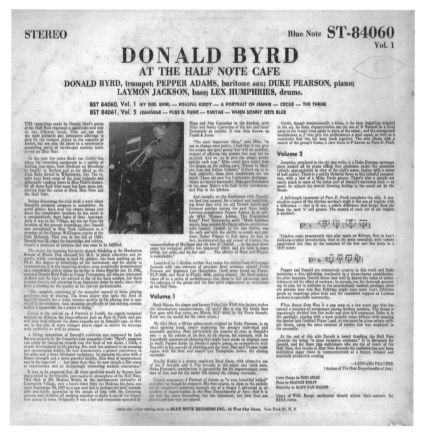

Figure 11.3. Blue Note Donald Byrd. Public domain.

Who wrote the thirty-three original compositions for the quintet during its four-year run? As it turns out, seventy percent were written by Byrd. Nine were composed by Pearson, Hancock, and Walter Davis Jr., the band's pianists. Although Adams wrote "Philson" and "Libeccio," it's not known if they were performed again by the working quintet.

Touring steadily for only a year with either Pearson or Hancock explains why Byrd–Adams is not well-known, especially as compared to other similarly constituted small bands of their time. Another reason for the group's lack of fame is because of the limited production runs of their studio recordings. "Those records are *brilliant,* but nobody in those days knew about those records because they were out of print," said Gary Giddins. "They just weren't available."

⌐

Beginning in early February 1959, Byrd and Adams began rehearsals for Monk's Town Hall concert on the twenty-eighth of the month. Rehearsals were conducted at Hall Overton's studio at 821 Sixth Avenue near Twenty-Eighth Street. "All the musicians wanted to get next to him," said saxophonist Charlie Rouse about Monk.

> He was like the master teacher. All different types of musicians, including drummers, trumpet players, all wanted to get with him. He was like the founder of all that modern thing. He had put the foundation down. His music is not really the easiest thing to interpret. He phrases differently from the regular norm of arrangers or composers and adds his personal touch to all his compositions. You have to play with him a while so you can get the right feel.

It took several weeks before the large ensemble learned Monk's new material. Eventually, only Adams's brief solo on "Little Rootie Tootie," the concert's finale, was included on Riverside's concert recording at Town Hall. Other than Pepper's iconic introduction to Mingus's "Moanin,'" his Monk solo would become the single most famous recording of his career.

"When we were rehearsing for the concert, there was talk—in fact, it was supposed to be definite—that a concert tour of about three weeks had been set up for the group that was to begin something like four weeks after the concert," said Adams.

We're to do the Town Hall concert, have three or four weeks, add some more pieces to the repertoire, have further rehearsals—paid for—and then go on this tour of concerts, primarily at colleges, I believe. That was the whole theory. That, in fact, was part of the package that I was approached with initially when I was asked to play in this band at Town Hall, which sounded fine. It was certainly enjoyable. The rehearsals were just great! We had a lot of fun. We go on, play the concert, and the immediate reviews that we received were so bad that all the rest of the concerts were cancelled.

Unfavorable reviews, written by John S. Wilson and Nat Hentoff in the *New York Times* and *Village Voice* respectively, negated two months of work, put an end to that band, and left Adams in a bind. His entire March and April schedule was dedicated to the Monk tour.

Negative or laudatory press has often shaped jazz. Ten years earlier, in the late 1940s, for example, "the jazz police—the emerging legion of jazz writers who were beginning to write critically about the music"—didn't like Leo Parker's bebop-influenced baritone solos, wrote Michael Segell. "The swinging lyricism of Harry Carney, whose resonant bari backed up Duke Ellington's orchestra for forty-seven years, had defined the stylistic boundaries of the bulky instrument. . . . The baritone was thought to be a harmonizing instrument, a section player, and when it broke out on its own for a chorus or two, its low, dusky voice was not to be displayed too prominently or for too long. It was like asking a walrus to sing."

A few years later, Gerry Mulligan's accessible, soft, and fuzzy tenor-like approach to the instrument changed its status, and, as a result, he became a darling of the jazz establishment. Their monomaniacal fascination with Mulligan at the expense of other baritone saxophonists was just one example of the winner-take-all ethos so common in US society. According to Robert Frank and Philip Cook who wrote about this phenomenon, "The top performers tend to monopolize pay and prestige, leaving little in the way of either gain or glory for the vast numbers of also-rans." Such behavior may have derived from Saint Anselm of Canterbury, the medieval philosopher. In the eleventh century, he advocated for God as the supreme being. Then, by utilizing ordinal numbers from two downward, he ranked also-rans, defining their relative importance to the almighty. Ten centuries later, Academy Awards, reality-show competitions, James Beard best-chef nominations, and annual jazz-magazine readers' and critics' polls are some of Anselm's progeny. In the late 1970s, when Adams's influence upon the field became undeniable, he finally surpassed Mulligan in *Down Beat's* jazz poll after thirty years as a runner-up. Upon Pepper's death, the torch was passed to Nick Brignola, and upon his passing in 2002, it was granted to Gary Smulyan.

~

In early November 1961, Byrd and Adams's final appearance as a working ensemble was in Kansas City. After their gig, the club went out of business, the band wasn't paid, and they had to drive 1,100 miles back to New York with their tails between their legs. Despite getting bilked, Shaw Agency demanded their fee and the union charged for travel dues. Adams expected his $1,000 payment for *Motor City Scene* to be waiting for him when he got home but Bethlehem had declared bankruptcy while he was traveling, and he never got paid for that either. Suddenly, Adams was flat broke.

When Charles Mingus heard about Adams's financial situation, he hired him immediately. Thus began a three-year association that lasted until Pepper's Mingus tribute album of September 1963. His work with Mingus was an important thread that gave him a sense of continuity during a turbulent period of his life. From 1961–1964, "I was officially homeless," Adams confessed. "I had an answering service as a mailing address and was living where I could live. It was very much a hand-to-mouth existence."

If Mingus had the opportunity to add a piece to his group, he would call Pepper to see if he was available. "I think it was partially because we *were* friends and he did like me, and he knew I'd come in and do a reasonable job," said Adams. "I think another reason is that I can sight-read E-flat parts, like for baritone, or I could take an alto and I could sight-read that. I could also sight-read bass-clef concert and I could make a pretty good job of transposing a tenor part or a trumpet part. So, if he had the wrong instrumentation or something, he could throw any kind of part in front of me and get at least a reasonably good job done."

Adams's first Mingus gig after Byrd–Adams's dissolution was in November 1961 at the Five Spot. At the time, Pepper was subletting Sara Cassey's apartment. Soon after moving in, the power was turned off because the utility bill remained unpaid. "As luck would have it, I was reading a Penguin edition of the collected letters of D. H. Lawrence," said Pepper. "Now, most of D. H. Lawrence's letters are appeals for money, so reading this by candlelight, in a sublet apartment that I'm not quite sure how I am going to pay for, was not really an ideal situation."

By the summer of 1962, Adams was working again at the Five Spot with Mingus, including August 27, the club's last performance before its demolition. Except for a week in Montreal, during all of October and the first half of November 1962, Pepper worked again with Mingus at Birdland. Adams had been subletting an apartment with Duke Pearson in uptown Manhattan, and he also worked in some capacity for United Parcel Service. "The work situation was very slow, and the financial situation was exceptionally grim," said Adams.

In October 1962, Adams was an integral part of Mingus's ambitious big-band concert at Town Hall. For some reason, the concert's original date of November 15 was changed to October 12, exerting additional pressure on Mingus to complete the music in time. Musicians were scrambling to finish arrangements, even working onstage the night of the performance. The concert and drama that led up to it "was a typical Mingus fiasco," said Jerome Richardson, who functioned as Mingus's concertmaster. "It was total chaos, the whole thing," agreed Snooky Young.

"I actually did some of the writing," said Adams. His one orchestration was "Please Don't Come Back from the Moon." "I was paid for it, of course. Paid very well, as a matter of fact. That part was nice. . . . There were a couple of really good things that we played that night. Not all of it was good, but the good things were not on the record."

Mingus's tendency to appropriate ideas from bandmembers at his recording sessions annoyed Adams and other musicians. Mingus "would write parts, and he would ask the musicians to make up a lot of the lines and parts—a composition—sometimes an arrangement, then Mingus would take credit for all of the writing," said Mike Jordan. "Before you know it, you had five different people collaborating on a tune that he was taking credit for." This was Mingus's "workshop" approach, over the years mythologized by jazz writers. Gene Santoro, the most hyperbolic of all, described Mingus's compositional approach as "the realization of the American dream in jazz form. . . . The workshops became a model of participatory democracy that attempted to re-enact and solve the quintessential American dilemma: how to allow maximum freedom to the individual without dissolving the group into anarchy." Instead, Adams decried this allegedly utopian method as "not knowing what the hell you're doing. I'm sure this is something Charles thought up as an excuse for not being prepared."

Besides the haphazard way that Mingus worked in recording studios, Pepper also disliked his stage personality. Mingus had already built a reputation for outrageous behavior that "a lot of people would come just to see," said trombonist Britt Woodman. Mingus "was an uncomfortable person sometimes to be around," explained Adams. "One always had to be a little leery, I think, because there was a line in his personality that *he* couldn't quite predict. . . . I think Mingus had an image of himself, that he felt compelled to try to live up to, as eccentric, but not enough to please himself, so he made up other stuff to go with it so as to be a true eccentric. When *he* would lose track of it, that's where I think he became dangerous. He was a pathological exhibitionist, and if lying would further his exhibition, he wouldn't mind indulging in it."

Mingus's public persona was "mostly a put-on," declared Elvin Jones. "He's really almost a shy man, and he tries to be boisterous to cover it up. Half the time he's frightened of one thing or another, like a little boy. But when he stops talking and starts playing, the virtuoso, the genius comes shining out. That's a different Mingus."

⤚

Just after Christmas, 1957, Adams moved into his unheated, fourth-story walk-up on East Sixth Street. At the time, Elvin Jones had to vacate where he was living, so Pepper suggested that he stay with him while he looked for another apartment. Jones stayed for more than a year, at least until Adams moved to 76 Jefferson Street in June 1959. "It was very compatible, very comfortable," remembered Adams: "We got along fine. Furnishings were, like, two beds, a television set, and a small kitchen. . . . It was great. The rent was, I believe, $55 a month, and we always managed to get it up and have it together. The phone bills: We figured, well, it's all going to average out in the long run, so we used to take turns paying the phone bill each month. . . . It was very groovy, very relaxed."

Occasionally, when they were low on cash and needed more time to pay their rent, Adams would ask Jones to talk to the landlord about it. "Pepper would disappear and let Elvin stay there and talk," laughed Oliver Shearer. " 'I ain't got no money, man,' he would tell him."

According to Lois Shearer, "They had a single, tiny, one-bedroom apartment, with two beds, one on either side of the room. The beds served as couches during the day." When Don Buday visited, he noticed the floor's strange slope. "I wouldn't say a 45-degree angle, but you felt like you were on a ship."

Elvin served as designated cook for the Sixth Street Detroit clique and would teach others how to prepare meals. One day he accidentally dropped a pool of liquid iodine into a pot of beans he was preparing. He scooped it out with a large spoon and said to his hungry friends, looking on in disbelief, "Don't nobody want to eat? They'll be more for us!"

Ray Mosca would often stop over at Pepper and Elvin's apartment after work when he was playing a gig in the Village. "They'd have a couple of tastes, we'd tell stories, and laugh and have fun, listen to music," he said. "They both read a lot. They were always reading books. They always had three or four books that they were reading at the same time."

Because he couldn't discuss politics and literature with some of his friends, Pepper would save that for Lois Shearer. To further express his point of view, "he would put up little cartoons in the bathroom or make dry political jokes or something, but he just brought a whole different aspect to the whole scene," said Shearer. "He was very gentle, and he was very quiet." Conversely, Jones was charismatic and occasionally brash. "Where Elvin went, everyone wanted to go," said Oliver Shearer.

During that time, Jones was doing drugs whereas Adams could barely afford to drink or buy pot. Elvin was "one of the most remarkable people for having a joint in one hand and a fifth of whiskey in the other hand, and had been up for three days, and shooting up and all that stuff, and having three chicks going at the same time," said Jay Cameron. "Absolutely fantastic energy with regard to all these things." One night he returned to his apartment completely stoned and started urinating on his bed. Pepper, already resting a few feet away, hollered at him, insisting that he use the bathroom down the hall. Indignant, Elvin said, "You don't like it?" at which point he pivoted and relieved himself on his roommate. "Pepper was furious," said Lois Shearer. "He came down and said he was going to move, but, of course, he never did." Adams "did not display emotions, which is why his coming to my apartment and being furious about Elvin was so unusual," she said.

⌣

On May 25, 1956, Adams stepped aboard Stan Kenton's bus in New York City and left for Boston's State Ballroom, his first gig with the band. Adams had been awaiting his union-card transfer to take effect. "For six months you were not supposed to take more than two jobs a week and you're not supposed to travel at all," he told Marc Vasey. "In those days the union was very strict on that," said pianist Richard Wyands. Because Pepper sur-

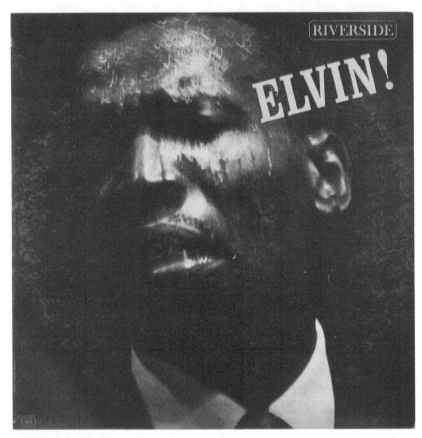

Figure 11.4. Elvin Jones. Recorded December 1961 and January 1962 in New York City, featuring his brothers, Thad and Hank Jones. Public domain.

reptitiously joined Kenton's band before his six-month interregnum ended in September, he submitted Elvin Jones's address of 202 Thompson Street and asked Jones to cover for him.

Although working with Kenton gave Adams a chance to be heard, especially at lengthy location gigs in Chicago and San Francisco, he wasn't sure it was the right step to take. For one thing, because Kenton historically featured alto saxophonists, he feared he might only function as a section player. Secondly, many of Kenton's charts didn't swing. Some could be "as ponderous as a Sherman tank," wrote Ted Gioia. Still, $150 a week was a decent wage and he'd be working steadily.

"There was a good deal of coldness at first," said Adams.

Sam Noto and Lee Katzman were immediately very kind and helpful. Several others were very aloof and let me know that they were stars and that I was just one of the workers in the band. This was not helped at all when, on the very first night, I got one solo to play, and without really thinking about it I played the way I normally do, which convinced a good portion of the band and especially Stan that I didn't know at all how to play a jazz solo. I remember exactly what I did. ["Intermission Riff"] was a twelve-bar tune that wasn't exactly a blues, but it was three bars of D flat major and a bar of D, and then three more of D flat and a bar of D, an E flat minor seventh to A flat seventh to D flat. It was easy as that. So, I jumped right in. I started right off on D major, running that against the D flat major to get a little tension going, which would be resolved in the fourth bar, but until then would be chalked-wrong on the blackboard. It's the sort of thing I've always enjoyed, and it's part of my playing, and I sat down very satisfied, thinking, "Gee, that was fun! I never played this tune before and it's a pretty dumb tune, but I found a way to make it interesting to myself." And then it was about three weeks before I got another solo because I had managed to convince everybody that I hadn't the slightest idea what I was doing. So much for ultra-sophistication! . . . Maybe I should have been more circumspect the first time around and played rather more like what they would have expected from their regular soloists? Now, looking back, I still think it's hilarious. I think I'd do it again.

Kenton was more concerned that Pepper wasn't a fast enough sight-reader. "I figured if I could read Poulenc's Clarinet Sonata, I should be able to read Stan Kenton's book," said Adams, yet Kenton was planning to fire Pepper after the second week. About the impending dismissal, Billy Root spoke with Lennie Niehaus, who functioned as leader of the reed section and was entrusted by Kenton. "Lennie never said much of anything, but when he said something, Stan listened," said Root. "He told Stan, 'I want him to stay right where he's at. He'll learn the book because he's got something.' And finally, after everybody told Stan he was a terrific player, Stan finally realized that he was a terrific player. But he was going to let Pepper go, and I was embarrassed 'cause I recommended him and I thought he sounded great to me. I thought, 'Boy, what a terrific player!'" True enough, by November's lengthy Macumba Club gig six months later, Adams had ten solo features, one indication of the respect the entire band held for him, though some, according to Pepper, were exceedingly jealous. Adams "was a genuine bebopper from Detroit," explained Mel Lewis. "He was the first one we had in the band like that. He had that blazing technique, and he could make runs, but he [had] that laid-back/catch-up feel. I've never heard anybody play like that on baritone." Lagging behind to create tension, then catching up when appropriate, was a common technique among vocalists but entirely new on baritone.

After some personnel changes, Lewis offered to room with Adams. The two ate, smoked, dressed, hung out together, and became lifelong buddies. Due to a fungal infection on his feet that he contracted three years earlier in Korea, Adams always wore two pairs of white socks. "He had to put this red crap on his feet every night," said Lewis. "The whole bed would be coated with stuff, I mean really heavy with the medicine he had to put on . . . It was like a wild shade of red, too. It was like a purply-red color. You could always tell what room Pepper was in because you could smell it out in the hall."

Kenton's musicians would meet in Pepper and Mel's hotel room to smoke marijuana and listen to records on Phil Gilbert's bulky, homemade victrola. "He was always smoking pot, but he was also smoking those Camels," said Lewis about Adams. "He smoked incessantly. . . . He must have smoked four packs a day or more, plus he was smoking pot, and he never used a filtered cigarette."

About Kenton, he "treated his musicians like gentlemen, and he knew how to draw the best out of you," said Mel Lewis, but Adams felt he had no sense of humor. "We totally disagreed on politics, on art, literature, cinema. You name any subject. We were at absolute poles and we got along beautiful! He considered me a communist, I considered him a fascist. I have never been a communist. I've been an extreme-left socialist all my life. I think he may well have been a fascist, however. His whole political opinion was all the lunatic-fringe right. . . . It speaks well of the man that he would accept my playing, and accept me as a person, and just cheerfully disagree on everything."

⏝

Adams, Mel Lewis, and Lee Katzman left Kenton's band after Thanksgiving 1956 and moved to Los Angeles to establish their new quintet. For four months Adams lived at Katzman's house with Lee's wife LaWanda, in Toluca Lake, twelve miles northwest of downtown Los Angeles. Both Adams and Katzman were impoverished. "The only thing that we had in the house was a couch and beds," said Katzman. Until late January and February 1957, when Adams started receiving checks from studio recordings that he did in Los Angeles, he made what little money he could by selling marijuana.

Adams's quintet rarely worked. Instead, as a suddenly in-demand sideman, he worked a few gigs, did a bunch of recordings, and sat in at numerous jam sessions. "Pepper was a new voice," said Lewis. "Pepper was the new cat, and, on the Coast, everybody was impressed with his playing."

By the mid-1950s, Peacock Lane, at 5501 Hollywood Boulevard and Western, had opened across the street from Jazz City. Adams played at both and attended nearby Monday nights jam sessions at Milomo. At 2829 South Western, Milomo had good food and, with Carl Perkins, Harper Crosby, and Frank Butler, an even better rhythm section. "All the guys used to come up there," said trumpeter Clora Bryant: Max Roach, Art Blakey, Ben Webster, Coleman Hawkins. Pepper also used to jam at Carl Perkins's house with Perkins and Leroy Vinnegar.

Additionally, about thirty blocks from Hollywood's Local 47 musician's union, there was a run-down building known as Bobby Doerr's Soup House that hosted Saturday night jam sessions. You'd enter by means of a fire escape and sessions took place on the second floor. "There'd be all these Mexicans there, and all this cocaine; enormous amounts of cocaine," said Adams. "A lot of good people would come by and play, so the jam session was fine. It was just the environment was so hectic. My God!"

Due to the similarity of their names and Adams's many recordings done in California during the fifties, he was often confused over the years with alto saxophonist Art Pepper. Complicating the issue was the fact that Art Pepper not only derived from Los Angeles but worked for quite some time with Stan Kenton. When Adams was mistaken for Art Pepper, he customarily distinguished himself by saying, "Yes, my sax is bigger," or "No, I never spent time at San Quentin."

As a means of returning to New York for his upcoming record date with John Coltrane and tour with Chet Baker, he joined Maynard Ferguson's big band for a month because they were playing gigs across the country, ending with a two-week engagement at Birdland. Ferguson's departure from Southern California also coincided with the end of Adams's six-month affiliation with Los Angeles' musician's union. Adams departed on March 23 for New York with Joe Maini, Jimmy Ford, and Bob Burgess. Ferguson had agreed to reimburse Pepper for car fare that he incurred driving three members of his band via Tucson, Omaha, St. Louis, Kansas City, and Minneapolis. It was a harrowing trip for Adams, since all three were heroin addicts who needed to stop along the way to buy drugs. Several times they left Adams alone in his car while he anxiously watched over their gear and awaited their return. After eleven stressful days, traveling 3,000 miles, they finally arrived in New York. Adams asked Ferguson for the promised compensation, but Ferguson refused to pay, saying, "You don't have that in writing." Adams promptly offered his two-week notice, something he was planning to do in any case.

After the Birdland gig Adams joined Chet Baker's group in mid-April 1957, working mostly in New York for the rest of the month. On April 20 Adams also led his first date for Prestige Records, though he's never been identified as its leader. Now better known as *Dakar*, with John Coltrane, Cecil Payne, Mal Waldron, Doug Watkins, and Arthur Taylor, it was first released as *Modern Jazz Survey: Baritones and French Horns* with the unusual running speed of 16 rpm.

At the beginning of May, Baker's group, with Elmo Hope, Doug Watkins, and Philly Joe Jones, headed west, first playing six weeks in Chicago, then two in Milwaukee and Minneapolis before making the long drive to Los Angeles for their gig at Peacock Lane. "Chet at that time was playing the best I think that he ever did in his life," said Friedman. "He had really good chops at that time, and he could play fast and hard, and he was really into a bebop thing but with a Miles kind of feel. It was great, and Pepper was the perfect counterpart to Chet."

While in Los Angeles, on July 10, 1957, Adams recorded his first actual date as a leader. With Perkins, Vinnegar, Mel Lewis, and trumpeter Stu Williamson, Adams had selected some of Los Angeles's best musicians. Adams together with Williamson's brash trumpet sound, a forerunner to Byrd and Adams, were a perfect match. Adams liked lyrical trumpeters as a counterbalance to his rhapsodic style, and Williamson, Katzman, Byrd, Baker, and Blue Mitchell all fit the bill.

Then, from July 16 until August 4, Adams played a three-week Chet Baker gig at the Black Hawk in San Francisco. For fourteen years at the northeast corner of Turk and Hyde, the famed club, owned by Guido Caccienti, "was leaky, unheated, dimly lit, badly furnished, and reeked of the petrified smoke of a million cigarettes." With the addition of tenor saxophonist Bob de Graaf, Baker had expanded the group to a sextet. Don

Friedman and Doug Watkins remained in the group and Philly Joe Jones was reinstated. One night during the engagement "Pepper took a break," said John Marabuto. "There was a bar next door where all the musicians went. When he came back, they were playing, and Mulligan was playing Pepper's horn. He didn't like that. Without asking him or anything." As Hank Jones pointed out, "*That* you don't do. That's a no-no."

Also on the trip, Doug Watkins was thrown out of his hotel because of the color of his skin. Adams, who was also staying there, left in protest. Because both suddenly needed a place to stay, Pepper called John Marabuto, who let them stay at his house in nearby El Cerrito. This was the first of many stays with the Marabutos over the years, a tradition that continued for the rest of his life.

Adams returned to Los Angeles on August 6, 1957, staying for a few weeks with Lee Katzman. Soon thereafter, Adams was named godfather of Katzman's daughter, Kellee, and throughout the years Pepper often visited when he was working in Southern California. While in town he recorded with Shorty Rogers and Bud Shank, then on August 23 for World Pacific recorded *Critics' Choice,* his second date as a leader. Adams hadn't been entirely satisfied with his playing six weeks earlier on his Mode session, but certainly offset it on "Minor Mishap," Tommy Flanagan's composition. Adams came out of the gate roaring with tremendous assurance and played equally well on Thad Jones's hip composition "5021," his dedication to the Blue Bird.

Back in New York, on September 29 Adams recorded Lee Morgan's *The Cooker.* At age nineteen it was already Morgan's fifth date for Blue Note. At twenty-six years old, Adams's first. The date, due to its widespread distribution, was many musicians' first exposure to Adams's playing. In November, Adams recorded *The Cool Sound of Pepper Adams.* This was the only "blowing session" that Adams had his name on as a leader. "I've always tried in my albums to present some kind of a statement, to have at least a couple of originals, minimum, and try to find some uncommon standards to play, and present an overall mood and change of mood and pacing, and present something that had some intrinsic value," said Adams. Instead, "It was just everybody going in the studio and play a little bit, and leave the studio, and then they make an album up out of it, so it does not add up that well."

⌐⌐

Soon after his arrival in early 1956, "Pepper created a sensation in New York because he outplayed Mulligan," said bassist Percy Heath. "Musicians

CRITICS' CHOICE **✱**

PEPPER ADAMS

✱WINNER: DOWN BEAT'S NEW STAR

Figure 11.5. Critics' Choice. Public domain.

appreciated Pepper not only as a person but also of his fantastic musician-ship," said David Amram. "Back in the fifties, all the real serious people in jazz knew that Pepper was 'the man' as far as his being able to take that harmonic approach that came out of the school of Detroit players, a lot of whom were influenced by Barry Harris, and being able to make it some-thing of his own." Bob Wilber was especially impressed with how Adams's playing had evolved since his teen years in Rochester. "I was amazed how much he had gotten into the modern scene, and with such expertise," said Wilber. "I was very proud of Pepper, the way he developed."

Adams's chief priority was to be heard on his instrument so he could acquire gigs of his own. Besides working a few small-group gigs with Oscar

Pettiford, sitting in at Cafe Bohemia and elsewhere with welcoming older musicians, or participating in jam sessions at Birdland and elsewhere, Pepper regularly sat in at informal loft sessions held throughout the city. One such gathering took place on Monday nights at painter David X. Young's place. Sessions never began before 11:00 p.m. Norman Mailer, Salvador Dali, or Willem de Kooning often dropped in with their entourage. Whiskey and marijuana were plentiful. Young, attractive, and available women were often in attendance. Although the sessions seem glamorous in retrospect, "the place was desolate, really awful," said Young. "The buildings on both sides were vacant. There were mice, rats, and cockroaches all over. You had to keep cats around to fend them off. Conditions were beyond miserable. No plumbing, no heat, no toilet, no electricity, no nothing."

Two miles across town, Larry Rivers and Howard Kanovitz, both painters, hosted jam sessions at their loft at 122 Second Avenue near St. Mark's Place. Clyde Cox's loft, on the third floor of a rundown building at 335 East Thirty-Fourth Street, was another venue. Sessions took place every night of the week. Still other sessions took place at 18 West Thirty-Seventh Street, where Zoot Sims and bassist Nabi Totah lived, and at bassist Peter Ind's recording studio on East Second Street.

At various Greenwich Village parties, David Amram would accompany Adams. The two would play, sometimes with a spontaneously added bongo player, or a drummer without his set playing brushes on a phonebook, or someone else reading poetry or singing a song. "I think he liked my enthusiasm, so we would go to different places just to get a chance to play," said Amram. "And then sometimes he would play piano and I would play the horn. . . . When Pepper played, even in the midst of the most raucous parties, everybody would quiet down. It was certainly the sound, and the intensity of what he was doing, and seeing, when he would pick up and play, the energy that he projected was so strong, that without trying to do anything to attract any attention to himself, which he never did, he would get everybody to be quiet and listen. He was always a tremendously strong player."

The best scene of all was Ken Karpe's Friday night jam session on East Twenty-Eighth Street near Third Avenue. It "served as a catalyst for some of the best jazz of the middle fifties," wrote Amram. "It was invitation-only, very high quality," said Adams. Oscar Pettiford parked a spare bass there. Most of the sessions ended at 7:00 a.m. but some lasted twenty-four hours.

Reminiscent of the weekly Detroit jam sessions held not that long before, all the new Detroiters in town attended. So, too, did many of jazz's best players: Monk, Zoot, Mingus, Max Roach, Clifford Brown, Percy Heath, Freddie Redd, Sonny Rollins, Cedar Walton, Hod O'Brien, Arthur Taylor, Philly Joe Jones, Idrees Sulieman. At those sessions, O'Brien heard for the first time Adams's "long, fluid, driving melodic lines," he said. "Pepper's playing had a particularly strong influence on me," he admitted. "I think that's where Monk became even more aware of Pepper's playing," said Amram. "He used to hear Pepper and really loved his playing."

Adams's move to New York coincided with the recording industry's adoption of 33⅓ rpm, 12-inch, long-playing records. This technological advancement allowed up to twenty-five minutes of music per side as opposed to less than five minutes on a 10- or 12-inch 78. The additional space allowed musicians to stretch out, replicating what they played on club dates. At the same time, recording technology had also improved, enhancing the listening experience even further. Ampex tape recorders, "probably the single most significant shift, revolutionized the radio and recording industries because of their superior audio quality and ease of operation over audio disk-cutting lathes."

The first record that Adams made in New York was the 1956 Savoy recording *Jazzmen: Detroit.* With his homies Burrell, Flanagan, and Chambers, and sponsored by Kenny Clarke, their earliest East Coast benefactor, the session gave the world a clear indication of what these twenty-something Detroit wunderkinds had brought with them to New York. Done on April 30 and May 9, 1956, just a few weeks before Adams shoved off with Kenton, "it was the first nationwide distribution of anything I had appeared on and had some artistic input on," said Adams. Kenny Clarke, then house drummer at Savoy Records, appointed Adams as contractor, who divided up the tune selection and arranging responsibilities among Burrell, Flanagan, and himself.

About living in New York, Adams cautioned David Schiff. "It's a rough city," he told him.

> You got to pay your dues. You go to play in these really crappy bars. The only way to get to play is to play these crappy bars and go and just sit in anywhere. Take the horn in your hand. Have it be a part of you and walk the streets. If you hear some music, go in and say, "Hey, can I sit in?" You can't be bashful. You got to really want to do this because if you have any doubt that you might not want to do this, the city will eat you alive.

Unquestionably, Adams knew he was extremely talented and wanted to succeed as a musician. But to realize his dream of becoming an innovative

Figure 11.6. Jazzmen: Detroit. Public domain.

jazz musician, it would take some of the grit, ingrained in his psyche, that he had inherited from his ancestors, particularly his sixth great-grandfather. In 1650, James Adams's will was mightily tested during the Battle of Durham, where four thousand soldiers were slaughtered, his subsequent exhausting march, at gunpoint, from the battle site to Newcastle, his incarceration and arduous ocean voyage to the New World, and, finally, seven years of backbreaking labor before he earned his freedom. As a survivor and rugged individualist in his great-grandfather's image, Pepper Adams, in his pursuit to be recognized as an original stylist, would certainly be battle-tested, too, during his remaining thirty years.

Chapter Twelve

Ad Astra

He was a towering figure, and had he been black he would be considered
one of the greatest people to play jazz on the saxophone.

—Dick Katz

What became of the teenager who was so bedazzled by Charlie Parker?
Did he accomplish what he set out to do in 1949? Yes, without
question, Pepper Adams succeeded in becoming a virtuoso, inventing an
original way of playing his instrument.

Judging from the many accolades he received from colleagues before
and after his death, Adams's prowess was equally esteemed by his elders,
contemporaries, and younger musicians. Among the old guard, Coleman
Hawkins was one of his biggest fans. "Hawkins admired Pepper," said Eddie
Locke. "He said, 'That cat is something else on that horn!' . . . He didn't
say that about many people; he didn't talk about many guys." Don Byas
also adored Adams's playing, and Milt Hinton, out of respect for Pepper's
intellect, dubbed him "The Master." About Adams, Dizzy Gillespie once rhe-
torically asked David Amram, "Man, that guy's phenomenal, isn't he?" And
backstage at the 1985 Adams benefit in New York City, Gillespie told Cecil
Bridgewater how much he admired what Pepper had done harmonically with
the instrument, how he had utilized the baritone sax in a different way from
other baritone players. "His playing was unbelievable, just fantastic!" agreed
trumpeter Clark Terry. "I never heard him jump into anything that stymied
him: any tune, any tempo, any key. He was a phenomenal musician, one

185

that could do anything. His rhythmic sense was superb, his melodic sense was fantastic. He was just a marvelous person and a marvelous musician."

Those born around the same time as Adams were just as effusive in their praise. "He is one of my heroes," said Bill Perkins.

> He's one of the true giants of jazz. He stood out in that rare group of jazz soloists, the great giants of all time, people like Bird and Prez—and John Coltrane has become that. I think Pepper was that on his instrument—and Diz. They're in an area where very few have done the creative work that they've done. Nobody is equal: There are some great young players around and they owe a great debt to him, but Pepper was monolithic in his playing.

Bob Cranshaw concurred with Perkins: "Everyone knew he was a superstar. The rest of the baritone saxophonists: *They* know! . . . In my book he's the Number One baritone saxophonist. I don't even think of anybody else." Phil Woods agreed: "Any baritone player that's around today knows that he was Number One," he said in 1988. "It's that simple. He was the best we had." Both Curtis Fuller and Don Friedman felt similarly: "He was the greatest who ever played the baritone saxophone," proclaimed Fuller. Pepper, asserted Friedman, "should be considered the number-one-of-all-time baritone player. Nobody ever played as many years at that level that I ever heard. There's no question about it."

Adams "was an excellent jazz soloist," said pianist Horace Silver. "He could handle any of the chord changes that you'd throw up in front of him. That's the mark of a true, great improviser. In my opinion, this is why any of the great jazz soloists get their reputation; because they're consistent." Bill Watrous said about Pepper, "Every time he played it was an adventure. His ideas and his conception of the stuff that he was trying to play was *totally* original." And saxophonist Junior Cook said about Pepper, "He was a virtuoso, without a doubt. He exemplified all the best things that any musician—jazz or otherwise—should aspire to: He had great tone, he had great time, and he had great taste."

For younger jazz musicians, Adams was a paragon of individuality. "There's very few stylists, real heavyweights," bassist Todd Coolman told Ron Marabuto about Pepper. "Maybe five of them. They're really rare. He's one of them." "Adams," said Bennie Maupin, was "a true master of his craft and absolutely one of the finest musicians of his generation." Gary

Smulyan acknowledged that Pepper "inspired me to make a life-long study of the instrument": "It kind of made me realize why I got into music. It was not to be a doubler. It was not to play all these instruments and get a Broadway show. It was to try to find a voice, and to express your life through an instrument. That was it. Pepper was the inspiration for that."

⌐

In *Outliers: The Story of Success*, Malcolm Gladwell explored how certain unique groups, and specific individuals within these groups, either became financially successful or, conversely, fell short of the success they deserved. Four concepts from his book are especially germane regarding Adams. First is Gladwell's thesis that genius is an innate attribute, but for that rare individual to do profound things to change the world, a series of "opportunities" must take place that act upon and inform such genius.

About Adams's intellectual capacity, there's no debate. "A more truly brilliant person I've never known," wrote Doc Holladay.

> Pepper could have had at least three PhDs had he pursued them through normal academic channels. His understanding of art, painting, sculpture, and other two- and three-dimensional media, complete with their respective historical contexts and significance, was clearly phenomenal. The breadth of his familiarity and comprehension of literary fields was almost legendary. . . . Not only was music his passion, but his mastery of theory, composition, history, and musicology was such that anyone who engaged him in discussions on these topics discovered quickly enough who was the master. . . . The best professors I've come into contact with as colleagues over the years know their subjects so well that information literally flows from their minds to their audience of one or a thousand. That was my impression of Pepper.

Peter Leitch felt much the same way. "I was in awe of him," he wrote. "He was amazing. He knew so much about so many things—all areas of music, visual art, literature, you name it—and he could carry on an intelligent, informed conversation about any of it." Mel Lewis compared Adams's intellect with Charlie Parker's. "I think it takes a tremendous mind to create a solo of the caliber that he comes through with all the time," he said. "I don't think he's any less a genius than Charlie Parker was, and Charlie

Parker was considered a genius." Hank Jones praised Adams's intellect and musicianship just as forcefully: "With the way he played the horn, Pepper was as close to a genius as you can find on earth." Jones placed him in the same exclusive company as his two brothers, Elvin and Thad, and also Art Tatum. "Pepper stands very tall among those giants," he said.

> When you say, "The man is a genius," that means that he's capable of doing things that nobody else is capable of doing, or at least relatively few people. Charlie Parker had that same thing. Charlie Parker had an endless flow of ideas, which he could execute flawlessly at any tempo, and with a tone that was impeccable. . . . I was just always amazed. I used to get the impression that there was nothing that he couldn't do. I got that same impression from Charlie Parker. There are probably things that he couldn't do, but, if there were, I don't think anybody ever invented them! . . . I never felt that I was up to his standards, to tell you the truth. I was reaching to play along with him. . . . He would extend your thinking, your abilities. That was part of the greatness of Pepper. He would make you *play.* He would make you think more creatively because he was thinking and playing creatively.

If Adams preferred, he could've been a writer, a mathematician, or an art, English, or music professor. Yet five things happened early in his life that propelled him to his future place as jazz's greatest baritone saxophonist: 1) his move to Rochester, and access to musical instruments in public school; 2) the opportunity to play professionally as a teenager during the Second World War; 3) his relocation to Detroit at the age of sixteen; 4) his discovery of the baritone saxophone at Grinnell's; and 5) his advanced status as a Detroit musician relative to other musicians in the US Army who were touring professionals. As Gladwell wrote, "Outliers are those who have been given opportunities and who have had the strength and presence of mind to seize them." Clearly, Adams did that.

Gladwell's second contention regarded the good fortune that comes from being in the right place at the right time. Although few before Adams had focused on baritone as a solo instrument, he believed that he could elevate the horn to be on an equal footing with other instruments. His timing was perfect. He could express his sophisticated harmonic sensibility and eventually play with a level of virtuosity never heard on baritone sax.

Pepper's quest to tame the baritone is in accord with Gladwell's "10,000-Hour Rule," his most famous tenet. "How long does it take to be good at something?" he asked. "To master a cognitively complex task, whether it's playing chess at an elite level, or being a brain surgeon, or a classical music composer, or a good computer programmer, requires, seemingly without exception, 10,000 hours of deliberate practice," said Gladwell. "10,000 hours is roughly four hours a day for ten years. So, you need to put in that kind of time before even the most innately talented of people can ever achieve elite status." And that's precisely what Adams did, beginning in December 1947, when he began sedulously practicing the baritone. Roughly ten years later, after logging more than 10,000 hours of work, he felt accomplished enough to move from Detroit to New York City, jazz's epicenter. Then, four months after his relocation, Pepper joined Stan Kenton's orchestra, kickstarting the upward trajectory of his remarkable thirty-year career.

Although Adams blossomed from instituting Gladwell's first three principles of success, disregarding the fourth one helps explain Pepper's lack of financial advancement. "No one—not rock stars, not professional athletes, not software billionaires, and not even geniuses—ever makes it alone," cautioned Gladwell. "Success is not exceptional or mysterious. It is grounded in a web of advantages and inheritances, some deserved, some not, some earned, some just plain lucky."

Adams did not have a "web of advantages." His family was not affluent, and his exclusionary relationship with his mother prevented him from acquiring political connections and valuable social skills so important for the growth of his self-esteem and future success. Certainly, as a well-respected professional musician, he was recommended by his peers for nightclub work and recordings. But he suffered from unlucky twists of fate, such as the abrupt ending of Byrd, Monk, and Thad Jones ensembles, and at several points in his career failed to leverage his good fortune that could have alleviated his financial misery.

In 1956, after quitting Kenton's band, for example, he lived for a few months in Los Angeles and earned more money doing sideman recordings than at any comparable four-month period of his life. Adams could have chosen to base himself there and capitalize on his newfound success, becoming, as Thad and Mel later did in New York, a well-to-do studio musician. Eight years later in 1964, Harry James offered Adams a $10,000 annual salary to join his Las Vegas based orchestra. Pepper declined his generous offer, worth $89,000 in today's money, not wanting to live there nor perform James's commercial dance music. Accepting the offer, if only for one year, would have provided him with economic security at a time of extreme hardship.

Gladwell's work helps clarify why financial abundance eluded Adams. Why he wasn't a household name can be explained six different ways. First, Pepper died much too soon. As pianist Eubie Blake, who lived to the age of ninety-six, once said, "If you hang around long enough, they get around to you." Ira Gitler said much the same about Adams: "If you survive for a long time and keep the level of your playing on a certain high level, after the youth that comes, say, after you've gained a lot of experience in your thirties and forties, and you're really a professional, and you still have your vitality—well, if you can keep that, and we've seen musicians that can do that—you start getting more recognition. You've been around that long, and more people know about you, and you're still playing at a high level. I think if Pepper had survived, it would have come more and more to him."

Had he lived another few years, a major label might have signed him, just as Verve did with fellow Detroiter Joe Henderson. Furthermore, like many of his colleagues, Pepper might have benefited from the widespread academic acceptance of jazz in the US that bloomed soon after his death. Considering his erudition and extraordinary contribution to jazz, he could have received an academic appointment, such as an artist-in-residence or professor of music post, that would have granted him even more financial stability.

A second factor that prevented Adams from being well known was the fact that throughout his career he functioned almost exclusively as a sideman. "A lot of people don't know a lot of the really great musicians because they were not bandleaders," asserted Tony Inzalaco. "Pepper was one of those people: A master musician, with a history of recording with so many different people and being able to make music at a very high level throughout his career."

Due to the historical bias that has always favored bandleaders, a significant disadvantage of being a sideman is that, once you get the chance to record under your own name, your albums are not readily available. Adams's LPs "were not easy to find," said Gary Giddins. Although his recordings as a leader were as artistically substantive as those made by many bandleaders, they were produced by small, independent labels that had scanty airplay, limited distribution, minimal advertising budgets, if any, and modest production runs that quickly went out of print.

A third determinant working against Adams's fame, psychoacoustic in nature, was the public's universal bias against low-pitched instruments. Adams felt "that if he played well, better than most everyone else, the world would discover him and reward him accordingly," said Ron Ley. But much like professional US athletes, in which the football quarterback and home-run slugger receive the bulk of attention, the jazz trumpeter, clarinetist, alto and tenor saxophonist, and pianist and guitarist are most conspicuous. The chief reason for this is that listeners generally favor higher-pitched instruments. "The average person on the street, when they listen, they hear the highs," explained trombonist Tom Everett.

> How often do you really hear a piano player improvise at length in the lower register, except for special effects, except for Eddie Costa? And then they do it more for textural type things and color things, because they realize that people lose the sense of line in the lower register . . . People don't hear it. It doesn't have the same impact. And it's an acoustical, physical fact that higher-pitched sounds and instruments—faster moving frequencies—move through the air faster and with less decrease of intensity. So, someone sitting across the room is going to get more impact from an alto saxophone than they are from a trombone or a string bass. It's a fact. Mathematically, if you pick up a book on acoustics, just look at what happens. Lower waves do not travel as far. If we put a tuba player and a piccolo player down at the end of the street and we ask them to both play a scale in their octave, after a while you're not going to hear the tuba player at *all,* or you're going to hear the tuba player *behind,* late, even though they are playing at the same time. The sound of the tuba travels slowly so it dissipates before it gets to you. That's why trombonists in our orchestras are always being yelled at by conductors for playing late. They're not playing late. They're playing instruments that take longer for the sound to move through the air, plus they're sitting in the back of the orchestra. So, most orchestral trombone players have just learned you always play a little bit on top of the beat so, to the audience and the conductor, it sounds like you're right there.

Despite the bias against low-pitched instruments, or the difficulty in articulating very low notes, Adams made the bottom register of his horn sing as expressively and dynamically as the rest of his instrument. And therein lies both his challenge to the listener and the essence of one of his greatest accomplishments. He pioneered the way to articulate very low notes, keep them in time, and play them, even rapidly, with a full sound that required a constant air supply.

A fourth reason why Adams was not popular during his lifetime was the perception that he wasn't marketable. "For ordinary success in music, almost everyone would agree irreducible amounts of talent and training are important," wrote Donal Henahan.

> But for extraordinary, flabbergasting success, nothing can take the place of a high E.Q., or Exploitability Quotient. Some musicians come by a high E.Q. naturally, some acquire it through diligent study, and yet others have it thrust upon them by canny managers. No matter, a high E.Q. is arguably the firmest foundation for a major career. . . . The surest mark of the high E.Q. musician is the regular appearance of his or her name in gossip columns and his or her person on television talk shows. However, it generally takes many years for a performer to develop an E.Q. worthy of being taken seriously by the producers of such programs. Long before that, the burgeoning young artist must be taken in hand by someone who understands the phenomenon of celebrity and its mysterious workings.

Adams, with his pale skin, geeky haircut, horn-rimmed glasses, and crooked front teeth, was hardly the glamorous-looking young artist who could have been coached and packaged as a promising client with a bankable future.

Not a savvy networker was a fifth element that exacerbated Adams's lack of celebrity. His experience with Stan Getz and Yusef Lateef at a West End Hotel after-hours jam session is but one glaring example. On the same night in 1955 that Adams manhandled Mulligan, Lateef also thoroughly outplayed Getz. Afterwards, during a break, both Adams and Lateef went over to Getz's table to say hello. Getz commended Adams, saying to those sitting at his table that here was the musician who obliterated Mulligan. With Lateef standing beside him, Pepper thanked Getz, then returned his compliment. Referring to Lateef, Adams said in his characteristically mild-manner style, "Thank you, Stan. Now let me introduce you to the man who did the same to you."

If Adams had not expressed his point of view, wouldn't a future alliance with Getz be beneficial? "The perception of greatness in jazz, as in the other arts, requires a consensus among the right people, money, and often a bit of self-promotion," wrote Peter Watrous. Adams's aversion to promoting himself, especially in ultra-competitive New York City, assured his impoverishment for much of his life, said Albert Goldman. "You can't be a wallflower in anything and expect to get ahead, and that's the way he did it."

An astute observer who knew Adams well, Goldman rejected Pepper's indifference to actively seek work and furthering his career as a tragic waste of talent. At the very least, couldn't he have implemented the advice of others who were doing better? Even in the lean 1960s, Adams's colleagues were getting gigs, teaching privately, or obtaining foundation grants and university appointments. It didn't help that Pepper had no personal management until the very end of 1981, nor ever worked with a public relations firm to create demand for his many skills.

Lastly, a sixth factor that moderated Adams's stardom was the complexity of his virtuosic style. "I think that might be, maybe, one of the reasons that Pepper wasn't recognized," said Don Friedman.

> When you have a lot of technique and you play a tremendous amount of music in a short time, the person who's listening has to be very tuned in to catch everything. Whereas, if a person plays like—I'll use Miles as an example. Miles has a tremendous appeal, and Miles, in my mind, also is a fantastic genius. But he can appeal to a tremendous mass because he plays in a way that anybody who likes music [can] pick up on what he's playing. He plays simple, a few things. Beautiful, soulful. His soul is so obvious whereas a guy like Pepper, his soul was not so obvious . . . You have to really listen to him to feel it. Otherwise, some person who wasn't a trained listener could just get the idea that they're hearing a blur of sound and not being able to really realize what they're hearing. If you're a musician and you're playing with him or listening to him, and you hear how his lines juxtaposed with the harmonic stuff that's going on underneath, then you realize what a genius this guy was.

Just as Miles Davis revamped jazz trumpet playing with his use of the destemmed Harmon mute, Adams revolutionized the approach to his instrument. "He reinvented the sound of the baritone saxophone," insisted Gerry Niewood. "You can hear Pepper play a couple of measures and you knew it was him. He had such a personal way of playing . . . His wit, his perfect swing, and the sound. I could always tell it was him." Not only was he "one of the handful of white musicians . . . really accepted by the African American community as a true master of the music," but Pepper was arguably the only white musician in jazz history who liberated his low-pitched instrument in much the same fashion as bassist Jimmie Blanton and trombonist J. J. Johnson did for theirs.

Like Julian Bream, David Oistrakh, or Andrés Segovia, Adams worked closely with composers, such as Thad Jones, Duke Pearson, Charles Mingus, and David Amram, who composed pieces especially for him. Amram, who wrote his *Triple Concerto* for Pepper, was planning to dedicate to him a sonata for baritone saxophone and piano. Alec Wilder was writing a saxophone quartet with Adams as one of its intended performers, and still other commissions would have surely come his way.

In the end, "The only thing that's sad about a Pepper Adams isn't that he didn't play 10,000 gigs, and make a million dollars, and screw six blondes a week," said Albert Goldman.

> The sad thing about Pepper is that you had the feeling there was a lot of very fine music in him that was never put down on record because he wasn't a star and there weren't that many people interested in "cutting" him. He was a remarkably gifted player in an age when everybody else of his generation or a little older was in decline. They had said it, they had done it, and they were just going around and around in circles losing altitude, whereas here's a guy who had *preserved* his talent, had never abused himself, who was as good or probably *better* than he had ever been, who had really deepened and gotten more interesting, and had a true spiritual development, which isn't common in the popular arts, and we didn't get but a small amount of it on wax. That's the tragedy. Pepper is somebody you feel bad about. Not because he died. We're all gonna do that. And not because he didn't make money or whatever. Not because he lived a loner's life. Simply because we didn't get what we should've out of that man. I don't think it's entirely the world's fault. He knew the game. He knew the world he was in.

"Ad Astra per Aspera," the Latin phrase for "to the stars through difficulty," serves as an appropriate metaphor for Adams's lifetime of achievement and his posthumous recognition as the supreme virtuoso of the baritone saxophone. The expression was adopted as the state motto of Kansas in

1861 upon the urging of John James Ingalls. "The aspiration of Kansas is to reach the unattainable; its dream is the realization of the impossible," wrote Ingalls. Isn't that essentially Adams's story? He conquered an instrument previously regarded as untamable. "Someone like Gerry Mulligan, and most of us, learned to adapt to the instrument," said Bill Perkins. But "Pepper took that instrument and he never conformed to its weaknesses." Because of his blinding speed, penetrating timbre, immediately identifiable sound, harmonic ingenuity, precise articulation, malleable time-feel, dramatic use of dynamics, and utilization of melodic paraphrase, Adams's reputation, now more than thirty years after his death, is very much on the ascent.

His career can be measured by a long, slowly ascending arc of success that increased exponentially once he left Thad Jones's orchestra. Without a doubt, his first six years as a traveling soloist were triumphant—a time when he burnished his legacy as a distinctive composer and virtuoso performer—making his dramatic three-year fall that much more lamentable. Nonetheless, he had a rich and influential thirty-year run. Consider for a moment the most notable jazz musicians of his era. How many stylists are there who are instantaneously identifiable and have had a profound effect on the art form? John Coltrane, Miles Davis, and Wes Montgomery spring to mind. Clifford Brown and Cannonball Adderley perhaps? Equally noteworthy is Pepper Adams, whose approach continues to serve as the lodestar for all his progeny.

Acknowledgments

I want to thank Al Gould, Steve Wood, Jim Merod, Pete Lukas, Eric Allen, Ken Kellett, Ronald Ley, Dan Olson, Nancy Thorne, Andrew Homzy, Mark Stryker, Rudy Tucich, Bob Blumenthal, Jeff Gottesfeld, and Joshua Breakstone for reading parts of the manuscript. Many thanks to John Vana, Frank Basile, Brian Priestley, and Leif Bo Petersen for critiquing the entire draft. Three readers in particular—Michael Pauers, John Gennari, and Barry Wallenstein—were instrumental in guiding the biography through to completion.

Many thanks to Chick Corea for his foreword, Erik Lindahl for the cover photograph, Frank Basile for assistance with photographs and documents, and Dan Olson for help with photographs and formatting the text.

I'm especially grateful to James Hall at the Rochester Institute of Technology. As part of RIT's School of Individualized Study Speaker Series, in 2015, Hall invited me to speak about Adams and his time in Rochester. Jim's kind invitation, and the school's generous stipend, supported my Rochester research. Many thanks to RIT's Office of the Provost, the College of Liberal Arts Department of Performing Arts and Visual Culture, and the Center for Media, Arts, Games, Innovation, and Creativity.

Further, I'm indebted to Jon Gudmundson at Utah State University for inviting me to participate in a 2017 residency honoring Pepper Adams. That experience kickstarted me to finally sit down and write this book after many previous attempts. Gudmundson was one of more than fifty professors since the 2012 publication of *Pepper Adams' Joy Road* who invited me to speak about Adams at their institutions. Thanks to them and their students, I was challenged with questions that spurred me to investigate new areas of inquiry.

I want to acknowledge the pioneering genealogical research done by Pepper Adams's cousin, Joie Gifford. I also benefited from groundbreaking research done by Frank Basile both on Adams's many gigs and the history of Selmer baritone saxophones. Moreover, Leif Bo Petersen's research on Charlie Parker was crucial in allowing me to understand Adams's experiences at Detroit's Mirror Ballroom, and in Kansas City while a soldier in the US Army. Also, his research on Fats Navarro and Lionel Hampton helped me pinpoint Adams's participation in Hampton's Junior Beboppers event in Detroit.

The author especially thanks the following interviewees for their wisdom: Pepper Adams, Claudette Adams, Ray Alexander, Marshall Allen, Barry Altschul, David Amram, Jorge Anders, Andy Anderson, Tony Argo, Lyle Atkinson, Steve Bagby, Jon Ballantyne, Danny Bank, Joe Baptista, Clifford Barbaro, Bill Barron, Kenny Barron, Billy Barwick, Charles Beasley, Marcus Belgrave, Hank Berger, Kenny Berger, Mark Berger, Bill Berry, Eddie Bert, Andy Bey, Walter Bishop Jr., Art Blakey, Dan Block, Hamiett Bluiett, Bess Bonnier, Beans Bowles, Joshua Breakstone, Cecil Bridgewater, Nick Brignola, Whit Browne, Clora Bryant, Don Buday, John Bunch, Ronnie Burrage, Charles Burrell, Kenny Burrell, Jaki Byard, Georgia Caddell, James Calhoun, Dolores Cannata, Lodi Carr, Gary Carson, Benny Carter, Ron Carter, Teddy Charles, Warren Chiasson, Denny Christianson, Joe Cinderella, Jimmy Cobb, Al Cohn, George Coleman, Junior Cook, Keith Copeland, Bob Cornfoot, Stanley Cowell, Bob Cranshaw, Stanley Crouch, Emilio Cruz, Eddie Daniels, Harold Danko, Peter Danson, Charles Davis, Richard Davis, Walter Davis Jr., Alan Dawson, James L. Dean, Al Defemio, Buddy DeFranco, Don DePalma, Ralph Dickinson, Larry Dickson, Len Dobbin, Jerry Dodgion, Michel Donato, Walter Donnaruma, Bob Dorough, Pacquito D'Rivera, Ray Drummond, John Dunlap, Jack Duquette, Tom Everett, Jon Faddis, Art Farmer, Mark Feldman, Tom Fewless, Diana Flanagan, Tommy Flanagan, Ricky Ford, Frank Foster, Don Friedman, Curtis Fuller, Frank Gant, Earl Gardner, Everett Gates, Gary Giddins, Joie Gifford, Steve Gilmore, Ira Gitler, Bob Gold, Lillian Gold, Albert Goldman, Bill Goodwin, Al Gould, Alan Grant, Norb Grey, Mark Gridley, Johnny Griffin, Paul Grosney, Lionel Hampton, Roland Hanna, Bill Hannah, Al Harewood, Billy Harper, Danny Harrington, Barry Harris, Beaver Harris, Billy Hart, Louis Hayes, Jimmy Heath, Percy Heath, Gugge Hedrenius, Joe Henderson, Jon Hendricks, Pat Henry, Bill Herndon, Michel Herr, Fred Hersch, Phil Hey, John Hicks, Billy Higgins, Dylan Hill, Doc Holladay, Major Holley, Andrew Homzy, Tim Horner, Clint Houston, Freddie Hubbard, John Huggler, Per Husby, Bobby

Hutcherson, Tony Inzalaco, Chubby Jackson, Hugh Jackson, Ira Jackson, Laymon Jackson, Milt Jackson, Charles Johnson, Howard Johnson, Bruce Jones, Hank Jones, Clifford Jordan, Mike Jordan, Sheila Jordan, Jeremy Kahn, George Kanzler, Dick Katz, Lee Katzman, Amos Kaune, Gene Kee, Ken Kellett, Maurice King, Jack Kleinsinger, Jimmy Knepper, Bob Koch, Ron Kolber, Howard Konovitz, Pat LaBarbera, Yusef Lateef, Hugh Lawson, Pete Leinonen, Peter Leitch, Phil Levine, Lou Levy, Mel Lewis, Cindy Ley, Ron Ley, Eddie Locke, Dean Magraw, Cookie Mandel, Dee Marabuto, John Marabuto, Ron Marabuto, Bennie Maupin, Andy McCloud, Andy McKee, Al McKibbon, Bernard McKinney, Hal McKusick, Spike McKendry, Jill McManus, Charles McPherson, Chris Melito, Lowell Miller, Billy Mitchell, J. R. Monterose, Doris Moreau, Mark Morganelli, Dan Morgenstern, John Mosca, Ray Mosca, George Mraz, Raymond Murphy, Mike Nader, Stephanie Nakasian, Frank Nash, Jamil Nasser, Gerry Niewood, Cisco Normand, Walter Norris, Fred Norsworthy, Sam Noto, Al Obidinski, Hod O'Brien, Niels-Henning Ørsted Pedersen, Jimmy Owens, Greg Packham, Don Palmer, Charles Papasoff, Stan Patrick, Bill Perkins, Gene Perla, Houston Person, Leo Petix, Bob Pierson, Allen Pittman, Vic Plotti, Herb Pomeroy, Mike "Q," Angel Rangelov, Rufus Reid, Jerome Richardson, Mario Rivera, Max Roach, Scott Robinson, Red Rodney, Mickey Roker, Sonny Rollins, Joe Romano, Jimmy Rowles, Patsy Ryan, Ray Santisi, Earl Sauls, Al Schackmann, David Schiff, Gary Schunk, Mitchell Seidel, Lois Shearer, Oliver Shearer, Horace Silver, Carol Sloane, Arlene Smith, Derek Smith, Gary Smulyan, Herb Snitzer, Lennie Sogoloff, Marvin Stamm, Charlie Starke, Alvin Stillman, Rory Stuart, Bob Sunenblick, Lew Tabackin, Arthur Taylor, Joe Temperley, Clark Terry, Toots Thielemans, Bill Titone, Fred Tompkins, Nabi Totah, Rudy Tucich, Mickey Tucker, Norris Turney, McCoy Tyner, Dave Usher, Eddie Vay, Vic Vogel, Kenny Washington, Bill Watrous, Bob Weinstock, Michael Weiss, Jon Wheatley, Andre White, Keith White, Bob Wilber, Buster Williams, James Williams, Leroy Williams, Skippy Williams, Claude Williamson, Glenn Wilson, Kellogg Wilson, Phil Wilson, Gunnar Windahl, Jimmy Witherspoon, Rayburn Wright, Mike Wolff, Phil Woods, Ed Xiques, Tony Zano, and Charlotte Zwerin.

For your assistance on the long and winding thirty-seven-year road, the author thanks Sandra Adams, Chris Albertson, Eric Allen, Tommy Banks, Mark Berger, Sika Berger, Roger Bergner, Edward Berlin, Monique Bielech, Sven Bjerstedt, Rien Boendermaker, Bess Bonnier, H. W. Brands, Laurent Briffaux, Cameron Brown, Jan Bruer, Al Bruno, Jim Buennig, Ronnie Burrage, Armin Buttner, Robert Campbell, William Campbell, Vince Carducci, Erin

Carner, Lodi Carr, Allan Chase, Denny and Rose Christianson, Noal Cohen, David Peter Coppen, Bob Cornfoot, P. J. Cotroneo, Josh Cross, Michael Cuscuna, Nou Dadoun, Rhys David, Paul de Barros, Rein de Graaff, David Demsey, Eddy Determeyer, Jeroen de Valk, Chris DeVito, Andrew Dewar, Larry Dickson, Danny D'Imperio, Jim Eigo, Dawn Evrich, Rich Falco, Tony Faulkner, John Fedchock, Dale Fielder, Mike Fitzgerald, Ken Franckling, Hans Fridlund, Will Friedwald, Gwen Fries, Keith Gerlach, Phil Gilbert, Ray Glassman, Bob Gordon, Jon Gordon, Kevin Goss, Bennett Graff, Frank Griffith, Wilhelm Hall, David Halliday, Tom Hampson, Thomas Hanney, Ole Kock Hansen, Danny Harrington, Jerome Harris, James Harrod, Rusty Hassan, Matt Havilland, Hal Hill, Jim Hill, Philippe Hirigoyen, John Horler, Thomas Hustad, Robert Iannapollo, Jocelyn Ireland, Steven Isoardi, Chuck Israel, Heidi L. M. Jacobs, William Jamieson, Mike Jordan, Ashley Kahn, Jeremy Kahn, Elena Kanigan, William Keeler, Bill Kirchner, Wayne Leechford, Carla Lehmeier, Ed Levine, Phil Levine, Devra Hall Levy, Aaron Lington, Eddie Locke, Dave Loeb, Jan Lohmann, Pete Lukas, Kirk and Lucie MacDonald, Jason Marshall, John Marshall, Yamaguchi Masaya, Ole Matthiessen, Melissa Mead, Mike Melito, Jim Merod, Joyce Middlebrooks, Mark Miller, John Miner, Anthony Minstein, Dan Morgenstern, Tony Mosa, Cyril Moshkow, Bob Mover, Kathryn Murano, Leo Murphy, Stephanie Nakasian, Michael G. Nastos, Alfie Nilsson, Dick Oatts, Ted O'Reilly, Phil Pastras, P. J. Perry, Leif Bo Petersen, Noah Pettibon, Christopher Popa, Bob Porter, Lewis Porter, Beth Prindle, Rob Pronk, John Reid, Howard Rees, Paul Remington, Osian Roberts, Espen Rud, Dick Salzman, Dave Schiff, Mario Schneeberger, Adam Schroeder, George Schuller, Todd Selbert, Cynthia Sesso, Warren Shadd, Ben Sidran, Mark Slobin, Ray Smith, Matt Snyder, Neal Starkey, Michael Steinman, Joel Stone, Mark Stryker, Anders Svanoe, Ate van Delden, Walter van de Leur, Rik van den Bergh, Stuart Varden, Gordon Vernick, Frank Villella, Tobi Voigt, Sheron Dixon Wahl, Gavin Walker, Ditmer Weertman, Ron Welburn, Sherry Wells, Jurre Wieman, David Wild, Brian Williams, Ed Xiques, Arthur Zimmerman, Tom Zlabinger, and Mike Zwerin.

Thanks to these organizations for their help: Burton Historical Collection of the Detroit Public Library, Detroit Historical Society, Massachusetts Historical Society, Detroit Public Library, Rochester Historical Society, Rochester Museum and Science Center, Salt Lake City Public Library, Sibley Music Library at Eastman School of Music, Centre for Swedish Folk Music and Jazz Research, University of Rochester Library, University of Utah Library, Utah State University Library, Utica Public Library, Smith College Library, and Braselton Public Library.

Sources

Quotations that derive from interviews conducted by the author are denoted by *GC*. *WPU* refers to material that is either currently housed or will be in the future stored at the Pepper Adams Archive at William Paterson University in Wayne, New Jersey.

Introduction

"The cradle-to-grave approach . . . events of it in sequence": Lomask, 38, 42.
"Biography need no longer . . . which sort themselves": Edel, 30, 196, 202, 30.
"A portrait in words . . . around him, or with both": Lomask, 2.

1. In Love with Night

"I knew of its significance even then": Rudy Tucich, *GC.*
"It was on the second floor . . . a place of wonderment to me": Rudy Tucich, *GC.*
"It was a night to remember": Oliver Shearer, *GC.*
"Pepper was ignoring everybody . . . from that night on, I think": Oliver Shearer, *GC.*
"The greatest I ever heard": Pepper Adams, *GC.*
"Somehow the name Arthur Honegger . . . ever heard of Honegger": Pepper Adams, *GC.*
"The stand-off qualities and the resistant fury of a stallion that dares you to break him": Iverson.
"I saw it as a wide-open field": Pepper Adams, *GC.*
"No one was playing jazz . . . do something entirely different": Pepper Adams, *GC.*
"She sits bestride the world . . . in American hands": Halberstam, 116.
"Going to Detroit at that time . . . in which to learn music": Pepper Adams, *GC.*
"Some guys take a solo . . . then you bring it up": Skippy Williams, *GC.*
"Those things make you a better musician . . . you're going to play better": Skippy Williams, *GC.*

201

"Pepper was a lonesome person . . . he lived for that horn": Skippy Williams, *GC*.
"I consider myself self-taught . . . from a bunch of people": Pepper Adams, introduction to "Body and Soul," 27 March 1978, *WPU*.
"She'd come by and watch me . . . he accomplished it": Skippy Williams, *GC*.
"Lovely person . . . some champagne at the house": Skippy Williams, *GC*.
"She told me personally that she really went with him for a while": Oliver Shearer, *GC*.
"Didn't like the system . . . if you happen to be free and brave": Ron Kolber, *GC*.
"It really plays well . . . take it home and try it": Pepper Adams, *GC*.
"We practically lived in there listening to music": Bess Bonnier, *GC*.
"Long, gracious room with big, tall windows": Bess Bonnier, *GC*.
"I always thought of him as kind of unhealthy": Jack Duquette, *GC*.
"He was always a little bit pale . . . never saw the light of day": Mike Nader, *GC*.
"When he'd buy a pack . . . dump them all in his shirt pocket": Tom Fewless, *GC*.
"He'd put a Camel in his mouth . . . until it was *all* over." Hugh Lawson, *GC*.
"I was on the GI Bill . . . make his notes": Bob Cornfoot, *GC*.
"No wonder the guy . . . scored in octaves": Bob Cornfoot, *GC*.
"She kind of hung out . . . when she was in that context": Jack Duquette, *GC*.
"It was a little different for me . . . felt a little funny about that": Hugh Lawson, *GC*.
"She looked pretty English or Irish . . . get to the real source": Oliver Shearer, *GC*.
"She started going with a friend of his . . . a skinny white girl": Curtis Fuller, *GC*.
"That was the best gig . . . to work in a bar": Pepper Adams, *GC*.
"In Detroit in those days . . . well before we were twenty-one": Danson, 4.
"There was a lot of playing in people's houses . . . this sort of thing": Pepper Adams, *GC*.
"They objected to my harmonic things": Danson, 6.
"Absolutely no respect for Duke Ellington . . . corny shit?": *Ibid.*, 6.
"Was drugs . . . excluded from that automatically": *Ibid.*, 6.
"White flight wasn't the only force . . . the cost of labor": Scott Martelle, 175.
"Firm and penetrating sound": Pepper Adams, as told to Peter Clayton, *WPU*.
"He was interesting": Beans Bowles, *GC*.
"He reminded me of Coltrane, in a way . . . it has a sweetness about it": Arthur Taylor, *GC*.
"Was kind of sheltered . . . Very Caucasian": Beans Bowles, *GC*.
"I had a chance for a gig in Sweden . . . my draft status was what it was": Pepper Adams, *GC*.
"I just went on and volunteered . . . I passed the physical": Pepper Adams, *GC*.

2. Now in Our Lives

"The work was hard, dirty, hot, and dangerous . . . constant hammering": Anon (Scots Prisoners).
"That's a hell of a feat . . . up a marble staircase": Pepper Adams, *GC*.

"The inside of my mouth . . . motorman's glove": Pepper Adams, *GC.*
"Kind of crazy, a terrible lush": Pepper Adams, *GC.*
"A vast, archaic, hectic kingdom . . . plunging waterfalls and wide, charging rivers": Haien, 15.
"Our whole family . . . being quite literate": Pepper Adams, *GC.*
"Everybody used to send . . . of their reading": Pepper Adams, as told to Albert Goldman, *WPU.*
"For more than a century . . . to the digital age": Johnston, 29.
"The earliest influence . . . got interested in [Art] Tatum": Anon, "Translation," *WPU.*
"I was taught sight-singing . . . been entirely different": Anon, "Translation," *WPU.*
"There was a period there . . . hotel in Louisville": Pepper Adams, as told to Marc Vasey, *WPU.*
"I was doing everything I could . . . pretty regular after school": Pepper Adams, *GC.*
"He had a real keen intelligence . . . this is quite remarkable": Everett Gates, *GC.*
"Rex was my favorite soloist . . . most inventive harmonically": Jeske, 29.
"He was playing the things . . . was what set him apart": Danson, 4.
"Stewart had this kind of a bleak . . . so I adopted some things from Rex": Ronzello, 36.
"Rex Stewart could play . . . why it worked": Pepper Adams, as told to Marc Vasey, *WPU.*
"Approach to chord changes . . . try to analyze it.": Pepper Adams, as told to Marc Vasey, *WPU.*
"I was studying more classical music . . . an entirely different ball game": Danson, 4.
"When I was a kid . . . of my playing": Pepper Adams, as told to Albert Goldman, *WPU.*
"Every day I think . . . Ellington meant a lot to Pepper": Gunnar Windahl recitation, *WPU.*
"Pepper was a very talented cat . . . people didn't appreciate him": Doc Holladay, *GC.*
"I collect jazz records . . . that lasted until he went to Detroit," Murphy, *GC.*
"The emergence of a collector's culture . . . listening and verbal expression": Gennari, 66.
"We talked about jazz . . . we read books about jazz": Raymond Murphy, *GC.*
"My biggest impression . . . right from the beginning": Raymond Murphy, *GC.*
"He didn't have much facility . . . he had that sensitivity to music": Bob Wilber, *GC.*
"Math I never had any trouble with . . . that was no problem": Pepper Adams, *GC.*
"You know where you have some precocious . . . man doing great things": John Huggler, *GC.*
"My, he was a little lost . . . glad we befriended him": Everett Gates letter to Gary Carner, *WPU.*
"He didn't have very much of a sense . . . a rather sad person": John Huggler, *GC.*
"The main stressors . . . lifestyle that most jazz musicians lived": Segell, 274–75.
"A hip jump band . . . He was killed in Korea": Pepper Adams, *GC.*

"One of the major reasons . . . an E. M. Forster article": Pepper Adams journal, 35–36, *WPU*.

"Pepper used to stop in there . . . get on the road": Leo Petix, *GC*.

"He played quite well . . . where they heard it first": John Albert letter to Gary Carner, *WPU*.

3. Inanout

"We all had to go . . . eight of combat engineer": Norb Grey, *GC*.

"He managed to get me called . . . in Kansas City [with] $3": Pepper Adams, as told to Albert Goldman, *WPU*.

"A shirt has to be hung up . . . some guys just won't put up with": Norb Grey, *GC*.

"He never went out of his way . . . didn't give a shit": Ron Kolber, *GC*.

"No one's sleeping in my bed . . . go to sleep": Ron Kolber, *GC*.

"I think his whole point . . . he stepped back from that": Doc Holladay, *GC*.

"But the only people . . . where I keep my pants": Ron Kolber, *GC*.

"But you can't leave your clothes . . . making us scrub it every day": Ron Kolber, *GC*.

"He never got into direct confrontation . . . a good reason for doing it": Ron Kolber, *GC*.

"Had all these tunes . . . got them from Barry Harris": Ron Kolber, *GC*.

"Pepper used the service as a school . . . taking a tune apart": Doc Holladay, *GC*.

"He attacked them . . . anything he wanted with it": Ron Kolber, *GC*.

"Here's a cat proceeding . . . players mostly did not": Pepper Adams as told to Albert Goldman, *WPU*.

"One of the newer people . . . needed people fast in Korea": Ron Kolber, *GC*.

"About the second day out . . . enough to make you sick": Pepper Adams journal, 4–5, *WPU*.

"The first day out of Seattle . . . days of the crossing": Pepper Adams journal, 1–2, *WPU*.

"We'd pitch in an open area . . . we'd put on a show": Al Gould, *GC*.

"The one vehicle that was the main one . . . 'Road to Ruin' ": Al Gould, *GC*.

"Marijuana was growing all over the place . . . get whatever they wanted": Al Gould, *GC*.

"A couple of times I hitched . . . had some good sessions": Tynan, 17.

"When the enemy broke through . . . We carried M-1s or M-2s": Al Gould, *GC*.

"Can you imagine how haunting an experience that would be?": Mark Gridley, *GC*.

"'Chinese Communist soldiers . . . bugles sounding in the pitch dark": Roth, 31.

"Going over on a troopship . . . realize something about casualty rates": Pepper Adams, *GC*.

"You might not realize . . . so many idiots in the world": Pepper Adams journal, 9, *WPU*.

"Gave him a lot of time to work on what he wanted to do with his horn": Jack Duquette, *GC*.

"Three or four years ago . . . be in premature capitulation": Pepper Adams journal, 21–23, *WPU*.

"A brief recession . . . to an 'automated' factory in Brook Park, Ohio": Lichtenstein, 290.

4. Twelfth and Pingree

"If the auto industry . . . that supplied the paints": Roger Lowenstein, *Brothers on the Line*.

"Miles would stand under the air conditioner . . . when he heard Thad play": Roland Hanna, *GC*.

"Lasted quite a few years . . . great, swinging music": Danson, 4.

"Certainly not the same . . . a blenderized drink": Pepper Adams interviewed by W. Kim Heron.

"The clientele at the Blue Bird . . . I felt no uneasiness at all": Bjorn and Gallert, 115.

"I learned a lot . . . takes some virtuosity to bring this off": Charles McPherson, *GC*.

"In the first half of the twentieth century . . . the city manufactured musicians": Slobin, 48.

"I had no idea . . . best goddamn baritone saxophonist in the world": Phil Levine, *GC*.

"Grinnell's had this thing . . . because of Grinnell's": Maraniss, 94–95.

"The family piano's role . . . the Grinnell Brothers Music House": *Ibid.*, 93–94.

"Public school music programs . . . an instrument in the third grade": Stryker, 11–12.

"There was a strong emphasis on learning . . . not sing on some level": Bennie Maupin, *GC*.

"Lawrence [was] a very good . . . a very good musician": Charles Boles, *GC*.

"You got there at something like seven . . . before 9:30 or 10:00 p.m.": Charles Burrell, *GC*.

"You started taking piano, harmony . . . You had your mother's consent": Charles Burrell, *GC*.

"When you finished Cass Tech . . . You were a finished musician": Charles Burrell, *GC*.

"There were a lot of private lessons . . . exposed to their playing": Bennie Maupin, *GC*.

"I had good teachers . . . people like Pepper, and Miles, and Coltrane": Curtis Fuller, *GC*.

"Detroit was like that . . . would always let you come up and play": Mike Coumoujian, *GC*.

"I think Frank Foster was probably . . . to Detroit when he came": Barry Harris, *GC*.

"He was becoming a pretty astute arranger . . . how to read his arrangements": Liebler, 21.

"I learned more about improvisation from him . . . He's a brilliant man": Whalen, 9.
"They discussed literature, politics, philosophy . . . these people are really different' ": Sheinen.
"Oh, you're an average kind of guy . . . It's not just notes and chords": *Ibid.*
"We would exchange music . . . we would rehearse a lot": Heckman.
"Because the contemporary kids . . . got to work at it": Pepper Adams, as told to Ted O'Reilly, CJRT-FM, Toronto, *WPU.*
"Every musician I know . . . something else going on there": Eddie Locke, *GC.*
"The friendship . . . you could go ahead and do your thing": Eddie Locke, *GC.*
"Pepper was a *player* . . . such a beautiful, beautiful cat": Eddie Locke, *GC.*
"A large number of musicians . . . could do that": Pepper Adams as told to Ben Sidran, *WPU.*
"I can remember many times when we've helped . . . Here, you take this' ": Billy Mitchell, *GC.*
"He didn't say . . . What's it gonna be, man' ": Eddie Locke, *GC.*
"One hundred fifty people . . . same sort of atmosphere": "Elvin Jones," *Notes and Tones,* 221.
"There existed a certain kind of elegance in those long, smooth, swinging phrases": Baillie.
"The night when he heard about Wardell . . . he was violent": Doc Holladay, *GC.*
"OD'd, and the guys around him panicked, threw him out in the desert": Buddy DeFranco, *GC.*
"If the guys he was with . . . he was anyhow": Gioia, 59.
"I heard them several times in person . . . wouldn't even consider it": Danson, 6.
"Stitt set the pace for articulation . . . were just at the highest level": Gerry Niewood, *GC.*
"He was the baritone player . . . keeping the instrument full at all times": Pepper Adams, as told to Albert Goldman at the Half Note, *WPU.*
"Carney I always admired . . . basic improviser": Pepper Adams, as told to Lucinda Choban, radio interview.
"I think he played better than the records tend to indicate": Pepper Adams, as told to Marc Vasey, *WPU.*
"Was a fine baritone player . . . extraordinary on the baritone": Pepper Adams, as told to Marc Vasey, *WPU.*
"Light, airy tone . . . I never liked": Rhoden.
"I found [him] extremely disappointing . . . and that made his time uneven": Case.
"I think it's a common tendency . . . with the way I heard Wardell playing": Danson, 5.
"When I was working with Miles Davis . . . he told a joke on somebody": Sonny Rollins, *GC.*
"Humair is quite conversant in the arts . . . no idea that Pepper was so hip": Phil Woods, *GC.*

"Pepper may well have encouraged . . . the take-out humiliation that Humair finally suffered": Ron Ley, *GC.*
"Meek . . . emotion that underlay his personality": letter from Ron Ley to Gary Carner, *WPU.*
"Dearest Pepper . . . love you, will never stop, P.": letter written to Pepper Adams, 1956, *WPU.*
"She never could quite get that idea . . . do things on his own": Bob Cornfoot, *GC.*
"Detested me since the day I was born": Claudette Adams, *GC.*
"Their relationship was unlike other . . . they were not close": Ron Ley emails to Gary Carner, 2012 and 2018.
"He did not like his mother at all": Gunnar Windahl, *GC.*
"Was his sound . . . loved what he did": Bennie Maupin, *GC.*
"Something that really turned me on . . . so inventive with his thought": Gerry Niewood, *GC.*
"They were in for a rough time . . . to come in and devour them": Major Holley, *GC.*
"Pepper really cut him . . . we were all rooting for the hometown guy": Mike Nader, *GC.*
"Him and Chet Baker came in . . . like a kid with that saxophone": Curtis Fuller, *GC.*
"That was a wailin' little band": Tynan, 17.
"A very unique place . . . The kids loved it. They could play chess": Curtis Fuller, *GC.*
"He heard a little something . . . he lived in was all white": Curtis Fuller, *GC.*
"He liked to run over a lot of Thad Jones . . . He just loved Thad": Curtis Fuller, *GC.*
"Coming up with Pepper . . . place on that instrument": Curtis Fuller, speech about Pepper Adams.
"At that time, it wasn't being done . . . a lot of things I'm playing": Curtis Fuller, *GC.*
"Playing with Pepper was pivotal . . . would have happened for me": Stryker, 104.
"Centralization of recording . . . into lasting professional success": Gennari, 128
"It was looking for broader . . . long run has been good": Pepper Adams, as told to Ted O'Reilly, CJRT-FM, Toronto, *WPU.*

5. I Carry Your Heart

"Was perhaps the evening's most poignant moment": Anon., *Down Beat,* 54.
"It was so beautiful . . . last time I was going to hear him": Mel Lewis, *GC.*
"Couldn't believe that a man that sick could play that well": Dick Katz, *GC.*
"I walked in, and he looked . . . the last time I was going to see him": Denny Christianson, *GC.*
"It's getting so bad, the horn weighs more than I do": Cisco Normand, *GC.*
"Sound in the hall was really big": Charles Papasoff, *GC.*
"It was a very emotional time . . . The drummer was in tears": Mike Jordan, *GC.*
"Pepper'll make you cry . . . few cats that can do that": Ray Mosca, *GC.*

"They shouldn't treat that": Gunnar Windahl, *GC*.

"Put him on a steamer . . . can never cure that": Gunnar Windahl, *GC*.

"I chose stuff that was compatible . . . and he did": Denny Christianson, *GC*.

"He didn't just smoke . . . world's biggest chain smoker": Don Friedman, *GC*.

"I scheduled the recording . . . He was very strong": Bob Sunenblick, *GC*.

"Dear Per . . . Skal!": Pepper Adams letter to Per Husby, *WPU*.

"I am sure the sequence of things . . . after he broke his leg": Diana Flanagan, *GC*.

"Gunnar called us . . . the furniture back in the house?": Diana Flanagan, *GC*.

"Really, really deeply disturbed": Bruce Jones, *GC*.

"Have you seen Pepper . . . I really want to see Pepper": Gary Giddins, *GC*.

"The band is up there . . . just watching the two of them": Gary Giddins, *GC*.

"Good evening and welcome . . . grind you down": Pepper Adams letter to the audience, 1985.

"As he was getting more involved . . . let this illness get in his way": Mark Feldman, *GC*.

"We live in a catch-22 here . . . basically what he had to do": Jack Kleinsinger, *GC*.

"Playing as forcefully as ever . . . but you could tell that he needed to rest": Bill Barron, *GC*.

"I tried to spend as much time . . . and [a baritone] is a heavy thing": Lew Tabackin, *GC*.

"I'd like to thank you . . . Things are definitely looking up": Pepper Adams, *Jazz-Times*, 26.

"Gelmann told me . . . was going to die soon afterwards": Bob Sunenblick, *GC*.

"He would have died all by himself": Bob Sunenblick, *GC*.

"The last two times I went to his house . . . couldn't go to see him anymore": Roland Hanna, *GC*.

"Whenever you talked to him . . . someone like him was very painful": Mark Feldman, *GC*.

"I thought maybe I should try . . . that had that sound of resentment": Diana Flanagan, *GC*.

6. Claudette's Way

"Had very strong maternal feelings for Pepper": Ron Ley email to Gary Carner, 2012.

"This was a very sad moment . . . in high esteem": Ron Ley email to Gary Carner, 2012.

"What has been happening to me . . . It's a good feeling": Danson, 9.

"I remember running into him . . . I had never seen it before": Hugh Lawson, *GC*.

"I went around with him . . . he'd be ready for three more": Keith White, *GC*.

"Pepper spoke more freely . . . he was sober. An introvert": Gunnar Windahl recitation, *WPU*.

"When he used to drink a lot . . . I always felt that he was depressed": Dylan Hill, *GC*.

"It was not always joyous . . . so he didn't drink too much": Gunnar Windahl narration, *WPU*.

"Once we played at a place . . . not very happy about that": Gunnar Windahl narration, *WPU*.

"Finally, we parted company . . . I gave him $100": Andy McCloud, *GC*.

"Occasionally I get *out there*": Pepper Adams, *GC*.

"I got a letter . . . signal of their relationship getting worse": Gunnar Windahl narration, *WPU*.

"Enigma, closed emotionally . . . didn't let anyone get close to him": Claudette Adams, *GC*.

"He'd tell you what was happening inside of himself with his horn, with his music": Jon Faddis, *GC*.

"It just seemed that there was no warmth": Rose Cornfoot, *GC*.

"Claudette seems to think that I have a mistress in every town": Pepper Adams, *GC*.

"He was a womanizer . . . she was, apparently, very jealous": Ruth Price, *GC*.

"Frustrated in their efforts . . . recognized by sheer pluck": Anon., letter to Gary Carner, *WPU*.

"I suspect a lot of his frustration . . . which he lost his cool": Anon., letter to Gary Carner, *WPU*.

"He seemed to be in excruciating pain, and was about to pass out": Dylan Hill, *GC*.

7. Joy Road

"Pretty much took me in . . . He was family": Ron Marabuto, *GC*.

"Was putting a book together . . . he could pace a whole night": Ron Marabuto, *GC*.

"They were the same tempos . . . real in-between tempos": Ron Marabuto, *GC*.

"He opened up my head to that way of playing": Cecil Bridgewater, *GC*.

"He got trickier with it, and more playful with it": Harold Danko, *GC*.

"He could take what a lot of us . . . mold it into pure platinum": Phil Woods, *GC*.

"Was one of the great ambitions of my life": Rusch (Bill Perkins), 1995.

"Sometimes I was very sad . . . dare take up the topic": Gunnar Windahl recitation, *WPU*.

"Did not like original material . . . talk them out of that": Pepper Adams, *GC*.

"He would send me a tune . . . gotta go all the way back": Ron Kolber, *GC*.

"Edgy and bright and buzzy": Scott Robinson, *GC*.

"Wheeler was a real individual . . . that was the attraction for Pepper": Kirk Mac-
	Donald, *GC.*
"He never struck me . . . would float on top of the time": Gene Perla, *GC.*
"Sense of time was uncanny . . . he had that": Keith White, *GC.*
"His time is very snaky . . . quarter-note oriented but phrase oriented": Phil Hey, *GC.*

8. Conjuration

"Because sometimes the slapstick kind of humor . . . in an entirely different key":
	Sidran.
"I think that is underrating him": Windell.
"I heard Pepper say . . . they were the giants of their time": Rusch (Seldon Powell), 7.
"There was a tremendous rapport . . . they laughed a million laughs": Marvin
	Stamm, *GC.*
"Harmonically, it was more modern, but it always swung": Jon Faddis, *GC.*
"You couldn't hire Pepper to come in . . . these bands was boring for him": Mel
	Lewis, *GC.*
"One of the greatest experiences . . . remember the feel of the tune": Gene Perla, *GC.*
"You couldn't very well ask . . . you can't do that": Rusch, (Mel Lewis, III), 16.
"Complemented each other and inspired each other": Rusch, (Mel Lewis, I), 8.
"There was a preponderance . . . and so did Nottingham": Rusch, (Mel Lewis,
	III), 16–17.
"Max's club was in pretty dire straits": Alan Grant, *GC.*
"Was going to charge $2.50 per head . . . they went for it": Holladay, 140.
"We played those nine charts and stretched them out": Bourne, *Jazz Journal,* 14.
"Even when the chart was the same . . . never knew what to expect": Bourne,
	Down Beat, 29.
"Used hand signals . . . an individual to improvise a background": Smith, 7.
"He used to do things like . . . one kind of lifting upward": Don Palmer, *GC.*
"He used to do things on held chords . . . being accentuated at different times":
	Don Palmer, *GC.*
"There was something magical . . . make it something different": Lisik and Allen, 92.
"No one ruled a band . . . we were all special": Bill Watrous, *GC.*
"He had an aura about him, and everyone had tremendous respect for him": Steve
	Gilmore, *GC.*
"I'd rather hear Thad miss a note than hear Freddie Hubbard hit twelve": Bjorn
	and Gallert.
"The two best soloists in the band were Thad and Pepper": Mel Lewis *GC.*
"In terms of taking the revolution . . . almost like they could not breathe": John
	Mosca, *GC.*
"Anybody who really loved this art . . . and it takes a lot of hard work": Tony
	Inzalaco, *GC.*

"Unfortunately, that band never had . . . it's pretty devastating": Rufus Reid, *GC.*
"The problem was both of them": Ed Xiques, *GC.*
"He just wanted to be a sideman": Ed Xiques, *GC.*
"The drummer is the leader of the band musically . . . was in heaven": John Mosca, *GC.*
"You couldn't talk to Thad . . . even bad conditions": Harold Danko, *GC.*
"With success comes a lot of responsibility": Jon Faddis, *GC.*
"Was always upset . . . would do things to sabotage that stuff": Jon Faddis, *GC.*
"Thad may have had a classic case of fear of success": Ed Xiques, *GC.*
"Every time we went to Florida . . . then he would create it": Rusch, (Mel Lewis I), 16.
"Had a preconceived idea before we went in . . . Thad was gone": Jon Faddis, *GC.*
"The guys in the band wouldn't even know . . . bothering us": Rusch, (Mel Lewis I), 16.
"We had a meeting one night in that kitchen of the Vanguard": Eddie Bert, *GC.*
"We were all involved in New York scenes . . . I couldn't leave town": Eddie Bert, *GC.*
"Little by little, the band became a lesser band for it": Bill Watrous, *GC.*
"Altogether very, very happy experience": Lisik and Allen, 168.
"As if we were a rock group . . . that many people": Billy Harper, *GC.*
"They got into my room . . . and put it backwards in the case": Ron Kolber, *GC.*
"There was a lady that Mel . . . keep up with the band": Billy Harper, *GC.*
"With Mel I think they might have had a method": Billy Harper, *GC.*
"In that sax section . . . as anything I've ever heard": Don Palmer, *GC.*
"You were just caught up in it . . . he still had that momentum": Earl Sauls, *GC.*
"I felt kind of bad . . . and I'd have six": Harold Danko, *GC.*
"Made no sense to me . . . he had in our band": Mel Lewis, *GC.*
"It's not running the book into the ground": Pepper Adams, as told to Ted O'Reilly, *WPU.*
"Strictly for survival . . . after a period of time": Pepper Adams, as told to Ted O'Reilly, *WPU.*
"Mel never forced the band . . . is to let the music be itself": Lewis, *Cadence,* 8.
"The perfect fill or set-up": Lisik and Allen, 113.
"It was really kind of like riding . . . there was that vacuum there": *Ibid.,* 110.
"That space that he would leave . . . easy for us to play the complex things": John Mosca, *GC.*

9. Civilization and Its Discontents

"That band could have been as good . . . too busy with chicks": Mel Lewis, *GC.*
"Was different from other producers . . . recordings went smoothly": Bertrand Uberall.
"I'm only responsible . . . to see that comes out well": Duke Pearson, as told to Ted O'Reilly.

"Was a romantic composer. He was like Puccini to me, the jazz Puccini": Tony Inzalaco, *GC.*

"Maybe we made $3 apiece . . . just enjoyed playing the music": Bob Cranshaw, *GC.*

"I think New York is great . . . another dimension to people's playing": Richards, 20.

"Birdland was a big meeting place . . . everybody would come down": Nabi Totah, *GC.*

"Those who played the clubs had free access to those playing the other club": Tony Inzalaco, *GC.*

"The music stopped almost . . . not that many gigs": Ray Mosca, *GC.*

"You used to go out . . . or two nights in Montreal": Ray Mosca, *GC.*

"There were assassinations . . . who tried to play for a live public": Schnabel, 12.

"The late sixties and early seventies . . . for a white jazz musician": Richards, 20.

"It got to be purely racial . . . as much as I wanted": Lew Tabackin, *GC.*

"Sometime in '67 . . . but it's a movement": Tony Inzalaco, *GC.*

"The sixties saw the perfection . . . inexpensive 45 rpm records": *Jazz: From Its Origins to the Present*, 376.

"In the late fifties . . . to 15–30-year-olds": John Gennari email to Gary Carner, June 19, 2019.

"Jazz music went all to hell . . . into some other form of music": Herrington, 28.

"I had always gotten good press . . . that they shouldn't bother": Pepper Adams, as told to Marc Vasey, *WPU.*

"A real jazz man . . . that's what I'm talking about": Eddie Locke, *GC.*

"The opportunity to record was only in England and very much on the cheap": Pepper Adams, *GC.*

"He thought it was underrated . . . proud of that composition": Gunnar Windahl narration, *WPU.*

"I like to use a strong melody . . . gives it a very bittersweet kind of quality": Danson, 9.

"Was a very brilliant up-tempo player . . . the Hamlet of the horn.": Albert Goldman, *GC.*

"I think that his tendency to double . . . He really was a master of that": Gerry Niewood, *GC.*

"Like a lot of guys do . . . you need to go to Notes Anonymous": Sidran interview.

"Some people say . . . He could do both": Don Friedman, *GC.*

"Are of the same party as those . . . a mystic as 'too full of God' ": Strickland, 102.

"The pieces sound . . . goes back to Duke with Blanton": Lewis Porter, email to the author, 2021.

"In the three years . . . at any period in my life": Anon., *Jazz Magazine.*

"If Pepper would have bought a bass clarinet . . . plus jingles and residuals": Mel Lewis, *GC.*

"That cat had one of the keenest and quickest wits": Ray Drummond, *GC.*

"He always had me in stitches . . . as a great American humorist": Frank Foster, *GC.*

"Could see the funny things, the ironic things": Bob Wilber, *GC.*

"If you copy from one person . . . it's research": Jerry Dodgion, *GC.*

"Toots was playing harmonica . . . even had to stop playing for a moment": White, 113.

"Pepper's right in the middle . . . It was very funny": John Mosca, *GC.*

"Most of the stage had been cleared . . . he had to stop playing": Chodan, C-1.

"He was lots of fun . . . get into any kind of mischief": Bess Bonnier, *GC.*

"He could get a little short . . . make comments he didn't care for it": Bob Pierson, *GC.*

"One musical discussion I had . . . no question about it": Per Husby, *GC.*

"He was always buried in a book of some kind": Frank Foster, *GC.*

"I hope you're a reader . . . funny besides": Pepper Adams letter written to Ron Ley, 19 November 1963, *WPU.*

"No matter where he went . . . he'd remember where they were from": John Marabuto, *GC.*

"He would talk to you . . . know what to say to him": Per Husby, email to Gary Carner, 2018.

"We could have periods of silence . . . gaps if somebody wasn't speaking": Cindy Ley, *GC.*

"We were from the radio generation . . . You listen": Ron Ley, *GC.*

"Thought that that was going to be the record that was going to put everybody over": Gary Giddins, *GC.*

"Mingus came to the date . . . couldn't believe that record dates were like that": Danson, 5.

"I remember walking up those steps . . . up these steps all the time": David Schiff, *GC.*

"Bachelor, alcoholic vibe": Ron Marabuto, *GC.*

"He loved talking to writers . . . the White Horse Tavern, the Corner Bistro": Mike Jordan, *GC.*

"I don't think anybody appreciates loneliness more than Pepper": Mark Feldman, *GC.*

"He was a very caring person": Rusch, (Per Husby), *Cadence,* 27.

"Had a crisis in his marriage . . . Sture and his wife not splitting up": Per Husby narration, *WPU.*

"He just couldn't let go . . . cared about these people": Rusch, (Per Husby), *Cadence,* 27.

"I just remember Pepper . . . the caring that he had in him": Jon Faddis, *GC.*

"The first American soloist . . . extremely friendly way of handling people": Per Husby, *GC.*

"It didn't feel like you were being pressured . . . felt like he respected you": Earl Sauls, *GC.*

"You can mimic anyone . . . your own sound and your own style": David Schiff, *GC.*

"Can you come to New York . . . you could be a great player": David Schiff, *GC.*

"I went up to his place and for hours and hours we'd play": David Schiff, *GC.*

"No, not really. I just want to play": David Schiff, *GC.*

"You can't play unless you learn . . . to voice for different instruments": David Schiff, *GC.*

"You got to learn your pentatonic scales . . . and all your majors": David Schiff, *GC.*

"The patterns in here are great . . . Pepper opened up my eyes and ears": David Schiff, *GC.*

"We spoke about how . . . copying other people": David Schiff email to Gary Carner, 2019.

"Agreed with my father . . . done and was doing": David Schiff email to Gary Carner, 2019.

"I practice telling a story . . . hear his voice telling me that": David Schiff, *GC.*

10. Lovers of Their Time

"I was very surprised . . . expect a proposal": Ruth Price, *GC.*

"He certainly was clear . . . the sweetest and most formal letter": Ruth Price, *GC.*

"He had a definite note of affection . . . physical warmth or hugging": Albert Goldman, *GC.*

"We both read all the German modernists": Ruth Price, *GC.*

"She was a very unusual, unusual girl . . . became involved with drugs": Arlene Smith, *GC.*

"As far as sex was concerned . . . like playing scales": Stan Patrick, *GC.*

"These people did everything for her . . . mean, nasty, and ugly": Bobbie Curtis Cranshaw, *GC.*

"She just loved the music, and I think she loved the life": Arlene Smith, *GC.*

"She knew everybody": Stan Patrick, *GC.*

"It was the only place . . . and get high again": Fran Kleinberg letter to Pepper Adams, *WPU.*

"If I ever needed anyone . . . not too good, is it": Fran Kleinberg letter to Pepper Adams, *WPU.*

"One very big advantage . . . be returned here": Fran Kleinberg letter to Pepper Adams, *WPU.*

"I don't feel that anyone . . . to understand me": Fran Kleinberg letter to Pepper Adams, *WPU.*

"This time, Pepper, I really hit . . . Love, Fran": Fran Kleinberg letter to Pepper Adams, *WPU.*

"Thanks so much for your letter . . . Love, Fran": Fran Kleinberg letter to Pepper Adams, *WPU.*

"Now that I have a record . . . even a little": Fran Kleinberg letter to Pepper Adams, *WPU.*

"I found letters . . . happy to destroy them": Claudette Adams letter to Gary Carner, *WPU.*

"She was my ex-girlfriend . . . They were in love": Curtis Fuller, *GC.*
"I had a small, little place . . . Elvin was always over there": Oliver Shearer, *GC.*
"Guys who knew him . . . kind of seemed outstanding": Jay Cameron, *GC.*
"Elvin was a little . . . sufficiently sexual": Lois Shearer, *GC.*
"You are rather nice . . . not speak so much": Rose Cobb letter to Pepper Adams, *WPU.*
"Tonight there is no hand . . . my heart that you do": Rose Cobb letter to Pepper Adams, *WPU.*
"Did I disturb you . . . to be close to you": Rose Cobb letter to Pepper Adams, *WPU.*
"It was an old, dilapidated warehouse": Emilio Cruz, *GC.*
"The front door was like the old refrigerator . . . the streetlight outside": Fred Norsworthy, *GC.*
"We all lost clothes . . . my radio, watch": Rose Cobb letter to Pepper Adams, *WPU.*
"God, I sure am lonely . . . have you come home": Rose Cobb letter to Pepper Adams, *WPU.*
"I love you very, very much . . . darling Pepper": Rose Cobb letter to Pepper Adams, *WPU.*
"Pepper, I can't come . . . Rose": Rose Cobb letter to Pepper Adams, *WPU.*
"Dear Pepper, What can I say now . . . Love, Rose": Rose Cobb letter to Pepper Adams, *WPU.*
"I think he tried it . . . ever got into it like his friends did": Mel Lewis, *GC.*
"The young lady followed me . . . broke her leg": Oliver Shearer, *GC.*
"You're asking me to choose between you and my music": Anon., *GC.*
"Music is my mistress, and she plays second fiddle to no one": Ellington, p. 447.
"Got what she wanted . . . when she wanted to be": Stan Patrick, *GC.*
"I think that was really a big issue . . . wasn't an attractive guy": Ron Marabuto, *GC.*
"You think they grow this way": Pepper Adams to Gary Carner, 1985.
"He wasn't a guy who was striking . . . as well as their ear": Albert Goldman, *GC.*
"If people are coming . . . who get a lot of attention": Don Friedman, *GC.*
"The external Pepper, the Pepper that Pepper presented to the world, was 'cool,' ": Ron Ley letter, *WPU.*
"To be cool . . . an artistic frame of restraint": Dinerstein, 39.
"He never was a ladies' man . . . because he wasn't attentive": Hugh Lawson, *GC.*
"I could see any woman . . . talk to really being interested": Rose Christianson, *GC.*

11. Urban Dreams

"Prior to the appearance . . . thought him to be black": Berendt, 213.
"Still followed in the [Hugues] Panassié idea . . . because he was white": Bob Cornfoot, *GC.*
"When Pepper first came to New York . . . that hard-driving kind of style": Horace Silver, *GC.*

"I learned how to play jazz . . . that's how to learn it": Eddie Locke, *GC*.
"I don't care, Locke. That's the truth": Eddie Locke, *GC*.
"Maybe if he had gone on out . . . he might have made it": Barry Harris, *GC*.
"The only thing that stopped . . . chopped his own head off": Arthur Taylor, *GC*.
"Pepper only associated . . . He became a part of it": Curtis Fuller, *GC*.
"Jazz man . . . lived in those joints with us": Eddie Locke, *GC*.
"A victim of reverse racial discrimination . . . entered into the picture": George Coleman, *GC*.
"Sometimes the wrong person becomes a victim . . . in philosophical terms": Lois Shearer, *GC*.
"He rose above all the muck . . . everybody liked him": Andy McCloud, *GC*.
"They could rehearse . . . whether Oliver was there or not": Lois Shearer, *GC*.
"I made friends with Bobby . . . jazz was fairly through with it": Lois Shearer, *GC*.
"Whitey's taking the music away . . . and they can't play": Lois Shearer, *GC*.
"Once you were OK . . . to me to be uncomfortable": Lois Shearer, *GC*.
"Bobby was very, very close to Pepper": Oliver Shearer, *GC*.
"Among all of us at that time . . . conversations among ourselves were happy": Lois Shearer, *GC*.
"Especially when Bobby was around. Bobby had all the records": Oliver Shearer, *GC*.
"Was trying to help Bobby out, keep straight": Joe Baptista, *GC*.
"He used to go by . . . somewhere else and get in trouble": Joe Baptista, *GC*.
"If you are a drug addict . . . go out on the street and find it": Gary Bartz, You-Tube interview.
"The Charlie Parker thing . . . more with personalities than professions": Mathews, 5–7.
"It had to be the pressures that caused us . . . was the most horrible thing": Richards, 7.
"I think the wear and tear . . . people that I was hanging out with": Richards, 7.
"I never felt that you had to do drugs . . . you didn't get the call": Mathews, 5–7.
"What does it do for you . . . which it wasn't": Michael Ullman, email to listserv, 2019.
"It slows everything down . . . get to that point, without that": Gary Bartz, You-Tube interview.
"Jazz was the music of New York . . . artistic New York": *The Color of Race*, 38.
"The capital of Western culture . . . untouched by the ravages of World War II": Dinerstein, 32.
"The old American colonial . . . the American art form *par excellence*": Rosenthal, 74.
"They felt that what we were doing was serious music": *Vibrations*, 262–64.
"When you opened the door . . . flood of color onto the street": Dinerstein, 354.
"The Beats . . . almost a passport into Beat society": *The Fifties*, 300–01.
"Most of the poets are slumming . . . learn anything about jazz": Gennari, 179.

"How dare they use jazz as a background . . . what the music was about": Lois
Shearer, *GC*.

"They used jazz as a background to make themselves look hip": Lois Shearer, *GC*.

"Consequently, most jazz musicians never got close to these people nor felt any
kinship with them": Lois Shearer, *GC*.

"I told him, 'Listen, on my solo, you just play in your key and I'll get it' ": Pepper
Adams, *GC*.

"Pepper could do anything": Mel Lewis, *GC*.

"At gigs . . . Pepper used to always do that to him": Oliver Shearer, *GC*.

"Used to wear off-the-wall shit . . . he dressed like a farmer": Mike Jordan, *GC*.

"But I already have a suit": Oliver Shearer, *GC*.

"Never maligned anybody unless it was in a humorous way": Anon., Timmons
Wikipedia article.

"Was just a real sweetheart . . . a sweetheart of a man": Anon., *Ibid*.

"If you want to say that anybody . . . also hooked up in economics": Mathews, 11.

"I arrived in Japan . . . I'd seen great improvement": Pepper Adams, *GC*.

"I love Pepper . . . and I loved him": Lois Shearer, *GC*.

"Blue Note seemed to want . . . arrangements and change everything": Pepper
Adams, as told to Marc Vasey, *WPU*.

"They were very interested . . . something that was saleable": Pepper Adams, as
told to Marc Vasey, *WPU*.

"Several times there were road trips so long . . . didn't cover the travel expenses":
Arnold Jay Smith, 115.

"Phew! Boy! The way they orchestrated . . . was just intense": Gerry Niewood, *GC*.

"When Pepper made those records . . . the middle of the hard-bop thing": Gary
Giddins, *GC*.

"Those records are *brilliant* . . . just weren't available": Gary Giddins, *GC*.

"All the musicians wanted to get next to him . . . get the right feel": Isherwood,
16–17.

"When we were rehearsing . . . concerts were cancelled": Pepper Adams, interviewed
by Ben Sidran.

"The jazz police . . . asking a walrus to sing": Segell, 119–20.

"The top performers . . . numbers of also-rans": Lind, 7007015 (national edition).

"I was officially homeless . . . a hand-to-mouth existence": Danson, 8.

"I think it was partially . . . at least a reasonably good job done": Pepper Adams, *GC*.

"As luck would have it . . . not really an ideal situation": Pepper Adams, *GC*.

"The work situation was very slow . . . was exceptionally grim": Pepper Adams, *GC*.

"Was a typical Mingus fiasco": Rusch, (Jerome Richardson), 11.

"It was total chaos, the whole thing": Young, 14.

"I actually did some of the writing": Pepper Adams, *GC*.

"I was paid for it . . . good things were not on the record": Pepper Adams, *GC*.

"Would write parts . . . a tune that he was taking credit for": Mike Jordan, *GC*.

"The realization of the American dream . . . dissolving the group into anarchy": Santoro, 917.

"Not knowing what the hell . . . an excuse for not being prepared": Pepper Adams, *GC*.

"A lot of people would come just to see": Bryant, 124.

"Was an uncomfortable person . . . wouldn't mind indulging in it": Pepper Adams, *GC*.

"Mostly a put-on . . . That's a different Mingus": Balliett, 47.

"It was very compatible . . . groovy, very relaxed": Pepper Adams interviewed by Albert Goldman, 1971.

"Pepper would disappear . . . he would tell him": Oliver Shearer, *GC*.

"They had a single, tiny, one-bedroom apartment . . . couches during the day": Lois Shearer, *GC*.

"I wouldn't say a 45-degree angle . . . you were on a ship": Don Buday, *GC*.

"Don't nobody want to eat? They'll be more for us": Oliver Shearer, *GC*.

"They'd have a couple of tastes . . . that they were reading at the same time": Ray Mosca, *GC*.

"He would put up little cartoons . . . he was very quiet": Lois Shearer, *GC*.

"Where Elvin went, everyone wanted to go": Oliver Shearer, *GC*.

"One of the most remarkable people . . . with regard to all these things": Jay Cameron, *GC*.

"Pepper was furious . . . about Elvin was so unusual": Lois Shearer, *GC*.

"For six months . . . you're not supposed to travel at all": Pepper Adams, as told to Marc Vasey, *WPU*.

"In those days the union was very strict on that": Richards, 8.

"As ponderous as a Sherman tank": Gioia, 145.

"There was a good deal of coldness . . . I think I'd do it again": Pepper Adams, *GC*.

"I figured if I could read Poulenc's . . . able to read Stan Kenton's book": Danson, 6.

"Lennie never said much of anything . . . what a terrific player": Rusch, (Billy Root), 14.

"Was a genuine bebopper . . . anybody play like that on baritone": Mel Lewis, *GC*.

"He had to put this red crap . . . could smell it out in the hall": Mel Lewis, *GC*.

"He was always smoking pot . . . never used a filtered cigarette": Mel Lewis, *GC*.

"Treated his musicians like gentlemen, and he knew how to draw the best out of you": Rusch, (Mel Lewis, II), 10.

"We totally disagreed on politics . . . just cheerfully disagree on everything": Pepper Adams, *GC*.

"The only thing that we had in the house was a couch and beds": Lee Katzman, *GC*.

"Pepper was a new voice . . . impressed with his playing": Mel Lewis, *GC*.

"All the guys used to come up there": Clora Bryant, *GC*.

"There'd be all these Mexicans . . . My God": Pepper Adams, *GC*.

"Chet, at that time . . . Pepper was the perfect counterpart to Chet": Don Friedman, *GC.*

"Was leaky, unheated, dimly lit . . . petrified smoke of a million cigarettes": Gary Kamiya.

"Pepper took a break . . . Without asking him or anything": John Marabuto, *GC.*

"*That* you don't do. That's a no-no": Hank Jones, *GC.*

"I've always tried in my albums . . . had some intrinsic value": Pepper Adams, *GC.*

"It was just everybody going . . . does not add up that well": Pepper Adams, *GC.*

"Pepper created a sensation in New York because he outplayed Mulligan": Percy Heath, *GC.*

"Musicians appreciated Pepper . . . to make it something of his own": David Amram, *GC.*

"I was amazed how much he had gotten . . . the way he developed": Bob Wilber, *GC.*

"The place was desolate . . . no toilet, no electricity, no nothing": Martin, 33.

"I think he liked my enthusiasm . . . always a tremendously strong player": David Amram, *GC.*

"Served as a catalyst for some of the best jazz of the middle fifties": *Vibrations*, 228–29.

"It was invitation-only, very high quality": Pepper Adams, as told to Ted O'Reilly, *WPU.*

"Long, fluid, driving melodic lines": O'Brien, 12.

"Pepper's playing had a particularly strong influence on me": *Ibid.*, 12.

"I think that's where Monk . . . really loved his playing": David Amram, *GC.*

"Probably the single most significant shift": Ted Gioia, YouTube.

"Revolutionized the radio and recording . . . disk-cutting lathes": Anon., (Wikipedia).

"It was the first nationwide distribution . . . had some artistic input on": Pepper Adams, *GC.*

"It's a rough city . . . the city will eat you alive": David Schiff, *GC.*

12. Ad Astra

"Hawkins admired Pepper . . . he didn't talk about many guys": Eddie Locke, *GC.*

"Man, that guy's phenomenal, isn't he": David Amram, *GC.*

"His playing was unbelievable . . . a marvelous musician": Clark Terry, *GC.*

"He is one of my heroes . . . the creative work that they've done": Bill Perkins, *GC.*

"Nobody is equal . . . monolithic in his playing": Rusch, (Bill Perkins), 1995.

"Everyone knew he was a superstar . . . don't even think of anybody else": Bob Cranshaw, *GC.*

"Any baritone player that's around . . . He was the best we had": Phil Woods, *GC.*

"He was the greatest who ever played the baritone saxophone": Curtis Fuller, *GC.*

"Should be considered . . . no question about it": Don Friedman, *GC.*

"Was an excellent jazz soloist . . . because they're consistent": Horace Silver, *GC.*

"Every time he played . . . was *totally* original": Bill Watrous, *GC.*

"He was a virtuoso . . . and he had great taste": Junior Cook, *GC.*

"There's very few stylists . . . He's one of them": Ron Marabuto, *GC.*

"A true master . . . musicians of his generation": Bennie Maupin email to Gary Carner, 2020.

"Inspired me . . . Pepper was the inspiration for that": Gary Smulyan, *GC.*

"A more truly brilliant person . . . my impression of Pepper": Holladay, 33–34.

"I was in awe of him . . . an intelligent, informed conversation about any of it": Leitch, 107.

"I think it takes a tremendous mind . . . was considered a genius": Mel Lewis, *GC.*

"With the way he played . . . as close to a genius as you can find on earth": Hank Jones, *GC.*

"Pepper stands very tall . . . he was thinking and playing creatively": Hank Jones, *GC.*

"Outliers are those who have been given . . . presence of mind to seize them": Gladwell, 267.

"How long does it take to be good . . . can ever achieve elite status": Malcolm Gladwell lecture.

"No one . . . ever makes it alone": Gladwell, 115.

"Success . . . some deserved, some not, some earned, some just plain lucky": *Ibid.*, 285.

"If you hang around long enough, they get around to you": Brozan, 6.

"If you survive for a long time . . . it would have come more and more to him": Ira Gitler, *GC.*

"A lot of people don't know . . . a very high level throughout his career": Tony Inzalaco, *GC.*

"Were not easy to find": Gary Giddins, *GC.*

"That if he played well . . . would discover him and reward him accordingly": Ron Ley, *GC.*

"The average person . . . sounds like you're right there": Tom Everett, *GC.*

"For ordinary success in music . . . and its mysterious workings": Henahan.

"The perception of greatness in jazz . . . a bit of self-promotion": Watrous, 28.

"You can't be a wallflower . . . that's the way he did it": Albert Goldman, *GC.*

"I think that might be . . . what a genius this guy was": Don Friedman, *GC.*

"He reinvented the sound of the baritone . . . could always tell it was him": Gerry Niewood, *GC.*

"One of the handful . . . a true master of the music": Kirk MacDonald, *GC.*

"The only thing that's sad . . . He knew the world he was in": Albert Goldman, *GC.*

"The aspiration of Kansas . . . realization of the impossible": Anon., "James John Ingalls."

"Someone like Gerry Mulligan . . . never conformed to its weaknesses": Bill Perkins, *GC.*

Selected Bibliography

BOOKS

Bjorn, Lars, and Jim Gallert. *Before Motown: A History of Jazz in Detroit: 1920–1960.* Ann Arbor: University of Michigan, 2001.

Bryant, Clora, William Green, Steve Isooadi, and Marl Young. *Central Avenue Sounds: Jazz in Los Angeles.* Berkeley CA: University of California, 1998.

Davis, Miles, and Quincy Troupe. *Miles: The Autobiography.* New York: Simon & Schuster, 1989.

Dinerstein, Joel. *The Origins of Cool in Postwar America.* Chicago: University of Chicago Press, 2017.

Edel, Leon. *Writing Lives: Principia Biographica.* New York: Norton, 1984.

Gennari, John. *Blowin' Hot and Cool: Jazz and Its Critics.* Chicago: University of Chicago Press, 2006.

Gladwell, Malcolm. *Outliers: The Story of Success.* New York: Little, Brown, 2008.

Gioia, Ted. *West Coast Jazz: Modern Jazz in California, 1945–1960.* New York: Oxford University Press, 1992.

Halberstam, David. *The Fifties.* New York: Random House, 1993.

Holladay, Marvin. *Life, On the Fence.* Oxford UK: George Ronald, 2000.

Homzy, Andrew. *Mingus: More Than a Fakebook.* New York: Jazz Workshop, 1991.

Leitch, Peter. *Off the Books: A Jazz Life.* Montreal: Vehicule, 2013.

Lichtenstein, Nelson. *The Most Dangerous Man in Detroit: Walter Reuther and the Fate of American Labor.* New York: Basic, 1995.

Liebler, M. L. *Heaven Was Detroit: From Jazz to Hip-Hop and Beyond.* Detroit: Wayne State University Press, 2016.

Maraniss, David. *Once in a Great City: A Detroit Story.* New York: Simon & Schuster, 2015.

Martelle, Scott. *Detroit: A Biography.* Chicago: Chicago Review, 2012.

McKelvey, Blake. *Rochester on the Genesee: The Growth of a City.* 2nd ed. Syracuse: Syracuse University Press, 1993.

———. *Rochester: An Emerging Metropolis 1925–1961.* Rochester NY: Christopher, 1961.

Mezzrow, Mezz, and Bernard Wolfe. *Really the Blues.* New York: Random House, 1946.

O'Brien, Hod. *Have Piano . . . Will Swing!* Charlottesville VA: HodStef Music, 2015.

Priestley, Brian. *Mingus: A Critical Biography.* New York: Quartet, 1982.

Roth, Philip. *Indignation.* Boston: Houghton Mifflin, 2008.

Segell, Michael. *The Devil's Horn: The Story of the Saxophone, from Noisy Novelty to King of Cool.* New York: Picador, 2005.

Slobin, Mark. *Motor City Music: A Detroiter Looks Back.* New York: Oxford, 2019.

Stryker, Mark. *Jazz from Detroit.* Ann Arbor: University of Michigan Press, 2019.

Sugrue, Thomas J. *The Origins of the Urban Crisis: Race and Inequality in Postwar Detroit.* Princeton: Princeton University Press, 1966.

Taylor, Arthur. *Notes and Tones.* New York: Putnam, 1982.

Ullman, Michael. *Jazz Lives.* Washington: New Republic, 1980.

Young, Al. *Bodies and Soul: Musical Memoirs.* Berkeley CA: Creative Arts, 1981.

ARTICLES

Anon. https://history.house.gov/HistoricalHighlight/Detail/36390.

———. "Nathaniel Q. Adams obituary." *Rome Sentinel,* June 22, 1929.

———. "Park Adams Obituary." *Utica Daily Press,* May 19, 1940.

———. https://www.geni.com/projects/Scots-Prisoners-and-their-Relocation-to-the-Colonies-1650-1654/3465.

———. Translation of French interview with Pepper Adams, *Jazz Magazine,* 1969.

Auslander, Philip. "Musical Personae," *The Drama Review,* Spring 2006.

Austin, Dan. "Fisher Building," *Historical Detroit.* https://historicdetroit.org/buildings/fisher-building.

Balliett, Whitney. "A Walk to the Park," *New Yorker,* May 18, 1968.

Betts, Kate. "Sex, Booze and Jazz in 1920s Paris," *New York Times,* October 14, 2016.

Bloom, Mike. "Pepper Adams," *Klacto,* January 1982.

Bjorn, Lars. "From Hastings Street to the Blue Bird: The Blues and Jazz Tradition in Detroit," *Michigan Quarterly,* Spring 1986.

Carner, Gary. "Pepper Adams's 'Rue Serpente,'" *Jazzforchung,* vol. 22, 1990.

Case, Brian. "Travels with a Baritone," *Melody Maker,* September 15, 1979.

Chodan, Lucinda. "Pepper Adams: Saxophone Great Playing for His Life," *Gazette,* April 19, 1986.

Cutler, Howard. "Sheila Jordan," *Cadence,* November 1987.

Danson, Peter. "Pepper Adams: An Interview," *Coda,* August 1983.

Fisher, Larry. "An Interview with Benny Golson," *The Note,* Winter/Spring 2020.

Frishberg, Dave. "Half Note Memories," *The Note,* January 1990.

———. "Memories of Al and Zoot at the Half Note," *The Note,* Fall 2005.

Haien, Jeannette. "The Wondrous World of Connemara," *New York Times,* July 15, 1990.

Heckman, Don. "String Theory," *JazzTimes,* July 1, 2007.

Hollis, Larry. "Frank Foster Interview," *Cadence,* April 1989.

Isherwood, Martin. "Charlie Rouse," *Cadence,* May 1988.

Iverson, Ethan. "Stanley Crouch, Towering Jazz Critic, Dead at 74," NPR.org, September 16, 2020, https://www.npr.org/2020/09/16/913619163/stanley-crouch-towering-jazz-critic-dead-at-74.

Jeske, Lee. "Pepper Adams," *Down Beat,* August 1982.

Johnston, David Cay. "Rochester, still a Cradle of Invention," *New York Times,* August 3, 2001.

Jones, Jack. "Thad Jones, Arranger for Basie, Dies," *Los Angeles Times*, August 21, 1986.

Kamiya, Gary. "The Blackhawk: San Francisco's Greatest Jazz Club," *San Francisco Chronicle*, April 29, 2022, https://www.sfchronicle.com/vault/portalsofthepast/article/The-Blackhawk-San-Francisco-s-greatest-jazz-17135567.php.

Lawrence, Joseph. "The Music Is: The Deep Roots of Detroit R&B," ed. Matt Groening and Paul Bresnick, DaCapo Best Music Writing 2003. New York: DaCapo, 2003.

Lesnik, Richard. "Charles McPherson," *Cadence*, February 1981.

Lewis, Alwyn, and Laurie Lewis. "Rufus Reid Interview," *Cadence*, November 1996.

Mailer, Norman. "The White Negro," *Dissent Magazine*, 1957.

Mastropolo, Frank. "Definitely a New York Hang: Jazz Musicians Remember the Five Spot Café," January 3, 2014. https://medium.com/the-riff/definitely-a-new-york-hang-jazz-musicians-remember-the-five-spot-caf%C3%A9-5d3f3d1e3e9d.

Matthews, Paul B. "Ronnie Mathews Interview," *Cadence*, May 1995.

Offstein, Alan. "Milt Buckner Interview," *Coda*, March/April 1977.

Paster, Dorian. "Letter to the editor," *The Nation*, March 25, 1991.

Piazza, Tom. "Jazz Piano's Heavyweight Champ," *New York Times*, July 28, 1996.

Rattman, Jay. "Jerry Dodgion Interview," *The Note*, Spring/Summer 2015.

Rhoden, Bill. "Pepper Adams Takes Sax to Bandstand Tonight," *Baltimore Sun*, March 1, 1979.

Ricker, Ramon. "Pepper Adams, Baritone Saxophonist," *Saxophone Symposium*, Summer 1978.

Ronzello, Robert. "Sittin' In with Pepper Adams," *Saxophone Journal*, Spring 1982.

Rusch, Bob. "Snooky Young Interview," *Cadence*, July 1986.

Russonello, Giovanni. "Curtis Fuller, a Powerful Voice on Jazz Trombone, Dies at 88," *New York Times*, May 14, 2021.

Santoro, Gene. "Mingus Ah Hum," *The Nation*, June 28, 1993.

Sheinen, Richard. "The Right Place at the Right Time: The Jazz Education of Charles McPherson," *Santa Fe New Mexican*, July 20, 2018.

Smith, Arnold Jay. "The Essence of Spice," *Down Beat*, November 3, 1977.

Smith, Arnold Jay. "Solo: Pepper Adams," *Jazz Magazine*, Spring 1980.

Strickland, Edward. "What Coltrane Wanted," *The Atlantic*, December 1987.

Stryker, Mark. "Chronology: Freddie Redd Steps Out of the Shadows." *JazzTimes*, June 10, 2021.

Tynan, John. "Doctor Pepper: Valuable Detroit Internship Helped Adams Find Himself," *Down Beat*, November 14, 1957.

Überall, Bertrand. "Take Five! Duke Pearson and Blue Note Records," November 20, 2021. https://americanart.si.edu/blog/take-five-duke-pearson-and-blue-note-records.

Voce, Steve. "Phil Woods Speaks to Steve Voce in 1996," *The Note*, Spring/Summer 2016.

Wikipedia: "Ampex." https://en.wikipedia.org/wiki/Ampex.

———. "Bobby Timmons." https://en.wikipedia.org/wiki/Bobby_Timmons.

———. "Eastman School of Music." https://en.wikipedia.org/wiki/Eastman_School_of_Music.

———. "Silver Stadium." https://en.wikipedia.org/wiki/Silver_Stadium.

Whalen, John M. "Yusef Lateef Interview," *Cadence*, October 1982.

Whitall, Susan. "Barry Harris Plays Up City Before Dirty Dog Jazz Cafe Performance," *Detroit News*, November 26, 2013.

LINER NOTES

Baillie, Mike. *Wardell Gray—Live at the Haig*. Fresh Sounds FSR–CD–157.

Gardner, Mark. *Dedication!* Prestige P–7729.

Porter, Bob. *The Big Sound*. Prestige P–24098.

INTERVIEWS

Bartz, Gary. "Gary Bartz Talks about Drug Use among Jazz Greats." https://www.youtube.com/watch?v=8KL1pbN9Gj0.

Chodan, Lucinda. Interview with Pepper Adams. Radio show aired posthumously in Montreal, 1987.

Clayton, Peter. Interview with Pepper Adams. BBC Radio, February 17, 1985.

Goldman, Albert. Interview with Pepper Adams, ca. 1969.

Heron, W. Kim. Interview with Pepper Adams, 1982.

Moyle, Will. Interview with Pepper Adams, 1978.

O'Reilly, Ted. Interview with Pepper Adams, CJRT Radio.

———. Interview with Duke Pearson, CJRT Radio.

Rowe, Mark. Interview with Nick Brignola, 1997.

Sidran, Ben. *Talking Jazz: An Oral History*. Unlimited Media, 2006. https://www.youtube.com/watch?v=T3HpWUJOSGs&t=312s.

Tucich, Rudy. Interview with Al Martin. WDET, April 28–29, 1990.

———. Interview with Billy Mitchell. WDET, April 28–29, 1990.

Vasey, Marc. Interview with Pepper Adams, November 1985.

MEMOIRS, SPEECHES, CORRESPONDENCE, TAPED REMEMBRANCES

Adams, Pepper. Journal, 1953.

———. Speech to the audience, June 20, 1976.

———. Speech to the audience, March 27, 1978.

Albert, John. Letter to Gary Carner, 1988.

Foster, Frank. Letter to Pepper Adams, December 11, 1952.

———. Speech about Thad Jones, September 2, 1986.

Fuller, Curtis. Speech about Pepper Adams, September 24, 2012.

Gates, Everett. Letter to Gary Carner, 1988.

Gioia, Ted. "How Important Really Is Miles Davis's 'Kind of Blue'?" https://www. youtube.com/watch?v=jPnkmuPgylg.

Gladwell, Malcolm. "Outliers: Why Some People Succeed and Some Don't." Lecture at Microsoft, 2009.

Ley, Ronald. Letter to Gary Carner, March 18, 1990.

Windahl, Gunnar. Taped remembrance about Pepper Adams, 1988.

FILMS, TV

Reuther, Sasha, dir. *Brothers on the Line.* 2012.

Suggested Recordings

These sessions showcase Adams as a soloist. See *Pepper Adams' Joy Road* for personnel and additional information (https://www.pepperadams.com/JoyRoad/index. html). Although it has been attributed to Duke Pearson or, more recently, Freddie Hubbard, trombonist Willie Wilson was the leader on *Dedication.* I also recommend *The Complete Solid State Recordings of the Thad Jones/Mel Lewis Orchestra* (Mosaic 151), though Adams solos on only a few tunes.

Adams, Pepper. *Encounter,* Original Jazz Classics OJCCD–892–2.

———. *Ephemera,* never released on CD. See YouTube or iTunes.

———. *The Master,* Muse-Impulse MCD–5213.

———. *Out of This World,* because its original tracks have been deplorably mangled on numerous bootlegs and CDs, consult the LP: Warwick W–2041.

———. *Plays the Music of Charlie Mingus,* Fresh Sound FSR–CD–604.

———. *Reflectory,* Muse CDMR–5182.

Byrd, Donald. *The Complete Blue Note Donald Byrd/Pepper Adams Studio Recordings,* Mosaic 194 and 195.

———. *At the Half Note Café,* Blue Note CDP–7–46539–2 and CDP–7–46540–2.

Fuller, Curtis. *Four on the Outside,* Timeless/Bellaphon SJP–124.

Garland, Red. *Red's Good Groove,* Jazzland OJCCD–1064–2.

Jones, Thad, and Pepper Adams. *Mean What You Say,* Original Jazz Classics OJCCD–464–2.

Jones, Thad, and Mel Lewis. *Thad Jones/Mel Lewis in Tokyo,* Columbia-Nippon COCY–80752.

Wilson, Willie. *Dedication,* Black Lion BLCD–760122.

Index

Adams, Pepper *(continued)*
of, 73, 74, 77, 80, 81, 82, 84; cigarette, smoking of, 16, 28, 34, 42, 45, 74, 76, 92, 93, 95–96, 132, 136, 176, 178; cliché, distaste of, 5; clothes of, 163; compose, composer, compositional work of, 91, 99, 128, 195; confidence of, 10, 131; continuity, in solos of, 65–66; contradictions of, 2–3; cool, trait of, 95, 152–53; *The Cool Sound of Pepper Adams* by, 179; craft, craftsmanship of, 66, 139, 186; *Critics' Choice* by, 179; debt to, 186; dedication of, 52; depressed, depression of, 33, 92; Detroit, relocation of, 12; diminished scale of, 98; Dodge, work of, 14; double-time runs of, 127–28; Ellington, Duke, influence on, 3, 32, 97, 129; *Encounter* by, 83, 134–35; enigma, enigmatic, trait of, 4, 93; *Ephemera* by, 126; erudition of, 103; Europe, contacts of, 91; Europe, gigs, travel, visit, trip, tour of, 62, 72, 77, 84, 90, 93, 101, 118, 124; exoticism of, 153; expertise of, 180; financial situation of, 97, 129, 170, 171; flexibility of, 162; Fort Leonard Wood; attendance of, 22, 39–44; frustration, felt by, 32, 90, 94–95; Fuller, Curtis, tutelage by, 55, 67–68, 139; fungal infection of, 176; genius of, 2, 187–88; glamor of, 127; Grammy, awards of, 90, 99, 142; Gray, Wardell, influence on, 15, 20, 58, 61, 111; great, greatest, greatness of, 12, 13, 21, 61, 65, 125, 130, 132, 138, 139, 165, 176, 185, 186, 188, 190, 191–92; Grinnell's, job of, 14–15; grit of, 182; hack work of, 91, 117, 132; hand-to-mouth existence of, 170; harmonic approach of, 180; Hawkins, Coleman, fondness of, 31; humor of, 43, 90, 92, 103, 132–33; ideas, abundant musical of, 128; impediments of, 157; individuality of, 139; influence of, 65, 67, 170, 182; instruction, approach of, 139; intellect, intellectual, intelligence of, 2, 26, 28, 65, 66, 94, 99, 185, 187, 188; intensity of, 21, 83, 181; intervals of, 139; intimacy, trait of, 33, 35, 65, 93–94, 149, 150; interview with, 2, 3, 13, 103, 129, 139, 155–56; isolation of, 33–34, 85; jealous of, 156, 176; Jones, Elvin and, 172–73; Jones, Thad, influence on, 43, 50, 67, 89, 90, 103–4, 105, 120, 129; journal of, 43; *Julian* by, 128; Lawton, mouthpiece of, 101; lead sheets of, 142; legacy of, xiii, 142, 195; letter by, 77, 80–81; 83–84, 134, 137, 141, 142, 144, 145; lifespan of, 36; *Live at Fat Tuesday's* by, 90; loner, loneliness of, 35, 136, 194; low notes, articulation of, 191–92; marginalization of, 156; marriage of, 89; marriage, dissolution of, 78, 92–96; marriage proposal of, 141–42; marijuana, used by, 45, 176, 177, 181; *The Master* by, 90, 99; maternal, lineage of, 25–26; *Mean What You Say* by, 106, 122, 136; memorial service of, 1, 145; mien of, 20–21; misimpression of, 62; *Modern Jazz Survey: Baritones and French Horns* by, 178; money of, 15, 28, 30, 40, 62, 76, 81, 82, 93, 129, 148, 165, 172, 177, 189, 194; mother-son relationship of, 65; *Motor City Scene* by, 170; move,

to New York of, 68; musicianship of, 163, 179–80; new voice of, 43, 177; nickname of, 29, 99; oeuvre of, 5, 91; originality, prized by, 3; ostracization of, 18, 157; Parker, Charlie, influence on, 10–11, 42, 60, 101, 156, 185; paternal figure, Thad Jones upon, 103; paternal lineage of, 23–24, 27; patterns of, 138, 139; *Pepper Adams Plays the Compositions of Charlie Mingus* by, 104, 136; phrase, phrases of, 10, 35, 38, 58, 65–66, 90, 102, 103, 111, 156, 195; pleurisy of, 84; pneumonia of, 82, 84; postcards of, 2, 134, 142; practice, regimen of, 10, 21, 33, 39, 42–43, 67, 138–39, 189; press of, 125; quiescence of, 134; quartet of, 128, 147; quintet of, 31, 103, 104, 105, 106, 107, 122, 136, 155, 162, 165, 167, 168, 177; *Reflectory* by, 90, 97, 99; relationship, relationships of, 3, 5, 43, 61, 65, 93, 94, 104, 114, 141, 142, 143, 146, 148, 150, 189; remoteness of, 65; reputation of, 83, 186, 195; resentment of, 96; reverence of, 116, 155; rhythm, concept of, 30, 38, 102, 111, 116, 186; self-absorption of, 136; self-taught musician, approach of, 13; Selmer, sax of, 20; sensation, in New York and Los Angeles of, 32; separation, marriage of, 93, 145; sex, attitude of, 146; sideman, status of, 3, 61, 132, 177, 189, 190; socialist, politics of, 14, 115, 176; soft-spoken, manner of, 3, 21, 62, 91, 153; sound, baritone of, 2–3, 10, 18, 20, 38, 43, 58, 65, 91, 101, 102, 139, 155, 181, 192, 193, 195; stature of, 101, 185; Stewart,

Rex, influence on, 29–31; studio dates, recordings of, 75, 83; success, lack thereof by, 5, 32, 189, 192; superstar, description of, 186; strike, participation of, 15; stubborn, trait of, 129–30, 133; studio, work of, 3, 31, 129, 131, 164, 167, 168, 177; stylist, style of, 3, 10, 11, 15, 32, 36, 37–38, 43, 98, 103, 111, 127, 135, 136, 137, 155, 166–67, 178, 183, 186, 192, 193, 195; swing of, 15, 43, 61, 128, 139, 193; talent of, 28, 32, 182, 189, 193, 194; teaching of, 137, 139; tenor saxophone of, 155; time of, 11, 15, 38, 58, 66, 102, 128, 186, 192, 195, mentioned, 116, 176; Timmons, Bobby, love of, 164; tone of, 13, 186, 188, mentioned, 3, 15, 58; transposing by, 170; traumas of, 34; *Twelfth and Pingree* by, 128; unattractive, trait of, 150–52; *Urban Dreams* by, 100; virtuoso, virtuosity of, 2, 4, 11, 29, 51, 128, 153, 172, 185, 186, 188, 194, 195; Wayne University, attendance of, 15–16, 21; Williams, Skippy, mentor of, 12–13, mentioned, 14, 29. *See also* Byrd– Adams, Thad Jones, Thad Jones– Pepper Adams Quintet
Adderley, Cannonball, 195
Aida, 132
Albert, John, 37
"Alice Blue Gown," 87
all-Detroit, band, group, rhythm section, 74, 134, 162; mentioned, 182
Al's Record Mart, 68
American Jazz Orchestra, 78
Ammons, Gene, 59
Ampex tape recorders, 182
Amram, David, 155, 161, 180, 181, 182, 185, 194; *Triple Concerto* by, 194

Dentz, John, 105, 106
Depression, Great Depression, 5, 12, 13, 21, 25, 27, 34
Detroit, 4, 5, 9, 10, 11, 12, 14, 15, 17, 18, 19–20, 21, 24, 25, 28, 31, 33, 34, 35, 37, 40, 43, 44, 46, 47, 49, 50, 51–57, 60, 62, 65, 66, 67, 68, 74, 87, 88, 118, 123, 125, 133, 134, 137, 146, 149, 150, 156, 162, 165, 173, 176, 180, 181, 182, 188, 189, 190; affluence of, 52; African-American homeowners in, 19; apprenticeship model of, 56; approach, non-judgmental of, 56; audience of, 56; auto, plants, industry of, 11, 19, 20, 49, 51, 52; Black Bottom in, 17, 19, 53; bond, immutable of, 57; boom, Art Deco architectural in, 9; brotherhood in, 56; Cass Tech in, 53, 54; culture, music culture of, 5, 12, 51, 54, 56; dance palaces in, 9; decentralization plans of, 19–20; Delray in, 66; economy of, 5, 19, 49; ecosystem, educational, of, 52–57; factory, jobs, work in, 15, 19–20; family income of, 49; freefall of, 25; freeway construction in, 19; generation, musicians from, 36, 51, 52, 55. 186, 194; geography of, 53; harmonic approach in, 180; informal, informality of, 52, 56; jam session, jam sessions in, 10, 14, 17, 40, 43, 57, 65, 181, 192; jazz players of, 54–55; jazz scene in, 51, 68; joints in, 54, 56, 125–26, 156; lending regulations in, 19; love and loyalty in, 57; meltdown of, 11; mentors, mentorship of, 15, 55, 58; Miller High School in, 53; money in, 68; Motown hit factory of, 51; munitions plants in,

11; musical training in, 46; music programs, public school in, 52, 53–54; Northeastern High School in, 53–54; Northern High School in, 54, 55; Paradise Valley in, 19; pianos in, 53; powerhouse of, 11; problems, racial in, 5; recession in, 47; recording industry in, 68; relations, race in, 67; scorn, by white players in, 19; workshop environment in, 56; white flight in, 19; wunderkinds from, 182; young players, milieu in, 12; zenith of, 19
"Dobbin,'" 71
"Doctor Deep," 101, 142
Dodgion, Jerry, 89, 105, 107, 108, 110, 113, 118; sight-reading of, 118
Dom, 121
Domicile, 128
Donahue, Sam, 54
Down Beat, 71, 170
Drummond, Ray, 132
Dublin Festival, 84
Duquette, Jack, 16, 46
Duvivier, George, 105
"Dylan's Delight," 74–75

Eastman, School of Music, 33; audience of, 33; faculty of, 28; theater at, 13. *See also* University of Rochester
Edel, Leon, 4
880 Club, 82
Elite, 33, 36–37
Ellington, Duke, 3, 12, 18, 20, 29, 30, 31, 32, 33, 60, 97, 129, 133, 150, 157, 169
"Elusive," 50
"Enchilada Baby," 99
Enja, 128
"Ephemera," 71; mentioned, 125–26
Ervin, Booker, 146

"Etude Diabolique," 97–98
Europe, move to, 10, 124; small-group jazz in, 125
Evans, Bill, 102
Everett, Tom, 191
The Explainers, 144

Faddis, Jon, 94, 105, 114, 115, 117, 118, 137; high-note chops of, 118
Farmer, Art, 123
Farrell, Joe, 107, 108, 114, 118
Farrow, Ernie, 53
Fat Tuesday's, 90, 99, 101
Feather, Leonard, 125
Feldman, Mark, 81, 85, 136
Ferguson, Maynard, 177–78; promised compensation of, 178
Fitzgerald, Ella, 2, 57
"5021," 179
Five Spot, 105, 124, 161, 162, 165, 170; demolition of, 171
Flanagan, Diana, 77, 78, 85–86
Flanagan, Tommy, 2, 50, 51, 52, 54, 57, 67, 68, 74, 77, 78, 79, 85, 134–35, 136, 179, 182
The Flashman Papers, 71
Ford, Jimmy, 178
Foster, Frank, 45, 51, 55, 74, 75, 79, 117, 132, 133; tritone substitutions of, 55
Friedman, Don, 74, 97, 128, 152, 179, 186, 193
Fuller, Curtis, 17, 51, 55, 66, 67–68, 139, 145, 156, 186; Bone and Bari of, 67; mentorship of, 67

Gardner, Earl, 117
Garner, Erroll, 157
Gates, Everett, 28–29, 32
Gates, Mrs. Everett, 31, 35
Gelmann, Edward, 73, 84, 85
Gennari, John, 33, 124

Getz, Stan, 141, 152, 192
Giddins, Gary, 78, 79, 136, 167, 168, 190
Gifford, Joie (cousin), 24
Gilbert, Phil, 176
Gillespie, Dizzy, 2, 9, 50, 80, 111, 159, 185
Gilmore, Steve, 110, 118
Ginsberg, Allen, 161
Gioia, Ted, 174
Gitler, Ira, 79, 190
Gladwell, Malcolm, 187, 188, 189, 190
Gleason, Ralph J., 162
Godot's, 125
Gogol, Nikolai, 134
Golden Getsusekai, 112
Goldman, Albert, 43, 127, 141, 152, 193, 194
Golson, Benny, 163
Goodman, Benny, 129, 143, 165
Goodwin, Doris Kearns, 5
Gordon, Dexter, 160
Gordon, Max, 109
Gould, Al, 45–46
Grant, Alan, 106, 109, 121
Gray, Wardell, 15, 20, 54, 58–59, 61; confident time-feel of, 58; death of, 58; lyrical sound of, 58; lyricism of, 111; precise articulation of, 58
Great Famine, 25
Grey, Noreen, 99–100
Grinnell's, 14, 20, 52–53, 188
Gulliver's, 97, 107

Half Note, 87, 109, 122, 135
Hamlet, 127
Hammett, Dashiell, 134
Hampton, Lionel, 117, 141, 144, 155
Hancock, Herbie, 167, 168
Hanna, Roland, 50, 54, 85, 89, 107, 116, 117, 126

Perla, Gene, 102, 107
Peterson, Oscar, 51
Le Petit Opportun, 84
Pettiford, Oscar, 31, 33, 164, 180, 181
Philadelphia International Records, 114
"Philson" 168
Pierson, Bob, 54, 133
Pit Inn, 112
"Please Don't Come Back from the
    Moon," 171
Porcino, Al, 89, 117
Porter, Lewis, 124, 129
Poulenc, *Clarinet Sonata* of, 175
Powell, Benny, 105
Powell, Bud, 51, 157
Powell, Seldon, 103
Prestige, 61; first date for, 178
Price, Ruth, 94, 141–42
Puccini, 122

"Quiet Lady," 71

race, racial, racism, racist, 19, 67, 124,
    153, 156, 161
Rains, Jack, 108
Reagan, Ronald, 91
Red, Sonny, 54, 55
Redd, Freddie, 182
"Reflectory," 97, 129, 142
Reid, Rufus, 107, 113, 118
Reuther, Walter, 14
Rexroth, Kenneth, 162
Richardson, Jerome, 107, 114, 118,
    171
Rivers, Larry, 161; sessions, hosted by,
    181
Riverside, 168
Roach, Max, 51, 177, 181
Robinson, Janice, 118
Rochester, New York: 4, 5, 13, 27,
    28, 37; Great Depression in, 5;
    economic solvency of, 27; economy

of, 5; industrial America in, 27;
    Irondequoit, suburb of, 27; jam
    session, jam sessions in, 31, 37;
    nightclubs in, 37; mentioned, 12,
    13, 14, 16, 17, 20, 27, 29, 32, 34,
    36, 93, 180, 188
Rollins, Sonny, 51, 55, 61, 122, 138,
    146, 182
Ronnie Scott's, 126
Root, Billy, 175–76
Rosolino, Frank, 53
Rouse, Charlie, 168
"Rue Serpente," 99, 129, 142
Ryan, Patsy, 89

Saint Anselm of Canterbury, 169
Sanders, Sam, 53, 55
Santoro, Gene, 171
Sauls, Earl, 99–100, 116, mentor of,
    137
Savoy Records, 31, 182
"Says My Heart," 101
The Scene, 105
Schiff, David, 136, 182; apprenticeship
    of, 137–39
Schopenhauer, 55
"Scratch," 50
Segovia, Andrés, 194
Seventh Avenue South, 99
Shah of Iran, 91
Shank, Bud, 124, 129, 179
Sharpe, David X., 125
Shaw Agency, 165, 170
Shearer, Lois, 146, 157, 158, 162,
    163, 164, 172, 173; loft of, 157–58
Shearer, Oliver, 10, 14, 17, 146, 149,
    158, 172, 173; loft of, 157–58
Shorter, Wayne, 107
Sidran, Ben, 57, 74, 103
Silver, Horace, 51, 155, 186
Sims, Zoot, 134, 135, 181; sessions,
    hosted by, 181